THE FORGOTTEN DAUGHTER

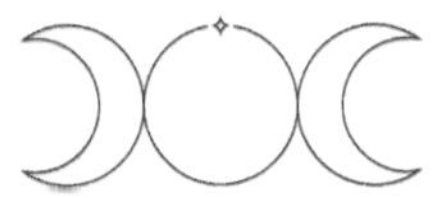

THE LOST COVEN BOOK THREE

E. O'MEAGHER

ISBN: 979-8-9883605-4-4 (paperback)
ISBN: 979-8-9883605-5-1 (ebook)

In loving memory of my grandmothers,
Joan and Donna

"She remembered who she was and the game changed."
Lalah Delia

Chapter 1

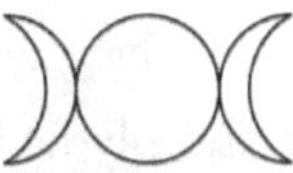

Frigid winds off Lake Erie battered against the spell, rattling it like shutters in a storm. A gust stirred up loose snow and sent it dusting across the frozen edges of the water. The flurries dissipated as they hit the invisible blockade around the yard.

If the neighbors noticed the snow refusing to touch the lawn, they kept it to themselves. It had only taken a day for the frozen covering that accumulated all winter to melt, leaving the grass a peculiar green for February. Copying Martin's spell had been a measured risk. But the backyard had become my only escape since we'd fled Halifax.

Grace took up the same spot she had all week, curled around my ankles in some twisted effort to comfort me. She refused to leave me alone, despite all my attempts to ditch her. Doors and walls, apparently, weren't a deterrent for Otherworld creatures.

Amity's book lay open across my lap, and the tea on the arm of the faded blue Adirondack chair had long lost its warmth. I ran my thumb over the blackened stone hanging around my neck. A habit, more than anything else.

I kept waiting for something to spark. For some heat to pierce the cold stillness. Waiting for the hum of magic to return.

But it wouldn't. It was gone, severed by the dagger that almost ended my life. The lost connection to the past daughters left me hollow. Without that power, there was no hope in getting my normal life back.

I pulled my sweater tighter at an imagined cold, crossing my arms to keep in whatever warmth I could. Despite the weather spell, a chill had settled into my bones and refused to let go.

Grace let out a small meow, and her tail twitched towards the house. I didn't bother looking. Lyra and Blythe had been taking turns trying to convince me to come inside and *talk*. It was pointless. No one was *talking* inside either. Arguing and snapping at each other, sure, but civil conversation? Not even close.

We'd landed in Cleveland after rescuing Lyra and made the hour drive to Sandusky, to the house mom left me. Wes and Chad were surprised by our late night—early morning arrival—but they'd kept their questions to themselves.

Trying to get situated had been the first hint at unsolvable friction. Eleven people, three bedrooms, and two and a half bathrooms wasn't ideal. Wes and Chad had tried to give up the primary bedroom for me, but I wasn't about to let them. Accommodating petty preferences almost sent me over the edge.

Leander refused to room with Rez, Lyra kept jabbing at Thea, and no one wanted to room with Sebastian. After I threatened to just kick everyone out, Wes stepped in and assigned sleeping arrangements.

In the end, he and Chad kept their bedroom, Jax and Leander went into a guest room while Rez and Sadiki took the other. Sebastian got the family room couch, and the last four of us had to make do with extra blankets and a few sleeping bags on the den floor.

A fresh, steaming mug of tea was set next to the cold one. I frowned at it as Wes lowered himself into the chair next to me. He hooked his cane around one of the arms and let out a sigh.

"We should try this spell back home," he said.

Home. A loaded word.

He shrugged to himself. "I suppose our neighbors might notice, though," he said, glancing at the house next to us. They were close enough that we could see each other in our yards, but it was nothing like the townhouse in Portland. "Maybe just the front walk," he continued. "So, we don't have to shovel as often."

I pressed my thumb against the crack in the ruby as hard as I could, the sting reminding me I could still feel. It was like I'd been walking through the last part of a dream. That stage just before waking up, where the lines of real and imagined blurred. Pain was the one thing I *knew* was real.

Grace stood and stretched, her long body arching, with a yawn that exposed sharper teeth than the typical house cat. She moved over to Wes to give his leg an expectant nudge with her head.

He scratched behind her ears, which earned him a loud, affectionate purr. She and the other two familiars appeared at the house a few hours after we arrived, which had taken some explanation and stirred some initial wariness from almost everyone. Familiars were one thing; Otherworld familiars called without clear intention were entirely different.

"How much longer do you plan on avoiding your guests?" Wes asked after a long moment.

I let out a harsh laugh. "*Guests* is a choice word there, Wes." We'd only picked this house because of the blood wards and other protections three generations of Boswell Blood Witches had placed on it.

I wasn't a host, and the other witches inside were hardly here on vacation.

"Friends, then," he suggested.

I shook my head and buried my chin in the high collar of my sweater. Friends didn't get friends killed. Vadim was gone because of me, and Rez had every right to hate me for it. Kane and I never got along, but he and Leander had been close; now he, too, was gone because he'd agreed to our plan to rescue Lyra. *Friends* was a worse choice of descriptors than *guests*.

"Em," he began. It was the stern tone I'd gotten when I'd used magic in front of Ian the first time. The tone I'd gotten when he'd caught me using magic to write a history paper. The tone of the uncle who had been forced to play father.

"You can't avoid them forever," he continued. "The property isn't that big."

Grace meowed in a way that sounded almost like an agreeable tone.

"Lyra is talking an intervention," he added.

I snorted.

"And maybe she's on the right track."

My knuckles blanched as I tightened my grip around the stone. Lyra could stage all the interventions she wanted. It wouldn't—couldn't—fix anything. But that didn't mean I doubted she would try.

"We—"

"What do you want me to say?" I demanded, turning to him. "I'm sorry? I screwed up?" Hot frustrated tears pooled in my eyes. "People are dead because of me. *Sorry* doesn't really cover it." I turned back away as the tears spilled over.

Sweater sleeves irritated the raw skin that hours of crying had already inflamed when I wiped them away. I couldn't differentiate the reason anymore; grief and frustration and anger all rolled into some new, nameless emotion that made me just want to walk into the freezing lake.

He didn't say anything, but I could feel his stare on me. "None of that was your fault," he said softly.

"I don't need to be placated right now, Wes."

He shifted in the chair. "You've been through a lot, it makes sense you—"

"And I *really* don't need to be pitied," I snapped, closing Amity's book and tossing it to the side. I pushed myself out of the chair despite the protest my stiff muscles made.

"Then what do you need?" Wes asked. "Because isolating yourself isn't it."

I paced a few steps closer to the edge of the yard, the edge of the spell, and watched snow skitter across the frozen surface of the lake with each gust of wintry wind.

Biting the inside of my cheek kept me from blurting out the answer to his question, and I pressed my thumb against the crack in the stone so hard it split skin, drawing blood. I squeezed my eyes shut against more tears, heaving a sob.

I hadn't been able to take a full breath in a week. My chest felt ready to cave every time I tried.

Grace rubbed her long body against my leg and looked up at me, her red eyes filled with a knowing that a normal cat could never have.

"I—" I took a shuddering breath and pressed a hand against the ache in my chest it brought on. "I can't feel them anymore." It came out so quietly, I wondered if he could even hear the words.

Grace let out a meow that reverberated through me, driving the cold away for a moment.

"I'm sorry," Wes said. He'd walked up behind me without even realizing. "I won't pretend to know what it's like," he continued, moving to stand in front of me. "But don't push the people who care about you away."

I crossed my arms and dug my toe into the grass. "I know you care," I muttered.

He put a hand on my shoulder. "I wasn't talking about me," he said with a soft smile. "Or, only me."

I shrugged off his hand and turned to look at the house. "I'll talk to Lyra," I agreed. "And Blythe."

He nodded slowly and picked up his cane to lean on. "And Jax," he added. "He's about to wear a hole in the floor with all his pacing."

I pursed my lips and gave him a short nod.

Wes frowned. "Em," he prompted.

I glanced out across the lake to stall. Jax and I had barely exchanged a handful of words since we left Halifax. I'd told him I needed space, and he'd given me that.

"It's just..." My hand went back to the fractured stone. "Maybe Isobel Jacob had a point."

He raised his eyebrows. "Since when have you believed in that?"

I half-shrugged. "It wouldn't be the first thing I was lied to about," I muttered.

He glanced back at the house. "Isobel Jacob's prophecy only becomes relevant if you let it." He gave Grace another scratch behind the ears before taking a few steps back towards the house. "Chad is making lunch. I'll see you inside in a few minutes."

I nodded and turned back to the lake, listening to the slight hitch in his breath with every step he took.

My family had spent their lives hiding from it, running and passing down the fear that we'd be found to each new generation. An anxiety as inherited as my power.

Wes had never put much stock in the words scrawled in Amity's book, and so he'd never wanted me to either. And I'd started to believe that he was right.

That was when my life had been my own. Before Wes's life had been put in danger because of me. Before Raven and Phoenix. Ian. Before Vadim and Kane. Before I had to flee my own home.

The fear, the running, the hiding, the grief. I'd accepted it all like the daughters before me because I'd thought that's what was required. A price for the magic our family was chosen to wield.

Now, grief had given in to a burning rage at the unfairness of it all.

Chapter 2

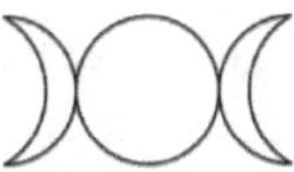

The old storm door screeched in protest at being used more in a week than it had in the last eight years. Our screened-in deck had seen better days. Upkeep hadn't been a priority since I'd moved away. Plastic totes filled with junk I hadn't gone through replaced most of the summer furniture, the space now a storage unit more than anything else.

I slid the glass door open as quietly as I could, but it didn't take more than half a second to realize I could have announced my arrival with a foghorn and still no one would have noticed.

Grace slunk in after me as I closed the glass door and hopped onto the love seat in the living room with the other two familiars. It shouldn't have been big enough to fit them all given their unnatural size, but she melted in seamlessly. It could have easily been mistaken for a black blanket, if not for the three sets of eyes watching the scene in the kitchen.

"Stop treating me like a fucking child!" Lyra's face was flushed, her fists clenched and shaking as though she was finding it hard to resist hitting her brother.

"I will when you stop acting like one," Leander snapped back. "This impulsiveness is going to get you killed!"

"You're not dad!"

Leander's face burned red, and he took a half-step towards her. "You didn't listen to him either, and look where that got you."

Lyra's bottom lip trembled, and I had a feeling it was from the effort of keeping herself from launching at him. "Fuck. You."

They may have been the ones shouting at each other, but the air was thick with wound-up tension from everyone. Sadiki sat at the head of the dining table, staring at his mug of coffee like he was reading his future in the dark surface.

Blythe stood next to Lyra, glaring at Leander, while Rez stood at the other end of the kitchen, feigning disinterest. But I'd seen that strategy before with Martin; he was ready to step in if Leander's anger turned on Blythe.

Sebastian was at the other end of the table, unable to hide a small smirk as he watched the fight continue. He'd been tentatively welcomed instead of left at the airport and, at that moment, I was questioning the decision.

Jax was next to Sadiki, his back to me. His shoulders tense, and I could picture his jaw flexing in the way it did whenever he felt the need to stop a fight but couldn't find a way.

My stomach tightened when I saw how close Thea was to him, hand resting on his arm like she did it all the time. She was trying to comfort him. Something I had never done because it had always been him comforting me.

"You can't keep doing whatever you want and expect no consequences," Leander warned through gritted teeth.

"Oh my—*Circe*, I'm not worried about a fucking demotion!"

His jaw clenched so hard I expected to hear teeth crack. "Kane is dead because of yo—"

I wasn't the only one who jumped when the mug hit the wall next to Leander's head. Shards of porcelain clattered to the tile. In the corner of my eye, I caught the cats stir for the first time since I'd walked in. Three pairs of otherworldly eyes narrowed on Leander.

Lyra's chest heaved with purposeful breaths, and her glare shimmered with tears. "Don't you *dare* put that on me," she hissed.

I thought I'd seen Leander angry before, but this was a silent fury that could rival my own. Only his was directed at the wrong person.

He turned and walked out of the kitchen, broken pieces of mug crunching under his feet. He caught sight of me and his anger switched focus quickly. I knew half of what he was yelling at Lyra for had been meant for me.

His attention drew everyone else's, and I felt their stares as I met Leander's glower. He took a few steps towards me and, in a blink, Grace was there in between us. She didn't make any other moves, didn't hiss, didn't swat at him, just stared in challenge.

He shook his head and brushed past me without another word. I could have been the one to speak, offer up some apology. Kane was dead because of *me*, and we all knew it. But defending myself was pointless. The rift was there, and I didn't have the energy to try to fix the irreparable.

Lyra's glare followed her brother until he disappeared from view, and we all heard the front door slam with more force than necessary. She wiped a tear from her cheek before moving to pick up the broken mug.

I caught the look between Blythe and Rez that clearly meant something to them, but I couldn't read the expression.

"So, are we having lunch or what?" Sebastian asked.

"That's it," Lyra grumbled, chucking the shards she'd collected back on the ground and rushing at him.

He knocked over the chair while trying to get away from her as Jax and Thea moved to intercept. They weren't fast enough. A crunch and a howl of pain sounded through the kitchen when her fist connected with

Sebastian's nose. He'd tried to get his own arm up in defense, but she was too quick.

Sadiki wrapped his large arms around Lyra and lifted her away from Sebastian before she could do any more damage. She struggled against his grip as he carried her to the opposite side of the room. Sebastian clutched his bleeding face with a whimper.

Jax started the scolding while Rez defended the action. Thea made a pointed comment about impulse control that brought Blythe into it, blaming Sebastian. Just one fight after another. Over and over.

Instead of making things worse, I used the commotion to slip into the den as Lyra let out a string of threats meant for Sebastian that drowned out nearly everyone else. Wes passed me in the hall, drawn out by the shouting.

He gave me a quizzical eyebrow raise. I offered a head shake and nothing more. There weren't words to adequately paint a picture of just how messed up everything was. He may not believe in Isobel Jacob's words, but clearly I was a catalyst for hostility between witches, intended or not.

I closed the door to the den and leaned against it, letting out a long breath. I'd let Wes convince me that coming inside had been a good idea. But it had only made things worse, and now there were six amped-up witches between me and the backyard. The den would have to do as a refuge. A refuge that was only a reminder of the shit situation I was in.

Boxes of mom's things that hadn't been moved to storage yet were shoved against a wall, the tattered lounge chair by the window was buried by dirty clothes and towels we'd ignored. And the floor was hidden by makeshift beds we'd pulled together.

I kicked one of the half-deflated air mattresses out of the way and shoved the small pile of clothes onto the floor before sinking into the chair and staring at the boxes of things I'd neglected.

The door opened, and Grace slunk in ahead of the one person I wasn't surprised to see but wished wouldn't have come in. Especially considering what had just happened with his brother.

Jax closed the door behind him as Grace made herself comfortable on one of the still-inflated beds. She laid her head on her crossed paws and looked between Jax and me like she was a mediator that had summoned us.

"Are you alright?" he asked softly.

I raised my eyebrows.

"I mean, after…" He didn't need to finish the clarification. None of us were *alright* after everything that had happened over the last few weeks. But he was trying to start a conversation after days of silence. But—fair or not—I couldn't help the twinge of anger every time I saw him.

"Can we talk?" he asked, shoving his hands into his pockets.

I shrugged. "About?"

He frowned. "Seriously?" he asked, an edge to his voice I hadn't heard before.

"Leander laid it all out pretty good, not sure what else there is to add."

He ran a hand over his jaw, days-old stubble making him look older—or maybe that was the stress. "You can't keep shutting me out," he said. "Not after everything we've dealt with."

Had he and Wes compared notes? I gripped the arms of the chair and looked out the window at the snow-covered front yard for a moment. "*Your* Council is the reason we had to *deal* with anything," I accused. "*Your* rules."

"You're blaming *me*?"

I ran a frustrated hand through my hair. "I'm blaming the people you work for."

He started to shake his head. "You're the one who ran," he reminded me. "You left without a word, and now you want to blame—"

"So, you'd rather I stayed and let Lenore kill me?" I asked, shoving myself back to my feet so would stop feeling like a child in trouble.

"That's not—the Coun—she's not the whole Council," he said.

"God, you're more delusional than I thought," I said, kicking another mattress out of the way. This room was getting too warm, too small.

"You didn't give any of them a chance," he snapped. "You didn't give *me* a chance."

I bit back the reminder that his own grandmother—a leader on his Council—had told me to run. "The chance to what?" I asked, pulling at the collar of my sweater. "Tell them what I was planning?"

The thing had been fine outside, but now it was too tight, itchy. I needed out of this room, or this sweater.

"I didn't say that."

"Fine," I snapped. "Tell me, Jax, what would you have done?"

His resolve faltered.

"Would you have helped me jump out the window? Pull a Lyra and drive the getaway car?"

"I—I don't—not if I thought it would have put you in more danger."

"And you wonder why I left," I muttered, yanking my arms through the sleeves of my sweater.

"You still could have—"

"What?" I practically whined, frustrated at the circular direction this conversation would inevitably take.

I yanked the stifling sweater off, leaving only the tank I had on under it, the cooler air finally able to slink relief over my skin. "What the hell do you *want* from me?" I muttered, tossing the sweater on the top of the pile of clothes.

His eyes widened as his gaze fell on my now bare skin. I frowned and glanced down; I'd forgotten about the scars. Raised and puckered skin that was healed as best it could, but the marks would forever be a reminder of the mistake that almost killed me and Blythe.

"What—"

"It doesn't matter," I said quickly, trying to shove my arms behind my back.

He caught one of them before I could manage it, though, and his golden magic sparked, sending pins and needles up my arm. "Who—"

I wrenched my arm free from his grip. "No one," I snapped.

He frowned. "Em, you can tell me what happened," he said, taking a step closer to me and reaching out again. Because that was his fix for everything. His magic, his power, helped and healed. It didn't hurt like mine.

I shook my head. "It doesn't matter," I repeated firmly, keeping the small distance between us. And it didn't, not to him. It was my mess and mine alone.

Hurt crossed his features. "Why can't you trust me?" he asked.

That bubble of anger boiled over, and no amount of focused breathing would put the lid back on. "I trusted you to keep Ian safe."

His face fell. "I never wanted him to get hurt."

I let out a humorless laugh. "Don't you get it?" I said. "It doesn't matter what we *want*."

He glanced at his feet. "I'm sorry about Ian," he offered and looked back up at me.

Grace let out a meow that sounded more like a low warning than anything else. If she was going to start interjecting in my arguments, she could leave. But when I looked over at her, her focus wasn't on me. Her red eyes were concentrated on Jax.

"I tried to—" His face froze, eyes wide.

Grace arched her back, hissing, hackles raised.

Jax's face contorted in pain, and he clutched his chest.

"Jax?"

He buckled. I rushed forward to grab him, but he was too heavy to keep upright, and we both crumpled onto the nearest mattress.

Grace continued to hiss like she was warding off some invisible force.

Sweat broke out across his forehead; his eyes rolled back in his head, his body seizing, and his skin burned under my touch.

Fear grasped my chest. "Lyra!"

Chapter 3

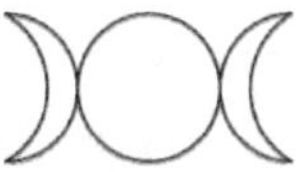

Jax trembled as his eyes fluttered shut, and he let out a groan of pain that made my breath hitch in panic. My own skin warmed against the feverish heat coming off him, and his forehead was slick with beads of sweat.

Grace scratched at the den door, claws leaving deep marks in the wood.

"For the love of—" I grunted as I tried to pull him up. "Lyra, get your ass in here!"

Lyra finally opened the door. "*Circe*, what the fuck is your—" She froze with her hand on the doorknob as Grace rushed by her, letting out a meow that made the hair on my arms stand.

"What happened?" she asked.

I shook my head. "I don't know, we were talking and he just collapsed."

She knelt and put a hand on his forehead. "He's hot."

"I know," I growled. "Help me get him up."

She nodded, and between the two of us, we managed to heave him out to the living room. Rez and Blythe looked around as we made our way out of the hall.

"Remind me not to argue with you," Rez teased.

"Shut up," I muttered.

"What happened?" Blythe asked, skirting around the counter to clear a path to the couch for us. Wes frowned as he pulled himself up from his seat at the kitchen table.

Blythe nudged Sebastian to get him up off the couch so we could put Jax there, but he didn't move. I almost shouted at him before I realized he was trembling, too; a sheen of sweat on his brow and his eyes darting beneath his eyelids meant Jax wasn't the only one who had gone down.

We managed to get Jax onto the love seat and his feet up, but it was still a tight fit. Grace leapt onto the back and lay down, tail twitching protectively over him.

Wes sent Blythe to get his bag upstairs while he looked over Jax.

"What happened to him?" Thea asked, drawn back into the living room by all the commotion.

"I don't know," I snapped.

Lyra looked between her brother and Sebastian and then back at me. "Leander..."

"Go."

She hurried to the front door, Rez at her heels. Wes pressed the back of his hand to Jax's forehead with a frown. Though his shirt collar was soaked with sweat, Jax shook like he was shivering from cold. A fever that came on this quickly could not be good.

Wes moved to Sebastian, frown never leaving his face. "Go soak some cloths in cool water," he said, nodding to Thea. "Cool, not cold."

She stared down at Jax but didn't move, like Wes's words didn't register.

"Thea," he said gently.

She started like he'd yelled.

"Cool cloths," Wes repeated.

She nodded and hurried upstairs just as Blythe came back into the room with a small duffel bag and handed it to him.

Sebastian let out a pained moan and shook so violently he could have fallen off the couch. Jax's breathing was labored, and Lyra hadn't come back with Leander. I glanced around the kitchen.

"Where's Sadiki?" I asked.

"He went outside to meditate," Blythe said, nodding towards the back door. It only took a second for us to silently agree we had to find him. Chad came with us, and we found Sadiki collapsed in the grass, letting out grunts of pain with each convulsion.

It took all three of us to get him back inside. We came in just as Rez and Lyra were hoisting Leander through the front door. He was covered in snow as though he'd fallen right into a bank; his head was low, chin to chest, the effort to keep it up was seemingly too much for him to bear.

Thea gently pressed a cloth to Jax's forehead, patting it carefully along his brow.

"Get them upstairs and into beds," Wes ordered.

After a quickly whispered spell from Lyra, they were each light enough for us to get them upstairs with little effort.

I stripped Jax out of his sweat-dampened shirt, but he could barely sit up long enough for me to do that. Head resting against my shoulder, he heaved a breath, and I could hear his lungs struggling to take it. Panicked tears pricked my eyes. I didn't know what was happening, but if the last thing we did was fight, I'd never forgive myself.

I shook the thought away. He'd be fine. They'd all be fine. They had to be.

"Here," Thea said, sitting on the other side of the bed and holding out a fresh shirt. Together we managed to get him into it, and I carefully laid him back on the pillow. He was so pale, he almost looked gray.

In the next bed, Sebastian let out a long moan.

"What happened?" Thea demanded.

I shook my head. "I told you, I don't know. We were talking and he just passed out."

"Talking, or arguing?"

I looked over to see her glaring at me. "What?"

"What, he say something that made you angry or something?"

I bit the inside of my lip to keep the trembling at bay. "You think *I* did this?"

She raised her eyebrows. Answer enough.

"You think I managed to do this to all of them?" I asked, nodding towards Sebastian. Was I angry? Sure, some of that anger was directed at the people in the house, but this wasn't what my power did.

"I honestly don't know what you're capable of," she said, taking Jax's hand in one of hers and running the other one along his brow, the movement was seamless, like she'd taken care of him countless times before.

Anger itched to show her exactly what I was *capable* of. I could make her leave this room. Make her walk into the frozen lake if I wanted. Jax pissing me off wasn't what she needed to be worried about.

"Wes needs you downstairs." Chad poked his head into the room and stirred me from the cruel thoughts aimed at Thea.

"Em?"

"Yeah, okay," I said and stood up, leaving Thea to watch over Jax. I took a steadying breath once I was in the hall and tried to shake off the anger-fueled ideas as best I could. Even if I had actually wanted to make Thea do anything, I wasn't even sure I could, not after the ruby was broken.

Wes was at the stove when I came down, stirring a simmering pot. Blythe and Rez each had a pestle and were grinding herbs.

"What can I do?" I asked.

Wes nodded to the pot. "Stir, don't let it boil."

I took over, and Wes limped to the four mugs set out on the counter. I watched the Tulsi leaves float on the top of the contents—Amla,

Moringa, licorice root from the smell—and let my mind wander to Thea and Jax upstairs.

Had she been right? Had my anger finally gotten the better of me and my magic had lashed out at those around me? I'd never intentionally hurt Jax, or Sadiki, or even Leander, but that didn't mean I hadn't done something inadvertently.

Small bubbles formed at the edges of the hot water, and I watched them form and dissipate, wracking my mind for anything that could mean this had been me. Had I been so consumed in the argument that I hadn't even felt my magic?

My hand automatically went to the stone hanging around my neck. No, it was impossible. Even *if* I'd somehow developed the ability to cause sickness like this, there was no way I'd have the strength to strike down four witches and not feel it. I'd be out myself, especially without the power of the talisman.

I didn't know what had made them sick, but I knew it wasn't *me*.

Wes had me take the mixture off the stove and we let the Tusli leaves soak a little longer before straining out four mugs of the tea. Lyra, Blythe, and Chad took them upstairs while Wes had me fill another small pot with water and put it on the stove to boil.

He put the crushed herbs, willow bark, and dried blueberries into four jars before filling them with vinegar.

"Once it boils, put the jars in and reduce the heat," he instructed.

I nodded my understanding, and he took his cane and went back upstairs. I stared in silence at the surface of the water, willing it to boil faster.

I knew the tincture from the smell. He'd made it for us and stored it in the pantry for in between doses of acetaminophen. Witches didn't get sick often, but when we did, it was intense.

Rez came up next to me and put a hand on my shoulder. "Sit," he said.

I shook my head. "The water needs to boil."

He nodded. "And it will, whether you're staring at it or not," he insisted. "Sit."

I didn't try to stop him from guiding me to a stool at the counter. Outside the window across from me, snow swirled through the air, kicked up by the seemingly endless wind off the lake.

I was numbly aware of Blythe coming back into the kitchen and taking the stool next to me. She put her head in her hands and let out a long sigh.

"You don't think..."

I turned to look at her. Her skin was paler than it had been earlier, and her hair had started to fall out of the short French braids she had in.

She took a deep breath. "You don't think Lyra's going to..."

I swallowed. "I don't know," I said quietly. For all I knew, we'd all end up passed out with high fevers without warning. My body gave an involuntary shiver as if to prove to itself that I wasn't overheating.

"Right," Blythe said, voice higher than usual. "They'll be fine." That part was quiet enough that I knew it hadn't been for me, but more a plea to the universe.

Rez put the jars into the boiling water before pulling out two mugs from the cupboard and clicking the electric kettle on.

I didn't like sitting and waiting for Wes's diagnosis, if there even was one. I crossed my arms on the counter and rested my chin on them. Too many people had died because of me; if anything happened to the rest of them, I'd wasn't sure I'd recover.

Rez put a steaming mug in front of each of us in what felt like too short a time for tea to be done, and I stared at the image on the porcelain, faded from years of washing. The logo for a diner mom and I used to frequent.

"Don't look so grim," Rez said. "It'll pass in a few days, a week max."

Blythe cupped her hands around her mug as I watched the nondescript shapes in the steam rising from the surface as if they held the answers I was looking for.

Like a stinging flick on the side of the head, his words registered. "What?" Blythe and I said together.

He shrugged. "Surprised it took this long to hit. But, I suppose when you're the Council's favorites, it was an argument."

"You know what's wrong with them?" Blythe asked.

He sighed. "I do."

"What is it?" I demanded.

"They defied the Council," he offered, leaning against the counter behind him. "Broke the Oath."

Blythe let out a frustrated growl. "For once in your life stop being so fucking cryptic!"

He crossed his arms with a half-smirk. "Your girlfriend will be fine," he teased.

"And the rest of them?" I pressed.

He glanced at the ceiling for a moment before looking back at us. "They'll feel like complete shit for a bit, then find out their expressed power is completely unusable."

My stomach dropped. "Why would—but that's—are you sure?"

He nodded.

"How are you sure?" Blythe asked.

He shrugged. "Because," he said. "That's what happened to me."

Chapter 4

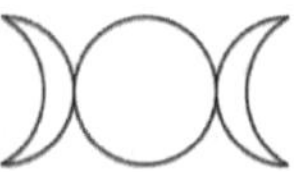

Blythe's eyes narrowed on her cousin. "I don't remember that," she
said.

"You were an Emissary?" I asked, looking between him and Blythe.
Lyra had let slip that he and Leander had been involved, but thinking
back, I realized neither of them had revealed *how* Leander and Rez had
met.

"Briefly," he admitted. "But try not to hold that against me."

Picturing him and Leander together had been hard enough, but imagining the man standing in front of me as an *Emissary* was nearly impossible.

"Back to the point," Blythe cut in. "When did you get sick like this?"

He sighed. "A few years ago," he said. "Before I opened the club."

Blythe frowned. "I thought..." She scratched the back of her neck. "I
thought Martin bound your powers."

I glanced at her. "Martin?" I rubbed my sore eyes. "Hold on,
why—what—what is going on?"

"You told me Martin was the reason your expressed power was dormant," Blythe continued, ignoring me.

Rez ran a hand through his hair. "He is."

I frowned. "But, then, how do you know what's going on with them?"

"And what does it have to do with you being an Emissary?" Blythe demanded.

"It's a long story," he said, turning to the stove and turning the heat off. He used tongs to take the jars out and set them on a towel to cool.

"Give us the CliffsNotes version," Blythe snapped.

He poured the boiling water out into the sink and set the pot on an unused burner. "My expressed power was bound because I broke the rules as an Emissary," he said. "And Martin could have stopped it."

Blythe and I exchanged a look.

"Okay, fine, give us the *abridged* version," she countered.

He shook his head and turned back to face us. "It doesn't matter why or how it happened," he said. "All that matters is that I know they're going to recover." He bobbed his head from side to side as if weighing options in his mind. "From the sickness, anyway."

"What is that supposed to mean?" I shot. If there was something else—not that there needed to be—we needed to know. Maybe we could stop it, or make it less intense, or...something.

He crossed his arms. "That finding out your expressed power is now buried so far deep inside yourself you can barely feel it isn't something you really *recover* from."

"Why would they do that?" Blythe asked.

"I told you," he said. "They broke the Oath."

She rolled her eyes. "Hardly see how running for your life is breaking an oath."

He shook his head. "It's not just an oath," he said. "It's the Council's way of curbing dissension. You agree to follow their orders, or you lose the use of your magic," he explained. "That way, even if Emissaries choose to turn against the Council, they wouldn't be able to do much else."

I clenched my fists against the counter. "That's awful."

He shrugged. "That's the Council."

"Martin isn't on the Council," Blythe said.

Rez raised an eyebrow.

"I'm not saying he's a gem of a person or anything," she continued. "But hard to hate him for something he has nothing to do with."

"He's a leader within the Assembly," Rez countered. "He could have intervened."

I frowned, I may not have known all the rules and inner-workings of whatever political system the covens had set up, but even *I* knew a member of the Assembly—what the Outliers called their version of a council—couldn't have done much if an Emissary broke the rules. The Outliers didn't have Emissaries.

Blythe crossed her arms. "What'd you do?"

"Nothing the two of you haven't done," he said. "Or Lyra, or her brothers."

"They wanted to make you an example," I muttered, glancing at the stairs. "All of you."

He nodded.

"And if Lenore's own grandson isn't safe from their punishment, there's not much hope for the rest of us."

I absently ran my thumb over the stone. "Can it be reversed?"

He frowned at me. "I don't know," he admitted. "But even if it can, it would take something incredibly persuasive to get the Council to reverse a decision like that."

"Something," I agreed.

(

As it turned out, Rez was right. Only the Emissaries fell ill, and after a few days, their symptoms got less intense. Still, with all four of them needing attention, the house felt smaller than it had before.

Despite Blythe's pestering, Rez still refused to give us any details about what he'd done to get his own powers bound. In the end, I decided it didn't matter much; the Council had made their choice. They had turned on their own, and there wasn't anything we could do about that.

Having three grandchildren of Council leaders on the chopping block was the only reason Rez could see that it had taken a full week for their powers to be bound. He assumed it had been a fight for a while. Apparently, the Council had to vote before any action could be taken—deciding if the Oath had been broken, or just rules. Rules, after all, were one thing. Betrayal was entirely different.

Wes did what he could to keep them all comfortable enough to sleep through the night, but even his skills couldn't stop the symptoms completely.

Chad and Rez were sent on a drugstore run when the acetaminophen ran out, leaving the rest of us to help Wes. Only, there was little to do. Every time I went to check on Jax, Thea was there. She'd even brought her sleeping bag into his room. I honestly couldn't tell if it had been to watch over him or to protect him from me.

She blamed me. We now knew why they'd gotten sick wasn't anything I did directly, but I could see why she still put the blame on my shoulders. He wouldn't have been in this position if it weren't for me. None of them would be.

Instead of pushing her out, I did what I knew how to do best. Clean. Clothes and sheets rotated through washing, drying, and folding. The kitchen was a disaster, thanks to the days of making teas and tinctures and no one caring much to put things away. I added the touch of sweeping and steam mopping the hardwood floors. Despite their illness not being a contagious one, the house still permeated sickly stuffiness.

I found an old eucalyptus and lavender candle and left it burning on the kitchen counter before opening the windows to the backyard to try to coax any kind of fresher air into the house.

No one tried to stop me. No one told me it was a pointless task, and I was thankful for it. It was like I was on the edge of some kind of emotional cliff, and one breath of strong wind would send me over the edge. I was either going to start crying or topple into an unrelenting anger. And I wasn't sure which was worse.

The den was in the worst shape for a room not occupied by feverish Emissaries. We all neglected it in the days we spent trying to keep them all comfortable. Lyra barely slept, and Blythe only did when Lyra did. I wasn't sure of the last time any of us actually got a full night's worth of rest.

I deflated what little air was left in the mattresses and rolled them to the side before vacuuming what floor space I could get to and cracking a window to let winter air in. The front yard hadn't been enchanted, but the icy chill was a welcome relief to start.

Our blankets and sheets were the last to run the cycle of wash-and-dry, so the mattresses stayed rolled away until they were completely ready to be made up again.

That left the boxes stacked around the far wall even more obvious, though. They'd been waiting for me to go through for years, but I'd never gotten around to it. I put a hand on top of the first one and stared at the faded black marker of a hastily scribbled label.

The den had been mom's office when we lived here. She'd had a photography business, and these were what was left of that. It hadn't been much, more a hobby that occasionally made money. She'd always wanted it to be more but never got the chance.

She loved it, and I loved helping her. She'd let me play assistant on some of the jobs: engagement sessions, senior photo shoots, even a dog's maternity shoot once. It was carrying her bag and keeping her water bottle close, but for an eight-year-old, it was the best job in the world.

I took a deep breath, pulled the tape off and opened the flap. Prints of her personal photos were on top. Us in the backyard a week before my thirteenth birthday. Pictures from the Christmas when Wes and Chad had come to visit. Images from Grandma Geri's backyard Summer Solstice party when I was five.

I searched each photo for an answer in the frozen faces. All the smiles, the memories, were slightly tainted now. How long had mom known we were bound to another bloodline? Had Grandma Geri been aware that whatever end we met, so did another witch? Had we hidden away because of the prophecy or because of *that*? Was everything a lie?

I put the photos back inside, chronologically, and set the box to the side. The next box was filled with used journals—least a dozen with faded soft leather covers. I took the top one out and opened to the first page. Her handwriting, neat and slanted, greeted me. The same handwriting in every birthday card, every note left in my lunch box, every grocery list she ever wrote.

I traced the letters of the first entry of the journal. A hello to a new one. She'd always said to treat a journal like a personal spell book. Treat it well, and it would hold your secrets better than anyone.

My fingers found the fabric bookmark at the bottom of the notebook. I twisted it a few times before pulling it to open to the marked page.

October, eight years ago. The day before my birthday. The day before she died. It wasn't an entry—not really. Just five words scrawled in a hurry:

I have to tell her.

Nothing else. No clue as to who she wanted to tell or what she wanted to tell them. Why had this been all she felt the need to write down that day? I flipped back to past entries and scanned them through. Some were long, ten pages even. And there was nothing in those that explained her last one.

Had I been "her" in that note? Was she planning on telling me about the binding at breakfast that day? I desperately wanted that answer to be yes. I'd spent years wondering what my life would look like if mom hadn't died, and now that question was back. If Blythe and I had known each other as kids, how different would our lives be?

With a frustrated sigh, I closed the journal and put it back into the box before grabbing two more, I flipped through them, looking for any mention of Osborne, Blythe, or the binding. If she had known about it, there was no way she wouldn't have written about it somewhere.

Forty-five minutes later, and I'd ripped open the other boxes to find all the journals I could. Most were spread out around me as I sat on the floor of the den, organizing them by years, trying to decipher when mom may have learned about the binding herself. But by the time I'd been through almost half of them, I was beginning to think Martin had just been trying to get a rise out of me; maybe mom didn't actually know anything about it.

As I started putting them back into boxes, I found another one, pressed against the side of the box, with something that looked like the corner of a paper bookmark sticking out of the pages.

Letting it fall open in my lap to the marked pages, I stared down at the Polaroid that had been used as a placeholder. Three women with their arms around each other, beaming at the camera. Mom was in the center, ruby hanging prominently around her neck.

I didn't recognize either of the other two women. They all looked so...young. The date written in black marker on the bottom noted it as two years before I was born.

She would have been seventeen. Seventeen and happy and having no idea what would happen in fifteen years.

I unclipped the picture and scanned the entry it had been with. Mom *had* been looking for a way to undo the curse, just like Blythe. Because this wasn't a journal entry like the others; these were notes on creating a spell.

Ideas scribbled out, notes in the margins, theories on how the curse had taken an entire bloodline. Only, the ideas were useless since it wasn't a curse. Undoing a binding and lifting a curse were too different to make any of her ideas helpful.

I turned the page. More notes and thoughts from mom. The name *Meg* had been jotted down at the top with a question mark and circled a few times. I frowned at it. The only Meg I knew of was a cousin of Wes, but what would she have to do with anything?

The door banged open, and I jumped, sending the journal sliding off my lap.

"I'm going to fucking smother him," Blythe snapped.

I took a breath to calm my pounding heart. "Who?"

"Sebastian," Blythe said, falling onto the chair across from me and slouching down in it. "He's moaning like death herself is breathing down his neck."

I reached for the journal. "You're surprised?" I asked. It was true, Sebastian had been the most vocal of the Emissaries. He'd successfully annoyed Wes so bad that he'd been given a little something extra in his tea to knock him out for a few hours. He was trying way too hard to be the one suffering the worst.

She took a long breath. "No," she agreed. "But it's annoying." She rubbed her face and sat up a little straighter as if trying to keep herself from falling asleep. "What are you doing?"

"Going through some of my mom's old stuff," I said.

She let out a long sigh. "Your need to organize scares me," she muttered.

I reached for the escaped picture. "Your apartment thanks me," I teased, reaching for the escaped picture.

She leaned over at the same time and picked it up. Staring at it and her frown deepened. "They did know each other," she said.

"What?"

"That's my mom," Blythe said, turning the picture around to show me. "On the left. And I assume that's yours, with the ruby?" She pointed to mom.

I nodded and took the image back, really looking at it. Now that I paid closer attention, I could see the resemblance to Blythe in the woman's face. The same eyes, nose, and smile—although Blythe smiled so rarely smiled it was hardly a shock I'd missed it.

"They look so young," Blythe said.

I nodded. "Seventeen," I agreed, not looking up. "You recognize the third girl?"

She shook her head. "But it has to be the third bloodline, right?"

I shrugged and chewed on my bottom lip. "Doesn't do us much good without a name." I flipped back to the page with the name Meg circled. Could that have been who mom meant? The third girl's name was Meg? Only, why would there be a question mark in her journal? Clearly, the three of them knew each other well.

Blythe grabbed a journal from the box. "Maybe she put it somewhere in one of these."

I bit the inside of my cheek. There was something personal about mom's journals that I wasn't sure I wanted anyone else to read. They were her inner thoughts, dreams, stuff about me as a kid. I opened my mouth to tell Blythe that I could do it alone, but the words stuck in my throat when her sleeve rode up and my eyes caught on her scars.

I just nodded and went back to reading through the one in my lap. Blythe curled her leg under her and began scanning another one. For all I knew, she might even recognize a name I didn't. She'd been aware of all of this for a lot longer than I had, after all.

Almost two hours later, and we had barely scratched the surface of mom's life before me. Part of that was me taking extra time to pore over the parts when she'd met my dad. It had nothing to do with the task at hand, but I couldn't help it. She'd never really given me much to go on with their relationship. I'd gotten snippets, at best.

When Blythe's mom's name—Dahlia—started showing up in entries, I tabbed them with the leftover office supplies I'd found. The journals were full of tabs for names we knew until, finally, after the sun had gone down and we could hear Chad starting dinner, we found a name that we could go off of. Given the timing, context, and proximity to mentions of Dahlia, we were confident we knew the first name of the third girl in the picture.

Marnie.

Chapter 5

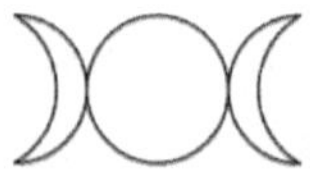

Almost a week passed, and the guys were just about over their fevers, but still not back to full strength. Although, according to Rez, they never would be. With this realization came a new wave of things to moan about, and I was beginning to wonder which task was harder: finding the illusive *Marnie* or getting Sebastian to stop complaining. If it wasn't the itchiness of the blankets, it was the temperature of his tea or the saltiness of the soup. Blythe wanted me to kick him out. Lyra wanted to kick something else.

Though they were over the illness that came with their punishment from the Council, we had burned through the majority of Wes's stash. Chad was able and willing to hit the drugstore for anything we might need, but admitted he didn't know the first thing about getting the supplies for our "witchy stuff."

So, after a hot shower to scrub away the frustration and tiredness brought on by days of Sebastian's whining and no answers about Marnie, I pulled a hat over my slightly damp hair and headed into the garage, armed with Wes's list.

I mashed the seat-heater button on and rubbed my gloved hands together. The garage and remote start made sure the car wasn't as cold as it could have been, but I hadn't let it run for long enough to be warm.

Putting the car into gear, I was ready to pull out when someone knocked on the passenger side window. Thea stood expectantly in a hat, coat, and grimace.

I re-parked and rolled the window down.

"Your uncle said you needed some help," she explained, tone suggesting she thought he was lying.

I glanced back at the door to the house. It *was* a lie. I didn't need her help, but it didn't take a genius to know why Wes had told her to come with me. Thea's overbearingness when it came to Jax had extended to Wes in the days since my attention had turned to finding Marnie. I'd overheard Wes muttering about it more than a few times. She wanted to make his tea, heat up his food, and she watched as Wes did anything to ensure it was right.

He wanted a break from her, and this was as good a reason as any.

I sighed. "Sure, that'd be great." Spending any kind of alone time with Jax's ex—especially one that thought I was some devious seductress—wasn't anywhere on my to-do list, but if it meant Wes could get a breath, I'd suck it up.

Her eyebrows pinched together, and her lips pursed; clearly, she hadn't expected me to say yes. But she didn't argue and climbed in. I waited until I heard the click of her seatbelt before backing out.

Sandusky was smaller than Portland by population, but that didn't mean I was any more comfortable driving. I'd avoided it as best I could after mom died. Ian had been more than willing to drive everywhere when he got his license, and especially after he got the Jeep. He wanted to show it off, so my lack of desire to drive became a non-issue.

That is, until Stanley—my old therapist—decided it would be a good idea for me to take the driving test and get a license as a step in the processing stage. I wasn't sure it actually helped me process anything. I'd agreed because it truly was impractical for me to not know how. Didn't mean I had to like it, though.

The nearest stop for the supplies we needed was about twenty-five minutes from the house, a co-op like the one in Portland on the lower level of an upscale French restaurant right on the water.

The restaurant itself was closed until late afternoon for dinner, but we weren't the only ones out for the day and ended up having to park a few blocks away or risk a ticket. I shivered as a chilled breeze swept across the snow-covered cemetery we'd parked in front of. After pulling my hat down further over my ears, I grabbed the reusable bags out of the backseat before locking the car.

On the drive over. it had been easy enough not to talk. We'd let the music fill the silence and kept to ourselves. But outside in the quiet cold, the awkwardness swelled like a balloon against a too-confined space despite the open air.

Even in gloves, the icy chill reached my fingertips, and I shoved my hands into my pockets against the sensation. I'd grown way too used to the spell on my backyard that held back the biting cold off the lake.

Wes had given me the correct phrase to get us in, but my French was worse than my German and, apparently, correct pronunciation was a requirement.

"Great," I mumbled and dug for my phone. We were about to find out if the access spell worked over the phone.

"French?" Thea asked, crossing her arms.

I nodded, using my teeth to pull a glove off my numb fingers to use the touch screen.

"Something about not doing harm with entry," I continued, pulling up Wes's number in the recent calls.

Thea nodded. "Aucun mal ne viendra de mon entrée."

I paused, finger hovering over his name and stared at her.

"You speak French?"

She flipped her hair over her shoulder and gave me a self-satisfied smile. "Bien sûr."

I tried not to roll my eyes as a dark purple door rippled into view. It wasn't hard to miss the smirk plastered on her face when she pushed through it. I shoved my phone back into my pocket and fought the immature urge to pull her hair.

Sandusky's co-op was set up differently from Portland's. Unlike unattended aisles of a grocery store, we stood in something with permanent stalls and an individual seller at each.

Sign-posts at the entrance to each row were in French and English, but that didn't mean it would make this easy. I knew where things were in Portland, but here I had no idea how it was organized.

Had I been alone, I would have loved to explore them all and take the place in. But while I was more than willing to give Wes a break from her, I really didn't want to prolong *our* quality time together any more than necessary.

Thea pointed to a row to our far left. "Fever reducers," she said.

"Right," I nodded. Wes's list was grouped by like items, the way I preferred it. Almost like he'd done it on purpose.

As we made our way over, I realized my initial assessment had been off. Everything was lumped similar to similar—that would help this to go quickly. And after about twenty-minutes of shopping, I'd crossed off a solid chunk of what we needed. That meant we'd, thankfully, be done faster than I first thought.

Thea purposely cleared her throat, and I had to physically choke back a groan. If she was about to tell me Jax preferred chamomile to peppermint, that impulse to pull her hair was going to win out. We weren't going to have to endure each other's company for much longer and all she needed to do was keep her comments to herself and we'd get out of here unscathed.

She cleared her throat again and my hand tightened on the bag in my hand.

"I—"

I saw her stick her hands in her jacket pockets out of the corner of my eye.

"I just," she took a deep breath and looked down at her feet. "I wanted to say, sorry," she said quietly.

My brain took a moment to fully register. I stared at the bag of Moringa in my hand instead of at her. Could I get away with pretending like I hadn't heard what she'd said? A condescending conversation I'd been prepared for, but she'd thrown me with an apology.

I bit the inside of my cheek.

"About the other day," she continued.

Swallowing, I slowly picked up another bag to compare weight versus price. I wasn't sure how much we'd end up needing before this was all through and doing mental math was preferable to having this particular conversation.

"For snapping at you."

Clearly, she was taking my lack of response as an invitation to keep talking. Sighing, I put the bigger bag into the small handbasket and turned to the next stall.

"I just thought you—"

"Are evil incarnate," I finished, turning to face her. "I'm aware."

A red flush crept up her neck. "I didn't actually mean that," she said.

"You made it pretty clear what you think of me at Sabbats," I said, adding a juniper and cedar cleansing bundle to the basket. The house was going to need a good smoke cleanse sooner rather than later.

She swallowed, and my eyes caught the movement of her turning the small amethyst ring around her finger. "Look, I was a mess when Jax broke up with me," she said. "I wanted someone to blame."

My stomach knotted; I picked up a jar of fennel and checked the price instead of offering a response. They'd been together when Jax and I met, and a small part of me had always wondered if he *had* broken up with her because of me.

"I didn't want to accept it."

I couldn't hold back the snort. "Doesn't seem like you have." I tossed the jar of fennel into the basket despite it not being on the list.

She bristled. "And it doesn't *seem* like you even want him." She crossed her arms. "Or was this your plan? Get him to sacrifice everything for you and then drop him?"

I rounded on her. "You caught me," I snapped. "Fleeing for my life, guess I've got them all exactly where I want them."

"Then, what?" she demanded. "What big plan do you have that has them all willing to follow you?"

I took a deep breath. "That's none of your business." I wished I felt half as confident as I sounded. Because the truth was, I had no idea why they'd all risked defying the Council, risked their *lives*, for me. But I wasn't about to give her the satisfaction of knowing any of that.

She took a deep breath and closed her eyes as if collecting herself. "Look, all I wanted to say was that I was sorry about snapping," she repeated, looking at me again. "I shouldn't have jumped down your throat just because of your magic. Okay?"

I started to shake my head but stopped myself. "Fine. You said it."

"You know you could—"

"Let's just get this done so we can get back," I urged.

She rolled her eyes but didn't argue.

It had probably taken a lot for her to apologize. No doubt why she'd been quiet for almost an hour, working up the courage to say something, and I'd completely brushed her off.

Call it mean-spirited or petty, but I sure as hell didn't want to accept it. She had no idea what it was like being judged for her magic. No clue what it felt like fearing reactions so much I had to hide. One half-assed apology wasn't going to fix anything.

The rest of the shopping trip was spent in a more tense silence than before. She followed behind me with crossed arms as I added more to the basket, completely neglecting the idea of comparing prices. After we paid, we headed back into the bleak February afternoon where the sun was struggling to break through the blanket of gray clouds.

We were a block from the car when the prick of a stare made my skin crawl. Thea and I stopped walking at the same time, exchanging a look to confirm we both felt it, before I glanced over my shoulder.

Four men in all black had stopped just behind us. They weren't dressed like they were out for a winter stroll, and their matching scowls were focused on us.

I couldn't help the groan. This was getting annoying.

"What?" Thea asked.

"Hunters," I muttered.

Her eyes widened as I grabbed her elbow and picked up the pace. The car wasn't far off, and all we had to do was get back to the house. Once we were there no one could get in without explicit invitation from me.

Of course, if they killed me before we did, then everyone in the house would be vulnerable.

"Run," I hissed at Thea, tearing off towards the car.

She kept pace easily with me, thanks to her long stride, but a kernel of panic set in when we found the direct path to the car blocked by two women.

I shoved Thea down a small alley between apartment buildings, and we ducked behind two large trash bins.

"How'd they find us?" she asked, peering over the bins.

I shook my head. That was a problem we'd deal with later. "Once we get to the car, we'll have to lose them in traffic," I explained, handing her the keys. She might not be Lyra, but she at least had some training on that kind of driving.

She stared at the fob in her palm. "Are you serious?"

"You got a better idea?"

She glanced at the entrance to the alley, where six figures moved towards us. Her gaze quickly flicked back to me, her head shaking in response.

I closed my eyes and focused on finding their energies. Or, at least, finding the weakest one.

My power was a flicker of what it had been. I was barely able to sense them, let alone capture them. It had been hard before, when I hadn't been using it often, but this...this felt impossible.

I pulled the necklace out from under my sweater and wrapped my hand around the broken stone, despite knowing it was useless.

"Sasha sends her best," one of them called, his voice sending a shiver over my skin. "She's sharpening her knife just for you."

Opening my eyes, I swallowed and forced my magic to focus on him and him alone. He was closest, and right now distance, wasn't my friend.

"Get to the car," I said through gritted teeth, shoving at Thea.

"What about you?" she hissed.

"I'll be fine," I lied as a wave of nausea hit. The alley pitched with the effort of barely holding one person. I leaned against the wall behind me to try to steady myself. I'd have to give her as much time as possible from here because there was no way I'd be able to run.

I took a deep breath and like muscle memory triggered by a well-known song, my lips formed the words, calling on the power of the past daughters.

But the ruby did not heat with power. The wall holding back the wave of magic I needed stayed unmoved.

Nothing but empty words now.

Chapter 6

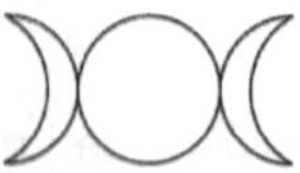

A frustrated tear rolled down my cheek, and I wiped it away before Thea could see it. I didn't want her to think I was scared. Fear was there, but it was anger that forced tears from my eyes.

"Sasha wants you to herself," the man continued—although, with my attempt at holding him, the words were strained. "But that doesn't mean we can't have some fun before she gets here."

"The other one is fair game," another voice said.

I caught Thea's eye and her set jaw. I wasn't sure how much experience she had with hunters. Lyra mentioned she wasn't an Emissary, but it was a slight comfort not to see fear on her face, even if she was faking it.

Thea looked to the clear opening behind us. "How long can you hold them off?" she asked.

I took a deep breath, another wave of dizziness hitting when I tried again to grab for full control, and wondered how big a lie she'd believe. "Not long," I finally admitted.

She gripped the keys. "I'll take what you can," she said and leaned around the corner of the dumpster. "Ready?"

I nodded, and she caught my elbow as the effort of standing nearly sent me back to the ground. Ready, but weak. Thea's confidence in whatever plan she had made me focus on not passing out so that she could take point.

It was like trying to walk on a boat in high winds; the ground rocked under my steps, despite my determination. I heard Thea move from behind me but didn't look around to confirm it.

I stopped in front of the advancing hunters and did my best not to vomit.

"*You're* the witch that killed Armin Scholz?" one of them taunted.

I raised my chin slightly and feigned surety. I had no idea what Thea was planning, and trusting that she had a plan was taking a lot. But I at least knew they weren't going to kill me until Sasha got here. It was an odd comfort, but a comfort, nonetheless.

A moment of clarity broke through at that. Thea's plan very much could have been to abandon me and head back to the house alone. She'd heard them say they were waiting on Sasha, which meant it bought her time to run. Leaving me behind to fend for myself.

All I had to do was hold off long enough for her to get back to the house and tell them what happened. I reached for my magic, letting it take the nearest hunter. The man who seemed to be in charge.

His steps were halting, jagged as my power connected to his energy. He could feel it too, I knew it. But his sneer never faltered. They knew what I could do by now. Surprise had been part of what made it easier to take them, but now that I wasn't a myth anymore, they were ready for me.

It was like being drugged all over again. Only this time, it was my own power doing it. It wasn't syringes but the lack of connection to the other daughters.

Mocking laughter filled my ears. If only my anger at that had been enough to light the spark. It used to be enough.

His laugh stopped short. Ice doused my skin and decay assaulted my nostrils. Nausea turned to bile as the stench of rotting flesh made my eyes water. A dark purple mist circled my ankles, crawling its way towards the hunters.

They all stared at me—or, rather, what was behind me, their eyes wide with fear. One doubled over and heaved as the mist found them. A shiver ran up my spine, this time because of what I couldn't see. Fear told me to stay put; morbid compulsion wanted me to turn around.

Guns were drawn from their coats and raised at me. Whatever had come for us scared them more than Sasha.

Instinct outweighed sense, and I let my magic lash out to stop them from getting a shot off. The mist's distraction made it easier to get some control, but it was still weak. I could feel fingers itching to squeeze triggers.

Sweat broke out at the base of my neck, and my head felt like it was being pressed between two rocks. I held on as long as I could, but eventually the effort sent me to my hands and knees.

Blood dripped from my nose onto the pavement, and I had to squeeze my eyes against the spinning world.

"Someone shoot it!"

"Shoot *what*?"

A feather touch across the back of my hand forced my eyes open. A spider scurried towards the hunters. I pushed myself back onto my knees and tried to shake the sensation off my skin. The pavement moved—no, it wasn't the pavement. More spiders hurried away from me, rushing towards the hunters.

Frenzied scraping came from the dumpster and trash cans. I let out a yelp and fell back as rats leapt from them. They bolted for the opposite end of the alley.

One of the hunters let out a screech and flattened himself against the wall of the building closest to him. Another one fired a shot off at the nearest rat.

I flinched and looked back at them. The purple mist was only getting thicker as it swirled around us. The hunters were scrambling, looking to shoot something that would get it to stop.

The leader's eyes narrowed on me as I used a trash can to pull myself up on wobbly legs. It didn't matter that I had *nothing* to do with what was happening. My magic didn't—couldn't—do this, but there was no way he cared about that.

He aimed for me.

Painful pressure wrapped around my ankle, and in the split second it took for me to glance down, too many things happened.

A dead vine wrapped around my leg and yanked—hard—slamming me against the pavement just as a shot hit the brick wall where my head had been. The vine snapped taut and dragged me backward, my chin scraping against the grit of the alley floor.

Clearing the ally, I glanced up and how thick the mist had gotten inside. Through it, I could only make out vague shapes of panicking hunters. I rolled onto my back and gulped down fresh air as fast as I could. My stomach roiled against too much air too fast. My throat stung against freezing air and the lurching dry-heave.

But I didn't care, I'd take a sore throat over the taste of rot clinging to my senses. I forced myself to sit up and my head swam thanks to both a bleeding chin and nose. My front was stained with its bright red stream.

Thea stuck out her hand to help me to my feet. When our skin touched I let out an involuntary shudder. Her touch was cold, clammy, and it sent a wave of dread through me.

She let go quickly once I was on my feet and turned to the running SUV. But not before I saw her eyes, glowing the same deep purple as the mist that had brought death and decay to the alley. The same mist— the magic—that had sent spiders and rats scurrying in terror.

I pressed my sleeve under my nose to try to staunch the bleeding. There was only one thing that scared creatures enough to flee like that.

Death Witch.

Chapter 7

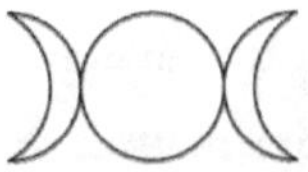

"It's just a bloody nose," I tried to say through the cloth pressed against my face.

"*You* don't get bloody noses," Wes countered, not letting me pull his hand away.

"Sometimes I do," I mumbled. He leveled a disbelieving look at me like I was a patient lying about taking her meds. Wes had two modes: doctor and uncle. When the two were combined, it was worse than either alone. Our silent stare-off ended with my loss, and I let him hold the cloth to my nose.

"I can at least hold it myself," I muttered, shoving his hand away. He waited until I put my own hand on it securely before giving me a firm nod and limping into the kitchen.

It had been a lot worse in the car, and I'd managed to get it relatively under control with the napkins in the glove box, but the stain on my coat and sweater had been enough to throw everyone into a slight panic when Thea and I walked through the door.

Questions were thrown out faster than I could answer. Why was I bleeding? Why was I covered in dirt? What happened to my face? Where were the supplies? Had Thea hit me?

All valid questions that I could have answered if anyone had let me. Instead, I was dragged to a chair and forced to sit while Wes took a look at me. The first time I'd tried to say a full word, the first cloth was shoved in my face.

Thea answered for us. Hunters. And no, she hadn't hit me. Although, I didn't miss the skeptical glance between Lyra and Blythe at that answer. I also noticed Thea conveniently leaving out the *exact* details about how we'd gotten out of the alley. She made it sound more like I'd tripped and scraped my chin while we ran. Which was arguably the most believable part of the story.

Even if I could have interjected, I didn't. Clearly, she wanted to keep what she'd done to herself. What I couldn't figure out was why. Probably just didn't want to admit to saving my ass.

"Is the shower free?" I asked, glancing around. Sebastian, Rez, and Sadiki were noticeably absent from the interrogation, and I really hoped none of them were using the upstairs bathroom.

"They're out," Lyra said around a mouthful of chips.

I frowned at her. "Now?"

She shrugged. "Sebs left right after you," she explained. "Rez and Sadiki followed him."

"Why are they—never mind," I said. "The hunters are still out there."

"I already told Rez," Blythe said.

"And in the case of one of them...I find myself not caring so much," Lyra admitted. "Besides, we all know they don't give two shits about the rest of us." She wiped her hands on her leggings, and I noticed the pointed glance between Jax and Leander out of the corner of my eye. "We should really check you for like a tracker or something," Lyra continued. She tilted her head back to pour the chip crumbs directly from the bag into her mouth. "I mean, how else do you explain how they found you, *again*?"

Wes set a mug in front of me. "Drink," he ordered.

I took a sniff and instinctively wriggled my nose against the nutty scent of dandelion root, but that only caused an uncomfortable tightness against the dried blood. I knew the tea would help, but it wasn't my favorite.

"Where's Chad?" I asked quickly.

"The store, getting stuff for dinner," he said. "And before you start, he's perfectly safe half a mile from the house."

I closed my mouth on the argument I was about to make. They were all too concerned with me right now. I was safe inside the house. The rest of them weren't.

Lyra crumpled up the chip bag and tossed it into the trash before rubbing her hands together. "I have a spell to reveal hidden tracers," she said. "Hold still, I don't want your nose to start bleeding again."

"I don't have a tracker," I snapped at the same time Blythe grabbed Lyra's wrist before she could even start with an incantation.

"Em," Lyra started. "C'mon."

"It's not some big secret where I'm from," I argued. "It wouldn't take more than a Google search to connect the dots."

Lyra frowned. "Well, that's boring."

"What do we do if they show up at the front door?" Thea asked, catching my eye. We both knew they hadn't seen the car or license plate, thanks to her magic, but she wasn't bringing that up and neither was I. That didn't mean we didn't have our risks, though. Especially if the others weren't across the threshold.

"Blood wards," Blythe reminded her before I needed to. "They don't only work on witches."

"All that does is keep them out of the house," I said. "Not off the property."

"I can extend them," Blythe offered.

I rolled my eyes. "That's not the point."

"Do it," Jax said, looking at Blythe. "Just let us know what you need."

Blythe raised her eyebrows. "You just sit there and look sickly, golden boy," she said as she slid off the stool. Lyra tried to turn her laugh into a cough, and I had to press my own lips tight to keep from cracking a smile. I even saw a slight upturn at the corner of Leander's mouth.

Jax frowned down at his hands on the table, mouthing *golden boy* to himself.

Blythe plucked the bloody cloth off the table. "This should do," she said. "Be back in a couple minutes."

"Blythe—"

"Drink your funky-smelling tea and let me do what I do best," she insisted.

"It's not *funky*-smelling," Wes muttered.

"If you're not back in five minutes, I'm coming out there!" I called after her.

She didn't respond but I saw her wave back at me and I knew that was the only acknowledgment I was going to get.

"They *are* finding us a little too easily," Leander said, speaking for the first time since we'd gotten back. "I don't like it."

"Maybe they're following you," Lyra suggested.

Wes stopped wiping the counters down.

Leander, Jax, and I stared at her.

"What—explain," Leander said.

Lyra rolled her eyes. "You showed up in Salem," she said, counting off on her raised index finger. "Sasha shows up." She put up another finger. "You show up in Halifax, Sasha shows." She put up a third finger. "Now here."

"Sasha wasn't there," I noted.

"But she was mentioned," Lyra said. "So, I'm counting it."

"We were at all three of those places, too," I countered.

"True," she said. "But we were hunter-free until the unit showed."

"What about Lunenb—" I clamped my mouth shut when Lyra shot me a dangerous warning look. But, based on Jax's face, the damage had been done.

"So, that *was* you," Jax said with a slight head shake.

I tried to give him an apologetic smile, but it was pointless to even try now.

"We suspected as much," Leander said to Jax as if confirming some suspicion from a separate conversation the rest of us weren't a part of.

"Okay, then," Lyra said. "Still doesn't count. Sasha wasn't there *or* mentioned."

I could hardly argue with her. Hunters all shared the same goal, for the most part, but the ones that followed us out of Lunenburg were different than Sasha. More fanatically religious, for one.

"Do I need to know more than I do?" Wes asked.

I shook my head. "We handled it," I half-lied. It had been handled, but very, very badly on my part.

He didn't look like he believed me, but he didn't press and went back to tidying the kitchen. I was starting to think my habit of cleaning to relieve stress wasn't all my own fault.

"Spill," Lyra continued. "We already know how you found us in Salem," she said. "Thanks for that, by the way," she shot at Thea.

"I just—it wasn't like—I didn't..." Thea looked ready to cry.

"Let it go," I said, earning a quizzical look from Lyra and more than one eyebrow raised in surprise from the others.

"It's done, move on," I pressed, more to Lyra than anyone else.

I caught Thea's eye, and she gave me such a small, quick smile, but I could have been imagining it.

Lyra shrugged. "Fine. Let's talk about Halifax," she redirected. "You *suspected* that we were attacked outside of Lunenburg?"

Leander nodded. "We weren't sure it was you until later. The Council told us they heard from a healer who had dealt with a witch that sounded a lot like you," he said, nodding to his sister.

"Nothing but utter perfection?" Lyra asked, tossing her braid over her shoulder with a flourish.

I rolled my eyes.

"Foul-mouthed and pig-headed," Jax offered with a smile.

Lyra flipped him off.

Blythe walked back into the kitchen and tossed the bloodied rag back on the table. "The ward around the property has been successfully extended." She unzipped her coat and discarded it over the back of the couch. "You are all very welcome." She climbed back on the seat next to Lyra. "And Rez says they're on their way back, so if there's anything you don't want the rest of the group to know, talk fast."

Thea used Blythe's return to slip away from the group, and we all pretended we didn't hear her go upstairs.

"The boys here were just about to get to the point and tell us how they found us in Halifax," Lyra said.

Blythe nodded, sniffing against the change in temperature, her cheeks flushed with cold. "Because Sasha's on their trail," she concluded.

Jax looked over at Leander. "I don't think we've decided that," he countered.

"Right, but Salem, then—"

"A healer told you Lyra was at Martin's," I prompted quickly. We could rehash the beginning of the conversation with Blythe later.

Leander nodded. "It took a few days for us to get permission to go up there," he said. "But when we did, Martin wasn't there to receive us."

"How formal of you," Lyra muttered.

Blythe nodded. "Because he wasn't at home."

I bit my lip. He hadn't been home because he'd followed us to Rez's to talk to us—me—about what I'd done at the Esbat.

"Still doesn't explain how you knew *we* were there," Blythe said, crossing her arms.

Jax looked at Blythe with something that could have almost been pity, and, for some reason, I had a feeling what was coming.

"Selvina," Blythe confirmed as if it were most obvious answer in the world.

Leander nodded. "She told us you had been staying with them but had left for Halifax before Martin."

"Bitch," Blythe mumbled.

Martin had promised that no one on the Council would find out where we were from him. Selvina had made no promises, and I guess without him there to enforce it, she was more than willing to sell us out.

It didn't come as much of a shock. It wasn't like Selvina Foster had even pretended to like any of us.

"And that's where you found us in Halifax," I concluded.

Jax nodded.

"When we heard Armin had landed there as well it was all the confirmation we needed," Leander offered. "Didn't take us more than a couple hours to find you."

"So, you were in Halifax *before* the hunters," Lyra said.

"Before Armin," Leander corrected. "We have no way of knowing when the others arrived."

I massaged my temples. "I don't think they've been a step behind," I said. "I think they've been *in* step with you this whole time."

Leander and Jax gave me identical frowns.

"Lenore and Armin knew each other a little too well," I explained. "I think she was telling them where you were headed."

"But—why would she do that?" Leander questioned, as if the idea was basically the same as me suggesting we all get matching friendship tattoos.

"Because she can't kill me herself without good reason," I said. "So, she sent the hunters to do it for her."

"That's...that's a risky accusation," Leander said slowly. "Without proof, no one is going to believe you."

Lyra let out a snort. "I believe her."

"Same," Blythe offered.

"No one who matters," Leander corrected.

"Asshole," Lyra said over Blythe's, "Fuck off."

I pulled the tie out of my ponytail that had all but fallen out anyway and ran a hand through my tangled hair.

"Explain how they found us here, then," Leander said. "She had no idea we were all going to—"

"*Dissent*," Lyra supplied with a smirk.

Jax rubbed his forehead. "Can we just all agree to be more careful?" he asked. "Avoid run-ins and keep to the house until this all gets figured out?"

Leander nodded.

Blythe grumbled something under her breath that I failed to catch.

Lyra crossed her arms.

Wes glanced at me.

I sighed. "No," I finally said. "I want another run-in, but on my terms."

"Em," Jax said with a shake of his head. "They want you dead."

I shrugged. "And until Sasha shows up, I could stand in the middle of downtown and be completely fine."

"Can I come," Lyra joked.

"No," Jax and Leander said at the same time, seeming to have completely missed her tone.

Lyra let out a half-chuckle. "*Circe*, what is with you two?" she asked. "I didn't think it was possible for you to be more uptight."

Leander shot a look at Jax, who let out a long sigh. "Opting for the most dangerous thing isn't funny," he said simply.

I downed the now lukewarm tea Wes had given me and shuddered against the poor temp and taste. "I'm not joking." I pushed the mug away and stood up. "From her point of view, I put her brother in a coma he may never wake up from and killed her dad," I continued. "She's not going to *let* anyone else kill me, and I can use that."

"We've been over this," Lyra said. "Life-and-death plans are to be handled by someone who is very much *not* you."

I shot her a glare.

"But once you let me take over," she continued, "I'm in."

"You don't need to be any more involved than you already are," Leander said, earning a pointed throat-clearing from Jax. Leander hung his head and exhaled pointedly. "The reasons she wants you dead mean she's hardly going to be reasoned with," he said to me, ignoring Lyra's questioning frown.

"I don't plan on *reasoning* with her," I said. "I plan on ending this, whatever way I have to."

The silence that followed was painful. They all understood my meaning, and I knew there had to be some who disagreed with it, but I was thankful none of them voiced it.

Lyra nodded but didn't say anything. She'd have my back, no matter how stupid my plan was. She'd tell me it was stupid but wouldn't try to talk me out of it.

"I don't really have a choice if I don't want to die," Blythe said, but her half-smile told me she was only half-joking.

"Don't underestimate her," was all Wes offered.

"I'll fill the others in when they get back," Blythe said. "You should go get cleaned up unless you want another round of explaining all...that." She gestured to me as a whole and was right. I no doubt still looked terrible and didn't need to rehash what had happened earlier. Especially since I couldn't quite remember the half-truths Thea had come up with.

"We'll go over specifics later," I agreed.

"Can we *please* talk about this?" Jax implored as I moved towards the stairs.

I shook my head. "I've made up my mind."

He pursed his lips against the argument I knew he wanted to have. And we would have it, that much I knew for sure. But that was a problem for after I had a hot shower and a long nap.

Besides, I had a Death Witch to thank for saving my life.

Chapter 8

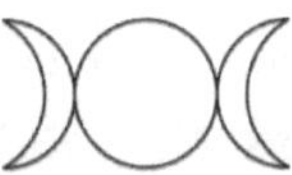

Muffled voices of a discussion followed me up the stairs. I'd dropped a bomb and left without giving anyone much opportunity to weigh in. But truth was, I didn't want anyone to weigh in. I was doing this with or without help.

It turned out Thea had already had the same idea I did about needing a hot shower. It was becoming a regular habit for me. Something about near-death experiences left the skin feeling like it needed a good scrub.

She caught sight of me in the mirror as I went into the primary bedroom to use that shower—it was the best in the house—and the red under her eyes told me she'd been crying.

She turned to face me and leaned against the counter, crossing her arms and biting her lip as it started to tremble.

"So," I started, closing the bedroom door behind me. "You're a Death Witch."

She nodded.

My mind flashed back to the brief contact my magic had made with hers in Sabbats. It had been rancid and cold, like, well, death. Had I given it more thought, it might have been easier to figure out, but I'd been more focused on reeling my own magic in than on what I'd felt from hers.

I yanked my sweater sleeve down as far as it would go and balled the end of it in my hand. "What kind?"

She was quick enough wiping the tear away that I almost missed it, and I realized after I'd asked that it wasn't really any of my business. My curiosity wanted to know more than anything. I'd never met a Death Witch before. Few had.

There were three types: Bone, Intercessor—or what mortals called mediums—and Necromancers. None had great reputations, and Thea admitting to being one was amazing enough. I knew I shouldn't pry any more.

She swallowed. "Did you tell them?" she asked, nodding to the door. "About..."

I shook my head, and that seemed to be a relief to her.

"Please," she said quietly. "Don't."

I frowned. "He—they don't know?"

She shook her head. "No one does." She glanced at the door as if scared someone had their ear pressed against it, listening. I moved further into the bathroom.

"I don't need to..." I took a deep breath. "I really just wanted to say thank you," I said. "For not leaving me back there."

Her eyes widened. "Oh. Yeah. You're welcome, I guess."

I nodded. "Mind if I get a shower?"

She blinked at me, clearly surprised at my dropping the conversation. But if she wanted to keep it a secret—especially from Jax—then who was I to push? I'd done that with Blythe, and it had resulted in more than one screaming match. I didn't have the energy for that on top of everything else.

"Yeah, sorry," she stepped to the side, and I caught the first good look at myself since getting back. The damp cloth had caught most of the fresh blood, but the napkins had done shit to keep it from staining my lips and chin.

Enough had gotten on my sweater that I could see why Lyra and Blythe had assumed a fist fight. I looked terrible.

I sighed and grabbed a washcloth to scrub away what I could before getting in the shower.

"Emaleth?" Thea began and I couldn't stop the flinch at my full name.

I turned back to her. "Yeah?"

"I'm a Necromancer," she said quietly.

My stomach dropped, and I tried to hide the surprise, but her grimace told me I hadn't succeeded.

"Oh," I croaked out.

She sniffed. "I just—" she straightened her back. "I wanted to say it, out loud."

"Okay."

She turned and walked out of the room, the door clicking loudly as it latched. I was too shocked to move for what felt like a full minute. Which was more shocking, I wasn't sure: her telling me, or that Thea—Jax's ex—was a Necromancer.

Slowly, I turned back to the mirror and absently cleaned what blood I could off my face before starting the shower and turning it as hot as I could. As steam filled the room, I stripped, and my mind went into overdrive.

Necromancers were rare. Not as rare as Blood Witches, but rare enough. Wes believed there were more than we knew because very few would admit to it. I wouldn't blame them; they had the worst reputation out of Death Witches.

Intercessors were saved the worst of the scorn because they could make a lot of money for a coven by connecting mortals and witches alike with dead loved ones. Bone Witches were historically notorious for robbing graves to cast their spells without exhausting themselves.

But Necromancers, they were the most dangerous. The last one I knew of went rogue sometime in the fifteenth century. He'd planned to raise some dead prince and use him to rule England.

A Scottish coven managed to stop him before he could gain too much power, but rumors that he actually managed to raise that prince were still circulating today.

Ever since, Necromancers were strictly regulated, and fewer and fewer were said to be born.

The hot water was doing everything for my sore body and nothing for the thoughts about Thea now stuck in my head. I'd seen her use her magic with my own eyes. My magic had detected what she was before I had. And she'd fully admitted it to me. Still, it was hard to reconcile what I knew about her with what her magic was. Every Death Witch—or enthusiast I'd met typically embraced the dark and macabre. Not that I'd met a whole lot, but still, Thea didn't quite fit the image I'd developed in my head.

But then, I was sure the Council had stricter rules than the ones introduced six centuries ago. If she was going to hide under their noses, looking the part was not the smartest idea.

I stayed under the water longer than I needed to, and I could feel the heat drying my skin out. Turning the water off, I wrapped myself in a towel and stepped out. Whether I wanted to admit it or not, Thea and I had more in common than Jax.

It looked like we'd both spent our lives hiding what we were from the Council and their perceptions of our magic.

(

My feet dangled over the arm of the Adirondack chair and Amity's book sat open in my lap, pages covered in sticky tabs and notes about the best use for each spell and some modifications that could be useful.

Wind swept across the frozen lake, sending snow eddying, frozen crystals sparkling in the sunlight. Absentmindedly chewing on the end of my pen, I watched as they were stopped by the spell guarding the yard.

"You *want* Sebastian in on the planning?" Blythe asked, running her hand along the slight arch in Rhi's back. The cat had perched herself on the arm of Blythe's chair, her length barely fitting.

I tapped the pen against the page and nodded. "At least some of it." Grace was curled up next to my chair, resembling a sleek black puddle more than a cat.

"So, now I have to make two plans?" Lyra asked, face tilted up to catch the warm sun, its rays reflecting in her mirrored sunglasses. Attie purred loudly, her front half draped across Lyra's crossed legs.

We'd moved outside for privacy and fresh air. The spell over the back-yard was still holding the temperature to a comfortable degree, and it was the best place to be. Especially after the idea of baiting the hunters had been floated to the rest of the group.

Chad asked if he had to do anything, and when told no, he went about prepping stroganoff to try to make the day a little better. He may not have understood much about what was going on, but he was probably the most supportive, outside of Blythe and Lyra. That didn't mean I couldn't sense his worry.

Jax had given up on trying to convince me to find another way to handle the situation, but he wasn't happy with me or Lyra and didn't even try to hide it. He seemed even more upset with Lyra's insistence on being involved, and, more than once, we'd found him and Leander talking in hushed voices that stopped as soon as they noticed one or both of us watching them.

Leander, too, had seemed to agree that there was no use trying to talk us out of it, but his approach was to be short with Lyra. Every joke she'd crack about "the worst that could happen" set his jaw on edge, and he'd snap at her to at least take it seriously if we weren't going to stop.

Rez and Blythe had it out in the den during dinner. We all ate and tried to discuss other topics to pretend like we couldn't hear every word. After fifteen minutes of the two of them screaming at each other, Blythe won out, and Rez grudgingly agree to help with what he could.

Sebastian went off about how completely unacceptable it was to provoke hunters. The Council had strict rules about Emissaries and hunters engaging, he argued. His indignation was far too forced to be convincing, and his storming out to "clear his head" was even less so.

"Think of it more like a bullet point to the bigger plan," I said.

"Let's not use the word *bullet*," Lyra muttered. "Can't I just knock him out and shove him in a closet again?"

I shook my head. "No, we need to be sure that Sasha knows that we're setting a trap."

"If we're going to have to pretend to include that asshole, I'm going to need something stronger than coffee," Blythe said. "I mean, did he really think we weren't going to notice him leaving the house like *all* the time?"

"Sometimes you just need to cry in private, babe," Lyra teased through a laugh. "Do you think exposing him is going to get him killed?" she added hopefully.

"No," I blurted. "I mean, that's not what I want."

"You're no fun," Lyra grumbled.

All three cats picked up their heads at the same time, ears focused on the neighbor's yard. I glanced over to see the car pulling out of the driveway. They weren't close enough to get a good look at what we were doing, but if they chose to look too hard, they might have noticed the lack of snow and ice and started to ask questions.

I found myself not caring as long as I was able to escape the cramped house for a little while. Grace stood and arched her back before walking a few steps away from the chair. She flipped onto her back and rolled in the grass, letting the sun warm her belly.

"How *is* your plan going?" I asked Lyra. She hadn't been forthcoming with her process, just telling us to read up on the books in case we had to deal with hunters and other witches.

"It's going," she replied.

I wrapped my hand around the blackened ruby with a sigh. "Well, I hope it takes into account that I'm pretty much useless." I'd told them more about the day the hunters found Thea and me—still leaving out the fact that Thea was a Necromancer. I hadn't wanted anyone else to know that my magic was practically non-existent, but if they were going to help me with this, they needed to know the full extent.

"What do you mean?" Lyra asked, pushing her sunglasses up onto her head and turning to look at me.

I shut the pen into the page of Amity's book. "Without this," I said, tapping the ruby, "I'm pretty much nothing."

Rhi slid off the armrest and Attie slunk out of Lyra's lap to join Grace in her sunbathing. Blythe stared at the ground in front of her, and Lyra looked at me like I'd just told her I thought the sky was purple.

"Is that a fucking joke?"

I shook my head. "This was the real power," I said. "I was just harnessing it."

"That's not how talismans work, Boswell," Blythe corrected. "They boost, they don't create."

"That's not—"

"You've never been *nothing*," Lyra said sternly. "You get what you put out. You've apparently decided you don't have power, so the universe is responding."

I frowned. That wasn't exactly fair; I hadn't *decided* anything. It felt more like the universe had been messing with me, not the other way around.

I ran my thumb over the gem. No one fully knew how talismans could work. Sure, there'd been enough made and used that we had a fairly decent grasp on the basics. But blood talismans—like everything else about blood magic—had been kept a close secret to keep other witches from replicating it.

For all we knew, John Osborne had created this one because blood magic got weaker with each generation and needed it. Just like Amity had, just like I had.

They could convince themselves the ruby had nothing to do with how powerful magic could be, but they hadn't been there. They hadn't felt the struggle to tap into mere scraps of mine and force it to do the bare minimum for me.

"Did you at least take into account the five witches without expressed power?" I asked, not wanting to fight with them about what I knew had to be true.

Lyra rolled her eyes and put her sunglasses back on. "Please, I'm not a complete fucking moron." She turned back around with a slight smile on her lips while the cats chased each other in the sunlight.

Chapter 9

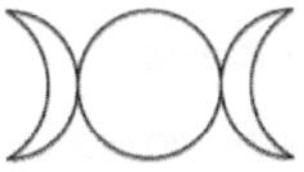

My sore eyes refused to focus on the page in front of me, no matter how many times I blinked. Black ink on yellowed pages blurred into indistinct lines. The harder I tried to find individual words, the worse it got.

Every spell book in the house was open on the dining room table, some tabbed, some not. Half-empty mugs of cold coffee sat among the notes we'd all made. I shoved one of the books away from me and rubbed my eyes. Stifling a yawn, I folded my arms on the table and rested my chin on them.

Morning had snuck up on us, and I couldn't remember how many ideas had been thrown out. We could have had a solid plan by now if Jax and Leander weren't so intent on striking everything down. It got to the point where Lyra was so frustrated she almost chucked another mug at her brother's head.

Wes and Chad had gone to bed at a very reasonable hour, leaving the rest of us to continue in as hushed tones as we could. Sadiki had sat down on the couch to "rest his eyes" but had started softly snoring half an hour later and hadn't moved much since.

Jax and Lyra's *discussion* on whether mugwort or yarrow would create a thicker smoke was finally cut off when Blythe decided we'd just use both. No matter what we brought up, he and Leander had a reason it wouldn't work. It was almost like they were intentionally trying to sabotage the whole thing.

Coming up with roughly a dozen non-lethal spells that anyone—expressed or not—could use had been the easiest part and met little argument from the group. The half a dozen Lyra original spells that she was the only one eager to test out had taken long and been the first strike against Leander's annoyance.

We were armed as well as we could be, but so far, we still hadn't figured out the most important part: how to get Sasha to find us and not make it look like we were searching for her.

"No matter what we do," Leander said with a shake of his head, cutting off Thea's idea of going back to the co-op, "She's going to think it's suspicious that you're out wandering around."

"Em's done way stupider things," Blythe offered.

Thea unsuccessfully turned her laugh into a snort.

"Hey," I muttered half-heartedly. She could have kept that thought to herself.

"I hate to agree," Rez said, leaning back in his chair and stretching. "About Sasha being suspicious," he added once I shot him a glare. "But we should give credit where it's due. Sasha doesn't strike me as ignorant as a lot of the other zealots we deal with."

"She's not," I grumbled. She may not have been Raven when it came to playing a role—Sasha hadn't even tried to hide her dislike for me from the beginning—but she was a step above the other hunters.

"No," Lyra agreed. "But she's fucking pissed. That tends to make people do shit they might not normally."

I knew that all too well.

"She's trained," Thea offered. "You really think she can't handle being angry?"

I stared at the flickering flame of the pine-scented candle burning in the jar in front of me, almost to the bottom. "It's not just anger," I said. "It's grief."

"For what?" Sebastian asked with a doubtful eyebrow raise.

"Her brother, her father, her pride. Pick one," I offered. "Grief and anger make for a dangerous combination." I was aware of how quiet the room had gone and could feel everyone staring at me. I focused on the flame in front of me. "You'd be surprised how little you care about consequences to just get that weight lifted for even a second."

No one spoke for a long moment.

"Like ignoring an obvious trap," Jax concluded.

I nodded against my folded arms.

Lyra shrugged. "We did."

"And Em almost died," he unnecessarily reminded us. He'd been tense this whole time; I could see it in how he sat, too rigid, like he was waiting for something to attack right now.

"But she didn't," Lyra said. "So chill out."

Leander let out a frustrated sigh. "You need to be less *chill*," he snapped. "You're taunting a killer and being too damn flippant about it."

"Kill or be killed," Lyra offered.

Blythe looked down at her hands, folded on Patience's open book.

Jax's head snapped to her.

Rez's cool demeanor hardened.

Leander's mouth parted in surprise.

Thea let out a small gasp.

Sadiki grunted in his sleep.

I picked my head up and ran a hand through my hair. She wasn't supposed to let that slip, at least not yet.

"You—the—you're going to kill her?" Jax asked slowly, looking between his sister and me.

I tied my hair up on top of my head. "I told you I was ending this."

"By killing her?"

"*She's* literally killed people," Lyra reminded him. "Like, a whole lot of them."

Jax took a deep breath and looked at Leander, who just shook his head, clearly in disbelief. "Killing her makes us just as bad," he said. "We should be better than that."

Lyra rolled her eyes. "*Circe*, what are you Catholic now? Witches don't do that whole 'turn the other cheek' bullshit."

"Doesn't mean we should start murdering people," Jax countered.

"Hunters," Lyra said. "Who would murder all of us without a second thought." She wasn't about to back down. Which is what we needed right now. At some point, the discussion had to end, and we had to put a plan into action.

"It's not an easy thing," Rez warned. "Are you sure?" He was looking at Blythe only.

She picked up her gaze to meet his. "Like she said, kill or be killed."

"What makes you think you *can*?" Sebastian snorted.

Lyra leaned towards him slightly. "What makes you think I can't?"

He folded his arms, but any bravado he thought he had was completely gone.

"If you plan on killing her, that only makes things more dangerous," Leander said. "I can't—"

"I'm not asking for anyone's permission," I stressed, leaning back in my chair and crossing my arms.

"None of us are," Blythe confirmed.

Thea rubbed her forearm through her sweater and glanced around at us like she wanted to add something. She gave a slight shake of her head and focused her attention on the table in front of her instead.

Leander rubbed the back of his neck and when he caught Jax's eye, I saw something fearful pass between them. Jax gave a half-shrug but didn't say anything, and I knew some silent conversation was happening.

"We still haven't determined how to get Sasha to come to us," Rez said, interrupting whatever the brothers were communicating.

Leander stared at him. "You're okay with this?"

Rez shook his head. "Not in the slightest," he admitted. "But I've done my best to protect Blythe up to this point. I'm not going to start telling her what to do." He winked at his cousin. "I think Martin has that role covered."

She let out a half-laugh. "That he does," she muttered.

Lyra looked at her brothers and raised her eyebrows. "See, now, why can't you two be that evolved?"

"We're not trying to tell you what to do," Jax said.

"We're telling you what *not* to do," Leander corrected, earning a glare from Jax.

"Just, think this all the way through before you jump into it," Jax added quickly, before Leander and Lyra could get into it. "You can be...impulsive, sometimes."

She rolled her eyes. "An all-nighter of planning isn't enough for you?"

Jax opened his mouth to add something, but Rez tapped his fingers on the table. "Let's see what they come up with before we start poking too many holes in it," he proposed, fixing Jax with a stern look. "I, for one, would rather not be excluded. Unless you'd prefer to have the three of them run off on their own. *Again.*"

Blythe scratched at her eyebrow piercing.

I bit the inside of my lip.

Lyra found something interesting on the table to scrape at with her fingernail.

"So," Rez continued with a nod. "Did you already have a plan or are we brainstorming together?"

I could practically feel Jax and Leander both wanting to argue, but to their credit, they kept their mouths shut. Truth was, other than just wandering around the city, I didn't know of a good way to make it look like Sasha found me and not the other way around.

"You could take the wards off the house," Sebastian suggested as simply as asking for no mayo on a sandwich.

"What?" Thea balked before I could.

He shrugged. "Just an idea."

"A bad one," Jax shot.

"I was trying—"

"No one wants to hear from room-temp IQ," Lyra said with an eye-roll.

I knew having Sebastian in on this part of the plan was technically my idea, especially if I was right and he was passing info to Lenore, but my patience with him and his voice was getting thinner by the sleep-deprived minute.

"Fine," he muttered and went to sit on the couch next to a sleeping Sadiki.

"Any other ideas?' Lyra said pointedly.

"If it weren't for the other witches, I'd agree with Thea," Blythe said. "They found you at the co-op before."

A wicked smile spread across Lyra's face and a shiver ran down my spine. "Just pick a nightclub," she suggested.

I shook my head at her.

"What? Near-death experiences tend to find you while you're out partying."

I tossed a pen at her. "Shut up."

She caught the pen, laughing to herself.

Rez drummed his fingers on the table. "It's not a terrible strategy."

We all looked at him.

He continued to drum his fingers to some unheard tempo. "You said anger and grief make people do stupid things," he explained. "How angry do you think she'd be if she thought you were out having fun instead of cowering in fear?"

I chewed it over. He wasn't wrong. Hunters used fear to intimidate. Their own religion used it to keep their believers in check. She wanted to be a threat to me, and if I acted like she wasn't, that could make her more likely to overlook the trap.

I could see the logic in it. Sasha *would* be furious if she thought I was getting drunk instead of hiding from her, but I had terrible luck at these places ever since that first night at Onyx. And the thought of giving whatever cosmic force that liked to pick on me an open shot made my stomach knot uncomfortably, but it was the only suggestion I could see working.

I nodded at Rez. "Yeah, okay, I guess that's the best idea we've got."

"Seriously?" Blythe asked, as surprised as I was that I agreed to it.

Lyra clapped her hands together. "Shopping," she said cheerfully.

"Keep it to a minimum," I warned.

"You should stay here," Leander insisted, looking at Lyra. "Run point on surveillance."

Jax watched Leander with a warning glance.

"Excuse me?"

Leander swallowed. "You're the best with the tech," he said.

"That's true," Jax added.

She laughed. "If anyone's staying behind, it's you two," she said.

"Lyra," Leander scolded. "Just hear us out."

"No," she said. "Your expressed powers have been bound, and neither of you cared to learn how to defend yourselves without them." She pointed to the couch with the pen. "Even numb-nuts over there was smart enough to do that."

"Hey!" Sebastian objected.

"You can't—"

"We just thought you might want to run the op yourself," Jax said before Leander could finish whatever he was about to say. "Since it was your idea."

She frowned. "Lack of sleep makes you two extra weird."

Jax nodded and glanced at his brother. "That's a good point," he admitted. "We should all get some sleep. We can revisit all this after a few hours."

My eyebrows pinched together. Lyra was right, he was being weird. I'd never seen him ramble. Tense and, occasionally, a little broody, sure, but nervous rambling was usually my thing.

Lyra sighed. "Okay, fine. I guess the weakest links need sleep." She uncrossed her leg from under her and slid off the table she'd been using as her chair. "And I'm sure your uncles and Sadiki are going to want to be filled in."

I nodded through a yawn I wasn't able to stifle. It had been a long night, and having the beginnings of a plan made my stomach pinch with a new kind of anxiety.

Despite exhaustion settling into my bones, I stayed up while everyone went to bed to at least attempt to clear the mess we'd left on the table. It was less about cleaning up and more about not leaving it for Chad and Wes. I stacked the spell books at one end of the table and the notes in a pile next to them.

The mugs and the carafe went into the sink without being emptied and the candle—all but a thin layer of wax now—went back into the cupboard. I half-wiped off the counters, draped a blanket over Sadiki, and shut off the lights before heading to the den to crash for hopefully the next eight to ten hours.

At the base of the stairs, I heard hushed voices; Leander and Jax were no doubt discussing how best to talk us out of our plan. Yawning again, I was ready to let them stay up even later to tackle that impossibility, when Leander's tone made me stop.

"...in a month," he whispered, a panic I'd never expected from him lacing the word. "We can't let her be this reckless."

I frowned.

"The only way you'll get her to cooperate is to tell her the truth," Jax said.

I turned to the stairs.

"Not yet," Leander pleaded. The desperation in his tone drew my foot to the bottom step.

A long sigh followed. "Fine," Jax said. "But tonight's not the night to decide anything. Get some sleep."

Leander—I assumed—snorted. "I won't be able to get much sleep until—"

"I know," Jax agreed. "But try."

With my foot poised on the step to go up, I stayed frozen in place, straining to listen to more. but all I heard was the creak of the floor and the click of the bedroom door latching closed.

What were they hiding from me *now*?

Chapter 10

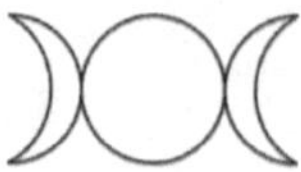

It took us all almost a full day of sleep to recover from pulling the all-nighter—and even then, I was still a little groggy as we explained the plan we'd come up with to Wes, Chad, and Sadiki. Wes and Chad reluctantly accepted the idea, but only as long as they were kept updated the whole time. I had a feeling they were taking Rez's approach and would rather be involved instead of arguing with us.

Difference was, Wes probably would have been the only one who could have talked me out of it. I'd never admit that out loud and give him the opportunity. Or worse, give Jax an ally that would work in his favor.

Sadiki agreed with the trap plan but kept to himself any opinions on what we were planning once we had her trapped. I had a feeling he would have agreed with the "kill or be killed" motto Lyra and Blythe had latched onto and that he was keeping quiet to maintain the peace.

Of all the conditions Jax, Leander, and Wes insisted on as far as our plan was concerned, there was one I didn't argue with: sticking to the house until we had a time and a place settled on. But that was only because I had already decided on doing that, mostly as an excuse to get out of shopping with Lyra.

After everyone had been filled in, Sebastian *suddenly* needed to leave the house by himself. Right on schedule. If he was trying to hide the fact that he was passing information to Lenore, he was doing a terrible job. His excuse? The scent of my chosen cleaning solution "gave him a headache." The least he could do was come up with a better lie.

The spells I needed for our plan were memorized, translated, and supplied. So, with nothing else to do but wait for Friday, I set my focus on trying to discern more about the elusive Marnie from mom's journals.

After all, if we made it out of this alive, that would be the next problem to tackle. Stop the hunters, undo the binding, expose Lenore, and get Ian's memories back. A checklist of the seemingly unachievable.

The first bullet point to item number two on my checklist was to find out who Marnie's daughter was and see what she knew about the binding. *If* she knew about the binding. Unfortunately, that task was proving more difficult than finding out what Jax and Leander had been whispering about.

I hadn't caught them discussing anything similar since that night, but I had noticed them acting strangely—or *stranger*—the closer we got to our planned night out. Leander seemed more worried and less angry, and, more than once, I'd caught Jax staring at Lyra like he was about to tell her that her favorite pet died.

The small part of me that was tempted to ask was largely overshadowed by my desire to avoid an argument with either of them before we tried this thing with the hunters. It was hard enough keeping the two plans we had going separate in my own mind; I didn't need to slip up and reveal that Lyra, Blythe, and I had our own scheme going.

I'd already confused who was going where in front of Thea and had to awkwardly cover it up by pretending it was due to lack of sleep, but I wasn't entirely sure she bought it.

So, I'd once again hidden myself away in the den to see if I could suss out the full identity of this "Marnie." She was only mentioned in a few passages through the years in mom's journals. The first note of her existence, chronologically, was not long after Blythe's mom's name popped up. Mentions of them both stopped roughly a month after Grandma Geri's funeral.

I'd kept my own scribbles about what mom had been doing and where she was when the names showed up. They ended up not being as helpful as I had hoped. I'd wanted to see if I could figure out where they'd met. If it had been a festival or event, I figured it would have helped narrow things down. The only issue was that nothing stuck out.

When re-reading passage after passage had gotten me nowhere, I switched to sorting through her pictures to see if there were any from an event that could help identify her. They were slowly becoming the last resort. If there was nothing in the years and years of images, I was going to have to let Lyra try a magical solution, and that, too, was going to be a stretch if all we had to go off was a first name.

Rolling out the stiffness in my neck that hours of sitting left me with, I set the last of the pictures from her eighteenth birthday to the side. I'd taken to organizing by year; if nothing else, they'd at least be in order.

A soft knock came, and before I could answer, the door slowly opened. I'd lost track of time, so for all I knew, someone was bringing me lunch—or was it close to dinner now? The light bleeding through the curtains meant lunch was a better guess.

Wes had been checking on me regularly. Blythe would pop in and offer to take over scouring the journals, and Lyra would pretend to help but ultimately end up focusing more on the clothes in the pictures than the people.

I looked up in time to see Jax slip inside the room, and my stomach flipped. I'd been trying to avoid him until after the hunter situation.

With a soft grunt, he sat down next to me, close enough for our arms to brush, and I tried to pretend it wasn't as distracting as it was.

"How are you feeling?" I asked, looking back at the pictures in my lap instead of his eyes. They all may have been over the illness that came with their "court-appointed" power binding, but Rez had mentioned it would take a while to feel fully normal again. And I doubted that staying up all night and stressing about death traps was good for any of them.

"Like I got dropped off a roof," he admitted. "But better."

"Good."

"How are you?"

I glanced over at him, frowning.

"You and Thea were the ones actually attacked," he reminded me.

"Oh, that," I said, waving his concern away. "I'm fine." And for once in what felt like years, it wasn't a total lie. Five months ago, I might have been freaked out enough to lose sleep, but now it was more of an annoyance than anything. Had I still been seeing Stanley, he would have forced me to unpack how recurring death threats and close calls weren't scaring me like they should.

And if I thought too hard about it, I found myself more freaked out by Thea being a Death Witch than hunters once again promising to kill me. Although, that was something I was keeping to myself as long as I could—or as long as Thea wanted to keep it a secret.

He nodded slowly. "I'm sorry I wasn't there."

I shrugged. "Not much you could have done," I said absently.

He flinched.

I closed my eyes for a moment at the embarrassment. "I didn't mean it like that," I backtracked. "It's just, they weren't really *trying* to kill me, so..." I bit my lip to physically stop the rambling.

"No," he said with a slight smile. "You're right."

I clenched my fist against the stack of photos to keep my hand from reaching for the broken gem I still wore. It wasn't the same, I knew that. I still *technically* had my magic, weak as it was.

He cleared his throat. "We never got to finish our conversation," he started.

I took a steeling breath. I'd been waiting—dreading—when he'd finally get me alone to have this conversation. The buffer of Lyra, or Blythe, or even Thea had protected me from this for the last couple of days. But now here we were.

I looked over at him and nodded. Might as well get it over with in case Sasha was more prepared than I anticipated.

"Before I—we—got sick," he clarified.

I blinked at him, surprised. "Oh. That."

He raised his eyebrows.

"Sorry, I just thought...the hunters..." I let the thought trail off. If he wasn't going to bring it up, then why would I?

He smiled but nodded. "You already know how I feel about that," he said. "And I wish you and Lyra would reconsider, but I'm never going to out-stubborn you two, so I'd rather talk about something else."

He took the photos out of my hands and set them on the floor on the other side of him before slipping one of his hands into my own

I swallowed against the warm and familiar sensation of his skin on mine.

He gave my hand a small squeeze. "We both said some things," he started.

My chest tightened as I looked at him. His blue eyes were duller than they should have been, like the binding that caged his magic also took that spark from him.

I took a deep breath. "We did," I agreed. "But nothing has changed in the last week, has it?"

He frowned at me. "Hasn't it?"

"Ian's memories are still gone," I said. "Lenore's Council is still after me." I pulled my hand out of his and put it in my lap.

"When they sent me to Salem," he began. "I didn't know what their plan for Ian was." He took a deep breath. "I—" he cleared his throat. "I thought you were with him."

I looked over at him, confused. "But you—" It took my brain a moment to catch up to what he was saying. "They sent you after Lyra?" I asked quietly.

He nodded. "They didn't think I would be able to be..." he started, his throat bobbing when he swallowed. "*Impartial* when it came to you." A flash of anger crossed his features, and I had to wonder what had happened to him after I'd left. I'd never given much thought about the punishment he could have faced after disobeying the Council and not dragging me in like Kane and Leander had wanted. I'd assumed Selene had stepped in on his behalf.

"Oh," I said, voice barely able a whisper.

"And they thought Lyra would be more likely to listen to me than Leander," he added. "When I found out you were with Lyra, it was too late for me to stop it."

I swallowed back the sob that tried to force its way out. "You didn't know," I concluded. Because how could he have? He was right. I hadn't trusted him enough. Lyra had even said Jax wouldn't let them take Ian from me, and he wouldn't have. But he had trusted that I wouldn't have let Ian go on his own. I'd been angry with Jax, but it was my fault. I was a stranger to Ian because I had decided to let him leave.

"If I had known what they were going to do to Ian, I wouldn't have let them," he continued. "I'm sorry."

My stomach tightened.

He moved his hand to rest on top of my crossed leg. His thumb started stroking small circles, the heat of his touch comforting.

I bit the inside of my cheek to keep my lip from quivering and looked down at his hand on my leg like it was the most normal thing in the world. Even before this, I had to admit I was being too harsh on him. He had no more power than I did against the Council. What had I, honestly, expected him to do?

I'd made Ian a target. His memory being stolen was my burden and mine alone.

I closed my eyes against the tears forming.

Jax's thumb wiped away a stray tear that had escaped, and his hand cupped my cheek. "We'll fix it," he said softly, resting his forehead against mine.

I opened my eyes to try forcing some words through the lump lodged in my throat.

His lips brushed mine, soft, delicate, but hesitant. His lips on mine, his hand on mine, his touch. It brought up all the times I'd wanted this. Him.

That want was still there anytime we locked eyes just a little too long, or when we sat so close I could breathe him in. It—*he*—clouded the reasons I couldn't give into what I wanted.

Because the moment I'd break eye contact or I'd shift away, those reasons would come rushing back.

I pulled back and shook my head slightly, trying not to let him see the tears flowing over.

"Em," he said so softly it could have passed for a breeze against a chiffon curtain.

Words were lost on me, and all I could do was shake my head again, knowing my silence had to hurt him.

But we were on opposite sides of an endless chasm, and no matter how large a part of me wanted to cross it and wrap myself in him, I couldn't—I *wouldn't*.

Not until we were done keeping things from each other.

Chapter 11

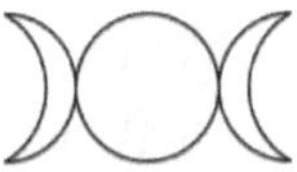

Stark white stood out against the dark industrial structures framing the two-story building. It resembled a colonial-style home more than a club. Black shutters pinned open on either side of the windows revealed revolving lights, and a neon sign with *The Gallery* in a script font hanging outside, were the only things that gave away the residential disguise.

It was further downtown and not surrounded by as many other late-night businesses as our first two stops. The first place had been a questionable Tiki-themed bar in the heart of downtown with an older crowd and watery piña coladas.

After an hour there, we walked a few blocks to a club hosting a Y2K night to bring in the college crowd.

Our secondary plan—the one the Emissaries weren't aware of—made stopping at multiple places necessary. We needed Sebastian to believe we were actually trying to draw Sasha out and not just expecting her to know where we'd be.

Or, that *had* been the plan. Now, it was almost midnight, and there had been no sign of Sasha or even a hint of the other group Thea and I had run into. We'd gone with the club idea because, my annoyance aside,

Lyra had been right. Danger had a knack for finding me at loud, dark, and crowded places. But, apparently, not when I was actually looking for it.

We'd all agreed, *The Gallery* would be our last stop of the night. And, after the woman checking IDs let us through, Jax and I made our way down the hall to the coat check.

Walking in, it felt a lot more like a museum than a nightclub. Had it not been for the thudding music in the walls, it would have been hard to tell.

The hall leading inside was dimmer in the center, illuminated only by the track lighting to draw attention to the anthropomorphic art displayed in large golden frames that hung on either side of the hallway. They were all dressed in large neck ruffs like the Elizabethan attire I'd seen in history textbooks.

Instead of the typical raccoons, foxes, or hunting dogs in bright clothes, however, they'd gone with grittier, less *desirable* animals. Rats, mice, and bats made up the gallery wall in more muted, Gothic colors.

I shrugged off the red leather jacket I'd worn over the cropped lace top and high-waisted jeans Lyra had picked out for me, handing it to Jax as we stepped up to the attendant.

Crossing my arms against the slight chill, I stared at one of the paintings while Jax made small talk next to me. The white bat was dressed in a comically large-collared jacket, ridiculous on its small frame. A clump of red spider lilies was pinned to the outside of the gray fabric, a morbid boutonnière. But the color was off, the red too deep, like open veins frozen in time.

Its unmoving eyes might have been fixed on the opposite wall, but they conveyed a sort of sad helplessness that made it almost impossible to look away, and my skin prickled uncomfortably.

"You good?" Jax asked, slipping the coat tickets into his pocket and sliding up beside me to let the next group move up in line.

I mentally shook myself out of the trance and faced him. "Yeah, just...yeah, let's go."

He nodded and slid his hand to the small of my back, the warmth from his touch sending a different kind of shiver up my spine. We hadn't been this close since the disaster of a *talk* in the den. I may have convinced a part of myself that stopping had been the right thing, that not letting him get too close was the most rational choice.

But there was an entire other part of me that had decided I was being completely idiotic about the whole thing.

And when his hand lingered at my waist as we made our way into the main bar the part that told me I was being stupid was making far more sense.

The space opened up to a large dance floor, with a bar that ran the length of the opposite wall. Both high-top tables and cocktail tables had been set up around the dance floor, most unoccupied. The flow of tables was interrupted by a set of stairs that went up to a sort of half-level with more seating and even fewer people. Another sign directed people to a rooftop bar, closed for the winter. That rooftop was one of the reasons Lyra had picked this place.

"We're almost to the ID check," Lyra's voice crackled through my earpiece.

"Two minutes out," Leander's grumble answered.

"Copy," Jax responded for the two of us, his voice in my ear and rumbling next to me.

"No one but us up here." Blythe.

After a beat, Rez added, "She means we're clear."

"That's what I fucking said," Blythe muttered, and I could picture the eye roll she must've given her cousin.

We found a high-top at the edge of the floor where we could still see the entrance hallway and the emergency exit door across from us. Jax gave my arm a comforting squeeze before heading to order drinks.

A metal menu holder displayed their specials. To compliment the gallery theme, their top drink was "Portraiture." A pawpaw mead that, based on the description, was meant to be a nod to both the Elizabethan era and Ohio's only native fruit.

I set the menu aside and glanced up in time to see Blythe at the railing of that half level where she had a great view of the entire bar and dance floor. She gave me a small nod and then refocused her attention on the entrance.

We'd grouped off for the night; a bound witch with a witch who could still use their expressed power. Blythe and Rez had gone in first to find a decent view of the entry and would be the first to see if our friends showed up.

Sadiki, Leander, and Thea were put together. Sadiki and Thea both had training like Lyra, and Leander refused to be left behind. I'd once again kept my mouth shut about Thea's power, as she wasn't offering it up—but hopefully, if things got sticky, she wouldn't hold back.

Lyra had put herself with Sebastian to keep an eye on him. There wasn't much she'd be able to do if his power hadn't been bound like the others, but she was itching to at least try to get another hit in, if presented the opportunity.

Jax and I were paired together. Lyra had passed off the reason as being that Sasha would be expecting it and therefore would help sell the "normal night out," as if any of this was *normal*. But I knew there were ulterior motives. Whatever was—or wasn't—going on between Jax and me wasn't exactly a secret, and I had a feeling Lyra was trying to play mediator. Whether that was because she thought she was helping me or because she didn't like Thea, I wasn't entirely sure.

My uncles, mostly Chad, weren't about to be left out. He had bought a police scanner app so they could listen in if the hunters had people in law enforcement here, too. I hadn't had the heart to remind him that we wouldn't know which communications were theirs and which weren't. This was Chad's way of being supportive.

"I got you the special," Jax said, setting a wine glass with a lemon-ade-colored drink in front of me. He moved to the other side of the table with his own pale ale.

"Thanks," I mumbled, rolling my thumb and forefinger around the thin stem to give my hands something to do.

He took a sip of his drink, glancing around the area. It wasn't the busiest place I'd been; Sabbats on New Year's Eve took that rank, but it was busy enough that I was nervous we wouldn't spot Sasha until it was too late, and then the plan to get her away from everyone else would be shot.

A group of girls on the dance floor drew my attention. They were jumping to the music, not really dancing, but laughing like this was the best night they'd had in a while.

I tried to remember back to when I felt like that. When the only thing I had to worry about was grades, or if I was getting invited to a party, or what to wear on an inevitably awkward first date.

I wasn't sure when I'd lost the hope that I'd ever get that back, but watching the group, I realized that was what made it so enviable: that I'd never have it again.

Jax pulled my attention away with a brief touch on my arm, and I looked at his slight frown.

He opened his mouth, but Lyra's voice cut him off.

"We're in," she said.

Jax paused a moment before answering. "High-top near the entrance," he directed.

"Copy," she responded, and I leaned slightly around him to watch Lyra move to the table he'd suggested while Sebastian went to the bar. None of us were *really* drinking, but we needed to look like we were.

"Just to the ID check," Thea's voice came next.

"Copy," Jax replied. "Head for the bar when you get in," he continued. "Gives a full view."

"I still don't like this," Leander offered, and I was sure I wasn't the only one who'd rolled their eyes in an eye roll in reply. He hadn't let up since we initially came up with the plan, and it was only getting more annoying.

"Keep it up and you can stay home next time," Lyra threatened.

My stomach knotted. I didn't like her even introducing the idea of a next time. I needed this to end—tonight. I took a long drink of the mead Jax had gotten me, and the mixture of tropical flavors coated my tongue.

"She's enjoying this a little too much," Jax grumbled.

My breathing became intentional as I stared at him. The music beat against my chest, steadier than my heart. She *was* enjoying this too much, but that was because she knew the full plan. He only had half the information.

The chasm widened in my mind as I watched his tense jaw work. I wasn't entirely sure what we were, or what I even wanted us to be. *If* we could be something. Because, he'd kept things to protect me; I'd done the same. And I knew we'd both do it again and again eventually getting stuck in a cycle that would only lead to the chasm swallowing us whole.

Someone had to be the first to break it.

Glancing to Lyra's table, then the bar, I watched as they all took their positions, waiting for trained killers to find us. Before I could talk myself out of it, I grabbed Jax's arm and yanked him away from our table.

"Em, what are you doing?" he hissed as I pulled him to a vacant table under the stairs.

Taking my earpiece out, I curled it into my fist. I didn't need anyone seeing or hearing us right now.

"Take out your earpiece," I whispered.

He frowned and glanced back at our now empty table. Turning back to me, he slowly pulled it out and put it in his pocket.

I took a deep breath. "Sebastian told them where we were going to be," I said hurriedly.

"How do you know that?" he asked.

I shook my head. "We just do." I peered out from the secluded spot to make sure no one was coming to check on us. "The point is, we—Lyra, Blythe, and I—have a plan to make sure he can't keep spying on us *and* to get Sasha off our backs."

He crossed his arms. "I thought that's what *we* were doing?"

I swallowed. "Not fully."

His chest rose and fell heavily, like he was trying to calm himself. "Em," he started.

"You were right before," I admitted. "I didn't trust you enough to tell you I was planning on running." I took a deep breath as hurt filled his eyes. "I told myself it was because I didn't want you to have to choose between me and your Council. And maybe that was partially true." I glanced around him to make sure no one was coming to look for us. "But if this is going to work, I have to do something and I need you to not try to stop me," I said quickly. I knew we didn't have enough time for me to explain in detail, but I wanted to give him enough.

His mouth parted. "What are you going to do?" he asked as if dreading the answer.

I put my hands on his crossed arms. "Something dangerous," I began. "You're going to be mad about it, but—" My phone buzzed in my back pocket, and I pulled it out to read an angry text from Lyra.

Put your fucking ear in!

Without giving Jax a chance to answer, I stuck my piece back in to hear the tail end of something Leander was saying. Jax slowly put his back too, but he never took his eyes off me.

"How long do you think until contact?" Thea asked and, having not heard the first part of whatever Leander had shared, I had no idea what to say.

"Oh, I'd say about a minute," Rez said. "Two if they get caught at coat check."

My stomach dropped.

"How many?" Jax asked without missing beat.

"Four," Rez said. "Five if the driver circles back."

"Is Sasha with them?" I asked.

"Can't tell," Blythe answered, but I knew she was lying. She had to if we were going to get Sebastian to bite.

"Then how do we know it's really them?" Lyra offered, laying on the fake skepticism a little too much.

Jax glanced in her direction despite not being able to see the group. It seemed to click quickly though, and his gaze snapped back to me.

"I'll go for a better look," Sebastian said quickly. And that's what we'd been waiting for. Jax made a move as if to go with him, but I put my hand on his arm and shook my head.

"I'm headed to the roof," I said. "See what I can get from there."

"Copy," Lyra and Blythe both said within a second of each other, and I knew they were on the move.

"Copy," Thea said, but hers sounded a lot more like a question.

"Are you all insane?" Leander snapped.

"Copy." Sebastian's voice came before we could answer Leander's question.

I pulled the earpiece out, placing it in Jax's hand before turning to leave, but he caught me around the waist.

"Dangerous?" he hissed. "This is suicidal."

I cupped his face in both my hands and gave him a quick kiss. "Trust me."

His eyebrows pinched together, and I thought he was going to argue. Instead, he pulled me against him and kissed me deeply for what felt like an eternity. But then he broke away, his eyes searching my face as if trying to memorize every line.

"Be careful," he said, voice filled with a soft pleading that nearly broke me.

But then, he let me go.

Chapter 12

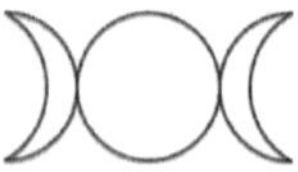

The path across the dance floor was not the least obstructed way to go, but it was the one that would hide me the best. I fought the urge to look back at Jax as I weaved between bodies to get to the other side.

The emergency exit door was poorly hidden behind heavy black curtains. I placed my hands on the crash bar and allowed myself one moment of hesitation.

"Keep us from harm, silence the alarm," I whispered. The metal heated under my hands briefly, and the second it cooled, I shoved the door open. No alarm sounded as I slipped through.

As soon as the door closed behind me, I was left in a large, quiet concrete hall lit only by strips of lights in the floor that gave off an eerie, dream-like, glow. A set of stairs, less decorative and wider than those in the main club, led up to the second floor and roof. I tied my hair back before rushing up, taking the stairs two at time.

I whispered the spell again at the door to the roof, combining it with Lyra's door-unlocking one, and stepped out into the cold February night. The moon was barely a sliver, while bright stars dotted the indigo sky.

Puffs of white breath clouded in front of me and gooseflesh sprang up my arms. I rubbed them to try to keep warm, wishing I'd kept my jacket with me.

The rooftop bar was closed up for the winter. Picnic tables were pushed to the side and partially covered in weeks-old snow and ice, the small wooden hut-style bar was boarded up, and poles that would normally hold string lights were left bare.

The emergency door was tucked into the opposite corner of the main entrance to the rooftop. A small, waist-high partition separated me from the seating area. I hopped up onto the small, raised platform—I could only assume was used for live entertainment—and carefully hurried over to where Blythe and Lyra were already crouched behind the low wall.

"What were you thinking?" Lyra hissed. "We use earpieces for a reason."

"Sorry." I blew warm air between my hands. "I had to—"

"At least tell us you were making out and not spilling everything," Blythe said as she put the finishing touches on her chalk rune circle.

I looked down at my hands. "Not *everything*," I countered.

They both groaned.

"You know he would have tried to follow me," I snapped. "This made it faster."

Lyra rolled her eyes. "Whatever you say." She pulled her hair back into a secure bun and I clamped my mouth shut on the explanation I wanted to give. Neither of them was going to believe me anyway.

Blythe handed me two small jars of ground-up mugwart, yarrow, rosemary, and garlic.

I held one in each hand. "*Calefac,*" I whispered. Once the heat from the command seeped into the jars, I shook them until a smoke began to form inside. It swirled around and around, growing darker and darker, turning almost black within half a minute.

The door leading to the club opened, and we peered over the edge of the partition to see Sasha stalk through, Sebastian right behind her, the light from the open door giving their outlines a white glow on the dark roof.

The door closed with a loud click, leaving us in darkness. We ducked as a flashlight beam swept across the rooftop.

"Where is she, Charlevoix?" Sasha asked and we heard the crunch of footsteps on the iced-over snow.

"She said she was heading up here," Sebastian said. "Maybe she got held up."

"Held up?" Sasha repeated mockingly.

"I doubt Jax would just *let* her go alone," he offered. "Man's got a problem."

The "I told you so" burned in the back of my throat but I kept it to myself.

"Touching," Sasha muttered, her footsteps getting closer. "If I have to burn this place to the ground to get to her, I will."

A long sigh. "I think that's excessive," Sebastian said.

"You're not here to *think*," Sasha said, turning back to face him and aiming the flashlight beam at his face.

Lyra clapped a hand over her mouth as she ducked back down behind the wall, shaking from the effort to keep her laughter quiet.

Sebastian squinted and held his hand up to try and block the light. "The deal was for her," he said. "The others aren't a part of this."

Thank the Mother for small favors.

"The *deal*," Sasha said, taking a step closer to him. "Was her life for yours." She lowered the flashlight. "That's all."

Sebastain took a half-step away and I had a feeling it hadn't been voluntary. "I can still pull the plug on this," he said, sounding more like a sulky teenager than a witch with any control.

Sasha laughed, titling her head to the night sky. "What in God's name makes you think you have any say here, *witch*?" She snarled the last word with such venom it made sent ice down my spine. "You're nothing without the protection of dear old grandmummy."

Sebastian stuttered. "You—you wouldn't even know where she was without us," he shot back. "We're the ones who got you this far."

She turned from him and swept the light across the roof again and we were barely able to duck out of the way in time.

"*And* we're the ones who made sure they're all powerless," Sebastian continued, clearly feeling more confident now that Sasha had moved away from him. But, none of us could have missed the change to *we*. As soon as he knew Sasha didn't care what he thought or did, he'd flipped the script to invoke Lenore. It was honestly pathetic.

Sasha's footsteps crunched closer to our hiding spot. "*If* your friends are as powerless as you claim, Marcus and the others will make quick work of them," Sasha said. Clearly, she didn't believe the others were bound. And why should she, especially if Sebastian still had his power?

She was too close. It was time.

I nudged Blythe and nodded when she looked over at me.

Lyra turned the small spell jar she had in her hand over itself as if itching to let it fly.

Blythe took out a small pocketknife and opened the blade to puncture the tip of her index finger and use the fresh flow of blood to draw one final rune in the center of the circle.

Once she'd replaced the knife, she held her hand over that rune, holding it half an inch from the surface and looked between us. Lyra gave one firm nod and with that, Blythe pressed her hand flat against the blood rune. The second she began muttering her spell, I could *feel* it working.

My magic—already weak—was being shoved down even further. It tried to fight, clawing at the invisible force trying to lock it away, but without the connection to the past daughters, Blythe's spell was more powerful.

I shook my head to clear the feeling and focus on what I needed to do, but it wasn't easy.

Lyra swallowed hard next to me. "Don't die," she said, voice shaking slightly. She felt it too.

"What's wrong with *you*?" Sasha demanded. Sebastian reaction to the spell pulling her attention from her search for me.

"Something isn't—I don't think—"

Lyra hurled her spell jar over the low wall.

I chucked mine a second later, and we all heard the glass shatter.

"What the fuc—"

Rancid smoke enveloped the rooftop and Sasha's words were cut off by a coughing fit brought on by the garlic and rosemary. My own eyes watered from the intensity of Wes's jars.

Before I could clear my head, Lyra pulled me up and yanked me around the wall. We sprinted into the heavy fumes. Lyra crossed behind me, heading for Sebastian as I rushed Sasha.

We connected in a slam of hard bodies, and I toppled over her before she knew what hit her. But it didn't take her long to recover and, before I could get the connection I needed, she rolled me off.

The smoke dissipated in a kick of wind as Lyra and Sebastian circled, hit for hit.

I dodged Sasha's kick and scrambled just out of reach; my knees going numb against the biting cold. Without *any* power, she had the upper hand. And now that she could see me, we'd lost what little advantage we had.

Her lip curled into a cruel smile as she reached behind her and drew a knife. I didn't think, just charged.

She swiped, and white-hot pain lanced up my side where the blade sliced through skin.

Doubled over, I tried to move away, but she was faster. The knife came down again. I turned. It nicked my arm.

Backed against the boarded-up bar, I clutched at my side, warm blood pooling under my hand. She glared at me with nothing but hatred in her eyes.

She lunged.

I kicked.

My foot caught her hand. The knife clattered to the ground, but my other foot caught an ice patch and I went down—hard.

My head cracked against the ground, stars bursting into my vision. Someone yelled my name.

Sasha's face swam above me. She dug her nails into the cut in my side, drawing a scream. Her laugh echoed in my ears.

Summoning all the strength I could, I grabbed both sides of her head. Her strong grip circled my wrists, trying to pry my grasp free. But I couldn't let go, not yet.

I pressed them harder and took a deep breath that made my side burn.

"*Aperi mihi animum tuum.*"

Sasha's nails dug into my skin, drawing blood.

"Memories found," I recited through hard-earned breaths. "Let them be bound."

She abandoned her attempt pulling my hands free, and I could feel her trying to climb off; still, I held.

It was getting harder to push out words. "Memories evoked, let—" Black edged into my vision. "—them be cloaked."

Sasha let out a pained cry and her whole body shuddered.

It wasn't as hard to fight her anymore.

"Memories found, let—" my head spun. "—them—" bile rose in the back of my throat. "—be—" heat scorched through my head. "—bound."

I could barely hear the last word. It was—I was weak. But it had to be enough. And, after an eternity hidden in a second pierced by Sasha's scream, I knew it had been.

The cold air vanished.

We plunged into weightlessness.

Chapter 13

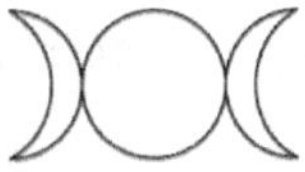

*N*othingness.

Blurry images from a childhood never experienced came into focus. Feelings I never had seeped into my core.

Falling deeper.

Our blonde hair flies behind us as we swing higher and higher, mom's gentle hand pushing us up and up and up. The elation when our stomach drops as we fall back down. We squeal for higher and higher. Alex is next to us, dad pushing him as he cries to slow down.

Deeper.

Our friends play tag after service on the front lawn. Grass stains our white tights after we take a tumble. Alex stands to the side, not wanting to play. Mom and dad talk with the other grown-ups. Doughnut crumbs on our pink sweater. The sun is bright and warm. Flowers are just blooming, and the air smells new.

Deeper.

Our new neighbor paints her front door purple. We go with mom to bring her muffins to welcome her. She invites us for tea. Dad tells us we shouldn't go. Mom says tea won't hurt anyone.

Deeper.

Our new neighbor has butterflies in her garden. We want to help her with her plants. Dad doesn't want us spending time with her. Mom says being different is harmless. Alex doesn't want to go over and help with the butterfly garden.

Deeper.

Our parents are fighting. Dad wants us to stop talking to the nice neighbor. Mom tells him to stop overreacting. She's sad, we can tell. Alex tells us it's our fault.

Deeper.

Our nice neighbor brings fresh-baked cookies when she comes over to watch us. Mom and dad have to go to the city. She meets us at the bus because they had to stay longer. Alex is rude to her. But we like her. She has fun stories.

Deeper.

Our friends play tag without us. Mom can't go to service anymore. Dad says she's too sick. She has lots of pills she has to take. The congregation prays for her. We cry ourselves to sleep. Alex yells at us to stop acting like a baby.

Deeper.

Our nice neighbor brought tea. Dad isn't nice. Mom thanks her. Dad yells at her like Alex yelled at us. We don't know why they're being so mean.

Deeper.

Mom is dead.

Dad is angry.

Alex is cruel.

Deeper.

Our nice neighbor is missing. The police come to ask dad about it. He doesn't care. Alex tells us not to cry because the nice neighbor is gone. He won't tell us anything else.

Deeper.

Our new home isn't as big and doesn't have a yard to play in. The new church isn't as bright. The pastor smells funny, and he talks about witches a lot. We ask Alex what a witch is. We don't make any friends.

No tag after service.

No swings on Saturdays.

No fresh-baked cookies.

Deeper.

Our pastor tells us about witchcraft. His sermons are about witchcraft. He denounces it and all who practice. We are all called to be the hand of God and purge the world of blasphemers. We've never met a witch before, but they sound horrible.

Deeper.

Our new school isn't a school. It's just us and Alex. We start traveling to a different city every few weeks. Dad recites the smelly pastor's sermons. Witchcraft is evil. It goes against God and everything He teaches. We have a duty to eradicate evil from His creation.

Deeper.

Our mission: find witches. We hunt and kill witches. We want dad to be proud of us. So, we do what God calls us to do. Alex isn't so mean to us anymore.

Deeper.

Our mother was killed by a witch and her evil concoctions. Killing witches is God's justice. They are foul, evil worshipers of the Devil and deserve punishment.

Deeper.

Our assignment is to find one of the worst kinds of witches. Even other witches fear them. Blood Witch. Alex doesn't think she's as dangerous as they say. We do. We know that witches can hide in nice neighbors.

Deeper.

Our source is a witch. She thinks helping us will protect her. It won't; she's just as heinous as the rest of them. We will kill the Blood Witch and anyone associated with her.

Deeper.

Our trapped witch is fighting back. Alex screams in pain. His eyes are bleeding. She will kill him. He's going to die at the hands of a witch, just like mom. The witch will die first.

Deeper.

Our mission failed. Alex's heart still beats, but his mind is trapped by a witch's curse. They say he might not wake up. This witch has to be punished—if not for God's purpose, then for hurting Alex.

Deeper.

Our enemy is our ally. We don't like it. Dad says it's necessary if we are to get righteous justice for Alex. The old witch is just as reprehensible, and we don't know why dad can't see it. She offers tea. We decline.

Deeper.

Dad is dead.

Killed by *that* witch.

It hurts to breathe.

We are alone.

Everyone is gone.

Rising.

Our grief clings to our being. Its claws bury deep inside, refusing to let up. Something tries to coax it away. Calls to us like a familiar lullaby we forgot we knew.

Rising.

Our pain eases, and the vise around our heart loosens. Bit by bit, grief dissolves into the darkness. We start to forget why we were angry. There was—is—a reason.

Rising.

Our flight to Boston is swallowed by the nothingness around us. We watched something on the plane. Or had we? Where are we going?

Rising.

Our school with no friends fades like a bad dream. Our years of traveling is wiped clean as a blank slate. Faint sermons echo in our mind, then are gone like smoke into a flowery spring breeze.

Rising.

Our nice neighbor's name is gone. Mom dying. Alex getting mean. Dad's anger. Like early morning mist fleeing a rising sun, it's gone before we grasp at it.

Green stained knees.

Doughnut crumbs.

New flowers.

Laughter.

Rising.

Falling.

Rising.

Falling.

Our blonde hair flies in the wind as the swing takes us higher and higher. We reach for the warmth of the bright sun...

☾

Bitter cold and pain greeted me as I pried my shaking hands from Sasha. She crumpled with a soft whimper, and I gulped in the cold air. Everything hurt. Things I didn't even know *could* hurt spasmed as I forced myself up.

My heart pounded, and drawing breath was more challenging than it should have been. I blinked sweat from my eyes and pressed my head firmly against the boards behind me, trying to ground myself in my own reality.

My skin was on fire while my veins burned ice cold. The sky was too dark. I needed to know I was here and not falling back into Sasha's memories. When I'd touched Phoenix's blood sigil, I'd seen flashes of his death, but that had been different. I'd been an observer; sure, I experienced what he'd felt, but I had still been *me*.

Sasha's memories swallowed me completely. Her pain was my pain; her grief, all-consuming. I held my hand out in front of my face and flexed my bloodied fingers. It was mine. Cold air stung. Still, I wasn't convinced.

Sharp pain like a needle to my temple shot through my mind just before a flash of someone else's memory crashed over me, drowning the present out. My stomach churned, and I squeezed my eyes shut against the visions.

How long had I been in her head? Hours? Days? Could I experience her life that quickly? Slowly, as pain completely unrelated to her memories surged, I opened my eyes again and pressed a hand to my side, letting the sting of a fresh cut remind me something about me was still very real.

Sasha stirred next to me.

I dragged myself away on instinct.

Her eyes fluttered open, and I watched her chest rise and fall. She rolled onto her side. Tears streaked their way down her dirt-smudged face; her hair had fallen out of the neat braid, and her eyes were no longer narrowed in hate, but wide and bewildered. With teeth chattering in a shiver, her fearful gaze found me, and gone was the deadly hunter, replaced by by a sad, lost child.

Her bottom lip trembled. "Where am I?"

Chapter 14

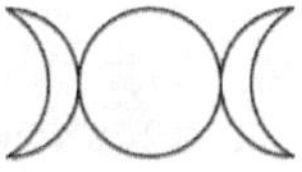

Jax pressed antiseptic-soaked gauze against the deep cut, and I sucked in a breath through my teeth at the resulting sting. Blood drenched paper towels were piled in the white sink of the ensuite, running the risk of staining the porcelain.

Jax had his own nasty cut above his eye that he refused to let anyone treat until I'd been taken care of. While our plan to make sure Sasha had no reason to come after me anymore worked, we'd mistaken her cronies for quitters.

It had taken all of us to get a disoriented Sasha off the roof, thanks to my bleeding out and Sasha's confused fear. Lyra had wanted to leave her—like we'd left an unconscious Sebastian—but with what I'd experienced and my guilt at how far back we'd sent her mind, I couldn't let myself do that.

"I think we got the bleeding stopped," Jax said, tossing the gauze into the sink with the rest of the bloodied things, my shirt included.

"Then will you go get that looked at?" I asked, nodding to his own face.

He shook his head. "It needs to be bandaged first."

"Wes can do that," I insisted.

"Em," he practically growled.

I pinched my lips together against another argument. There were enough scrapes and bruises to go around. The four other hunters hadn't been merciful, especially once they found Sasha trembling in a corner. We'd had to fight our way out of the club—or, everyone else had.

The dizziness from blood loss wasn't the only thing keeping me from doing anything. Flashes of Sasha's memories kept jolting me in and out of the present. It happened right when a hunter took a swing at me, and I was so wrapped up in it, he got a clip in on the side of my head.

Thea managed to let out enough of her power to have them scurrying away. Death wasn't something *anyone* wanted to feel. She'd chosen a particularly chaotic moment, still clinging to her secret. But I knew it was her. I'd felt it before, and it wasn't something I'd ever forget.

Jax opened the jar Wes had given him. "She could have killed you," he chastised under his breath.

"But she didn't," I reminded him. "And now, we don't have to worry about her anymore."

He stirred the contents of the jar, an antibacterial poultice of Wes's own invention that worked well enough on cuts, bruises, and mild burns.

"It was a bad plan," he muttered angrily, using the small spatula to spread a good helping across my cut.

I closed my eyes against the tingling relief of the instant cooling that spread up the wound. That relief was quickly interrupted by another flash of Sasha's memory. I flinched as I—we—*she* braced for a *disciplinary* hit from Armin.

Jax's fingers feathered across my cheek, and I opened my eyes to meet his. "Em," he said, softly this time.

I swallowed. "All good," I lied through a forced smile. "Just dizzy."

He frowned as he tucked a strand of hair behind my ear. "Head still hurt?" he asked, gently rubbing small circles on my temple with his thumb, a similar movement to something he would have done had his power not been locked away. I ached for the golden warmth of his magic, desperate for something to sooth the sharp pain of Sasha's memories.

I closed my eyes and leaned against his palm like a touch-starved cat. "No," I murmured.

He sighed. "Liar," he countered gently.

I opened my eyes to catch him searching my face as if he could will golden magic to form by determination alone. With a small shake of his head, he dropped his hand, and I let out a soft whimper at loss of his grounding touch.

Picking up clean cloth bandages, he wrapped them around my midsection, taking care to keep the poultice from rubbing off. It was already getting uncomfortably sticky as it worked to seal the wound.

A wave of dizziness hit, and the bathroom dissolved, giving way to a vision of a giggling Sasha chasing after a yellow dog. Sucking in a breath, I grabbed Jax's shoulder as lightheadedness and my throbbing temples threatened to topple me onto the floor.

He put a steadying hand on my waist, holding me firmly in place. His fingers flexed against me as if he was just as worried as I was about me falling back into Sasha's childhood memories.

I gave his shoulder a gentle squeeze as the flash subsided and the stinging turned to a dull headache. "She had a dog," I said through a sob.

Jax caught the tear on my cheek and wiped it away. The unexpected emotions were almost as bad as the pain. To have this reaction to the memories of a killer was troubling, to say the least. But I'd tumbled too far down, and the spell's aftereffects made me watch helplessly as an innocent child was tainted by a spiteful monster, forcing me to bear witness as religion-fueled hate corrupted a girl who just loved to swing.

Jax's hands went to my temples again, tracing those small, slow circles. "Did Martin's pages say anything about it?" he asked, keeping his voice low, as if he thought speaking of too loudly would make the throbbing in my head worse.

We'd come clean in the hour or so since we'd gotten back to the house. And while Jax's relief that I'd been lying about my murder plans was obvious, it was slightly overshadowed by his clear frustration at me trying a complex spell I'd never done before.

Leander joined him in that irritation—irritation that quickly turned into full-on anger when Lyra made a joke to lighten the situation. Her brothers hadn't always been the biggest fans of her crazy ideas or insistence on trying brand-new spells, but they were getting way too testy way too quickly. I wanted to blame it on the loss of their expressed powers, but something told me it was more about the loss of control.

I grimaced. "I didn't exactly get that far," I admitted. Most of the spell had been in Latin and I'd translated enough for me to use it effectively. But I'd deliberately stopped translating before I got to the potential rebound warning, because if I'd known the consequences, I might've backed out. Although, with another painful flash of Sasha rolling around in the grass with her dog, I was really re-thinking that stupid decision.

"So, you have no idea how long it's going to last," he concluded. "Or if it's ever going to go away."

I shrugged but immediately regretted it when the bandages pulled uncomfortably.

He shook his head and helped me carefully pull a clean t-shirt over my head—Chad's if I had to guess based on how large it was.

"I get why you kept it from me," he said, propping his hands on either side of my legs. His tone suggested otherwise. "But, next time you tell me to trust you, I'm going to have a harder time letting you go." He put his head down with a sigh and gave it a slight shake. "You scared me tonight," he confessed, looking back up at me.

"I scared myself," I admitted. "But, at least I didn't put anyone in a coma this time." My joke didn't land the way I'd wanted it to. There was no twitch of a smile, no smoothing of his worried brow.

I ran my finger along his creased frown, and he closed his eyes like it was my touch that was the healing one.

I held his face in my hands. "Jax," I whispered.

He opened his eyes, face close enough I could feel his breath.

"You don't need to protect me from everything," I murmured.

"Just yourself," he grumbled with a small smile.

"Occasionally," I agreed so quietly that if he hadn't been half an inch from me, he might not have heard it.

He let out a low chuckle, and his warm breath brushed against my skin, sending a shiver racing through me. We were too close and too far apart at the same time. I wasn't sure if he leaned in or if I pulled him to me, but the moment our lips touched, it didn't matter. There was no hesitancy to this kiss. No delicate question in his touch.

His grip dug into my hips like he was afraid I'd disappear if he even thought of letting go. My fist curled around the front of his shirt, clutching him to me. And the last few hours vanished. The days I'd spent avoiding him were nothing now. All that matter was his lips, his touch. Him. Us.

Wrapping my legs around his waist, I felt his fingertips trail down my exposed thigh. Feather-light touches grazing my calf. Chills spread wherever his hand went, and heat curled in my stomach. There was a reason we shouldn't be doing this, but I couldn't quite remember what it was.

Cupping the side of my neck, he placed slow, drawn-out kisses along my jaw, and I let out a breathless moan as I tipped my head back.

I tensed as sharp pain built behind my eye, threatening another Sasha memory. Flashes of an awkward first kiss tried to break through. Gritting my teeth, I fought to keep it away. I didn't need that right now.

"Em?" Jax whispered against my neck, concern edging into his tone.

I let out a frustrated whimper.

"Em," he soothed. "You need to rest."

I shook my head. "I'm fine," I whined.

He placed a gentle kiss on my lips before holding my head in his hands, thumbs poised once again at my temples. "You're getting worse at lying," he said simply.

I sighed and opened my mouth to argue when someone very intentionally cleared their throat from behind us. I peered around Jax, expecting a smirking Lyra. Instead, my stomach dropped, and I gently pushed him away from me.

Thea stood at the entrance to the bathroom with her arms crossed, but the hurt in her features betrayed the unaffected stance. Jax flushed, red blooming on the back of his neck. He took a very deliberate step to put more distance between us.

A gurgle of an apology stuck in my throat. I wasn't even sure what I'd be apologizing for exactly, but it felt needed.

I slid off the counter. "Thea, we were—"

"I think I got the gist, thanks," she said brusquely, looking at Jax instead of me. "Is the shower free?"

I nodded.

Jax cleared his throat. "I'll just clean this up." He scooped up the bloody mess in the sink and tossed it into the trash.

She slung the towel over her shoulder while she waited for us. Jax put his hand on my lower back as if to guide me out of the bathroom, but I was frozen to the spot, staring at Thea's arms. The light had caught them when she'd moved the towel, and it was taking my mind longer than I wanted to admit to register what I was seeing.

White, raised, burns. From the back of her hands to her wrists, licking up her forearms in tendrils.

Just ike mine.

"Are those—how—what happened?" I asked.

"Em," Jax warned quietly, putting a hand on my arm.

She pulled the towel off her shoulder to cover her arms again. "None of your business," she snapped, but the bitterness was less convincing with the slight tremble in her bottom lip.

I shoved Jax's hand off and took a step towards her. "No, those are burns," I said.

"So?"

"So, how'd you get them?" I asked. An unwanted possibility forming all too clearly in my mind. I needed her to answer so that my brain didn't find that distressing conclusion on its own.

Thea's throat bobbed when she swallowed.

"All yours," Jax said, catching me under the elbow and steering me out of the room. I tried to pull away, but he held on tight, practically dragging me into the hall. He shut the bedroom door and rounded on me.

"What is wrong with you?" he asked.

"Me? What's wrong with you?"

He ran a hand across his jaw. "You can't just ask people how they got scars," he chided.

I frowned at him. "Do you know?" I demanded.

He crossed his arms and glanced over his shoulder at the closed door. "She doesn't like to talk about it."

"*She's* not," I countered. "I'm asking *you*."

He studied my face for a moment before sighing. "Spell gone wrong," he finally offered.

My stomach clenched. "When?"

His eyebrows pinched together. "What?"

I flinched as another memory jolt hit. Sasha, surrounded by flowers, in our—her favorite butterfly dress as a soft summer breeze lifted her hair. I rubbed at my forehead to get it to stop.

"You don't need this right now," he said, moving around me. "Maybe Wes has some tea to help you sleep."

"I don't want fucking tea," I snapped, resisting the childish urge to stomp my foot in frustration. "I want answers."

He turned back to face me. "Why does it matter?" he asked as if this was an argument about the rules to some stupid board game.

"Because she—it just does," I said. "Or, it might." I still hadn't told him what I'd done and how it had hurt Blythe.

He scratched at the back of his neck and looked down at his feet. Even in the dim lighting of the hallway, I could see the struggle plain on his face. He wasn't one to betray secrets. That was partially why we were in this mess.

"A few weeks ago," he admitted. "She came to the post with bad burns, looking for a healer." He shifted on his feet, clearly uncomfortable. But I didn't have the bandwidth to feel guilty about it right now.

My mind swam with a thousand possibilities. It would be too easy. Easy and incredibly messy. I ran a hand absently over my own raised scars as if I could read an answer in them.

"Spell gone wrong," I repeated to myself.

He nodded.

I moved around him, but he caught my arm before I could get to the stairs. "Are you going to clue me in?"

I shook my head. "No."

"Seriously?" he hissed.

"Not...yet," I offered.

"This is getting old."

It was getting old, but *he* was hardly in a position to call me out for that. Not when he and Leander were still having hushed conversations they didn't include anyone else in. I wanted to remind him of that, but considering he'd just spent the last half hour or so cleaning up my blood, I decided he could have his frustration, for now.

"It's just," I leveled with him. "I need to be sure first."

He sighed. "Fine," he said, waving his hand towards the stairs.

"Thank you," I said, reaching up to give him a light kiss on the cheek before hurrying downstairs. Being *sure* was a luxury these days, but it was more than that. Fear had gripped my mind, and I found myself hoping that fear was crazy.

☾

"That's fucking crazy." Lyra's brow knit together, and she stared at me like I'd just told her I'd decided to become an Emissary.

"How hard did that hunter hit you?" Blythe added.

I'd managed to pull them away from the others and into the candlelit backyard without any questions, thanks to Wes insisting on finally checking Jax's cut.

Lyra's reaction was what I'd expected—and half-hoped for. Voicing the theory was hard enough to do, let alone sell. But I knew a part of it was Lyra's dislike of Thea as a whole.

I pulled on a sweatshirt over Chad's over-sized t-shirt. "I'm serious."

Lyra tossed her damp hair over her shoulder. "That's what's concerning," she muttered.

Grace, Attie, and Rhi had each taken one of the chairs and watched us as closely as we could be watched. Only their bright eyes gave them away as more than shadows.

"How can you be sure?" Blythe asked. "Burns aren't exactly uncommon with witchcraft."

"I know that," I snapped. Spells and candle work alone meant small burns were a regular occurrence for most witches. *Small* being the key word. "But they're *exactly* like ours."

"Which could be from anything," Lyra insisted.

"You know as well as I do *coincidence* isn't a thing with us," I said. "And if it was from something normal, why be so defensive about it?"

Blythe frowned. "I thought you said Jax told you it was a spell gone wrong?"

I nodded. "It was, just not hers."

She rubbed her lower arm absently and I tried not to let the guilt of my mistake overshadow the importance of what I was trying to work out.

"Blood loss can cause confusion," Lyra offered.

I rolled my eyes. "I didn't lose that much blood," I countered, flinching as yet another Sasha memory shot through my own. Another day on the swing set, this time getting as high as she could before jumping off. Pain lanced through my wrist as she landed one jump wrong.

Lyra and Blythe both raised their eyebrows in unison.

Shaking the pins out of my arm, I looked between them. "Fine," I said. "If that's the only thing we have in common, I'll drop it." I turned to Lyra. "How old is she?"

Lyra rolled her eyes. "Em, we're all around the same age."

"When's her birthday?" Blythe asked.

Lyra rubbed her forehead. "Really? You too?"

"Humor us, sunshine," Blythe said with a half-smile.

Lyra pursed her lips like she didn't want to offer an answer. Attie let out a soft meow.

"October," Lyra finally gave up. "Thirty-first."

I stuffed my balled fists into the sweatshirt pockets, pressing my nails into my palms to keep my mind focused on this conversation and not the sensations of Sasha's childhood.

"Parents?" I asked.

Lyra shook her head. "Em, I know where you're going with this, but it's impossible," she said. "If she was from a lost bloodline, the Council would have figured it out way before *us*."

I shook my head. "You said she didn't make it to Emissary," I countered. "So, if she was playing it safe, why would they have bothered looking into it?"

Lyra crossed her arms. "Her mom died when she was thirteen in some freak accident at a Samhain festival." She held up her hand to stop anyone from commenting. "But her dad is alive," she continued. "In prison, but very much alive."

"Prison?" Blythe and I blurted in unison.

Lyra shrugged. "There was this thing with a freelancing Necromancer that, shocker, didn't end well," she said with a wave of her hand as if going to prison for messing with necromancy—freelance or not—was no big deal. "Point is, she doesn't have dead par-*ents*."

I opened my mouth, fully prepared to reveal Thea's Necromancer secret.

"My dad's not dead either," Blythe said with half a chuckle before I could get half a word in.

I blinked at her. "He's not?"

She shook her head. "Ditched when I was seventeen, but still alive."

"So, not everything needs to match up," I offered, looking back at Lyra.

"The important shit does, Em," Lyra countered. "Like magic."

I frowned.

She sighed. "You and Blythe both have the same expressed power as the original member of the coven, right?"

We both nodded.

"Thea doesn't even *have* an expressed power," she continued. "So, there's no way she could be the same."

"Yes, she—you're assuming the third member also had an expressed power," I argued. "We don't even know for sure who the third member was."

They both fell silent, leaving only the scritch of ice on ice from the lake beyond the spell.

There had been thirteen total members of the Triple Moon Coven at the time of Amity's assumed death. Records memorialized the other twelve witches who died the same day. History told us hunters were responsible, but we knew it had been Mary's desperate attempt to stop Isobel's prophecy.

Marnie was the only modern-day hint we had at the third bloodline of Amity's first coven—her bound coven. Patience Osborne's name hadn't been in any of the memorial records, so chances were neither was the third witch.

"She had to," Lyra said. "I mean, two Blood Witches weren't going to invite a non-expressed into their coven."

I frowned. "Why not?"

"Well, because—it's—you know what, never mind," she said, focusing on playing with the end of her braid.

Blythe and I exchanged a glance.

"Lyra, what is it?"

She shrugged but continued to separate the hair left out of the braid like it was her job.

Blythe's face relaxed as if she'd just figured out the answer to a riddle. "You're jealous," she concluded.

I looked between her and Lyra. "No," I said. "You're not...Lyra?"

Lyra tossed her braid over her shoulder. "No," she said, crossing her arms. "Maybe." She uncrossed her arms. "Okay, kinda."

"Seriously?"

She threw her hands up. "Yes, fine. I'm not thrilled *Thea* gets to be in your special little coven, okay?"

My mouth dropped.

Blythe let out a laugh and then clapped her hand over it with an apologetic look towards Lyra. "Sorry," she said, still through a slight chuckle. "It's just...c'mon. You *want* to be a part of the death coven?"

"Death coven?" I shot back.

Blythe gave me a half-shrug.

My arm tingled as Sasha's memory of getting her cast removed interjected. I closed my eyes briefly and forced it to the back of my mind. We'd have to figure out how to get that stopped if I wanted to get anything else done.

Lyra let out a long sigh. "I just thought, after all this, I could be, you know, a part of it, or whatever," she admitted.

"You are," I blurted before I could stop myself or get interrupted by another Sasha memory.

Blythe raised an eyebrow at me.

"Not the death part," I clarified quickly. "I just mean—look, *if* I'm right and Thea is the third bloodline, we just need her to undo the binding. It's not like I'm inviting her for slumber parties."

"Except..." Lyra nodded to the house with a slight smile.

"You know what I mean," I said, aiming a playful kick at her.

"Should we ask her?" Blythe suggested. "See if she knows who Marnie could be?"

I shook my head. "Not yet," I said. "If she freaks out and leaves, we're screwed. I think we first need to see if we can figure out who the third member was and link them to Marnie."

Lyra grimaced. "And then connect them to *Thea*." She shuddered dramatically.

"You both say that like it's easy," Blythe scoffed.

I shrugged. "Easier than it would have been if we didn't know there were two covens," I said. "Besides, it wasn't like there were a million people in The Colonies back then. We should be able to at least narrow it down."

"True," Blythe agreed with a slight incline of her head.

"And then Thea gets in?" Lyra grumbled.

I shook my head. "You think I like the idea?" I asked. "That I might be bound to my—Jax's ex?" I took a deep breath.

Lyra pressed her lips together like she was trying not to laugh. "Okay, you've got me there."

"Besides, we're only doing this to undo the binding," I said firmly. "*No one* is resurrecting any covens here."

Blythe gave Lyra a playful shove. "Yeah, but even the death coven could use a little sunshine."

Lyra smiled.

I shook my head. "Stop calling us that," I muttered, rubbing my forehead as if that could dispel the vision of Sasha sobbing in the vet's office as her beloved dog was put down. Sorrow gripped my chest, her emotions crashing over my own.

I really hoped Wes had some tea that would help me sleep.

Chapter 15

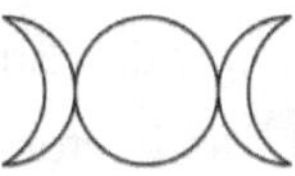

Pages crinkled under me as I rolled over, trying to get more comfortable. I didn't remember falling asleep because that had not been the plan at all. We'd gone through nearly all of mom's journals for what felt like the dozenth time, the spell books I'd brought, and Blythe's books, comparing notes.

If mom had been working on undoing the binding, she had to have written down *something* that could help. And, between all the books, the little bit of history class Lyra remembered, and Selene coming through and sneaking us some of the records the Council had, we were able to narrow it down.

Luckily, Salem Village hadn't been hugely populated back then and the witches who worked for the Collective did an excellent job of keeping track of their own kind, especially after the trials. That kind of registry was part of what caused the rift between the Boswell sisters in the first place.

Two witches disappeared from Salem records around the same time as Patience. Lydia Toothaker and Abigail Nurse. Mom's own research had determined that Abigail had remarried when her first husband died and moved back to England with him. Abigail Nurse became Abigail Whittle and lived a relatively long life with children and grandchildren. Her line was accounted for.

Lydia was proving to be an unknown. Toothaker was her married name, and there was record of a daughter, but that was it. After sixteen-ninety, there was no accounts of her or her daughter. Not even a mention of either of their deaths.

Just like Amity and Patience, Lydia had been practically erased. And that's the last thing I remembered before waking up: trying to find a connection between her and my own ancestor. Or even her and Thea.

But while timing was in our favor to call her the mysterious third member, there was one wrinkle that kept me searching. As far as anyone knew, Lydia didn't have an expressed power—something that had made my argument for Thea's connection more convincing to Lyra and Blythe.

Only, *I* knew that Thea had an expressed power. And if Lyra was right about those kinds of specifics matching up, then there was no way Thea could be the descendant of the third line. Unless Lydia had been a secret Necromancer. Not completely impossible, even back then they weren't widely accepted, but I had a feeling *someone* would have made a note of it.

All we were able to scrounge up about Lydia and her magic was that she was a sought-after spellwright. Witches would travel from all over for one of her custom spells for everything from finding lost items to changing the weather. Apparently, they still taught some of her spells in Collective schools as a standard.

I rubbed my sore eyes before reaching for my phone. Almost three in the morning. Sleep didn't stay as long these days, and I didn't need Stanley to tell me why.

Attempting not to crumple my paper notes more than I already had, I carefully rolled off the air mattress and stood, swaying slightly on the spot as dizziness rippled the room around me. I closed my eyes against the sensation, waiting for it to subside.

It had been a couple days since the club, and while the jolts of Sasha's memories had stopped interrupting my day, they'd been replaced with regular dizzy spells and fatigue like I'd never experienced.

Wes bought an iron supplement the last time he and Chad had gone to the store, hoping it would help. He was doing his best to keep me from completely falling apart, but supplements weren't going to fix the kind of stress I was under.

I finger-combed my hair before putting it back into the hair tie in a less frazzled mess and yanked a sweatshirt over my head, not even sure it was mine. Scooping up the notepad and journal I'd been working on, I stepped around a sleeping Lyra and Blythe, their mattresses pulled together to make up one bed.

Thea had taken the vacated couch when Sebastian fled back to Lenore and the Council. It had nothing to do with comfort, as that couch was hardly better than an air mattress. It was all to do with avoiding me. And she'd been fairly successful at it after she'd caught me with Jax in the upstairs bathroom.

I dimmed the lights as low as I could to make sure I didn't wake her up and went to make my tea as quietly as possible. But, every footstep and clink on the counter was like a whip crack in the too-quiet house.

I even used the single-serve coffee maker to heat my water because would make less noise than the kettle—something I hated doing, as the water was never quite clear of coffee.

Sitting down at the table, I blinked the sleepiness from my eyes and flipped to the last page I'd left off on in mom's journal. The one with the name of the third woman in the picture. *Marnie.* A woman who could be of Lydia's line, hidden from history like Blythe and I were.

Rereading it for the hundredth time wasn't getting me anywhere, but I'd convinced myself I was missing something mom had left written between the lines. A hidden message she left for *only* me and I just hadn't found it yet.

Stifling a yawn, I tapped my pen on the edge of the journal and stared at the passage, losing the words for the page.

"Got any more of that?"

I dropped my pen when I started and looked up to see Thea standing at the table, hands in the large pocket of an oversized sweatshirt, hair falling out of a bun, and dark circles under her dull purple eyes.

I glanced at my steaming mug and then back at her. "Uh, yeah," I said. "Sorry, did I wake you up?"

She shook her head. "Can't sleep," she explained, voice rough from lack of sleep. She slid into the seat across from me.

I nodded as I stood to make her a cup.

Thea rested her chin on folded arms and stared ahead without focus. She looked about as tired as I felt.

As I busied myself with the tea and honey, stirring it carefully, I glanced back at her. She shook herself from her staring and found my notes.

"Is this what you three have been up to the last two days?" she asked, cocking her head to the side to try to read them.

I nodded as I set the mug down in front of her. "We're trying to find someone," I said.

She cupped both hands around the mug and blew on the top of it. "Who?"

I ran my finger along the edge of the worn journal page and watched her, wondering how much to say. I'd seen the damage being bound caused in real-time. Admitting it was my fault she had those scars wasn't going to smooth anything between us. Especially after she'd walked in on me and Jax.

She sniffed and looked down at her tea. "It's none of my business," she said quietly and made to get up.

"No, Thea, it's not—" I took a deep breath, trying to think of the best way to start this conversation. "It's just...complicated," I settled on. It was pretty much stating the obvious, though. Everything was *complicated* these days.

She nodded slowly, but I could tell she thought it was just a way for me to continue to keep her out of it. And Lyra wanted to keep her out of it. She still wasn't convinced Thea was connected to this and only wanted to bring it up when we had irrefutable proof.

But fresh eyes were what I needed at this point. We all had our own ideas about how we wanted this to go, and that's what put us at a standstill. We needed someone who didn't have an inclination towards confirmation bias. I'd hit a wall and needed a boost to get over it. And, there was a solid chance that Thea *was* involved, so we were going to have to tell her at some point.

I looked back down the hall to the den where Lyra and Blythe were still sleeping. "Blythe and I are..." I started, turning back to face Thea. "Bound."

Her eyebrows pinched together as her own gaze flicked to the den.

"As in, life-or-death bound," I offered.

She blinked at me. "Oh."

I couldn't know where she thought this was going, but that clearly hadn't been it. "We think our ancestors messed up a spell and now we are trying to fix it," I continued.

She took a tentative sip of tea and winced slightly at the scalding temperature.

"And, uh," I swallowed hard, bracing for the next part. "We're pretty sure there's a third witch bound to us." I watched her face for any flash of recognition. "So, that's what we've been working on. Finding them."

Thea nodded slowly. "But you haven't," she concluded. It wasn't a dig, just a confirmation.

I shrugged. "Not yet, but we think we've narrowed it down."

She rested her chin in her palm and continued to try to read my hurried handwriting upside down.

"We think they're from Lydia Toothaker's line," I prompted.

She reached towards the piece of paper closest to her. "The spellwrighte?" she asked.

Nodding, I slid the paper closer, letting her pick it up to read better and watched as she scanned my progress. "Genealogy records aren't available?" she asked, handing the notes back.

I shook my head. "Not to me, anyway." The Council probably had something on her, but if they did, they were keeping it secret from even Selene.

"That sucks."

I frowned. "You don't have any ideas?" I asked.

She took another sip of tea. "Why would I?"

"I just thought maybe because..." I paused. "You worked with the Council and stuff." I wimped out of bringing up her scars again, caught between two goals.

On one hand, I wanted Thea to be the third witch so we could undo the binding, and I wouldn't have the outcomes of two lives hanging over my head for much longer. On the other, I wanted Thea to be as involved as little as possible because I *really* didn't want Jax's ex magically bound to me.

"So did Lyra," Thea reminded me. "And her dad would know all that stuff."

I cleared my throat. "Right, but you were a lot more into that stuff than she was, so I figured..."

She chewed on her bottom lip. "Is that what she told you?"

I started to shake my head.

"Because I wanted to be an Emissary," she continued. "I wasn't using her to get there."

I frowned. "Thea, she didn't say that," I insisted, confused. I knew Lyra had her issues with Thea, but I'd never asked, and she never brought it up.

"Right, because Lyra's so reserved about her feelings."

I stared at her for a moment longer than was comfortable. "Look, I don't know what happened with you and Lyra or you and Jax," I said. "But I figured, at the very least, you paid more attention in class than Lyra." I already *knew* she'd paid more attention in class; this was *Lyra* we were talking about. But it was as good a way to try to get what I needed as any.

Her face softened. "Oh."

I pulled the corner of the Polaroid out of the book I'd stuck it in. "Best lead we have," I said.

A flicker of something like panic crossed her features but vanished quickly.

"That's my mom," I said, pointing to her in the image. "And Blythe's."

Thea's bottom lip quivered.

"And that's someone named Marnie," I continued softly.

She flinched like I'd slapped her. "Good for her." The slight hitch in her voice gave her away.

I tapped the image and took a steadying breath. "Your mom?" I asked as gently as I could.

She swallowed and focused on the tea in her mug instead of me or the picture. The house creaked as it settled around us. I didn't need her to say it; her reaction had told me everything I needed to know.

"They knew each other," I added. "I think they were trying to unbind the lines."

Her jaw clenched.

"*Our* lines."

She shook her head. "You're insane." Half-whispered, it sounded less like a harsh accusation and more like a soft hope.

I nodded to her arms. "Your scars," I said, rolling up my own sleeves. "Blythe and I both have them, too."

Her eyes widened as she caught sight of the raised white lines covering my forearms, and her shoulders rose and fell as though she was concentrating on breathing. She sat like that for almost half a minute.

"You—you're—you're wrong."

"It's too much of a coincidence if I am."

"What about the other person?" she asked, nodding to the picture between us. "It could be them."

I looked at it too, frowning. "There's three people in the picture."

She rolled her eyes. "Someone had to *take* it."

"I..." I picked it up and stared at it. I'd been so focused on the subjects in the picture, I hadn't given a second thought to whoever took the photo. The women were all standing too far from the camera for any of them to be holding it. Maybe my mind had automatically written it off as Grandma Geri—but that couldn't have been right. Mom's entries around that time had said she and Grandma had been fighting. Mom had been "staying with friends."

"The scars," I said lamely.

"Lots of witches have burn scars," she snapped.

It was the same thing Blythe had used to poke a hole in my theory. "Identical ones?" I shot back.

Her jaw worked to come up with a retort. "I'm not—we're not. No."

I took a deep breath. "Fine," I said. "Prove me wrong, help us find the third part of the binding."

"How do you expect me to do that?"

"Do you have any books from an ancestor? Around the late sixteen-hundreds?"

She blanched and looked down at the tea, shaking her head. "No," she said quietly. "It's...gone."

"What do you mean gone?" I asked, panic edging into my voice. If we couldn't get her ancestor's book, proving she was the third line would be moot. Sure, Lyra could *probably* write her own unbinding, but that could take years to get right. And I wasn't ready to hide out for *years*.

She heaved a sigh. "The Council took everything," she said. "When my dad was arrested."

Lyra had mentioned something about her dad being in prison. But, if the Council took it, that didn't mean it was gone-gone, just out of our reach. Out of reach, I could work with; destroyed, I couldn't.

"Did they keep it?" I asked, grabbing a page of notes and a pen to jot down anything she knew. But when she didn't answer, I looked up to see tears swimming in her purple eyes. My stomach knotted. I'd stepped in it, forgetting why her father was arrested.

"Sorry," I stumbled. "I didn't mean to bring up...sorry."

She wiped a tear away with the sleeve of her sweatshirt. One that looked a lot like Jax's. All Lyra had told us was that after her mother's death, Thea's father had hired a freelancing Necromancer, and an arrest followed. It didn't take much to fill in the gaps.

Except. "He didn't *hire* a Necromancer, did he?"

She sniffed and rubbed under her nose. "No," she said through a sob. "I tried to...but she—" Thea bit her trembling lip and looked up at the dim light above the table. "I couldn't do it."

And her father covered for her. He chose prison over risking exposing her power to the very Council who claimed to safeguard witches. My mother embraced the cycle of running and hiding from the magical community to ensure I wouldn't be condemned for my power. Blythe's mother accepted Martin's control to keep Blythe off the Council's radar. Right or wrong, we'd all been protected because we had power the Council wanted to control—or destroy.

Thea and I weren't necessarily friends, but still, I felt for her. I couldn't imagine what it had been like for her. I knew the pain of that loss. When mom died I'd tried to find something that magic could do to fix it. And there was no getting over the fresh wave of grief when I learned that, even with all the magic I had, there was no brining her back.

But Thea, she did have that power. She was supposed to have control over death. She should be able to bring people back, and knowing she tried and failed was something I would never be able to comprehend. That failure would have broken much older witches.

A thirteen-year-old witch, however, likely wouldn't have had the strength to fully raise someone. But that wouldn't have stopped me from trying, either. And the guilt after her father was taken from her because of something she did, I couldn't imagine.

I felt sorry for her. The way I felt sorry for myself and Blythe. We all shared in the heartache.

Because we'd all been born into a tragedy not of our own making.

Chapter 16

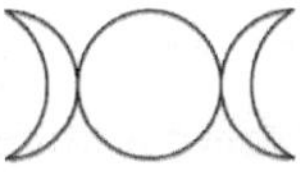

The only sound left in the kitchen was the faint tick of the wall clock that hadn't been set to the right time in years. My tea had lost all of its heat, but I didn't want to get up to make more. I'd been prepared to, well, not *dislike* Thea, indifferent sure. But now? Now I was feeling guilty over judging her too harshly.

And I wished she would have confided in Lyra about what really happened with her dad. Maybe then she wouldn't have felt as alone.

I took a sip of the chilled tea and tried not to wince. "You were young," was all I managed to say.

She shook her head with a sniffle. "It wasn't that," she said. "I knew I *could* do it." She took a sip of her own tea with shaky hands. "But it was like my magic was blocked or something." She rolled her shoulders. "Still feels like that a lot of the time," she admitted. "Like it shouldn't take as much effort as it does."

I frowned. "Blocked?" I repeated.

She nodded.

I chewed on my bottom lip as my heart sped up. That's how it felt for me too, especially since the talisman had been broken. Even with that, it hadn't been *easy* to use. And the drain afterwards took a larger toll than I liked to admit.

I stood up, and her eyebrows creased.

"Hold that thought," I said and hurried back to the den. A new theory was forming in my head; not an entirely new one, but one that, if I was right, meant maybe—just maybe—it wasn't only me who couldn't fully access their magic.

Shaking Blythe's shoulder, I got nothing but an annoyed grunt until I shook harder, and she blinked up at me.

"The fuck, Boswell?"

"We need to talk," I pressed.

"Now?" Lyra grumbled, face half-buried in the pillow.

"Yes."

Lyra rolled over and pushed herself halfway up, glaring at me. "Somebody better be fucking dead," she said. At the same time, Blythe muttered, "This better be fucking important."

I hopped up and went back to the kitchen, their shuffling and grumbling following me. Lyra frowned at Thea but said nothing as she pulled herself onto a stool and crooked one leg underneath her. Blythe slid into the seat at the head of the table and raised an expectant eyebrow.

I glanced at Thea. "You need to tell them."

She looked at me like my hair had caught fire and I was refusing to put it out. "I don't know—why?"

"Tell us what?" Lyra demanded.

"About your mom," I prompted.

Thea shook her head. "There's nothing to tell," she said pointedly. "She's dead."

"Is that the big reveal? Dead mom?" Blythe asked. "Welcome to the fucking death coven."

I rolled my eyes. "You really need to chill with the death coven shit." I looked back at Thea. "I know it's asking a lot, but please."

She shook her head. "I'm not—"

"Either you do or I will," I said. "At least now the guys won't get to weigh in." Her eyes narrowed, and I knew she understood I meant one guy in particular. Was that particular tactic in poor taste? Yes. Did I care? No. She wanted to keep her magic a secret, I got that. But we were at the point where secrets were going to lead to early graves for us all, and I wasn't going to let that happen without a fight.

"Okay, what are we missing?" Lyra puzzled through a yawn. "Fess up or I'm going back to bed."

Thea picked at a chip in the ceramic mug with her fingernail, avoiding looking at any of us.

Lyra sighed and hopped off the stool. "Don't wake me unless someone is dy—"

"Thea's dad didn't hire a Necromancer," I blurted. "He was covering for—"

"Seriously?" Thea snapped, eyes flaring a deep purple. Clearly, I'd struck a nerve. Good.

Lyra frowned as she climbed back onto the stool. "Qu'est-ce que c'est, covering?"

Blythe rubbed the sleep from the corner of her eye.

Thea's glare sent ice down my spine. If anyone could have a look that killed, it was a Death Witch. But I held her glare with my own determined one. This was coming out one way or another. I'd hoped giving her the chance to tell the story was enough, but there were too many secrets now. At this point it seemed every secret led to a deadly consequence, and I was more than over it.

Thea swallowed and tore her gaze from me to look at Lyra. "For me," she confessed. "I was the one who tried to raise her."

Lyra was so still, I was tempted to check for breathing. I'd never seen her take so long to process before.

Blythe beat her there. "But, that means—"

"You're a fucking Necromancer!" Lyra's voice was just a little too loud.

We hushed her with a collective "*Shhh*," before all pausing to listen for any noise from upstairs indicating the guys had been woken up. I wasn't sure I'd be able to come up with even a halfway decent lie for our impromptu meeting.

"Yes," Thea confirmed after it was clear no one else had heard Lyra. "Happy?" she jabbed at me.

I crossed my arms.

"Let me get this straight," Lyra began, closing her eyes and pinching the bridge of her nose. "You've been a Necromancer this whole time and never told me?" She cocked her head to the side. "But you told the *hag* who stole your boyfriend?" she asked jerking her thumb at me.

Thea shifted in her chair. "It wasn't like that."

"Hag?" I repeated.

"Her word, not mine," Lyra offered like that was supposed to make me feel better about the insult. "Then what *was* it like?"

"I was upset," she muttered with a half-apologetic grimace.

"Was it *like* you told Jax and not me?" Lyra asked, hurt creeping into her tone.

"Again, hag?" I insisted.

"I. Was. Upset." Thea paused before she continued, "And no, I didn't tell Jax."

"Well, I guess you lying to *everyone* is slightly comforting," Lyra shot.

"Your dad threw mine in prison for *hiring* a Necromancer," Thea reminded her. "What do you think he would have done to an actual one?"

Lyra chewed that over. "Is that why you started dating Jax? Get in good with dad?"

"What?" Thea sputtered. "No." She looked at me. "Is this what you wanted?"

I shrugged. "Well, you know us *hags*."

She rolled her eyes. "You need to—"

"I'm assuming Em had a point to this?" Blythe asked firmly, raising her voice just enough to get our attention without disturbing the sleepers on the next floor.

I crossed my arms. "I did," I agreed.

"And that point was?" Blythe prompted. "Because I doubt it was fighting over who kept what from who."

"The point is me, just a hag trying not to die over here," I mumbled.

Blythe let out a long sigh. "Thea's sorry she called you a hag before she knew you," she said. "Besides, I've called you way worse."

I gaped at her. "Seriously?"

She shrugged. "I thought you knew about the curse and didn't care," she explained. "Now that I know you're clueless, we're good."

"Curse?" Thea squeaked.

"Binding, sorry, old habits," Blythe corrected.

"I'm not clue—" I stopped myself with a long inhale and even longer exhale, forcing my brain back to the reason I'd yanked them out of bed. "Thea said when she tried to raise her mom, she couldn't," I started.

"You were thirteen," Blythe said simply.

Thea shook her head. "It's always been like that," she said. "But that was the first time I tried to get passed it and just, couldn't."

"Have you tried since?" Lyra asked.

We all looked at her.

"What?" she sassed with a shrug. "It's a fair question."

Thea let out a huff. "No, Lyra, I haven't tried to raise anyone from the dead since my mother."

I tapped the page Blythe had torn from Martin's book. "I think that's what this meant by our powers being bound, too," I explained. "None of us can tap fully into it."

"That would explain a lot," Blythe agreed.

Lyra rubbed her face and sat up straighter on the stool. "No, uh-uh. I don't buy it." She yanked the tie out of the end of her hair. "I heard you threatened to bind Sebastian's line for, like, eternity." She used her elbow to point at Blythe while she gathered her hair back into a bun that wasn't completely falling out.

Blythe smirked. "Empty threat," she said. "I figured he didn't know I couldn't do shit. I've never managed a full blood binding." She glanced at me for a moment. "Not for lack of trying."

I frowned. "Did you—"

"Like I said, didn't work."

Lyra gaped at her. She turned to me. "You fucked up a whole lot of hunters only, like, what, a month ago?"

"That was—"

"I swear to *Circe,* if you say it was the fucking moon, I'm going to hit you."

"The talisman," I finished pointedly. "It was the only reason I got through the block. Which is why I can't now."

She let out a breath and slouched slightly, the exhale seeming to have deflated her. "That's—but...damn it, I hate it when you make sense."

"Me too," I mumbled.

Thea looked between Blythe and me. "So, you think we're all bound and that makes our magic not work?"

Blythe shrugged. "Looks like it."

"Is that it?" Thea asked tentatively.

"Nope, as an added bonus, if Boswell dies, *we* both die," Blythe confirmed simply.

We watched Thea as she took it all in. It was a lot; I wasn't going to pretend like it wasn't. And I wouldn't blame her if she needed to take a few minutes to fully process. I was still processing a lot of it myself.

Her mouth parted and then closed. "So, you found a picture of our moms and now you think I'm a part of this...this—"

"We've been going with death coven," Lyra offered with a smirk. "So, you should feel right at home."

Thea's eyebrows shot up.

"No, *we* haven't," I hissed. "Our lines are bound, yes. But if we can get our hands on the last part of the original binding, we can undo it."

"We think," Blythe added.

"Solid seventy percent chance," Lyra offered.

"And the other thirty?" Thea asked, raising an eyebrow.

Lyra caught my eye and then looked down at her own hands instead of answering. We weren't sure what failure would look like. The binding staying in place, sure. Making it worse somehow, probably. Dying in the attempt, possibly. But none of that would matter if we couldn't get our hands on the last third of the original spell.

"Well, it doesn't really matter, since I don't have any of my family books," Thea said, sitting up a little straighter. "Like I said, they took everything when my dad was arrested."

"And by *they*, you mean my dad," Lyra mused slowly, glancing at the ceiling. She let out a dramatic sigh and slid off the stool. "Get a pot of coffee going, we're going to need it."

"Why?" I asked.

"Caffeine makes the brain go vroom-vroom," she said, patting the top of my head as she passed by.

I swatted at her hand. "Where are you going?"

"To wake up the boys," she declared. "Unfortunately, we've hit the point where we actually need them for something."

☾

Leander jammed the coffee carafe back into the maker with more force than necessary. "You can't just walk into Stromford," he said, turning back towards the table, "and expect no one to raise an eyebrow."

The guys hadn't exactly been thrilled when Lyra woke them up at half past three in the morning, but frustration quickly pivoted to anger when she told them *why* we were getting them up.

"Gee, thanks for stating the fucking obvious," Lyra snapped. "I'm not stupid." Attie jumped onto the table in front of Lyra, arching her back for attention. Lyra ran her hand along the cat's spine but didn't take her eyes off her brother.

"Could have fooled me," Leander muttered, and I honestly couldn't say if it was Attie or Lyra that leveled a hiss at him.

Grace had curled up in my vacated seat, chin on the table, watching everyone, her red eyes flicking to each new speaker like she was taking everything in. Rhi lay out in front of Blythe, large paws hanging over the table's edge, eyes fixed on Thea, who had moved seats when the animal had taken to staring at her.

"This is exhausting," Leander added, taking a sip of coffee.

"Oh, I'm sorry, are you tired of dealing with the fallout from your *colossal* mistake?" Lyra mocked. Waking everybody up had seemed like a good idea at the time, but now I was thinking we should have just gone back to bed and dealt with all this at a more reasonable hour.

"*My* mistake?" Leander shot back, setting the mug down on the counter so forcefully that liquid sloshed over the side and I swore I heard porcelain crack.

"You told the Council about Em," Lyra countered. "Big. Fucking. Mistake."

He took a deep breath, nostrils flaring wide. "I was doing my job," he said, bracing himself against the counter.

They're bickering was *exhausting*.

"Your job is—"

"Regardless of how we got here," Rez interrupted. "I have to, unfortunately, concede your brother has a point."

"I don't need your help," Leander snapped.

Rez fixed him with a glare that had me worried they were about to start throwing things at each other now. "You 'doing your job' has fucked up enough lives," he said coolly, but I could hear a slight tremor in his voice. "Don't you *dare* brush me off."

Leander's jaw was so tight I imagined teeth cracking. "You—"

He put his hand up, cutting off whatever Leander was about to say. "Jumping from dangerous situation to dangerous situation isn't healthy and is hardly maintainable," he said to us, leaving Leander fuming.

Lyra rolled her eyes. "Calling this a *dangerous* situation is a smidge dramatic, even for you."

"How is breaking into a prison not dangerous?" Leander asked through a sharp, skeptical laugh that had me wondering if the amount of times we'd interrupted his sleep was starting to take a real toll on him.

Lyra let out her own bark of laughter. "Breaking in—they have visiting hours, dipshit."

He let out a huff. "Not for fugitives."

"Then I guess it's a good thing I can look like anyone I fucking want."

We'd been at it for almost an hour. After we'd filled them in on why we'd woken them up, things had devolved quickly into fighting. Jax had already poked a hole in our idea when he brought up the fact that we didn't *actually* know whether Lydia's book was in the confiscated materials from the arrest—something Thea couldn't confirm either. All she knew was that any books that had been in her father's possession at the time were taken.

From there, we'd decided we would need to come up with a few possible locations to hit at once. If Lenore and the Council caught on to what we were looking for, it could be over before it began.

That's when the bulk of the arguments began. Seized items from witches the Council arrested were put into a warehouse of sorts attached to Stromford Prison. Getting in sounded simple enough using Lyra's glamour and old-fashioned lies, but finding what we needed was more challenging. And if the book wasn't there, it complicated things.

Rez had floated going back to Martin and forcing him to answer questions. We already knew Martin had a version of the entire spell; if we knew how he got it, that could give us the lead we needed. Both Blythe and I agreed that would be a last resort. There was no telling what would get back to the Council if Selvina was in a mood.

Sadiki offered to reach out to some of his connections outside of the Collective. He'd apparently spent a good amount of time with witches who "collected" rare magical items through less-than-ethical ways prior to becoming an Emissary.

"I still don't understand why this has to happen right now," Jax said.

"Impending death isn't a good enough reason for the golden boy?" Blythe snapped.

He shook his head. "I don't mean—I just—once Councilwoman Charlevoix finds out exactly what happened to Sasha, she's going to find another way to get to you," he said, looking at me. "We need to lay low."

"That's why we need to do it now," I argued. "The more time we give her to cover her bases, the harder it's going to be for us."

He massaged his jaw. "But—"

"The longer we wait, the higher chance she gets at a three-for-one," I said.

"I'm just asking you to wait a couple more weeks," he insisted.

"What's going to change in a few weeks?" Thea asked, frowning at him.

He shot an apologetic grimace at Leander, who stood frozen, staring at Jax and the grenade he seemingly just dropped into the conversation.

"Nothing," Jax muttered. I knew I wasn't the only one who caught that his comment had been an unintended slip. And, looking around, I realized I also wasn't the only one who was confused about it.

"Ignoring whatever *that* was," Lyra pressed on, clearly not as fazed by her brother's behavior as the rest of us. "Em, what do we got?"

I pulled my focus from watching another silent exchange between Jax and Leander to the list I'd been keeping.

"Stromford," I read. "The Aspese Syndicate. And Martin."

Lyra frowned. "That's it?"

I nodded. "Unless someone else has an idea?"

"Try cousin Meg," Wes said, walking into the kitchen with a hot water bottle under his arm.

I turned to him. "What?"

"Meg," he repeated, dumping the contents into the sink and setting it to the side. "She collects rare and antique books. Might have an idea or two. Some of her books might even have the answer to where Lydia's ended up."

Lyra frowned at him.

I let out a sigh. "How long have you been listening?"

He shrugged and made his way to the table. "You aren't exactly being quiet," he said with a grin. "And for what it's worth, I think you're right. You don't want to give Lenore any more time to regroup."

Jax let out a disapproving snort.

"Is there something you'd like to share with the class?" Lyra snapped.

His jaw clenched, but he shook his head.

"Great," she muttered. "Cousin Meg?"

I shrugged. "She's like a magical history buff and likes to collect. There's a solid chance she knows where it is or knows someone who knows."

"Or has it?" Lyra prompted.

I bobbed my head side to side. "Probably not, but…"

"I'll call her later," Wes said, giving my shoulder a light squeeze. "But she might not have time to go through everything herself."

I nodded. "I can go out there," I offered. Lyra might have been able to look like anyone, but I certainly couldn't. And this was the best excuse for not going with the other groups. With my power pretty much non-existent and me still recovering from Sasha's memory dump, methodically going through old books at Cousin Meg's seaside cottage sounded like the perfect retreat.

"I'm sure she'll be happy to see you," he said, placing a light kiss on the top of my head. "Try not to stay up too much later."

I nodded. "We'll try to keep it down."

"Sure," he said with a skeptical grin. "Go easy on them," he added to Lyra before turning back to the stairs.

Lyra smirked. "Alright then," she said, rubbing her hands together. "Add your history nerd of a cousin to the list."

I already had, but I didn't have the energy to correct her; Meg was into history, but *nerd* wasn't exactly the adjective I would have used to describe her. Then again, describing Cousin Meg was like trying to describe the ocean to someone who'd never seen it. Not impossible, but hard to do it the justice it deserved.

"Buddy system," Lyra declared. "Sadiki, you and the grumpmeister will hook up with your Syndicate contacts and—"

"We're not splitting up," Jax and Leander said at the same time, a matching panic edging into their tones that I hoped was due to the lack of sleep.

Lyra crossed her arms. "What part of 'hit as many things at once' aren't you two grasping?"

Jax looked down at his feet.

Leander flexed his hands as if he was itching to put a shield up. "Then I'll go to Stromford," he said.

Lyra opened her mouth.

"And you can go with Em," Jax offered.

I frowned.

Lyra looked between them. "If I 'can't just walk into Stromford,'" she said, lowering her voice in a poor impression of her oldest brother, "then what in the fuck makes you think *you* can?"

He hesitated for a moment, his gaze flicking to Rez. "I know someone who works there," he said. "Owes me a favor."

Rez snorted.

"And you're just sharing this *now*?" Blythe asked.

"I didn't want to encourage the idea," he said simply, crossing his arms.

Lyra rolled her eyes. "Fine, you can come with Thea and me."

"What about—" Jax started.

"I. Can. Look. Like. Anyone." Lyra said dramatically clapping her hands between each word. "What is with you two?"

"Nothing," Jax muttered while Leander mumbled something that sounded a lot like "Doesn't matter."

"Good then. So, Thea, Leander, and me will head to Stromford." She looked around as if waiting for more arguments. When none came, she nodded at me, and I made a little note. It wasn't like this was going to be hard to remember, but Wes and Chad were going to want to know where everybody was supposed to be in case things—as they tended to—went sideways.

"Blythe, you and Rez will hit up gramps Foster," she continued. "Sadiki, you and Jax will hook up with the Syndicate people."

Jax looked around, frowning. "That means Em's on her own."

Lyra nodded. "At her cousin's. Oh-so very *perilous*."

He started to shake his head. "That's not a good—"

Lyra threw up her hands. "You fuckers are impossible!"

Sadiki chuckled deeply. "It's alright, Lyra," he said. "I should go alone. Bringing one of Castor's sons into the Syndicate will not loosen lips."

Lyra nodded. "*You* are my favorite right now."

He raised his coffee mug in a toast to her.

She looked around at the group. "Last time now," she said and took a deep breath. "We'll go and see if we can get into the storage unit with the confiscated items at the prison," she said, waving a hand among the three of the Stromford group. "Sadiki will meet with his Syndicate contacts, *alone*." She added the last word with a punctuated glare at Leander. "Blythe and Rez will try to squeeze some information out of Martin, and Em and Jax will go see the nerdy cousin."

I finished my notes and looked up.

"Any other complaints?" she asked.

Thea's mouth parted like she was about to offer one, but closed it without a word and sat back in the chair with crossed arms. And it didn't take a genius to figure out what about Lyra's groupings had her upset.

Chapter 17

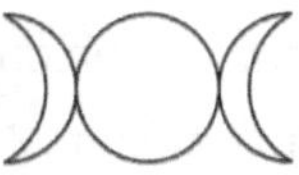

White Cedar Island sat six miles off the coast of Bar Harbor. Cousin Meg was one of the just under two thousand people that called the island home year-round. Memorial Day to Labor Day that number easily tripled. And that's when they'd have two ferries running every half hour, but in February they had only one leaving every two hours from before six to just before eight.

We'd missed the last ferry before the hour lunch break by fifteen minutes and had to find a way to waste time until next one. Bar Harbor, Maine, like the island, was a well-known summer destination. There were hardly any tourists during late-winter, and many of the shops had reduced hours for the off-season. Instead of walking the streets, we settled for the terminal's vending machine coffee and whatever it tried to pass off as chai.

We were among the dozen or so others on the crossing, all huddled inside the first-floor interior of the ferry to stay warm. About halfway through the choppy waters, however, I had to go up top for fresh air to ease my churning stomach. The icy wind stung my cheeks as I watched the snowy island come into view.

We docked at Nock's Landing and were directed to follow the signs to the welcome terminal. An iron sign, still wrapped in white string lights glowing dimly against the gray daylight, and a large wooden pirate statue donning a pink heart on its hat left over from Valentine's Day greeted us.

That was just a taste of what the ferry terminal offered. Unlike the one we'd left, the island's was an introduction to their theme: pirates. Art, murals, display cases of things common during the golden age of piracy, it was like stepping into a mini museum. All to draw the crowds.

Because, White Cedar Island had more than small town charm and rocky beaches to draw in tourists. Sometime in the late eighteenth century, a few gold coins were found, and rumors that they were part of some massive treasure started immediately. From there, it became an obsession for a lot of fortune hunters. Bits of jewels and more coins had been found over the centuries, yet the big prize remained elusive. But that was blamed on a mysterious curse that would keep the treasure hidden until enough people died.

Wes didn't believe in the hype or in the curse. Chad tried to get me to help him come up with a spell to find it when I was fifteen.

Most of the passengers who had walked on with us split off to find their cars in the residents' parking lot. A couple with fuzzy hats and expressions that told me they hadn't prepared for this weather were waved down by the shuttle for the local inn.

I pulled my phone out to find Meg's number. Wes had let her know we were coming, and I'd kept her updated about what ferry we'd caught, but she wasn't exactly known for her punctuality.

A horn honked twice, drawing my attention, and I looked up to see a light gray Land Rover flashing its lights at us. A woman in her mid-thirties opened the door and stepped halfway out, waving to us.

"That her?" Jax asked.

I nodded and waved back as Jax grabbed our bags. Maneuvering through the other crossers and delivery trucks, we hurried over to meet her.

Despite the grayness of the afternoon, Meg pushed round black sunglasses on top of her head, sweeping the long layers of her dark-brown windswept hair away from her face.

Her black pointed boots, cuffed boyfriend jeans, black shirt, and long green cardigan looked out of place in the sea of parkas and duck boots. That was Meg, always looking perfectly confident wherever she was, while also giving off the feeling of being *slightly* out of place.

Her smile was warm, and wide enough that it stretched the scar on her upper lip, making it more noticeable. Her long nose and round cheeks had a smattering of freckles that I'd never seen her cover with makeup, and as she tossed her waist-length hair out of the way to grab our bags, I noticed the shiny burn scar on her neck. I was sure I'd seen it before, but now that I had my own scars, it stood out more. I'd never asked how she got it.

"Good crossing?" she asked, a touch of an Irish accent to her words, thanks to being raised by a great-aunt from Galway. She tossed the two duffels into the back of her car.

"A bit rough," I admitted as she shut the back.

"Nothing a bit of tea won't fix," she said, putting her hands on her hips. "Let's get a good look at'cha, now."

I stood awkwardly in the cold while she gave me a once-over. "You look older," she said, blue-gray eyes narrowing on my face.

I shrugged. "It's been over a year."

She shook her head. "Hmm."

I wasn't entirely sure if that was the sound of approval or not, but I suppressed a shudder under her continued appraisal. Meg wasn't that much younger than Wes, but every time we met, she gave the impression she was able to sense more than she let on. She was a Hedge Witch like

Wes, but that didn't mean she couldn't have traits in her lineage that gave her a boost in instincts.

She said nothing else, instead turning to Jax. "You're the friend, then?"

He nodded. "Jax," he said extending his hand to her.

Her eyebrow hitched slightly, but she shook it. "Grand then. Let's get'cha out the cold." She opened the passenger door and leaned the seat forward before jerking her chin towards it, signaling for Jax to climb in.

The running car was warm, and I sank against the soft leather as Meg pulled her sunglasses back over her eyes and sped out of the lot so fast Lyra would have been jealous.

"I'm thrilled to see ye now," she said, turning at a four-way stop without even pretending to tap the brakes. "But it's not exactly peak season, and Wesley was a bit vague on the phone."

Wes had purposely been vague at Lyra's suggestion. The night we'd gotten back from the bar, Lyra had done a bug sweep of the house and our devices, but that didn't stop her from being just a tad paranoid that Sebastian had left *something* behind to spy on us. Add that to the fact that Lenore no doubt already knew everything Sebastian did, and we weren't willing to take any unnecessary risks—or, at least, any more of them.

We had the surety that Meg wouldn't go around telling anyone what we were up to. Wes had been impartial to the Collective and the Council before all this. As long as they stayed away, he didn't care to give them much thought. Meg, however, was *loudly* opposed to their entire existence, especially after a couple glasses of whiskey.

Still, the fewer people who knew the full extent of our plans, the better. The Council most likely wouldn't find any real connection between Meg and me, as she wasn't actually anyone's cousin but instead an old family friend of Wes's. But after what happened with Ian, we wanted to be as careful as we could.

"We just had some history questions," I said, "and were hoping we could look through your books."

"Public libraries not cutting it?" she teased.

"Your spell books," Jax clarified from the backseat.

Meg pulled her sunglasses down her nose with a slender finger to stare at him in the rear-view mirror—long enough where I wanted to grab the steering wheel to keep us on the coastal road as we wound close to the edge of land and water.

"You're Castor's, yeah," she said, pushing her glasses back up and returning her attention to the road. It wasn't a question or even an accusation. Just a simple statement that sent my mind reeling.

I glanced back at him, but he looked as confused as I did. Wes had let her know a friend would be coming with me but had left out his name. There was no reason she should have known who Jax was, let alone his father.

"You know my father?" Jax asked.

All Meg gave him in response was a shrug and turned up the music. Hurried strings filled the car and she tapped her fingers in time with the tune as we settled into a comfortable silence.

Soon, we came around the bend with a small sign that identified the part of the island known as Kitte's Cove. It was the only place that had a stretch of sandy beach open to the public and where the majority of the vacation homes had been built. Year-round residents tended to live in or close to Nock's Landing, where the bulk of the businesses were. Kitte's Cove had a population of two this time of year: Meg, and Walter the one-eyed inn-keeper who would always give me red licorice ropes when I came to visit.

Meg's gray-shingled cottage was the quintessential seaside home. A wrap-around porch where driftwood and heart cockle shell art hung from the underside of the roof and on the sides of a dark purple door. A small bell, carved with the image of three ravens in flight, trilled in the cold breeze as we made our way up the steps.

She led us through an unlocked door and dropped our bags next to the dark olive velvet couch. The cottage wasn't overly large. Two levels, but only two bedrooms, with an open concept kitchen and living area on the first floor featuring large glass windows and French doors that opened to the back side of the porch and gorgeous ocean views.

A stone fireplace stood opposite us, flames leaping to life with a flick of Meg's index finger. Peat mixed with the heavy cedar aroma from the thick wood mantel and beams in the room. Hints of lemon, lavender, rosemary, and vanilla from the simmer pot on her stove tickled my nose.

Meg pulled the sleeves of her sweater up her arms. Another scar wrapped around her wrist and up her forearm, the extent of it still hidden under her sleeves. "Kitchen," she said, waving her hand to her side in a mini tour, various crystal bracelets clacking together with the movement.

Her kitchen was small enough for the cottage, but large enough to not feel cramped. In the middle stood a small butcher block island with shelves to hold a variety of cooking and spell books. A small breakfast nook was tucked next to a window to watch the waves. Drying herbs hung from the underside of the shelf built into the wall behind the farmhouse sink. Jars of crushed herbs sat on top of the shelf, ready for use.

The cupboards were windowed with clear glass to display all that was housed inside. Everything from the expected tableware and bags of coffee grounds to jars of mugwort and nettle.

There was no mistaking a witch lived here, and that was Meg. She wasn't worried about hiding what she was, and I found that comforting after months of being hunted for what I was.

Meg turned over the black onyx bracelet she wore on her right wrist, the black a stark contrast with the amethyst one stacked with it, but what stood out the most was the antique bangle with a small emerald in the center. "Bathroom is upstairs to your left, guest room to the right." She eyed us. "Only the one bed."

My neck heated.

"Couch is fine," Jax said before I could figure out what to say. It wasn't like Meg was a prude, but Jax and I hadn't talked about "us" since Thea walked in on us, and I wasn't sure sharing a bed was the best way to break that ice.

And it wasn't for lack of trying. But Jax had been uncharacteristically quiet on the flight from Ohio. Every time I'd tried to ask him about it, he'd just say he was tired. I'd spent my fair share of time avoiding people—him—to know what that looked like. What I couldn't figure out was what exactly I'd done to earn it.

"Right," she moved into the kitchen and pulled out a copper teapot. "I'll have some biscuits, then," she added, filling the kettle at the sink. "Unless you need something more substantial."

I shook my head. "Tea is fine," I replied, trying my best not to immediately jump into searching through her collection. It had been over a year since we'd seen each other, and I didn't want to be rude. She put the kettle on the stovetop next to her simmer pot and clicked the flame to life as I shrugged out of my coat and hung it on the driftwood coat rack she had next to the door.

"So," she began turning back to face us. "What's the story?"

I glanced at Jax to see if he wanted to jump in first, but he was conveniently avoiding eye contact with me and instead looking at the frames on the wall next to him.

I turned back to Meg, who was nice enough not to comment on the lack of interaction between Jax and me. "We're trying to find a spell book that's pretty old."

She watched Jax over my shoulder for an uncomfortable amount of time before her eyes came back to me. She nodded and motioned to the stool at the island across from her. I kicked off my shoes—despite Meg keeping hers on—and sat down while Jax continued to take his time examining what was hanging on Meg's walls.

"Define 'old' for me, yeah?" she said, pulling a jar of loose-leaf tea from one of her cupboards along with a sage green teapot.

"Late seventeenth century," I said.

She nodded, adding a couple scoops of the tea to the infuser attachment in the pot.

"That's a bit of a ways back," she admitted. "Those that survived the hunts were kept in families." She tilted her head side to side as if considering options in something. "Or lost. Anyone in particular?"

I bit the inside of my cheek. I knew we'd have to give her more information at some point. Narrowing down to even a decade wasn't going to be helpful, considering how many books had been destroyed by hunters around that time.

I felt heat creep up my neck and knew Jax had given me his attention, but I refused to look away from Meg. I swallowed. "Lydia Toothaker," I offered.

She propped her hands on the edge of the counter, sage nails tapping on the hard surface as she considered me.

Then, an odd smile curved her lips, and her stare focused behind me. Turning, I saw Jax shifting uncomfortably under her gaze. He looked ready to bolt but seemed unsure of the best way to do so. Was I missing something?

"Castor doesn't have a mind for that?" Meg asked.

He swallowed so hard I saw his throat bob. I turned back to Meg, who wore the expression of a teacher who had caught a student cheating and was waiting for him to confess. There had to be something I was missing.

"Last we—they—knew, it was at the Chicago post," he said. "But that was before the fire in—"

"I know when *the* fire was," she cut in, emphasizing the article.

His jaw clenched.

I was *definitely* missing something.

Her smile returned to normal, and she drummed her fingers on the counter faster as if to a song only she could hear. "I can't tell you for sure where the Toothaker book ended up," she admitted. "Rumors that it survived the fire were confirmed about fifty years later. Some broker for a rare item—" she paused as if considering her words before continuing, "—*connoisseur* tried to sell it for three times its value."

Jax and I exchanged a glance. That sounded a lot like the group Sadiki had gone to talk with. Maybe they would have a lead.

"It was, let's say, *liberated* before a sale could be agreed upon," she continued.

"Liberated?" Jax repeated slowly.

Meg shrugged. "The stolen was stolen," she offered with a soft wink. "Don't have a mind for what happened to it from there. We'll see the occasional claim of ownership, but so far those have all been proved forgeries."

"People *forge* spell books?" I asked.

She shook her head. "Important spell books," she corrected. "Toothaker was a powerful spellwright. A few made their way to use these days, but imagine what kind of spells and concoctions her original work would have?"

I wasn't the best at writing spells and preferred to stick with the ones I knew would work. But Lyra loved to come up with her own and if she even had a quarter of the skill Lydia'd had, then those spells definitely could do some serious damage.

"So, you have no idea where it could be?" Jax ventured sounding almost relieved. I tried not to take it personally. He probably thought the sooner we finished here, the sooner he could go back to avoiding me.

The kettle whistled behind her, and she let it whine for a moment, still staring at him like there was some silent understanding between the two of them about not saying something in front of me. It was eerily similar to the way he and Leander had been having silent conversations lately. And it was frustrating to say the least.

She turned off the stove and poured the water into the tea pot, the warmth filling the small space and spiced tea overwhelming the rest of the scent of the cottage.

"Oh, I be having ideas on me," she said, turning back to face us. "But considering their power, I'll be keepin' 'em to myself."

I frowned before opening my mouth to ask what that even meant, but she held up a hand to stop me. "I'll ring up a few friends, see if they've got a mind for it," she offered. "Discreetly," she added when I knew my face betrayed a panic at the notion of bringing even more people into this.

"As promised," she said. "You are welcome to look through the collection. See if any of them'll help."

She nodded to the back door and moved for it. I grabbed my shoes and quickly yanked them on, hopping after her. She led us down a path clear of snow but patchy with ice to a padlocked shed beneath a snow-covered white cedar tree.

She pulled a key from around her neck, taking a moment to untangle it from the other chains that held crystals and silver jewelry. After she popped the lock off, and after opening both doors, she stood to the side to let me look inside.

"All yours," she offered.

Shelves bowed from weight, shelves partially off the wall, and overflowing boxes on the floor greeted me. Teetering piles of books in the corner looked ready to topple at the first strong breeze and both spines and pages were facing out as if shoved in whatever space they'd fit. And I thought Blythe's shelf had been bad.

I took a step inside—calling it a step was generous, as only the front half of my foot could find space—and stared at it all. I knew she was a collector, but this was not what I expected at all.

"These are all spell books?" I asked quietly.

Meg leaned against the open door and crossed her arms, gazing at the inside proudly. "Spell books, journals, rantings, you name it."

"Where'd you get them all?" Jax asked, craning his neck to take in the lot with me when I turned to face them again.

Meg shrugged. "Here and there," she said and glanced at her watch. "I've got a meeting," she said. "Bunderbuss delivers 'til seven if you need something before I'm back."

My stomach dropped. "You have to go?" I'd been counting on her help and after seeing the state of the shed I needed it.

"Sorry, love." She held out the key to me. "Between the two of you, you'll be able to find what'cha need, then," she said as I took the key from her. "Lock up when it gets dark."

She turned back up the path while I stared after her, the key to days—if not weeks—of work curled in my hand. She stopped halfway up the path and turned back to us. "If you can't reach me by mobile, send Cormac and he'll find me."

I nodded and turned back to the books, the weight of what we were about to attempt sitting on my chest. Even if the owners of all these had put names and details in, it would still take hours to peruse each for a mention of Lydia or the Triple Moon Coven. All we could hope for was another group finding something first.

"Wait," I muttered, turning back to the house Meg had disappeared into. "Who's Cormac?"

Chapter 18

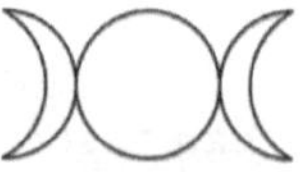

We had a week until the full moon, but it was still bright enough to reflect off the dark ripples of the ocean outside Meg's cottage. Every time a wave disturbed the surface, the movement caught my eye and pulled my thoughts back to the first night we'd tried to undo the binding. The moon, the crisp coolness of a winter night, mixed with salty air.

I tossed the book I'd been skimming back into the box of its rejected companions and rubbed my sore eyes. Between trying to decipher old handwriting, the faded ink, and the inadequate lighting, my eyes and mind were strained.

I leaned back against the couch. "This is useless," I muttered. We'd been at it for over five hours, the sun had set hours ago, and the "Treasure Map" pizza from Blunderbuss had long passed an eadible temperature.

Meg texted to let us know she got stuck at work and then had a client dinner, so she wouldn't be back until late.

When Jax asked what she did that kept her busy on a Saturday, I had to admit I wasn't entirely sure. I knew she ran the historical society, or maybe served on its board, or something like that. Meg's actual profession remained a mystery to me. She'd inherited a chunk of family money from her great-aunt, so I got the impression that a lot of what she did was because she enjoyed it, not for the money.

Once our fingers had gone numb from the chill and we found it hard to turn the pages, we'd taken to lugging armfuls of books into the cottage. I'd lost count of how many we'd actually managed to go through. Her system was, well, books. It stopped there. She hadn't even managed to organize by century, and it made my head ache more than the poor lighting.

Any other time, it would have been interesting to spend a few weeks here—preferably in the summer—to go through and catalog the collection, but we were here to find what felt like a specific grain of sand on a beach.

Meg's collection was all magically preserved against decay, which explained why she kept them in a shed the way she did. Still, the least she could do was fix the shelves.

"We've barely been through a quarter," Jax said, not looking up from the book in his lap.

I reached into the unsorted box to pull out yet another book and opened it. Correct year, wrong location. "That's my point," I said, scanning the first few pages. The scribblings of an English witch's tests on nettle versus garlic in curing something called *hard pulse disease*. "At this rate, it'll be peak season before we finish." I closed the book, tossed it in the reject pile that was getting larger by the hour, and let out a frustrated sigh. "Nothing from the others?"

He picked up his phone and glanced at it. "Nothing yet."

"I need a break," I muttered and used the couch to pull myself up. Stretching my back out from sitting too long, I stifled a yawn. "Refill?" I offered, nodding to the practically empty mug in front of Jax.

He shook his head and replaced the book he'd been reading with a new one from the pile. I bit the inside of my cheek and walked to the opposite wall to get the ache out of my stiff legs.

I examined the framed photos on the wall. Some of the newer ones were from the last time I'd visited. Meg, Wes, Chad, and me on the beach. Chad and me posing with the wooden pirate at the ferry dock. Further up the wall, the older the pictures got. Wes with Meg before I came to live with them, maybe even before he and Chad met.

Meg with two women I didn't know outside her cottage. A shot from a local paper of Meg walking a group of tourists around the island. She never seemed to age the expected way. She was always just...Meg. Maybe that was part of the appeal of island living; less stress to age you.

The photos turned from black and white to sepia images of stiffly posed women in nineteenth-century dresses. Meg's ancestors. They all had the same-shaped eyes and nose as hers. I moved to the mantel where framed artworks were propped up. Drawings of the island before it became a town. An old cottage on the coast of what I assumed was Ireland. A sketch of three laughing women wearing dresses you'd find in movies about pirates and holding large mugs.

I squinted at the sketch. They all looked remarkably like the women in Meg's picture outside her cottage. Movement from the corner of my eye pulled my attention, and I turned in time to see Jax setting his phone back down next to him with his eyebrows pulled together.

"That them?" I asked.

He shook his head and went back to the book he had in his hands without even looking at me.

"Oh," I mumbled. Crossing my arms, I watched him for another moment before stuffing my nerves down and forcing the question out of myself. "Are you mad at me?"

He froze in the middle of turning a page and frowned at me. "What?"

I let out a half-breath. "Are you mad at me?" I repeated. "Because you've been super quiet and, I get it, you didn't like this plan. But, to be fair, it was as much Lyra's as it was mine."

He shook his head. "I'm not mad."

"You seem mad."

"I'm just—"

"Tired," I finished for him with an eye roll. "Jax, you know how many times I've used that lie?"

He held my gaze, and heat crept up my neck the longer he stared. "I'm not mad," he said again, tone softer this time.

"Okay," I conceded. My next question, though, I both wanted an answer to and wanted to avoid an answer to. It had been rolling around in my mind since the flight. A part of me had hoped he was mad; that would have been easier.

"Is it because of Thea?" I asked, frustrated at my own slightly shaky voice.

He blinked at me. "Thea? What—what are you talking about?"

I shrugged. "After we, you know. And then she..." I took a deep breath. "I just thought maybe you were worried about hurting her feelings or something."

He smiled. "Are you?"

"Kind of," I admitted. "I mean, we're not friends, but that doesn't mean I want to be all couple-y and in her face."

He nodded slowly. "Because it's selfish?" he asked quietly.

I opened my mouth, but no words came out, just a half-strangled noise, wanting to agree but also not. I hadn't expected this to circle back to *that* conversation. But in truth, the fears I'd had about giving into my feelings for him, with everything going, on were still there.

Nodding, I moved around the low coffee table and sat back down on the couch, grabbing a throw pillow with a raven printed on it and hugging it to my chest, inhaling the peat smoke that clung to the fabric with each breath through my nose.

I watched him out of the corner of my eye while he stared at the book in his lap. We sat like that for what felt like an eternity but couldn't have been more than a couple minutes.

Sighing, I tossed the pillow aside and reached for the stack of books we still had to get through and grabbed a new one. I shouldn't have brought it up.

Jax caught my wrist, and the warmth of his touch shot up my arm. We hadn't been this close in days, and I hadn't realized how much I'd missed it.

Swallowing, I forced myself to meet his eyes.

"You're not selfish," he said softly.

I couldn't stop the disbelieving snort.

He moved closer and took the book out of my hand, setting it on the edge of the coffee table. "You're not," he insisted. "But, I think I might be."

I started to shake my head, but he released my wrist to cup my face in both of his hands. "I want you, this," he said simply, and my heart skipped. "I'm sorry if I've been distant, it's just—" he stopped and shook his head slightly. "I'm sorry."

I frowned. "What?" I asked, wanting to know what he'd stopped himself from saying. An excuse? An explanation?

"It's not important."

"Jax," I started.

His fingers traced along my jaw as he leaned closer. "It's not important," he said again, voice barely above a whisper, his blue gaze holding mine.

My stomach knotted, but I pulled his hands away. "I think it is," I said. "So, why won't you tell me?"

He sighed and hung his head for a moment before looking back up at me. "Family stuff," he said with a forced half-smile. "Leander's worried."

I frowned. "That's nothing new."

He let out a breath of a laugh. "I guess that's fair." He rubbed his jaw and moved to scoot away from me, but I held his free hand, keeping him close.

"You've dealt with all my family stuff," I reminded him. "You can talk to me about yours."

He glanced at the front door and then turned to me, a fake smile plastered on his face. "I think you're right, we need a break," he said, pulling his hand out of mine. He stood and went to the kitchen. I turned on the couch to watch him open the fridge with a frown.

"You think your cousin has anything to drink?" he asked.

"Jax," I started.

"I mean, other than whiskey," he added with a slight chuckle. "Don't need the hard stuff yet."

"Are you serious right now?"

He closed the fridge and looked at me. "I do think we need a break, yes."

I bit the inside of my cheek to keep the frustrated growl from escaping. I'd always been the one to avoid certain topics. Especially with him. We'd been down this road before and the last time it was my fault. He never pushed, so did I have any right to now? The truthful answer was no. But that didn't stop me.

"I'm sure she's got wine somewhere," I said. "But are we really not going to talk about this?"

"Em," he pleaded, pulling out an open bottle of white wine and setting it on the counter. "There's nothing to talk about. I'm just stuck between Leander and Lyra, like always." He started opening cupboards.

"It doesn't feel the same as always," I muttered.

He set two glasses on the island. "Well, we haven't actually known each other that long, have we?"

My stomach sank, and the hurt burned. "I guess not," I agreed as I stood. I nudged a book that had fallen on the floor out of my way and moved around the couch. "Enjoy your drink."

He frowned. "Where are you going?"

"Bed," I snapped before taking the narrow stairs two at a time to the second floor. Shutting the door to the guest room, I didn't bother turning on the light, just fell onto the mattress and stared at the shadows from the almost full moon sliding across the ceiling. I could hear the wind moving the trees outside, and could pretend I could hear the crash of the waves too. Anything to keep my mind from replaying that disaster of a conversation.

He was right. We'd only known each other for what, three months? For all I knew, this was how he normally reacted when his siblings put him in the middle of their stuff. How well did I actually know him? Or Leander or Lyra, for that matter. We'd been through so much together that I wanted to believe we were close, but if life-and-death situations were all we had, what would happen once those were gone?

The sooner we heard from another group, the faster we could leave. I wanted to check in with Blythe to see how things were going on her end, but I'd left my phone downstairs. Rubbing my face, I let out a frustrated sigh. This was going to be awkward.

After rolling off the bed, I crossed to the door and opened it to see Jax standing outside, hand raised like he'd just been about to knock. We stared at each other for a second longer than needed.

"Your phone," he said, holding it out.

"Thanks," I mumbled, taking it and turning it over in my hands. I'd been prepared for awkwardness but thought I'd have a few more minutes before I was going to have to face it. I glanced down at the phone and checked the notifications for missed calls or messages. Nothing.

"I'm sorry I snapped," I said, finally looking back up at him.

He took a few purposeful breaths. "It's not that I don't want to talk to you about it," he explained. "It's that I don't want to talk about it at all."

Sighing, I walked back into the room and tossed the phone onto the nightstand. "Okay," I said, turning to see he'd followed me inside.

"It's just a lot," he said. "With them, my dad. I just want to not think about it."

I crossed my arms. "Your dad? What does your dad have to do with Leander and Lyra?"

He rubbed the back of his neck. "Nothing—it's just—there's a lot going on with...stuff."

I fell back onto the bed and resumed watching shadows. "Stuff, right."

"Em," he said, the mattress depressing as he sat down next to me. "It's complicated, and dragging you into it is the last thing I want to do."

I chewed on my bottom lip and turned to face him. "But, you're fine being dragged into all my complicated?" I asked.

He shrugged. "I like your complicated," he said.

I snorted.

He lay down next to me, our hands close enough I could feel the heat of him, but far enough we weren't touching. "It's more exciting for sure," he said softly and I could hear the smile in his voice.

I took in his shadowy profile, illuminated only by the moonlight bleeding in from the sheer curtains and the light we'd left on downstairs. He might have been smiling when he said it, but his brow was creased as it so often was these days. His jaw clenched as though he hadn't had a moment to relax, ticking near his temple at some unspoken thought.

Without thinking, I reached over and ran a finger lightly over that ever-present crease to try to smooth it. His eyes fluttered shut and he let out a long breath.

"You'll get wrinkles if you're not careful," I teased, trailing my finger to the space just at the edge of his eyes, where it would crinkle when he smiled.

He caught my hand. "I'm sure Wes has something for that," he said before placing a light kiss on my palm before releasing it.

It fell to his chest as I propped myself up on my elbow to better look at him. Even in the darkness, I could see lines that hadn't been there when we'd first met. Like he'd aged years instead of weeks. I wondered whose *complicated* caused it, mine or his.

"Jax?"

"Hmm?"

"You *can* talk to me, you know," I said, looking down at my hand on his shirt, tracing small circles along the slightly textured fabric. The side of my face warmed when I felt his eyes on me.

He didn't say anything and his stare went back to the ceiling. "Not now," he said softly. "But, not never."

I took a deep breath. Maybe that was all I deserved. *Not never.* Swallowing, I pulled my hand from him. "Not never," I accepted with a small nod. Reluctantly, I dragged myself back to my feet.

He sat up with a frown.

"A lot more books to go through," I said, waving my hand towards the door.

He gently pulled me in to stand between his legs before I could make for the door. He looked up at me with a playful grin. "I thought we were on a break," he insisted.

I put my hands on his shoulders. "Break's over," I teased.

He shook his head. "Five more minutes," he fake whined as his grip moved to my waist to pull me even closer to him. The heat from his body radiated through mine, despite the chill of the upstairs room.

My mouth had gone very dry and I was having a hard time forming complete thoughts as his hands slipped under my sweater. His thumb ran the length of the partially healed scar from Sasha's knife and it sent a shiver through me.

"Ten more minutes?" he whispered.

I swallowed and started to shake my head.

He kissed the scar gently and I sucked in a breath as blood rushed in my ears. There was something my brain had decided before this. Before he...wasn't there?

My eyes flittered shut. "Jax," I warned breathlessly.

"Yes?" he said innocently. As if he wasn't completely aware of what he was doing to me.

I let out an involuntary moan as his mouth continued further up my stomach, his hands resting just below the band of my bralette. "The books..."

He nodded. "Will still be there in half an hour."

I looked down at him, tilting his face up to mine and seeing a little of the spark I'd so desperately missed in his blue eyes. Before I could think too much, I pressed my lips to his, wrapping myself around him. He let out a soft breath and pulled me on top of him as he fell back onto the bed.

Right, wrong, it didn't matter right now. It would at some unknown hour. Because no matter what we felt in this moment, there was a lot to figure out. With me, with him, with *us*.

But that was tomorrow's problem.

Chapter 19

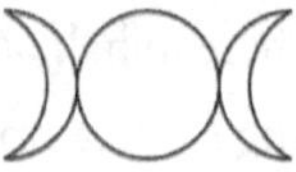

That unsettling feeling of being watched pulled me from an uneasy sleep. Heart beating faster than it should have, I blinked at the dark windows outlined by ice, waiting for something to show itself. The gentle groan of the cottage settling around us and Jax's steady breathing next to me were the only sounds pricking my ears. I took deep breaths to try and slow my heart rate, but my mind kept waiting for the creak of a footstep or the rustle of clothes.

A sliver of moonlight fell on the floor through the slight crack in the curtains. Nothing jumped from the shadowy corners or the small closet, yet my brain was convinced Jax and I were not alone. Carefully sliding out from under his arm, I sat up and took a full look around the room. Jax let out a soft grunt but didn't wake up.

Sighing, I moved out from the comforter and let out a slight shiver as my bare feet hit the cold hardwood. Gooseflesh rose on my arms in the chilled air now that I wasn't comfortably warm next to Jax. I grabbed the first shirt I found in the dark and pulled it over my tank and sleep shorts.

Softly closing the door as I stepped into the hallway, I took a deep breath as that unnerving sensation eased slightly. The rest of the cottage was dark. The crackling fire downstairs had been put out, and I felt a twinge of guilt as I made my way downstairs. We'd fallen asleep without coming back down and hadn't cleaned up at all. The least we could have done was toss the cold pizza.

I didn't think it had been too late when we'd gone to bed, but I didn't remember hearing Meg come home. And she *had* come home, since the mess we'd left was gone. I didn't want to be an even worse guest and wake her up, but whatever had interrupted what little sleep I was getting had replaced tiredness with a frustrating alertness, and I was hoping Meg had some kind of tea to help with that.

A faint warm light bled from lights under the kitchen cabinets. My eyes adjusted to the new light as I went to fill the kettle while the soft click of a clock emanated from the living room. Cringing as the water hit the pot too loudly in the still cottage, I filled it enough for maybe a cup and a half before turning the tap off.

After turning the stove on, I filled a glass with water and gulped some down to soothe my dry throat. A second later, I froze, the hair on the back of my neck rising as the feeling of being watched returned. Lowering the glass slowly, I waited for movement from anywhere in the room. The clock stopped its ticking.

Shaking myself from unfounded fear, I took another sip.

"Hi."

I inhaled the water, startled by the not-quite human voice that broke through the hushed living room. Coughing to clear my throat, I set the glass down and took a tentative step towards the direction I thought I'd heard the voice. It was late and I was tired and on edge. It could have been my imagination.

"Hi," it repeated.

Something inhuman was in the living room. It was the only explanation for the voice and the sensation creeping up my spine. I took another tentative step.

"Hi."

Swallowing, I shoved the anxiety swirling in my gut down even further. "Hello?" I whispered, hoping I wasn't going to get a response.

The kettle whistled behind me, and I nearly jumped out of my skin. Heart pounding, I hurried to remove it before it woke anyone up. I was losing it, talking to shadows.

"Pretty girl," the voice rasped.

My hand went to the powerless ruby around my neck out of instinct as I tried to decide if I had enough of my own power to fight whatever was in the house or if I should wake someone up by screaming.

"Don't mind Cormac," Meg said as she walked into the kitchen, giving me the third startle in the last five minutes. "He's a shameless flirt." She leaned against the counter across from me with a small grin. Her hair was in a loose braid that fell over the shoulder of her satin emerald pajama set.

"Cormac?" I repeated slowly, looking between Meg and the dark corner of the living room.

She nodded and, in a swish of plumage, a large black bird glided out of the shadowed corner and landed on the island in front of me, clicking its beak in an impression of a laugh. He hopped closer to Meg and bent his head down. She ran her hand against his smooth feathers.

"Never seen a familiar before?" she asked.

I shook myself from my staring. "No, I have, I just wasn't expecting it—him."

She nodded slowly. "Can't sleep?" she continued, moving around the counter to pull out a jar of loose-leaf tea.

I nodded, keeping Cormac in sight. Something about the bird's unnaturally green gaze made my skin prickle. There was a familiarity to it that had me wondering if it had been his stare that woke me up.

"Bad dreams?" Meg asked, busying herself with making the tea. "Or just not tired enough?" Her knowing glance swept across my shirt, and I tugged the sleeves of Jax's henley to my knuckles.

"Just...a lot on my mind," I said, burning embarrassment rising up my neck. We hadn't heard Meg come home, and I'd wanted that to be because we'd already fallen asleep, not because we'd been in the middle of...

"That bad?" Meg teased, handing me a steaming mug.

"What! No! It was—no," I stumbled, suddenly very warm in the chilled cottage.

She chuckled. "Only havin' the craic, love."

I cleared my throat uncomfortably. "You have a familiar?" I asked, jerking my thumb at Cormac, desperate for a change in subject. Meg wasn't some Puritan by any means, but we didn't know each other well enough for *that* conversation.

She smiled like she knew exactly what I was doing—not that I was being that smooth about it—and just nodded. "Not nearly as fun as yours," she said, earning a chastising beak click from Cormac.

I let out a sigh, thankful she'd allowed the change in topic. "Wait, mine?"

As if on cue, Grace leapt onto the island, red eyes glowing softly in the dimness. Cormac let out an indignant squawk and glided to another counter. Meg chuckled as she went to comfort the cooing bird.

Grace padded over to me, and I scratched behind her ears, gaining a loud purr. "What are you doing here?" I asked her.

"What a familiar does," Meg said simply.

I looked up from Grace in time to see Meg toss a very time-worn book onto the island. She leaned against the counter behind her and crossed her arms.

Frowning, I reached for the book. "What's this?"

"Lydia Toothaker's book," Meg offered with a half-shrug.

"*You* had it?" I accused. If she'd had it this whole time, why hadn't she just told us? Why make us spend hours going through everything else?

"No," she said. "I think its whereabouts are a better question for your *leannán*," she added, eyes flitting to the ceiling when she emphasized the last word. A term clearly in another language and I wasn't entirely sure I wanted to know its meaning. It wasn't hard to guess *who* she was referring to, though.

"Then, how is it here?"

She sighed. "Between Cormac and Grace here, they found it," she explained. "They're quite the little team, apparently."

Cormac gave the end of her hair an affectionate nip with his beak while Grace let out a soft meow.

I stared at the cat. "You can do stuff like that?"

Meg laughed "Creatures from the Otherworld don't play by the same rules as us, yeah."

I frowned at Grace. "Then why didn't she just *do* that?" I muttered. She sat and blinked at me as if I'd just asked her why the sky was blue.

"Did ye ask?"

I took a deep breath. No, I hadn't thought of asking my cat if she not only knew where the book we needed was, but also if she could get it for us.

Meg let out a soft chuckle. "Something you'll learn is that our familiars are connected to the magic in this world much differently than witches," she explained. "Don't be afraid to ask for their help." She stroked Cormac's feathers, and he leaned into her touch, green eyes gazing up at her like a fully content puppy might.

"I just assumed they did what they wanted," I grumbled as Grace lay down on the counter in front of me.

Meg shrugged. "Oh, they do," she agreed. "But they only respond to a worthy call, so if she didn't want to help, she wouldn't be here."

Grace blinked at me with a look that told me I was being judged for having to be told this information in the first place. Like the knowledge of how familiars worked was supposed to be commonplace. But if she was that smart, didn't she know familiars were rare these days?

I swallowed. "I wasn't the one who called," I admitted. "Lyra did." I left out the part where Lyra had done so after too much wine. Whether we were deemed worthy or not, wine-drunk casting was rarely a good thing.

"One in the coven calls, all in the coven call."

I stared at Grace, who looked so much like a typical house cat it was hard to imagine her as anything else. But her bright red eyes and massive form meant she was anything but *typical*. She could find missing books and seemingly teleport to wherever she wanted. If a worthy witch—or coven—were able to call a worthy familiar, what did the death coven manage to call?

"Lost in your head?" Meg asked.

I looked up to see her watching me with a slight grin on her lips, one that somehow matched Cormac's expression. Her hand went flat on her chest and she rubbed circles around it as if trying to ease a pain. She stopped when she caught herself and lowered her hand.

"Just...yeah," I replied, looking down at the book in my hands. The one I wanted to open and keep closed at the same time.

"Right, well, turn out the lights when you're done," Meg said with a soft sigh. She turned towards the stairs as Cormac swept back to his corner perch. "Don't stay up too late. No matter what you find in there."

I glanced up, confused at what she might have meant, but she'd already rounded the corner and was out of sight. Placing my hand on the soft, worn cover, I wasn't sure when my heart started beating too fast, but it wasn't long before I could hear my pulse in my ears instead of the tick of the clock or Cormac adjusting his large wings.

Swallowing, I opened the cover to the first page, yellowed with age and covered in the tidy scrawl of Lydia Toothaker's handwriting. Gently, I turned to the next page and the next, trying to find the one spell that we needed. It took a lot to not get distracted by the titles of the other spells she'd invented—ones for problems that modern technology fixed for us now, but at the time would have been revolutionary.

My heart skipped when I saw what I needed. The Triple Moon binding spell. Right there, written in centuries-old ink. Finally, something good had happened. I'd managed to find it without nearly dying; maybe my luck was turning.

But the further I read, the more the cold air around me grew suffocating, and my stomach dropped when I read and reread the final line. A frustrated scream built in the back of my throat.

Lydia Toothaker wasn't the third member of the coven.

☾

The crossing back was a far smoother ride. At no point did my stomach feel the need to eject the full Irish breakfast Meg treated us to before driving to the ferry terminal. No fog obscured the water ahead, and I could just make out the outline of Bar Harbor from the top deck.

It was cold, but I'd bundled up as much as possible and taken to staring ahead as we made our way back. Even though there were only a dozen other people on this morning, it felt cramped inside. Lydia's book lay in my lap, open to the page that made it clear we'd been wrong. Sure, Lydia being the third member had been a guess, but it had been such a good one I'd gotten my hopes up.

But I'd pored over the last spell Lydia Toothaker recorded in the book, a three-part coven binding spell. Only it wasn't her name attached to the third part. Because she hadn't been the third member, she'd just been the one to create the spell.

The family tree in the front of the book was even less helpful. It had her grandparents, parents, and her daughter, but that's where it ended.

Next to her name was her birth date and a death year; she had been twenty-one.

Her daughter was born the same year she died, but she had no death recorded. Had that been because her daughter had lived, and the book hadn't been passed to her to continue the tree on the front pages? Or had her daughter died not long after her mother, and no one thought to write it down?

I ran my hand over the page of the spell, as if touching it would give me the answers I needed. As if the rough, aged paper and rise of inked words held secret messages the eyes couldn't see.

We may have found the original spell—different in a few key places from the one Martin had—but, without the third bloodline, it wouldn't matter. It didn't matter how convinced I was that Thea was still the third bloodline if I didn't have proof. And trying the unbinding again without being *sure* wasn't something any of us would be open to.

We hit a wave that sent the ferry rocking slightly, and I watched the mainland get closer. What would happen if I just didn't get off? Got a return ticket and hid on the island with Meg? We could say I drowned or something. It wouldn't be the worst life; Meg seemed to enjoy herself.

And Lyra could have Lydia's book now that we found it. She'd like it. There were so many spells in the first part that Lydia had perfected. One to change the color of fabric instead of buying new, a spell to change the texture of hair, and one to clear acne—or "face spots" as she called them.

A shiver ran up my arms despite my thick coat. Late winter in Maine was always cold and wet—it's what made summers so attractive—but I never remembered being *this* cold.

"It's warmer inside," Jax said, sliding into the bench next to me.

"I know," I mumbled.

He passed me a steaming paper cup. Meg had sent us with a thermos of hot whiskey for the trip back. I took a tentative sip, letting the spice and honey coat my tongue and the relief of the heat spread to my toes.

Jax put an arm around my shoulders as I stared down at the diluted amber liquid in the cup. I took a deep breath of the chilled, salty air.

"Find anything else?" he asked, nodding to the book.

I shook my head. After I'd managed to process things, I'd woken him up to show him the spell and, to his credit, he'd listened to my less-than-coherent rambling with as much attention as he could muster after being violently shaken awake.

But once the full weight of what I was trying to get out hit him, he'd practically ripped it out of my hands to flip to the family tree page. I didn't get the chance to explain anything else before he rushed to grab his phone. Whatever call he needed to make at two o'clock in the morning was one he felt didn't need to be in front of me.

What she'd implied before I'd woken him up hadn't been easy to ignore; her odd comments about his father, all but accusing him of knowing where the book had been replayed in my mind and made it extremely hard to fall back asleep. But that didn't stop me from pretending when he finally came back into the room.

And her parting words at the ferry terminal only made things worse. Advice I wasn't sure what was brought on by and what do to with, but they were there like a song stuck in my head on repeat and nothing I thought of could clear it.

Few men can be trusted with your heart. And none with your power.

The knot in my stomach tightened. Our entire stay with Meg I knew Jax had been keeping something from me, but I hadn't thought it had been anything Meg would have had a clue about. But maybe that was just one more thing I was being left out of.

"Jax," I started, facing him. If I let the knot fester much longer it was bound to turn into an ulcer at some point.

He lowered his drink and raised his eyebrows at me.

"Why did Meg think your dad would know where the book was?"

His jaw tightened, and he pulled his arm from around me. "Because he works for the Council," he said unconvincingly.

"She didn't say the Council knew," I said. "She asked specifically about your dad."

He took a stalling drink, and his gaze focused on the water while I stared at his profile. "Lots of witches talk like they're the same thing," he explained.

My grip tightened on the cup in my hand. He was talking like the Emissary I'd first met, every word a carefully rehearsed company line.

"What aren't you telling me?" I asked softly.

He huffed a breath. "Nothing."

"Jax, I'm not stupid," I said. "You and Leander have been acting weird, and don't tell me all that stuff with Meg wasn't off." I picked at the lip of the paper cup and felt him tense next to me. He continued to refuse to look my way. "At first I thought it was because of whatever was going on with us," I continued. "But now..."

"Em," he warned.

"Was she right?" I pressed. "Did your dad know where this was?" I held up the book between us for emphasis.

He grabbed it and tossed it onto the bench on the other side of me. "It's not—" he started, rubbing his jaw. "He's not—he doesn't tell me everything," he finished.

My chest tightened at his answer. "So, he could have?"

"Em, please, I can't."

"Why not?"

He downed the rest of his hot whiskey in one go. "Because I *can't*."

My stomach lurched as a strong wind kicked up, tossing the waves in angry swells the closer we got to land.

"Trust me," I concluded, leaning back against the bench and sniffing against the cold.

"That's not it," he said.

"Then what?"

He crumbled the paper cup in his fist. "It's not *about* you!" His voice filled the upper deck, and I stared at him. He'd never raised his voice like that before, and I wasn't sure which hurt more—his words or his tone.

The whirring engine of the boat and a rush of wind filled the silence his outburst left. He was breathing heavily, both fists clenched. He stood without a word and strode back down to the inside of the ferry without looking back.

Chapter 20

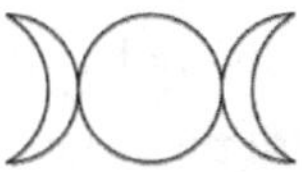

The house smelled like Chad's orange sweet rolls and lemon Lysol when we walked through the door. There were fresh vacuum lines in the den carpet and folded sheets on the air mattresses, and the windows were open to the backyard to let in fresh air. It was far less stuffy than when we'd left.

Jax went upstairs as soon as he could without even looking at me. We hadn't spoken since the ferry, not that I'd given it much effort. We'd been picked up after Blythe and Rez on the trip south; between Blythe's ranting about how useless Martin had been and her recounting the massive fight about Selvina telling the Council where'd we'd gone, I wouldn't have been able to get a word in anyway.

Sadiki was staying in New York a few extra days. Apparently, even asking for help from the Syndicate meant you owed them a favor, and they'd called his in immediately. He was vague even with Jax on the specifics of that favor.

Lyra, Thea, and Leander had already been picked up from their location and brought back to the house. They'd done what they needed to do and got out of there quickly. Lingering near a Collective prison wasn't the smartest of ideas.

I dropped my bag on the laundry room floor and unzipped it to dump the contents into the machine. I'd only brought two changes of clothes and only worn one, but separating it all felt like too much work, so it was all getting washed. I left everything at the bottom of the machine until we had a full load to run.

Lyra and Thea had gone out for groceries—apparently, their time in jail bonded them— and wouldn't be back for a bit, so there was no point in sharing what I'd found until then. That didn't mean the need didn't itch like a bad rash.

Chad had gone with them to stop at some specialty grocer to get the ingredients he needed for his big dinner plan that he didn't trust anyone else to get. We always joked that cooking was his own version of witchcraft.

When I came back into the kitchen, I saw Jax and Leander at the far end of the backyard, talking where no one could overhear them. I watched while answering Wes's questions about the island and Meg with one-word answers. His voice sounded further away than the kitchen table.

I clutched the mug of undrunk tea, forcing myself not to march out there and demand answers from them both. Meg *had* known something, and Jax admitted to keeping it from me. But he'd said—rudely—that it wasn't about me. There was only one other person they'd lie for.

Wes suggested I take a nap. Despite not getting much sleep at Meg's after she'd given me the book, I didn't think my mind would turn off enough to get any kind of rest, so instead I went upstairs and took an extra hot shower.

I replayed the trip in my mind as I stood under the stream of water. Every word, every little movement of Jax's, for some hint at what he and his brother were so on edge about. Finding Lydia's book was supposed to have been the balm to our problems, not bring new ones.

Wrapping a towel around myself, I stood in front of the steamed-up mirror and stared at my hazy reflection. Meg had said I looked older. Maybe she was right. Months of stress could probably age you.

With a sigh, I wiped some of the condensation away from the mirror and went through the steps I would have if this were any normal day. Cleansed my face, moisturized, sunscreen, all of it. I even blow-dried my hair for the first time in what felt like forever. It wasn't much, but it lent a little bit of normalcy to my mind.

I pulled on knit pants and a long-cropped sweater instead of ratty sweats and a T-shirt with holes in it. When I finished, the mirror was clear and I double checked my reflection. I was crumbling around the edges, ready to break, but at least I didn't *look* like it.

Everyone had returned by the time I came back downstairs, and Lyra was digging into one of Chad's sweet rolls while Rez helped Wes put the groceries away.

"You look fancy," Lyra teased around a mouthful of roll. "Gotta hot date or something?"

I slid into a seat across the table from her and gave her a weak smile. "Or something," I muttered.

She frowned. "I thought you said you found it?"

I'd texted her and Blythe that I'd found the book, but that was all. The rest needed to be something we discussed in person. Mostly because I hadn't been able to find the right words then.

"We did," I confirmed.

She licked frosting off her finger. "Then why aren't you happy?" she asked.

Blythe took a seat next to her with a fresh cup of coffee. "Yeah, I thought I was the pessimist?"

I sighed and glanced at the back door. I hadn't seen Leander or Jax upstairs, so I had to assume they were still out back. "It's not exactly what we needed," I said, standing to grab Lydia's book off the coffee table where I'd left it. "Slight issue." I opened it to that final spell and slid it over to them.

Lyra wiped her hands on her leggings before pulling the book closer at the same time Blythe leaned over to read it.

"It's the binding," Lyra said. "I don't see what the problem...oh."

"Oh," I agreed.

"Fuck," Blythe muttered.

Lyra flipped back to the front of the book and read. "Cool spells, though."

"So, what happens if we try to undo this and I'm wrong about Thea?" I asked.

Lyra shrugged.

"It won't work," Blythe said. "And'll probably hurt."

I glanced around the room. "Where is Thea?"

"Outside with Jax," Lyra said absently as she continued to scan the pages of Lydia's book.

A twinge of jealousy burrowed into my gut. Was he going to tell *her*? Did she already know? They had known each other a lot longer than we had; maybe he didn't feel like he needed to keep things from her.

"*Circe*, she was talented," Lyra breathed. "She mixed...I wouldn't have even thought to..."

Blythe cleared her throat. "The unbinding?" she prompted.

Lyra looked up at us like she'd forgotten there was anyone else in the room. "Sorry," she mumbled and flipped to the back of the book. "Yeah, looks like the ingredients are pretty similar to the ones we got at Martin's. Possibly a few mistranslations." She bit her lower lip in concentration and turned the book sideways to read the scribbles in the margins.

"Can we trust you're not going to try it with tea bags this time?" Rez asked, leaning against the counter with a mug of coffee.

Lyra flipped him off.

"If you hadn't assigned us a babysitter, we could have gotten what we needed," Blythe reminded him.

"Because that would have gone over well with Martin," he teased, giving her a wink.

Wes aimed an exasperated sigh at me. "Do I want to know?" he asked.

I grimaced. "Probably not," I admitted. If Wes knew we'd tried a spell without making sure the ingredients were correct, I'd never hear the end of it. He'd taught me better.

He shook his head and pursed his lips, but I knew he wasn't actually mad. Letting Lyra try to unbind us with poorly separated tea bag herbs was maybe the least dangerous thing we'd done lately.

"No tea bags," Lyra agreed. "I can't wait to dip my hands into this."

"That's not going to happen."

We looked around. Leander stood at the sliding door, arms crossed and face set. Jax and Thea slid in behind him.

Rez lowered his coffee before he could take a sip and frowned at Leander.

Blythe's eyes darted between the three of them, mouth slightly parted.

Lyra raised her eyebrows. "That was kind of the point of the field trips," she said.

"Something we indulged, but no more."

"Now you sound like dad," she accused.

Leander took a few steps forward and reached for the book.

Lyra snatched it up before he could touch it. "Okay, what gives, grabby?" she snapped. "You *want* the three of them to be bound?" Her eyes narrowed on her brothers, and I stared at Jax, despite him avoiding my eye contact.

Rez's gaze had gone dark as he stared at the two brothers, the question seeming to have struck something inside of him.

"It's not that," Jax said quickly.

Thea ducked around Leander and moved to the kitchen, where she busied herself with making a cup of coffee while Wes stood, staring at the group of us like a concerned parent.

"Then what is it?" I asked.

Leander looked at me briefly and sighed. "We don't want you bound, but Lyra can't be the one to undo it."

"Why not?" Lyra asked slowly, looking between her brothers.

"Because you can't," Leander chided.

She laughed. "Yeah, no, that's not a reason."

Jax glanced at Leander, who gave him a small shake of the head. Some signal indicating that they weren't going to—or weren't supposed—explain. But that wasn't going to happen, not now, not when we were so close.

"Either someone explain why Lyra can't do the spell or get out," I snapped.

Everyone's eyes fell on me. I wasn't *really* going to kick anyone out, but it was nice that my voice was firm enough that it was believable.

"Lydia's daughter—" Jax started.

"Jax," Leander warned.

"Lydia's daughter," Jax repeated, shooting his brother a glare, "was adopted by her brother. Her line continued."

Lyra's brows knit together. "So, she *was* the third member?" she asked, gaze flicking to Thea. "Then who the fuck is Sybil?" she asked, holding the book open in front of her and tapping the part of the spell with the label.

Sybil had been the name attached to the third part of the binding in Lydia's book. Each part was for a specific witch: Amity, Patience, and Sybil. Yet another new name we didn't know anything about.

Jax shook his head. "She wasn't a member of the coven," he corrected. "She wrote and performed spells for them."

"No shit," Lyra muttered. "What does any of this have to do with *me*?"

Leander took a breath. "You," he said, as though that single word pained him, "are the last witch of the Toothaker line." He crossed his arms. "A line cursed to die before they turn twenty-two."

The tick of the wrong clock, the slosh of the washing machine, the drip of the coffee maker. It all seemed too loud, too slow to be real. I was hyper-aware of my own breathing and the peaks and valleys in the woodgrains of the table under my fingers.

Then a thousand questions burst into my mind, all vying to be asked first. They churned and writhed, and I couldn't discern one from the other. In a moment, the questions subsided, and one thought broke through: Meg knew. *That's* what she'd implied when she thought their dad would already know where the book was, why she told me to ask Jax, the pointed stares. Everything. I didn't know how she knew, but she knew.

I flinched at the sudden pressure around my shin and glanced down to see Grace slinking between the chair legs to rub against my leg. I hadn't seen her since the island and frowned down at her.

Rhi had appeared next to Blythe, the top of her head rubbing against Blythe's elbow.

Attie stood between Lyra and her brothers, her back legs slightly bent as if preparing to pounce given any provocation.

"Mom's still alive." Lyra's voice was too loud against the unnatural quiet that had settled in the room. "And definitely *not* twenty-one."

Jax looked down at his feet.

Rez's expression had softened from dangerous warning to genuine confusion and hurt as he watched Leander straighten his back.

"Your mother died when you were two." Leander's tone was softer than his stance would have given away. He wasn't trying to be hurtful, but I couldn't see how it wouldn't be.

Laughter bubbled from Lyra's throat, and she clapped a hand over her mouth to stop it from spilling over as we all looked at her. She shook her head, still covering her mouth. "So," she began, still trying to contain her laughter. "You're saying I'm *actually* adopted?" She didn't try to stop it anymore and let the laughter out. I couldn't help the smile that curved on my own lips as I watched her wipe a tear from her eye from laughing so hard.

Blythe pressed her fist into her mouth, but her shaking shoulders gave her away.

"This isn't funny," Leander scolded.

"Were you ever going to tell me?" she asked, laughter fading into a hard accusation.

"Dad—"

"*Your* dad," she corrected bitterly.

Jax swallowed. "He didn't want you to know," he explained. "Wanted to avoid it hanging over your head."

She rolled her eyes. "What about Gram?"

Leander sank into the chair in front of him as if she'd taken all the fight from him with that one question. "She is *our* grandmother."

Lyra nodded slowly. Attie hissed a warning when Leander slid his hand towards Lyra as if to comfort her. Lyra yanked her hand away and pressed her palms over the book.

"My mother?" The determination on her face was as sharp as I'd ever seen it, but her voice wavered slightly. I wasn't even sure everyone caught it. But Blythe's slightly downturned mouth told me at least she had.

"Our Aunt Estrella," Jax answered, sticking his hands in his pockets.

My stomach turned to ice. Thea had pointed out that there had to have been a fourth person to take that picture of our mothers. Had it been Lyra's? Had they all been in on the attempt to stop the cycle we'd been born into? I watched Lyra's face as she processed in real time.

Lyra closed the book and tucked it under her arm as she stood. "Right." She glanced around the table. "Anyone else have a deep, dark secret they'd like to share?" Neither Leander nor Jax would meet her stare. Rez was still watching Leander like he'd never seen him before. Thea had been stirring her coffee for way longer than necessary, and Wes caught my eye for a moment.

"No?" Lyra confirmed. "Good, because I have work to do."

"Lyra," Leander started. "You need to—"

"Do me a favor, *bro*," she snapped. "Don't ever fucking talk to me again."

She stormed to the den, Attie at her heels, and slammed the door hard enough to get her point across. No one was going to follow her, not yet anyway. Tears brimmed in Blythe's eyes as she fidgeted with the hem of her sweater sleeve.

Rez lifted his mug to take a sip, but his hands were shaking, and I wasn't sure if it was out of fear or anger. I suspected both. Because that's what was swirling in my own mind. Fear for Lyra and anger that she'd been lied to—that we'd all been lied to.

Maybe we *were* the death coven.

Chapter 21

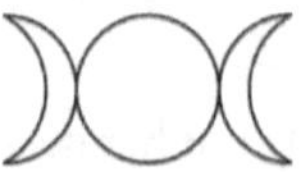

Low voices pulled me from sleep. I blinked against the sun, surprised it was already up. It felt like I'd only crawled into bed an hour ago, if that. I buried my face in my pillow and breathed into it, letting the warmth of my own exhalations heat my face for a few moments before rolling over.

Lyra and Blythe were sitting on the floor, their mattresses rolled up and pushed to the side to make more room for their massive amounts of notes. Four books were in front of them, all open on the same spell: Amity, Patience, Lydia, and Sybil's. The visit to Stromford had been a worthwhile trip after all.

The items the Council confiscated from Thea's dad had included a book from her ancestor—Sybil Graeves. The family tree in the front had a line from her to Thea's mom, Marnie, and finally Thea. And, just like the other three, it included the binding spell.

In the aftermath of Leander and Jax's revelation, Lyra wasn't willing to let her keep that book to herself. She'd practically ripped the book away from Thea after an unconvincing protest. I could understand why she'd want to keep herself out of whatever we were, but even she couldn't stay in denial. We were connected, whether we wanted to be or not.

Only, translating and making the modifications Lyra thought we needed had taken longer than we'd thought, and we were running out of legal pads.

Lyra ripped off the top piece of paper and crumpled it up before tossing it to the side. She clicked the pen in her hand a few times, staring down at one of the books. One leg was folded under her while the other stuck straight out in a stretch, and she bent at the waist to get a better look at the weathered pages. Her hair was in a knotted mess that might have been a bun hours ago.

Blythe was on her back, knees pulled up to her chest, a legal pad covering her face. Had it not been for the occasional grunt of frustration, I would have assumed she was asleep. Her hair fanned out around her head in short waves that hinted at it having been braided at some point.

The carafe from the coffee maker sat between them, nothing but dregs left in the bottom, surrounded by ripped and crumpled paper.

"We have recycling," I croaked.

Lyra used the pen to point to the bin by the door. The small blue container already was overflowing with bunched up paper. We were definitely out of legal pads.

I sat up and ran a hand through my hair. I'd gone to bed with it still damp and was now paying the price. Cringing as my fingers hit a particularly bad knot, I worked my way through it. "How long have you two been up?" I asked.

"Hours," Blythe muttered without moving the pad from her face.

I tied my hair up, still partially tangled but, I'd deal with that later. "Have you eaten?"

They both stayed silent, and I took that as a no. Sighing, I pulled my sweatshirt on and crawled off the air mattress much easier than I had before. Like the others it was new since the trip to Meg's and hadn't partially deflated overnight.

I grabbed the empty carafe. "Time to take a break and put something other than battery acid in your stomachs."

Lyra shook her head. "I'm so close. If I take a break now—"

"You won't collapse from exhaustion," I finished, stepping around her crumpled notes on my way to the door. "But it'll take me twenty minutes to get food going."

She nodded but didn't look my way. I nudged Blythe with my foot, and she pulled the pad away from her eyes to glare at me. I gave the glare right back, nodding my head towards Lyra.

Blythe sighed and nodded. That was all the agreement I was going to get. I may not have been helpful with getting this spell to usable shape, but if they thought I wasn't going to make sure they took care of themselves, then they clearly didn't know me.

After a quick stop in the bathroom, I headed for the kitchen, where I found Rez already up, dressed, and mixing pancake batter.

"I wondered where that had gotten off to," he said, nodding to the carafe in my hands.

I wiped out the silt stuck to the bottom before rinsing it clean and refilling the maker. "I think they've been up all night," I said, dumping out the filter with its damp grounds before replacing it with a new one.

He let out a long sigh. "They can't keep this up."

I scooped fresh coffee grounds into the filter and closed the lid. "Try telling them that." I stared out the window above the sink and saw the neighbor on her back porch. Large coat over pajamas, coffee in hand, dog sniffing around the yard. The sun's rays bounced off the frozen lake, making the world seem brighter than it was.

I stifled a yawn.

"How is she?" he asked.

Sighing, I hung my head with a slight shake. "How do you think?" I replied, looking over at him.

For five days, Lyra had managed her silent treatment with her brothers—cousins, rather. She'd maintained it with the rest of us for almost two before Blythe got her going on a rant.

We'd all tried to keep out of her way, let her process the way she needed to. But now, that processing was bordering on obsession, and if she didn't let up soon and get some rest, someone was going to have to step in.

"Did you know?" I asked, turning around and leaning on the counter.

He set the mixing bowl down. "Why would I have?"

I watched him turn on the griddle, searching for the lie in his response, this homey version of him a far cry from the club owner I'd first met. "You and Leander were...close."

He propped his hands on the counter and let his head hang. After letting out a long sigh, he turned to me. "Leander and I were—*are*," he ran a hand through his unstyled hair, pushing the black waves away from his face before concluding, "complicated."

He'd feigned indifference before, usually around Martin. When Blythe was threatened, that facade would slip ever so slightly, hardly noticeable if you weren't looking close enough. But now it was like that one word he'd chosen to use gutted him.

I swallowed. "I get *complicated*," I started.

"No offense," he said, stormy eyes fixing me with a hard stare, "but the little dance you and Jax have going is hardly difficult to decipher."

"I didn't mean it like that," I mumbled. "I just meant...I'm surprised Leander didn't tell you."

"Does he strike you as the type to toss family loyalty out the window and divulge their biggest secret because we were, *close*?"

I bit the inside of my lip. "No."

"We don't always tell the people we love everything," he said. "And maybe that's the problem," he added, more to himself than me. He stared at the floor for another moment before shaking himself out of whatever thought had kept him still and turned back to the bowl of pancake batter.

I watched him stir it again, despite it not needing anymore. I really couldn't argue with him; we didn't tell people everything. He hadn't told Leander about Blythe. Jax had kept the secret about Lyra from me. And I was keeping Thea's secret from him. That cycle which crumbled more from the edges of the chasm, reared its head yet again. *Complicated.* A word slowly losing all meaning.

Leander wouldn't have betrayed his family secret, that was true. But Jax wasn't like his brother. He'd already shown he was willing to skirt the edges of the rules when he stayed with me in Portland. It was selfish to think I was different and deserved different. But I found myself wanting to be selfish these days and had no explanation as to why.

If I made it out of this alive, I was going to have to seriously considering going back to therapy.

Rez sprayed cooking oil on the griddle, and I clicked the electric kettle on. The hiss of the batter on the hot surface and the roil of heating water filled the kitchen. Instead of standing in silence, I grabbed a skillet out of the cupboard and found the bacon and eggs in the fridge.

Rez and I cooked side by side as if this were a completely normal thing. I wondered if he felt what I did, having found out Leander had kept such a big secret from him. Was he hurt, betrayed? Or did he feel relieved at not needing to feel guilty about keeping his own family secret from Leander?

The ginger tea helped settle my aching stomach, and soon the smell of cooking food coaxed the rest of the house awake.

Chad set the table, Rez put out the food, I opened the orange juice, and Wes poured coffee. Lyra, no doubt forced out by Blythe, had all the books and notes in her arms when she sat down; she stared at them, ignoring the rest of the table.

The little conversation we had was limited to the weather, Wes asking again how Meg was, and if we thought spring temperatures would be kind and come early this year. My uncles were trying to make things less tense, and I loved them for it. Awkward family meals weren't something we were used to.

Chad's contribution to keep the silence at bay was updating us on Mama Bell's trip to Florida and how his sister was doing. When that failed to keep up the conversation for more than a couple minutes, he brought up the Bruins's chances as playoffs were only a couple months away.

Rez did his best to try to help, by answering questions and offering his own opinions on topics where he could; in the end, it failed to do anything to ease the painful strain in the group that made the food hard to swallow.

We cleared the table, and I waved off Chad's attempts to do the dishes. Rez and I had cooked and house rules meant neither of us should be the ones to clean up, but I needed something to do with my hands and Chad, thankfully, obliged.

Lyra and Blythe returned to their notes once the table had been wiped down. At some point, the TV got turned on. Wes folded towels. Chad updated his blog. Thea curled up on the couch with a novel.

The dishwasher didn't take long to load, but I took my time scrubbing the pans, taking my frustration out on the gunk that clung to them. The fresh pine-and-lemon scented soap filled my nostrils and reminded me of summers long gone. Winter had lasted a decade in my mind already.

How had everything gone so horribly wrong so fast? My birthday felt so long ago, I found myself barely able to remember it. It was supposed to have been one of the best days of my life; instead, one decision, one change of plans, had set off a chain reaction that wrecked everything—and everyone—around me. And no matter how much I wanted to envision my life going back to normal, I couldn't avoid the gut-wrenching feeling that things were going to get a lot worse before it got better.

After rinsing off the skillet, I set it to the side to dry and peeled off the rubber gloves and draped them over the faucet head. On autopilot, I put half a pump of lotion from the nearly empty bottle we kept on the sill and rubbed it into my winter-dry hands, staring without seeing.

Lyra let out a frustrated growl that turned into a deep-throated almost-scream, and I turned to the table just as she chucked the pen across the room.

"I'm out of paper," she snapped, balling her fists around the one piece still left on the pad.

"I'll go get more," I volunteered, moving back to the den to run a brush through my hair and change into real clothes. I came back into the kitchen to see Lyra trying to scribble out ideas on a paper towel. Obsession may have been too gentle a word.

"Anyone need anything?" I asked the room at large. A few absent "*no's*" and head shakes were all I got. I pulled my coat off the hook at the door to the garage and, after putting it on, shoved my feet into my boots.

I went to grab the keys out of the dish, but Jax's hand covered mine. He wore his own coat and a tentative smile.

"Jax," I started.

"I just want to talk," he said quietly.

"We could have talked a week ago," I said. "At Meg's. Or *before* Meg's."

He frowned. "I couldn't explain then," he offered.

My gut twisted between wanting to continue to let him sit in his guilt and wanting answers.

"Fine," I said.

He smiled again and held up the keys. I took them and stuffed them in my pocket. My hand was on the doorknob, ready to turn when I stopped.

Turning on my heel, I headed back into the kitchen, brushing past his confused look. I snatched Lydia's book out from under Lyra's hand, holding it away from her as she lunged to take it back.

"Hey!"

"You'll get this back after you've gotten at least four hours of sleep," I said, tucking the book under my arm. "And nothing less."

Blythe folded an arm over Patience's book like she was worried I was going for it next. "It's going to take you that long to get paper?" she asked, her accusatory gaze flicking to Jax behind me.

"No, but that's hardly the point," I said.

She rolled her eyes. "I don't know who you think you—"

"Same rule applies to you," I directed, swiping Amity's book before either of them could react. "Four hours *minimum*."

Blythe pouted at me while Lyra glared daggers. I mustered the sternest look I could and turned my back on their silent protests. It may not have been the most impressive display, but the last thing we needed was *three* over-tired witches attempting an eleventh-hour spell.

Chapter 22

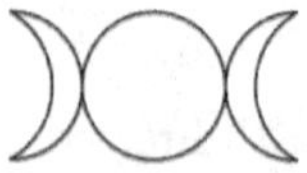

Saturday shoppers were out in full thanks to timing and the sun warming the day for the first time in weeks. I put the car in park and grabbed the reusable bags off the backseat before making my way to the entrance of the office supply store.

Jax jogged slightly to catch up and fell into step next to me, hands stuffed into his coat pockets. It had only been a little over a ten-minute drive, but despite his reason for coming, he hadn't even tried to talk. We just sat and listened to the dull hum of whatever podcast channel Chad had been listening to.

I grabbed a cart from the corral and wheeled it through the sliding doors which opened with the soft whoosh of rubber on floor. The subtle hints of paper, industrial cleaner, and new leather filled the air space, and I couldn't help but take a deep breath. It was the kind of smell that reminded me of back-to-school shopping and the childhood I'd had here.

It was enough that the twinge of loss pinched at my chest. Not as bad as it had been in the first year since mom died, but enough to cause tears to prick my eyes. I blinked them away and focused on what we were here to do.

My old therapist, Stanley, had always said grief never fully goes away after a loss. The pain lessens, giving way to memories that illicit happiness instead. And for the most part, he'd been right. Being in the house and going through mom's things had made me feel closer to her—despite finding out what she'd hidden from me. But I hadn't been prepared for a place as benign as *this* to trigger a grief for what never was.

Taking deep breaths, I pushed the cart into the first aisle we needed and grabbed a couple packs of legal pads, large and small. I could feel Jax staring at my back as he followed my course, but if he thought I was going to break first, he was wrong. I wanted answers, sure, but that didn't mean I couldn't be petty about getting them.

"You think Lyra's ever going to talk to us again?" he asked as we turned down the aisle filled with pens of all colors, inks, and models.

I sighed and grabbed a pack of cheap ones off the hanging display. We didn't need the fancy ones if Lyra was just going to run through them in a of couple hours.

"She's pissed," I said, tossing the pens into the cart on top of the legal pads.

He nodded slowly. "I know."

"You lied to her," I reminded him.

"I know," he repeated.

"You lied to me."

"I know."

I turned to face him, one hand squeezing the plastic guard on the cart handle so tight I could feel the embossed store logo pressing into my skin.

"Are you going to explain why, or did you just want to come to get away from her?"

He stuck his hands in his pockets. "I didn't *want* to keep it from her. Or you." One shoulder rose in a half-shrug. "My dad made us promise to not tell anyone, for her protection."

I turned back to the cart and pushed it to the next section. "You ever notice how that's always the reason we keep things from each other?" I asked. "Doesn't seem to work out well in the end, though." The last part I added to myself more than to him.

Because I really thought I'd done something that night in the club. It may have been a last-minute confession, but I'd thought maybe—just maybe—if I told him what we were planning instead of keeping it from him for his *protection,* then we could all move forward.

But it turned out he was keeping something even bigger from everyone the whole time.

"I want to explain to her," he continued, leveling with me as I examined the sticky note options. I would want the multicolored pack for labeling and sorting, but they were a little more expensive.

"So, why aren't you doing that now?" I tossed the multi pack into the cart.

"Hard to do when she won't even look at me," he offered, rubbing the few days of stubble that had collected on his jaw; the only indication that he, too, had been having a hard time dealing with this.

"Jax," I warned, sensing where this was going. "Don't put me in the middle." Getting me out of the house to explain his side so I could help him, and Leander convince Lyra of, well, anything wasn't going to end well.

"I'm not trying to," he said. "But she needs to listen to someone."

"You and Leander need to fix this. I can't." I held his gaze for a moment longer than I needed to. "Don't ask me to take sides."

His jaw tensed. "Because you'll take hers?"

"Yes."

He raised his eyebrows at my complete lack of hesitation. I'm sure he'd expected a different answer—or more likely, a non-answer. And a few months ago, that's exactly what would have happened. But I was over and done playing both sides. Over trying to see all the points. Lyra had been lied to about her own life, just like Blythe and I had—and even Thea, too. I was over it all.

"Why did your dad even want her to be an Emissary?" I asked before I could stop myself, pretending to look at the options for colored adhesive flags.

Mom had lied to me about the binding, about being the last Blood Witch, about Blythe. And I'd never get to know *why*. Her journals would only give me so much. Lyra, at least, had the chance to get some answers.

She may not be ready to ask the questions for herself, but I was.

He was quiet for long enough that I didn't think I was going to get a response. And in truth, he might not even have known why his father did what he did.

"I think he figured it would draw more attention if he *didn't* push her like he did with us."

I picked up some of the flags without really even seeing them. I didn't look at the size or the price, just tossed them in with everything else. "Even though she didn't want to?" I asked, facing him again.

A small smile touched his lips. "She always wanted to travel," he said. "Meet other witches with different abilities. I doubt she'd admit it, but being an Emissary was her ticket to do that."

I raised my eyebrows.

"But, no, she never really wanted to be an Emissary. At least, not in the way the Council uses them." He glanced at his feet. "Especially after Willowhill."

I picked up a pack of note cards. "Willowhill?" I asked, racking my mind for any mention of that from Lyra or anyone else.

He grimaced like he hadn't meant to say that—at least not to me. "Assignment before we met you, didn't go well," was all he offered.

I added the cards to the growing pile of unnecessary office supplies in the cart. None of the siblings had talked much about their assignments before the one that merged our lives. I had a blurry memory of Lyra mentioning Roanoke, but that had been an example of a *less* exciting one.

I wanted to press, wanted to know what about that assignment had put Lyra more at odds with her family's expectations, but the look on his face made me waver in asking for more.

I tapped my fingers on the plastic cart handle. "How long have you known?" I asked, choosing not to ask him anymore about it quite yet.

He frowned.

"That she wasn't your sister?"

He flinched slightly. "Dad told me when I was ten," he said. "Leander knew first."

Pushing the cart around him, I moved to the snack aisle, more for something to do other than standing and staring at him. "Is that why he doesn't like me?" I asked. "Too much risk?"

Jax huffed out half a laugh. "He likes you just fine."

I snorted.

"He does," he insisted. "But, yeah. You were supposed to be an easy assignment." He rubbed the back of his neck, but I didn't miss the slight blush creeping into his complexion. "You not following the rules gave Lyra an excuse not to. Then, when it was clear you weren't going to come without a fight, things took a turn."

"He thinks our friendship is going to get her killed."

He nodded.

I'd assumed Leander's *irritation* when Lyra and I got closer was simply because I wasn't willing to follow their rules and protocols, that it was directed at me and only me. But now, I saw things a tad differently. I'd put myself in danger and Lyra followed, even offering some dangerous ideas of her own.

I'd never asked her to do any of that. She'd come up with it all on her own, and no one—Leander included—could have argued that Lyra would do anything she didn't want to. In his eyes, though, I was the excuse she needed.

I stopped the cart in the middle of the aisle as the days since we first met ran through my mind in a new light. Turning back to face him, I checked to make sure there weren't other people too close. "That's why you stayed," I said, the realization dawning on me. "And didn't get in trouble."

He frowned.

"After Armin showed up in Portland," I reminded him. "You didn't go back with Leander, and I thought you were going to get kicked out or something," I continued, my mind replaying that day and the weeks after. "But you didn't because you stayed to make sure Lyra was okay."

He shifted on his feet, hands in his pockets. "That was part of it, yeah."

"And Salem." I faced the shopping cart again, and began pushing it mindlessly down the aisle, not even registering fully what part of the store we were in. "You came after Lyra, not me."

"Dad wanted her back safe," Jax said, voice close enough behind that I knew he'd followed me.

"Leander didn't want to come?" I asked bitterly.

Jax moved in front of me, stopping my aimless wander. "Em," he said softly. "It wasn't like that." He shot a glance to either side of him now that we were clear of the aisle. Checking, like I had, that no one was eavesdropping on us. "It's just that he and Rez have a...complicated history." There was that word again. "Dad didn't want that getting in the way."

"Seems like your father has this all figured out," I muttered, but the anger that was there when we first started talking about all of this wasn't there anymore. Because now that I knew, I couldn't hold onto the anger that I'd had since hearing Kane tell me that Ian's memory was gone. I'd blamed Jax for not protecting him, for not going to him instead of me. But how could I possibly be upset that he'd chosen his family over mine? Lies aside, Lyra was his family, and if they all believed she had the proverbial axe hanging over her head, how could I honestly ask them to risk her life over Ian's memory? He might not remember me, but at least he was alive.

"He thinks so," Jax said, stepping to the side so that we could continue down another aisle—why, though, I wasn't sure. It wasn't like I was shopping anymore.

"Selene let her go with me," I reminded him.

He pursed his lips. "Gram never quite agreed with how dad handled Lyra," he said. "Wanted her to experience life, regardless of the risk."

"Then why not tell Lyra herself?"

Jax sighed. "Aunt Estrella left a Will," he explained. "Lyra was to be dad's responsibility, and I don't think even Gram wanted to challenge her daughter's last wishes."

A new anger that wasn't only for Lyra bubbled in my chest. "Did that Will include lying to her?" I snapped before I could stop myself. I knew the bitterness that lashed out at him wasn't fair. I was dealing with my own family secrets, and I didn't need to take it out on him.

Jax had the decency to look embarrassed.

"Because if it did," I continued, trying to keep the acid from my tone, "Lyra deserves to know *that*."

She deserved to know all of this, but we both knew she wasn't ready to hear it. Not until her father—uncle—was there to tell her everything Leander and Jax couldn't. She was angry and had every right to remain in that anger as long as she needed to.

He started to shake his head but stopped himself. We both suspected the answer. That his father had been the sole decider in how to deal with the responsibility his sister had left to him. He'd been the one to keep Lyra in the dark about everything and made his sons complicit in the lie.

I'd never met their father, and I wasn't sure I ever wanted to. He, like the Council, seemed to *demand* control and order. Two things I, clearly, was not. All three of his children forsaking the Council's orders in favor of a rogue witch wasn't something I could imagine he was handling well.

"So, your family knew Lydia wasn't the third member of the coven?" I concluded.

He shrugged. "I guess."

I shook my head. "That's why Meg thought your father knew where the book was," I continued. "But..."

His eyebrows pinched together. "How did *she* know?"

An errant shiver ran down my spine, and I couldn't help the slight reaction. Something told me that Meg might know a lot more than she was letting on, and we'd asked her all the wrong questions.

My phone buzzed in my pocket, and I pulled it out, expecting a request for something from the store or a stop for something other than black coffee for once.

I groaned as I read and sent a quick reply.

"What's wrong?" Jax asked, and I pushed past him, quickly turning the cart.

"We need to get back," I said. "Before Lyra kills your brother."

Chapter 23

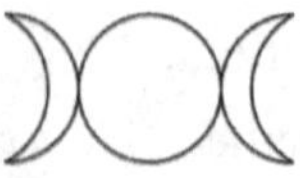

For the second time since getting to Sandusky, I found myself walking into a fight between Lyra and Leander. Their raised voices met us as we walked through the door from the garage. I kicked off my shoes and tossed the keys into the bowl as Jax hurried ahead of me to find out exactly what they were yelling about now.

After hanging up my coat, I carried the bag of office supplies into the kitchen, wondering which one of our mugs was going to be claimed as a casualty. I set the bag on the counter and took in the sides of the argument—literally. Which, also, meant my instructions for Lyra and Blythe to get some sleep had gone ignored.

The two books I hadn't taken were open among the spread out, used legal pads, and behind them stood Lyra, Blythe, and Thea. On the other side of the table, Leander and Rez stood, both wearing the same expression of someone who'd just been slapped. I didn't need to know what had started the whole argument; the visual alone was enough to know this wasn't going to be good.

"I still don't understand why you think you get a say in this," Lyra argued, arms crossed. Even with sleep-deprivation evident under her eyes and hair that looked like it hadn't seen a brush in days, she was still intimidating enough.

"It's too risky," Leander stated. "It's not a spell that's used."

"Because no one knew about it!"

"What's too risky?" Jax asked on top of my question, "What spell?"

Lyra and Leander didn't stop glaring at each other, but everyone else turned to at least acknowledge our presence.

Rez answered first. "It seems your sister wants to try a spell that," he paused, glancing at Leander's profile, "no one knows whether it or not it has successfully been cast before." His hands were in his pockets, his body relaxed like this was a simple business meeting, but his drawn brows and set jaw betrayed his concern.

"*Cousin,*" Lyra corrected sharply. Her glare found Rez. "Every spell doesn't work until someone tries it."

"And how often do those go wrong?" Leander snapped. "You're *not* doing this."

Lyra let out a harsh laugh. "Not up to you."

"Okay, can we back up here?" Jax asked, noticeably taking a few steps towards Leander and Rez's side of the table. "What spell are we even talking about?"

I moved to the books on the table. Patience's and one I didn't recognize but assumed had to be Sybil's. Notes on the nearest pad told me Lyra had found another legal pad somewhere; her hurried notes were hard to discern, but four words at the top were clear and dark from repeated tracing: *How did it happen?*

"How did what happen?" I asked, looking up at Blythe.

Lyra uncrossed her arms and slid Sybil's nook over to me. "The binding."

I frowned. "Don't we know that?"

She shook her head. "No. We can guess based on the spell itself, but I want to *know.*"

"I'm confused," Jax admitted.

Rez pinched the bridge of his nose. "They want to cast a spell to see what happened in the past."

I felt my jaw drop. "Time travel is—"

"Impossible, we know," Blythe interjected. "But we think we can combine a few spells to get us what we need."

"What kind of combination would get you that?" Jax asked, earning a glare from both Leander and Rez.

Lyra and Blythe both looked at Thea. She sighed but pointed to the book Blythe had put in front of me. "There's a spell to connect with the dead in Sybil's book," she replied.

"Mix it with the blood-to-blood Seer spell in Patience's and we have a new spell that we think will work."

"*Think* being the keyword there," Leander said. "A spell like this has never been attempted."

"Without a Death Witch involved, it's even more likely to go wrong," Rez added.

Thea's throat bobbed with a swallow, and she closed her eyes for a brief moment as if steeling herself. "*I* am a Death Witch," she admitted. The creak of the house settling with the with the new warmth of the day, filled the room. I'd never seen Rez fully surprised; he'd always hidden it well, but Thea's revelation put true shock on his face.

Jax looked between her and me, hurt lacing into his frown. He seemed to quickly process the fact that they were the only three who were surprised. I felt his hard stare but refused to look at him.

He no doubt saw me as a hypocrite. I'd just given him a hard time about lying to Lyra and me, but now he knew I'd been keeping something from him. Outing Thea and her magic was not the same, though, and there was no way of convincing myself that I would have been doing it for the right reasons if I had told him.

Leander's mouth wordlessly opened and closed as if he could inhale the truth out of the air. "You're—you—a *Death* Witch?" he sputtered. "Since when?"

"Birth, moron," Lyra countered. "The point is, we have what we need. A Death Witch and the blood connection of everyone that was there."

"Blood magic and death magic," I muttered quietly, scanning the page in Sybil's book. Blood magic, as misperceived as it was, took the essence of life and manipulated it; either from the witch doing the casting or the witch—or mortal, apparently—being casted upon. Blood was life; for the witch their magic was in their blood, making it even more a part of that life. A Blood Witch could hold control over life which was, in part, why we were feared.

Death Witches dealt in the opposite. They could cross a boundary no other witch could. Death magic was essentially the balance to blood magic. There were very few records—ones that could be trusted—where a Blood Witch and a Death Witch interacted magically. I didn't know of a time, *ever*, where they combined their magics.

"I have to reiterate my agreement with Leander," Rez pressed. "It's too dangerous. There's a reason these types of magics aren't mixed."

"According to who?" Blythe asked. "The Collective? Martin? Everyone who's been lying and keeping us separated and bound for *generations*?"

He crossed his arms. "History speaks for—"

"*Their* history," I corrected. "It said Amity died childless. Completely left out Patience and Sybil's involvement." I slid the book back to Blythe. "Our own families kept it from us," I continued, waving a hand at the three other witches in this mess with me. "So maybe we shouldn't trust everything *history* has to say."

Jax sighed. "I get that," he said slowly. "But this—"

"I'm in," I cut him off, ignoring whatever he was going to try to argue, because it all came down to Lyra being right. This wasn't their decision. It was ours.

"Great," Lyra said. "Four against three. We win."

"But—"

"It's not up for a vote," I said. "If Thea and Blythe are willing to try, then so am I."

Thea and Blythe both gave firm nods.

Rez shook his head. "Recklessness disguised as independence doesn't help anyone."

"Oh, shut up," Blythe snapped. "You of all people don't get to lecture us on recklessness."

His jaw clenched in a bout of anger I hadn't seen before. "Recklessness got my friend killed."

My stomach seized, and my throat seemed to close against my attempt to take a breath. The sensation of Vadim's blood on my skin prickled in my memory, my vision tinged a slight red as my magic stirred.

I grabbed the back of the chair in front of me to steady myself and swallowed past the imagined block in my throat. "And if we don't try *something*, Blythe will be next." I gritted my teeth, fixing him with a stare.

He held my gaze, the stormy gray of his eyes holding me in place. Vadim's death, Phoenix's, even Raven's would all haunt me for the rest of my life. But this was a necessary risk. As if he could read the thoughts behind my eyes, he gave me a stiff nod but said nothing.

"You'll get yourself killed," Leander warned, the words sounding more like a plea than anything else.

Lyra crooked an eyebrow. "I'm not twenty-one for another two weeks, so apparently I'll be *fine*."

I let out a breath somewhere between a sigh and a laugh.

Blythe's mouth parted as she stared at Lyra.

Thea shook her head.

"That's not funny," Jax said.

Lyra re-crossed her arms. "It's really not, is it?"

"Please," Leander started. "Think this through."

"I think you lost this one, boys," Wes said. We all turned to him. I hadn't realized he'd been standing in the hall, listening this entire time.

"You're okay with this?" Jax accused, waving his hand at the four of us.

Wes shook his head, and my heart sank. "No," he admitted, moving further into the kitchen. "But that's neither here nor there." He rested both hands on the top of his cane. "It's their lives, their magic, and their binding. That makes it their choice and theirs alone."

The whole time I'd lived with him, he'd done everything he could to protect me. The rules, the wards, keeping me hidden when my magic would be the strongest—but he never took away my choice, not really.

"Wes," I started, feeling a need to explain why I had to take *this* risk despite everything he'd done for me.

He held up a hand to stop me. "I did what your mother asked," he said. "I kept you safe as best I could. But I think we both know now she had her own secrets." He sighed. "Why she didn't share them with me, I'll never know, but you have more than earned the right to decide how you want to learn about them yourself."

My eyes welled with tears, but I managed to keep them from falling as I moved to hug him. "Thank you," I whispered as he wrapped an arm around me and squeezed. "For everything."

He nodded and let me go, and I saw tears glistening in his own eyes. "Doesn't mean I'm about to let you do this with *tea bags*." He shot a pointed look at Lyra over my shoulder. "What do you need from me?"

"Ha!" Lyra declared as I turned back to face the group. She aimed a triumphant eyebrow raise at her bro—cousins. Leander threw up his arms and stomped off. Rez stood with his arms crossed; he may have accepted defeat, but it looked like that didn't necessarily mean he was willing to help. Jax frowned at me for a moment longer before brushing past me and heading upstairs.

I stared after him, waiting for that inevitable push of guilt that would urge me to follow him and and force him to understand why we needed to do this. But it never came.

If the neighbors thought it odd the four of us were outside standing in a circle with candles, they kept it to themselves. I couldn't imagine what it may have looked like to them if they were watching from their windows. Or, maybe it looked exactly like what it was: witchcraft.

The last time Lyra, Blythe, and I tried something like this, we'd been hiding on rocks along the ocean. The backyard was far more exposed, but it was the only place big enough to accommodate what we were attempting.

Huron Lighthouse's beacon swept the icy surface of the lake in timed intervals. Above us, the silver light of the full moon covered our little circle. Despite my magic being more dormant than I was used to, I thought I felt it stirring under the light.

We'd spent the rest of the day re-working the two spells into one and, with Wes's help on herbs and Chad making sure we stayed well-nourished, it was as productive a day as it could have been, even with the others refusing to help. Once we had it as perfected as it could be, Lyra even agreed to take a nap.

When the moon rose, it was time, and we positioned ourselves. Four witches, four directions for the added boost of magic. I was at the southern point, red candle lit and dripping wax onto my hand. Across from me Thea was at the northern point with a black candle, Blythe to my right with blue, and Lyra to my left with white. Despite the climate control spell, a shiver ran up my arms, gooseflesh rising underneath my sweater.

It was like a subconscious part of me knew the power our circle held, even if I wasn't fully aware of it. I took a few steadying breaths; the flame in front of me flickered slightly with each exhale.

Despite their reluctance to help, Jax, Leander, and Rez had come to the backyard to watch. I wasn't sure if it was to ensure we didn't die in the attempt or to sabotage us, but either way, they kept a healthy distance. Wes and Chad watched from the porch, their unwavering support fortifying my decision.

"Ready?" Lyra asked, voice quieter than I expected.

Nods all around.

She nodded back, looking at me. "Remember, focus on the binding and *only* the binding."

I swallowed a deep breath and pricked my finger to draw blood. Holding the candle out in front of me, I pinched my finger with my thumb and held it over the flame, letting a drop fall onto it, thinking about the binding and everything it had taken from us.

My magic stirred. "Blood calls to blood through time," I began. "Daughter calls to daughter. Show me mine." The flame turned blood red, and the flicker of heat warmed my fingers. The backyard grew a little hazy. I swayed, but something strong—hands, maybe—held me up.

"Death calls to death through time," I heard Thea recite. "Daughter calls to daughter. Show me mine." Through the blurriness, I saw a flicker of purple flame across from me. A fog settled in my mind, slowing my thoughts and making my toes go numb.

"Blood calls to blood through time," Blythe said, sounding further away than I remembered her being. "Daughter calls to daughter. Show me mine." Her candle burned a bright red, and the yard vanished in a swirl of black mist.

Something pulled taut at my midsection, and I was tugged backward. My stomach dropped as if hitting that first plummet of a roller coaster, and I squeezed my eyes shut, bracing for the inevitable hard landing.

Chapter 24

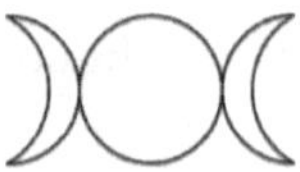

I expected death to feel different. Was I dead? I wasn't sure *what* I was, but it didn't seem like dead. Slowly opening my eyes, I blinked up at a deep indigo sky with impossibly bright stars staring down at me. I couldn't remember if I'd ever seen so many. Branches from trees framed the view but didn't detract from it..

Carefully, I sat up, relieved to not feel anything broken. Squinting around the darkness, I tried to make out something that would tell me where I was. I could make out trees—a lot of them—but that was it. It was warm enough that I knew I probably wasn't in Ohio anymore, at least not in the winter. But no, the sky was too clear for it to be anywhere near a city.

Brushing leaves from my sweater as I rolled to my feet, I waited for my eyes to finish adjusting to this level of darkness. A full moon hung in the sky, making that adjustment easier, but I was used to more light pollution than wherever this place was.

It didn't take me long to realize, however, that I was completely alone. We'd all done the spell, yet three distinct people were missing. Had we messed it up? Instead of showing us the binding night, had I spiraled to the night of Amity's birth—or sometime equally unhelpful?

Rustling came from the brush behind me, and I turned to face whatever was coming. We were supposed to be in a memory—or something like it—so I wasn't sure if I was going to need to fight, or if I even could.

My heart pounded and my mind reeled. We'd jumped into this too quickly. The guys were right, and we'd accidentally landed in the Otherworld or something. I really didn't want to have to face Leander and his smug "I told you so." Then again, if this *was* the Otherworld, we'd never see him again, so that was a nice silver lining.

Blythe struggled free of the plant life and froze when she spotted me, letting out a sigh of relief. "Thank *the Morrigan*, I thought we fucked this up," she said.

"Shhh," I hissed, glancing around as she moved to stand next to me.

"Why?" she whispered back.

"Because..." I muttered, rubbing my arms as the prick of unseen eyes skittered across my skin. An unnaturally warm breeze swept through the trees, the branches creaking in its wake. This place, wherever it was, was *off*. Like the air knew we were trespassers.

We both stood in silence, listening for any indication we weren't alone—recognizable figures among the trees, or a distant call from a familiar voice. Lyra and Thea did the spell, as well, so they should be here. My nerves tightened the longer the silence remained unbroken.

"Should we look for them?" Blythe asked.

As if on command, a fire burst to life not even ten yards from us. Voices—laughter— carried over on the breeze. Blythe glanced at me for confirmation that I'd heard it too. I gave her a short nod, and we headed in that direction.

Nestled in a clearing among the trees, a fire burned in a stone circle, the flame flickering blood red and black. Clearly, conjured by the two women standing around it. I recognized one of them instantly. Her dark red hair flowed freely down her back, her bright eyes red like mine, her long nose the one inherited by many of the Boswell daughters.

I glanced over at Blythe, who stared at the other woman like she'd seen a ghost. And for all I knew, that's exactly what this was. Ghosts of our ancestors, replaying the night it all went wrong.

I nudged Blythe with my elbow to get her attention.

Is that...? I mouthed, afraid of either apparition hearing me.

She nodded quickly before we both turned back to the scene unfolding before us.

"They are late," Patience said, tossing something into the fire that made it spark a deep purple, illuminating a scowl I'd seen Blythe wear more than once.

"Lydia must wait until Simon and the baby are asleep," Amity told her, stated like a reminder given often.

"Sybil said she would be here," Patience continued.

"Your mother should rethink your name," Amity teased, "for you lack it."

Patience tossed a small stick at Amity. "Perhaps I would simply like not to draw the attention, or ire, of your mother."

Amity spun in a circle, face lifted to the sky. "You fear my mother, Patience Osborne?"

"The whole village fears your mother," Patience grumbled.

Amity laughed, and the sound stirred my magic like a long-forgotten lullaby. "I can handle my mother."

Patience glanced around. "I do not like that she is late," she repeated in a murmur.

"Sybil would be late for her own funeral," Amity said in a tone that suggested there was a private joke behind the words.

Patience's lip lifted in a smile, the first to cross her face since we'd seen her.

Another woman walked into the circle of firelight. Her dirty blond hair pulled into a braid that fell below the waist of her simple black dress, her eyes a brilliant but dark purple, I shivered as her magic filled the space.

I'd only had a small taste of Thea's magic, but if this was what a fully powered Death Witch felt like, I never wanted to experience more than that.

Her magic felt *off* compared to my own, rousing an impulse to shrink away and to keep it as far from me as possible. This had to be what they meant when they said Blood Witches and Death Witches rarely worked together. We were *too* different. Yet, our ancestors seemed to have overcome that difference. What had gone so wrong that history erased it?

"Hello, sisters," Sybil said, pulling the leather cord from around her hair and letting it fall out. "It is a beautiful night."

Amity stopped turning in a circle, and Patience crossed her arms. They both smiled at the woman.

Thea stepped out of the low brush next to me and I flinched as she swatted at something next to her face. Blythe and I both stared at her.

"Spiderweb," she muttered as she crouched next to us. "Are those your ancestors?"

We nodded.

"Patience was just expressing her concern at your tardiness," Amity said, pulling our attention back to the clearing. She resumed turning in slow circles under the full moon.

Sybil ran a hand through her hair. "Then, perhaps, your mother should have considered a different name for you," she said with a smirk, earning another laugh from Amity.

"Jest at my expense all you like," Patience said, crossing her arms. "But if we take too long and Mary gets word of this, she will not take the slight in stride."

Sybil shook her head. "Your fear of the Boswell matriarch is astounding, considering her power is no match for your own."

I exchanged a glance with Blythe as Thea continued to watch the scene in front of us. They were joking around, sure—but with that small interaction, we learned both that Patience was more powerful than the famed Mother Witch *and* that Mary Boswell probably had told her daughter not to do exactly what they were about to attempt.

Patience shrugged. "Her twelve other daughters together could easily match me."

"Would you please not speak of my sisters *here*?" Amity said bitterly. "I wish to keep one place as my own."

Neither woman spoke, as if in silent agreement.

"Has Lydia yet to arrive?" Sybil asked after a moment.

"The moon has not reached the peak," Amity noted and the three of us all looked up. The light from the moon was out, but it wasn't directly above the clearing yet. It wouldn't be long, though. And both our groups were missing someone. Is that what happened? Had they waited too long to start, unwilling to let another month pass?

A branch snapped, and we—ancestors included—turned towards the sound. A tall woman walked into the circle; her light blond hair tied back in a low ponytail hanging over her shoulders and golden amber eyes, the same ones I recognized from my dreams after Phoenix's death.

She'd been the third woman in the mirror, I knew it. Three of the four women in the clearing had somehow made it into my subconscious when Jax had put me under. Why not four? Why hadn't I seen Sybil?

"Forgive me," Lydia said, accepting Patience's hug as she entered into the circle. "Hope would not go to sleep."

"You arrived at the perfect time," Amity reassured her, sweeping a hand at the sky.

"Babies are fucking annoying," Lyra said, coming up behind us. I spun on my heels to face her at the same time Blythe reached up as if to pull her down.

Lyra gently pushed her hand away. "Why are you hiding in the bushes?"

I pointed to the clearing.

"They can't see us," she said. "Or hear us. I could punch Lydia in the fucking face and nothing would happen."

Blythe frowned. "You punched your ancestor?"

"I said I *could*."

"Shut up," Thea snapped, nodding to the clearing.

Lyra, with a pronounced roll of her eyes, crouched down next to us as we faced the clearing again.

"We should get into position, then," Lydia said, pulling her book out of a leather bag at her side.

"We *are* sure this decision is prudent?" Patience asked, no doubt still trying to avoid the *ire* of Mary Boswell.

Lydia winked at her. "Trust, sister."

"I trust your skill," Patience said, moving as the others did to form a circle around the fire. "It is the intention of our actions I waver on."

"My mother would never allow me to be bound to an Osborne," Amity said, digging out her own book. "If she learns of your existence, she'll drive you from the village as she did my father." She tossed her hair over her shoulder. "Am I alone in my desire to not allow her to have that power over us?"

"I do agree with you on that," Patience interjected.

"As for Sybil," Amity continued, "if the others knew a Death Witch of her power were here, they would turn her over to Samuel and his hunters without pause."

"You do not have to say it with such carelessness, Amity," Lydia scolded.

Amity shook her head. "I do not intend offense," she replied. "It is the simple truth. We are feared for our power as solitary practitioners. The community would rather see us hunted than joined as a coven." Her red eyes burned. "If none of you truly believe that, then we can go to my mother now and state our case."

A part of me broke for them; outcasts just trying to find some way to feel less alone. But this, this was not what happened, and we knew it. Something, some force, was about to see that Amity's first—and, arguably, only—coven would be erased from the history we knew.

With none of the women offering any arguments, we watched as they prepared for their binding spell—similar, so far, to how we'd done it during the Esbat, only Amity and Patience positioned themselves differently. A cauldron had appeared seemingly, out of nowhere, and they added the same ingredients we had, sans tea bag additives.

They stood, Amity, Patience, and Sybil, holding hands after they each cut their palms to allow blood to touch blood. Lydia played the same roll as Lyra, standing in the center of the circle with the cauldron. She began to read the spell we already had.

Lyra leaned forward, unblinking, as she watched them preform the spell. An explosion could have rocked this dream-memory-thing, and I doubted it would have broken her concentration.

A gust of hot wind roared through the trees, and a clap of thunder echoed through the cloudless night. Heat flooded my body, and all the hair on my arms stood as magic crackled through the clearing.

A mist of red, black, and purple shrouded the four witches. Fissures of gold cut through like bolts of lightning.

"That's not what it looked like for us," Blythe whispered in awe.

I nodded in agreement.

The mist swirled higher and higher, a plume reaching for the moon just as it crested overhead. I clapped my hands over my ears trying to block out the intensity of the ringing, but the sharp sting meant it wasn't *external*. Despite the pain, I couldn't look away from the column of magic.

It slammed back to the ground, shaking the forest floor and leaving us in deafening silence. The mist dissipated, like an early morning fog chased away by the heat of the day, until it was gone completely.

Slowly, I lowered my hands, and the creak of the trees in the breeze and the spit of the fire replaced the painful ringing.

A cry pierced the night, and I flinched at the shrillness against my sensitive ears. Next to me, Blythe was staring at the clearing, all the color drained from her face. Thea had a hand clapped over her mouth, silent tears rolling down her cheeks. Lyra was...gone.

I looked around for her, but she wasn't with us anymore. Like she'd vanished with the mist. Another cry tore my focus back to our ancestors, and bile rose in my throat.

Amity heaved sobs on all fours as her eyes and nose bled.

Patience cried loudly, arms wrapped around herself, rocking back and forth, the corners of her mouth and ears stained red with blood.

Sybil's arms were covered in cuts, streams of blood trickling down them, and she let out another cry of pain and went to her knees.

But Lydia...Lydia lay lifeless in the center of the circle.

With a gurgled sob, Amity dragged herself to Lydia's body and drew her into her arms. "No, no, no," she cried.

"Is she—"

"Gone," Sybil declared, and I wasn't the only one who let out a gasp.

Patience shook her head. "She—she cannot be!"

Sybil just gave them one nod.

Patience shook her head more intensely.

Amity cradled Lydia's head. "Bring her back," she choked out, tears cutting through the blood on her face.

Sybil's eyes went wide. "I cannot."

"Try," Amity pleaded.

"You said it yourself," Sybil cried. "They would hand me over to be killed without a thought!"

Amity shook her head. "No one would know."

"You ask too much this time, Amity."

"We would keep it secret," Patience said. "She is your friend. Your sister."

Sybil shook her head. "It is not a secret easily kept," she said. "She would not be as she was."

Thea choked out her own sob next to me.

"She is gone," Sybil repeated. "There is nothing to be done." She turned to leave.

"Do not walk away!" Amity's voice deepened with a power I recognized, having wielded it myself. Her eyes burned a deep red.

Sybil turned, her own purple eyes blazing—whether with anger or power, I wasn't sure. "You cannot force me, Blood Witch," she warned, and I flinched as if the harshness of those two words had slapped me themselves.

"Life holds no power over death."

My stomach dropped as the weight of Sybil's words rushed over me. Amity hadn't just been threatening Sybil; she'd tried to *control* her. But Sybil, being a Death Witch, was immune. Life and death. Balance always.

Amity, out of grief, or rage, or sheer pride, did not seem to care. She sent her magic barreling towards Sybil with such force it knocked me backward, clutching at my chest like *my* magic was trying to come to her aid. But that was impossible—it had to be—because this had already happened, and we weren't there. Were we?

"Amity, no!" Patience moved to try to step between them, but she wasn't fast enough.

Sybil took a half-step back as if Amity's magic had been a physical force shoving at her. "How dare you!" She regained her step and raised her hands.

"Sybil, please! Stop this!" Patience was crying again, but it happened in an instant. A scythe made of purple mist took form and slashed down just as Patience turned, attempting to stop her friend. The magic blade caught her across the face, and she crumpled to the ground.

She clutched her cheek, fresh blood dripping between her fingers. She looked up at Sybil, clearly hurt in more ways than one.

Sybil's anger wavered as she took in what her magic had done. "I do not want this," she said. "Any of it."

"Then raise her," Amity demanded again. "Or Patience will bind you."

Patience's eyes went wide, and her head swiveled to Amity. "What—no!"

"If she will not use her power to bring Lydia back to us, she is unworthy of it."

Sybil's mouth parted in a hiss of anger.

Patience glanced between her two friends, tears spilling over, the look of defeat on her face broke my heart.

Patience shook her head. "No." She stood firm against the other witch.

"Then both of you, get out," Amity growled, magic deepening her voice once again.

"Amity, ple—"

"If either of you are still in the village by first light, I will turn you over to Samuel myself."

Thea gasped.

Blythe cursed.

The ground pitched under me.

Sybil stood her ground. "I will not allow *you* to run me out of my own home."

Amity removed herself from under Lydia's body and stood, drawing to her full, considerable height. Her eyes flared, an unfelt wind whipping her hair around her as power radiated. My chest seized again.

Patience stumbled backward, tripping over a rock and hitting the ground hard. She didn't come back up, and Blythe's presence vanished.

One moment, the light pressure of her shoulder was against mine. and the next it was gone. I was too scared to look away to confirm it.

Logically, I knew Patience wasn't dead; her recorded death date and Blythe's existence told me that. But fear rarely gave into logic.

Amity stepped over Lydia's body. "I swear this to you, Sybil Graeves," she began, drawing a knife. The power bleeding through her voice was almost inhuman. She continued towards Sybil, who had gone still.

"That until you rectify what you could have in this moment," she continued, cutting the heel of her palm to summon fresh blood, "or my line ends..." She snatched Sybil's wrist, slashing the witch's palm before pressing it to her own.

Sybil tried to struggle away, but Amity held her with an abnormal strength.

"You will never know peace," she swore, yanking Sybil so close their noses were practically touching. "Your daughters will never know peace." Her eyes blazed, and Sybil let out a cry of pain. "Death will be your *curse*."

Thea buckled at the same time Sybil did. The fire behind Amity burned blood red, and the ruby around her neck sparked enough for me to feel the heat, even from our distance.

The light faded, and Amity released Sybil so roughly the woman fell to the side.

Panting, Sybil glared up at Amity. "You are as vile as your father."

A cruel smile spread across Amity's face. "My father would not have let you live."

Sybil rose to her feet and glanced at an unconscious Patience, then Lydia's lifeless body. "It is not only my line you have destroyed this night," she growled. "Mark my words, *Boswell*."

Sybil spat at Amity's feet before turning and storming out of the clearing. In a rush of jarringly frigid wind, Thea vanished, leaving me alone to watch as my ancestor collapsed to the ground and let out a scream that caused a burst of red power to singe the trees around her, scorch the ground under her, and send pain lancing through every part of my being.

Chapter 25

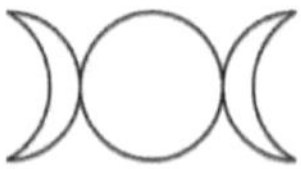

An invisible hook yanked me back to the present with such force it felt like a part of me was left behind. White dots burst into my vision at the sudden lack of red, raging light, and I tried to blink away the wet tears that clung to my lashes.

Heat from Amity's magic clashed with the chill of the night, and I could still somehow feel the surge of her power gripping at the inside of my chest. I couldn't stop shaking, and there was no way to know which was the cause.

Wisps of clouds slid across the moonlit sky; as the ringing in my ears subsided, I listened for anything to orient myself. The stars weren't as bright. Was I back in the yard?

I rolled to my side, groaning against the pain that pierced through every muscle. Shoving myself up, I swayed in place as the ground pitched under my feet.

Jax swam into my vision, his brows creased as he looked over my face. He was saying something—at least, I thought he was. His mouth was moving. Dull sounds were coming back, but I couldn't *hear* anything.

He held my face in his hands, mouth working again, and I stared at his lips, trying to read the words he was saying. It was no use. I shook my head against his grip, trying to clear away whatever was keeping me from understanding. Everything was muted and distant. I squeezed my eyes shut and swallowed hard. My ears popped , allowing some sounds to become sharper. It still sounded like I was on an airplane, but at least I could start to pick out individual voices. There was a lot of shouting. I opened my eyes and quickly scanned the grass for Lyra and Blythe. I needed to make sure they'd come back, too. Everything we'd seen in the spell felt too real, and I couldn't shake it off.

Jax took a few steps away from me, voice low, and I saw his fingers flexing as if trying to summon his magic. What was going on?

Another shout reverberated, this one closer to me, and I turned in time to see a tall figure rushing my way. Sharp pain across my cheek sent me stumbling. The shock brought my hearing back to jarring chaos.

"The fuck!"

"Thea!"

"What are you doing?"

I rubbed the ache on the side of my face and found the glow of Thea's purple eyes glaring death at me. She raised her fist and took two steps in my direction. I backpedaled as both Jax and Leander moved to get between us, and a long, low hiss echoed through the yard. Grace popped in next to me, hackles raised and looking much more the Otherworld creature than house cat.

Thea's fist fell to her side, clenched hard, and her chest heaved.

Jax took my chin and tilted my face towards what the little light radiated from the porch. "Are you okay?"

I blinked, unsure what he could possibly mean by that question. I'd just been sucker-punched by a Death Witch after watchin my ancestor grieve the death of her friend by terrorizing two others—I was so far from *okay,* it was laughable.

His scowl deepened before he rounded on Thea. "What was that for?" he snapped.

Thea was visibly shaking. "Because *all* of this is her fault!"

My eyes caught a form on the ground. Blythe sat, hugging her knees, her eyes staring wide ahead of her. A trickle of blood, now dried, ran down her forehead from an injury that wasn't hers. Rez crouched next to his cousin, arm wrapped around her shoulders, while Rhi stood next to her with eyes firm, as if daring anyone else to come too close.

"What are you talking about?" Jax demanded.

"Her ancestor—"

"Exactly," he said. "Not her. Attacking Em isn't going to help anything."

"Keep defending her," Thea shot. "She's just as bad, watch."

I shuddered under the accusation.

Jax turned back to me and pulled me into him, clearly thinking the reaction had been from fear. I took a trembling breath against his shirt, inhaling his familiarity to remind me that I was here. I was back. I wasn't in the woods, watching as my family ruined another.

"You—" his started, voice rumbling in his chest against my ear.

"Get inside," Wes ordered before Jax could finish. "Before the neighbors call the cops." I had no idea what the spell had looked like from this side, but Wes's tone was firm and filled with a worry I hadn't heard in years.

Jax didn't move, but I heard everyone else shuffling in the grass and even Thea's cynical snort. But still, we didn't move.

"Em," Jax said softly, but I still flinched at the sound. He held me away from him, eyes searching my face. "What happened?"

I shook my head. "We—I—it's all wrong," I choked through a sob. My own voice was too loud in my ears. Shivers that felt more like electric shocks ran along my spine.

"What is?" he asked, tucking my hair behind my ear with a frown.

"Jax!" Lyra called.

"In a minute!" he snapped back.

I swallowed, suddenly very concerned with what would make him snap at her like that.

"No, we should go," I said.

"Em, you can take a minute."

I shook my head and took a deep breath, trying to compose myself. "I'm the *last* person that gets to take a minute." Moving around him, it took me longer than it should have to get back to the porch, even with Jax's help.

Grace slowed her pace as she marched in front of us protectively. And as we stepped onto the porch, I glanced back out at the yard and couldn't stop the gasp that escaped me.

A large circle had been burned into the ground where we'd been standing, the grass a black mass under the full moon. We'd seen what had started all of this centuries before we were born, but what price had it demanded?

The lights were too bright in the living room as Jax helped me onto the couch. Blythe sat at the other end, Rhi perched on the armrest next to her, staring at the flames in the electric fireplace. One hand was wrapped around a steaming mug, the other holding a blanket around her shoulders. The red in her eyes was brighter than I'd ever seen.

Rez stood behind her like a sentry. Anger would be understandable, but the fear that laced the air in the house was unexpected, and the urge to ask what they'd seen when we were under burned in my chest. But I couldn't quite find the right words.

Thea leaned against the chair across from us, arms crossed and face set, eyes blazing a deep purple as a faint mist curled around her fingertips. I tried and failed to suppress the shiver at the power radiating from her. It was all focused on me, and for good reason.

Lyra stood in the small space between us as if ready to tackle her if she came at me again. I almost wished they'd just let Thea hit me again; maybe that would at least expel some of the tension.

Leander stood next to Lyra, hands in his pockets and jaw working. He wanted to say something. I was ready for the lecture, the scolding, anything to keep me grounded to the here and now.

I hissed as ice-cold pain hit my cheek. Jax knelt next to me, holding an ice pack to my face and occasionally shooting Thea a glare that she returned completely unfazed. I put my hand over his and nudged his hold on the ice pack away, pressing it to the dull ache in my cheek. He sat on the armrest and continued his face off with Thea.

"What happened?" Leander asked, clearly not able to keep his questions in any longer.

Lyra glanced at him. "Yeah, I thought we'd all come out at the same time."

"This is why you don't do experimental spells," Leander muttered.

"You wanna get hit too?" Lyra growled at him. "I remember seeing them do the spell, then I was back here with this panicked idiot." She jerked her thumb at Leander.

"You all vanished," Rez said. "In some glowing haze that left quite the mark in the grass. Excuse us if we were a little concerned."

"Vanished?" I croaked. "We weren't still here?"

They all shook their heads, and Lyra and I exchanged a glance. She'd made the joke about how she could punch her ancestor without her noticing—but if we'd actually left, if we'd actually been there, was that true?

"You don't think we were..." Blythe left the question hanging in the air.

Lyra shook her head. "I landed smack in the middle of Lydia's house with a screaming baby," she said. "They would have noticed."

Leander frowned. "Time travel is impossible," he bit out.

"Let's back up," Jax said. "Lyra, you said you saw the spell, then you were back here. Why only you?"

Thea aimed her glare at me. "Ask *her*."

Lyra raised her eyebrows.

Anger surged in my gut. "Amity wasn't the *only* one there."

"No, she—"

"Wasn't the one who refused to save Lydia," Blythe interjected, snapping out of her stupor. "Or did you forget that part?"

Lyra's eyes went wide. "Lydia died," she breathed. "That's why I came back first."

"Sybil wasn't the one dishing out blood curses," Thea shot back, and the room went quiet.

Wes made a slight gasping sound that he covered with a cough.

Leander's eyes flicked from me to Thea.

Jax's arm went around my shoulders.

"She's right," I mumbled.

Chad held a mug of steaming tea in front of me, and I set the ice pack down so that I could wrap both hands around it. He gave the top of my head a light kiss and went back to the kitchen to busy himself with more tea.

"Amity cast a blood curse?" Lyra asked slowly. She looked at Blythe. "Patience?"

Blythe shook her head, then closed her eyes as if that movement was painful. Her hand went to the back of her head, and I wondered if she still felt the effects of Patience's injury.

"I saw Lydia dead," she finally said. "Then Amity and Sybil fought about raising her." She swallowed. "Amity...she..."

"She threatened to have Patience bind Sybil," Thea finished for her. "Tried to use her power on her. Patience got knocked unconscious—"

"Which is when you came back," Lyra nodded to Blythe.

"—that's when Amity decided cursing my family was a great idea."

"But that doesn't make sense..." Lyra mused.

"It's true," I croaked. "Amity was...yeah."

Lyra ran a hand over her face. "Are you sure it was a *curse*, though?"

"I know what I fucking saw," Thea snapped.

"Sure Thea, just like you *knew* you weren't bound to Em," Lyra said. "Or just like we *knew* you were a Death Witch." She finished with an impressive eye roll.

Thea stood, matching Lyra's height as more purple mist gathered at her fingers and the swirl of death made my stomach churn.

"It wasn't just her," I said. "I saw it too."

Lyra didn't look away from Thea. "Curses aren't easy to just *do*," she said. "For regular witches, they take time, planning, careful execution, or they can rebound."

Thea didn't back down. "Amity wasn't a regular witch."

Lyra shook her head. "Only one powerful Curse Weaver could pull something like that off without *any* prep," she explained. "And even then, it's highly unlikely it would work if they were as emotionally fucked up as Amity was."

"But not impossible," Thea accused.

"C'mon, Amity wouldn't have been able to manage leveling a curse *that* specific, that lasted *this* long all while pissed off and grieving. Don't be fucking stupid."

I swallowed slowly. Lyra had a point. There was a reason curses weren't commonplace. They had a nasty habit of rebounding, even if the caster took every precaution they could think of. Curse Weavers were the only ones known for their specific abilities to avoid rebounds. And they were all gone.

"What else could it be then?" I asked quietly.

"Tell me *exactly* what happened," Lyra said.

Thea and I exchanged a glance and, after a beat—and with some input from Blythe—told Lyra everything that had happened after she'd come back from the spell. When Thea finished, Lyra looked at me expectantly.

"She was…" I wasn't even sure how to describe what Amity had done or been after Sybil left the clearing. "Just, raw power." My chest tightened and my magic sparked. I rubbed at the sensation, trying to ease it.

"*Circe*, this thing is layered." Lyra ran a hand over her face, "so, based on all that…" She waved her hand through the air between Thea and me. "Not a curse."

Thea snorted.

"Not *technically*," Lyra continued. "More like a hex. But if Amity used *those* words…" She looked to me for confirmation and I nodded. "It's one that she also put on her own bloodline."

I frowned. "She hexed her own line?"

"Unintentionally."

"Does it matter?" Thea snapped. "The point is, *she's* the reason we're all in this mess."

"Only part of it," Lyra said quickly. "The coven binding is the reason you're in this mess, Amity just, sort of, tacked on an addendum." She chewed on her bottom lip. "A tricky one, sure, but nothing we can't fix. I think. I hope."

A headache was building behind my eye that had nothing to do with getting punched.

"I don't think you can fix this," Blythe said. "Amity turned her own blood against itself with that hex."

I flinched and looked around at her. "What did you just say?"

Blythe shrank away. "I didn't mean…I just—sorry," she muttered.

I shook my head. "No, you said she turned her blood…shit." I handed Jax my mug and tossed the ice pack aside, mind racing.

"Em, what—"

I left them murmuring in the living room as I made my way to the den as quickly as I could. Which wasn't very fast, considering I had to use the wall to support myself.

We'd always assumed what she'd meant. Everyone always assumed they knew what she meant. Mary Boswell, the Collective. My family, *Blythe's* family. Everyone. It had been decided. But after tonight...

I fell onto the air mattress and dug out Amity's book from under the clothes I'd tossed aside earlier. I cracked it open and reread the words for what felt like the thousandth time; only, after what I'd seen, they took on a whole new meaning.

I went back to the living room, returning to worried stares, and held out the book—open to Isobel Jacob's prophecy. Lyra frowned at it.

"It was there the whole time," I said.

Lyra looked at Jax like she was worried I'd lost my mind. "Yeah, we know."

I shook my head. "Read it," I instructed. "And put it in the whole context."

She took the book, her eyes scanning the prophecy as I sank back onto the couch, still too dizzy to stand.

Her eyebrows rose. "No fucking way."

I nodded. "Exactly."

"What?" Thea demanded.

I took a deep breath. "Isobel Jacob's prophecy about the thirteenth daughter," I started. "It didn't apply to one, but three."

"I think that spell messed with your head," Leander grumbled.

"The prophecy hasn't been fulfilled," Rez said. "By either of you." He nodded to Blythe and me in turn.

I shook my head. "The prophecy was realized three centuries ago," I explained. "But no one knew because the coven binding was kept secret."

"Can someone *please* explain what is going on?" Leander said loudly.

"With the thirteenth it will begin," I recited. "At their binding, the course is set for strife beyond amends." The words flowed like a well-rehearsed song. I'd seen them, heard them so much in my life, I knew them without reading them. But we'd always been told it was the reason we'd been running, hiding over generations.

I felt Jax's body tense next to mine, and Blythe turned to watch me.

"Blood will turn on blood," I continued, emphasizing those words. The words Blythe had used.

"And only when the covenant is restored will that which was shattered find its mend," Blythe said next to me. She put a hand over her mouth, and Rhi let out a soft meow next to her.

"What does this have to do with anything," Leander growled.

"They think the prophecy was referring to that night," Rez offered. He sighed. "Was Sybil a thirteenth daughter?"

Thea's face was still hard, but it was no longer as angry as it had been. She gave us one short nod, and the air rushed out of my lungs.

"They did it to themselves," I said.

"That's why they were so worried Mary was going to find them," Blythe said, and I nodded in agreement.

"What about the last part?" Lyra asked.

"I think that part actually does apply to us," I said. "It was never about a war among covens. It was about what happened in *one* coven."

"One the Collective didn't know existed," Jax added. "So, they'd never be able to figure out what Isobel was talking about."

"Great, so we have to—what? Restore the 'covenant' and that fixes it all?" Thea said, throwing up her hands. "How are we supposed to do that?"

We all looked around, each hoping the others would somehow have the answer. None came, and I sank further into the couch, fatigue taking over as the adrenaline faded.

Lyra clapped her hands together. "Well, we can start with making sure you all don't die," she announced. "At least not at the same time."

"You think you can still undo the binding?" I asked her.

"And the addendum?" Thea added under her breath.

"No," Lyra said. "And maybe."

"No?"

She shook her head.

"That's what this whole risk was for!" Leander shouted, although it sounded a lot more like a whine than anything else.

Lyra shot him a glare that made him shrink back slightly. "I can't *undo* the binding," she admitted.

"Why not?" Blythe said. "The law of—"

"Reversals, I know," Lyra said. "The problem is that our ancestors royally, and I mean *royally*, fucked this up. Lydia's death became an element of the binding. Which is why I think it never lost steam over the centuries."

I felt my mouth drop.

"They *accidentally* used a life to bind their coven?" Rez asked.

"Yes," Lyra said matter-of-factly. "So, unless we know someone who wants to be a willing sacrifice, we're definitely screwed on a complete undoing."

"If you can't undo it," Jax said, "then, they're just all going to be bound together for the rest of their lives?"

Lyra shook her head. "I think I can shift it."

"No," I objected quickly. "We're not putting this on anyone else."

Lyra rolled her eyes. "No shit," she said. "We're not going to put it *on* anyone. We're going to put it *in* something." Her eyes went to the dark gemstone around my neck.

I instinctively covered it with a hand. "It's...it lost its power," I said pathetically.

"It lost *a* power," Lyra corrected gently.

I wrapped my fingers around it, the jagged edges where it had split rough against my skin. Power or not, it was still something that connected me to them. All of them. Mom, Grandma Geri, everyone. Without it, what would I have left? Tears pricked my eyes.

But then, Amity's anger and fury swam into my memory. The heat from her power, the haunting intensity of her demands on the witches she called friends—sisters, even. She'd tried to curse one, force another to bind the other.

She'd been the start of our bloodline. A kind, but flawed, witch I'd been told—we'd all been told. She was supposed to be nothing like her father or the Blood Witches history sought to villainize.

Maybe that was true in the end, once she had to come to terms with what she did. But what I saw made my heart ache at yet another lie I'd been fed. She used her power to threaten and hurt the people she was supposed to care about. Her power—her magic—became more important.

I ran my thumb along the crack in the stone. One crack, three pieces. Swallowing, I tugged hard at the chain, feeling the clasp snap behind my neck. Giving it one more firm squeeze, I held it out to Lyra without a word, the last line of the prophecy playing in my mind.

With the thirteenth it will end.

Chapter 26

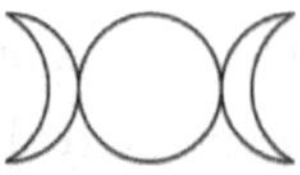

Pulling my hat further over my ears against the wind, I made my way down the path between headstones. The newer plots were arranged more neatly than the cracked and aged.

I wasn't the only one out; others used the cleared paths to get their morning jog in or chat with a walking partner. Maybe they, too, had loved ones buried here and were visiting. Maybe they just liked the quiet a cemetery provided.

I skirted the double headstone of a couple that died within a day of each other, complete with etched pictures of them when they were younger, and moved further into the grave markers. These were more maintained as their loved ones were around to leave flowers or pull the occasional weed.

A little halfway down the row, I stopped and turned to the small headstone with her name.

Grace Anne Boswell.
Beloved friend and mother.

She'd been reduced to a four-word platitude for passersbys. But what else could it say?

Keeper of dark family secrets.

Blood Witch.

One of those *Boswells.*

No, there wasn't enough space to tell the world what she was. What it lost that day. What we lost. What *I* lost.

The temperatures were staying high enough that some of the snow had gone, and dry enough that dead leaves collected at the base. I knelt and brushed them away with a gloved hand. It wasn't much. I hadn't visited in years.

Wes had been good about ensuring a flower delivery to the site every year on the anniversary—my birthday. He'd lost someone that day, too. I should have visited more, but it wasn't as if she wasn't everywhere. This was just the place that marked where her physical body had been laid. Her spirit, her essence, had returned to nature like all witches are destined to.

She was in the soft snowfall, the buds flowering in spring, the gentle lap of waves at the beach. Her power had been in the talisman before it broke. And despite knowing that wasn't all of her, it still hurt having that part of her gone now, too.

I sat back on my heels and stared at the stone marker. "Why didn't you tell me?" I whispered, knowing I would get no response.

It was an unfair question. Because if she had, would that have changed anything? Or had Amity's choices sealed the fate of the daughters who would come after her?

She'd known. She had worked with Blythe's mother, Thea's, and maybe even Lyra's to no success. Only another falling out that had them keeping their relationship a secret from another generation.

We'd all inherited a legacy of death and lies, and no matter how hard I tried to imagine why they'd all kept it from me, all I had was anger.

Towards mom, Grandma Geri, Amity, Lenore, myself. An anger that refused to be doused and had my magic roiling beneath the surface. It longed to be stretched, to lash out. I wasn't sure if I was fueling it or if it was the other way around.

I'd needed to get out of the house for that reason. Every quip from Leander telling us to not be reckless, every worried glance from Jax, and Rez's quiet pleading with Blythe—it all set my teeth on edge. It was like Amity's rage that night had seeped into my veins and refused to let go.

I knew the stages of grief. I'd been in them all, multiple times. It wasn't a ladder for climbing out. Grief was a rotating door, and you never knew which section you were going to get.

Acceptance, until the song on the radio reminded you of them. Denial, ripping through you after a too-vivid dream where you could have sworn you felt their touch years after the loss. Grief was ever-present. It never went away; it only eased until you could see through the haze.

But, in the days since the spell that gave us a chance to watch what our ancestors had done, that haze was tinted red and harder to see through. I was both wronged and responsible, and that, above all, was what made the anger burn like acid.

"Please," I whispered to the slab of rock. "Just tell me why."

Tears fell, and I sniffed against them and the cold. Still, I knew I wouldn't get an answer. I picked up a leaf and ran it through my hands.

"Lyra thinks she can fix this," I said, turning instead to explanation. "Not completely, but it's a start."

The rock stared back.

"We have to go back to Salem, though," I continued. "Proximity and all."

Truthfully, we had no idea if that would matter. But Lyra's theory was that the more we could replicate from the original spell, the better our chances. With a few exceptions; new moon instead of full, our positioning, her wording. She'd tried to explain it to me, but I had only been half-listening.

"Wes gets the house if..." I swallowed, unsure if I should tell her how I spent the first part of my day.

If I died, the blood wards on the Sandusky house would break, eliminating it as the safest place to be, but that didn't mean I needed it falling into the pits of the mortal system either.

I'd found a lawyer who would see me on short notice and didn't ask too many questions about why a twenty-one-year-old was making a Will to ensure her property and inheritance went to the only family she had. The family books, however, went to Meg. I didn't need the Collective coming after Wes for those, but somehow, I knew Meg would be able to keep them safe.

Either pessimism or pragmatism drove the idea. Perhaps a little of both. It didn't matter, though. It was settled, and no one could change that now, especially since no one knew I'd done it.

The papers were signed. If I didn't come back from Salem, the house, the money, everything would belong to Wes and Chad. They could sell it, rent it, burn it down for all I cared.

"He was the right choice," I said, watching the leaf in my hand instead of looking at her headstone. "To take me in. So, in case you had doubts, you picked right." I let out a watery chuckle. "No surprise there, right?"

A soft breeze swept through the grounds, kicking up dried leaves and sticks. I heaved a sigh and held the leaf out, letting the wind take it, and watched it dance through the air for a moment.

Standing, I brushed my pants off and pulled off a glove to place my bare hand on the stone, cold seeping into my skin. Another breeze sent my hair tickling my bruised cheek.

See you soon. The words tumbled through my mind like an unwanted echo. I wasn't sure where they came from or why they intruded now. But the uneasy feeling they came with sat like a rock in the pit of my stomach.

☾

An empty Sabbats was the only place protected enough for us to all spread out. Rez had converted the bar area to a staging arena. We had no doubts that Lenore knew we were back. The moment we touched down in Boston she would have been informed by any number of her spies.

We weren't naive enough to think Sebastian hadn't confirmed the binding. I had my own suspicion that she'd known all along, but proving it didn't matter anymore. She knew we were back and why. Killing me before we could finish was her only way to keep control now. Therefore, timing was key, and the dread that washed over me at the cemetery had only increased when we'd gotten into town.

I'd tried to convince Wes and Chad to stay in Ohio, behind the blood wards that still worked. In the end, I'd lost the fight, and they'd come with. I still didn't like the idea of them being involved—let alone this close to the Council—but I was running out of energy to fight with *everyone.*

Wes and Lyra had spent over an hour taking stock of the herbs we already had and the ones they'd need to get before the spell. Chad was in the kitchen with Rez, cooking. Because that's what he did for the people he loved when there was nothing else to do. Cook.

He couldn't fully understand the gravity of what we were trying to do, no matter how well Wes tried to explain it to him. But he knew enough that worry creased his brow every time he looked at me.

I flinched as Lyra pried the ruby free of its setting with the blade of a knife, the pieces clattering to the bar with an unnatural echo. The silver setting had been the only thing still holding it partially together.

Lyra swept the three pieces into her hand, catching my eye. She mouthed an unnecessary apology. I reached automatically for the space where it had hung. When my fingers found nothing, my hand dropped.

Jax set a hot tea on the table. "Sadiki's about an hour and a half out," he said, sliding into the seat across from me.

I nodded. We needed all the help we could get to make sure Lenore wasn't able to interrupt us once we got started. I still wasn't sure what favor the Syndicate had asked of him, but when Lyra had called to tell him we needed his help, he hadn't hesitated.

Jax reached up and his fingers lightly traced the bruise Thea had left. "Wish you'd let Wes take care of that," he muttered.

I caught his hand and pulled it down to the table, holding it in my own. "It's fine," I said. It still ached, and the bruise was obvious, but I didn't want it to go away because a part of me felt like I deserved it.

He wrapped his other hand around mine and brought it to his lips. "You sure about all this?" he asked after a quick glance at Lyra.

I stared at him, that ever-present anger bubbling. "If Lyra was the one bound to me, would you be asking that?"

He froze, then knit his eyebrows together. "What do you mean?"

I sighed. "If Lenore trying to kill me meant your sister would die too, would you be trying to talk me out of this? Trying to talk *her* out of it?"

He removed his hands and folded them on the table in front of him. "No," he admitted quietly. "But I'd still want to make sure it was safe."

"I haven't been safe since the day I was born," I pointed out. "Neither has Lyra, or Blythe, or Thea."

He shook his head. "Why does everything have to turn into a fight?" he muttered.

"I don't want to fight with you," I told him. "But you can't keep playing protector. At some point, you have to realize there's nothing you can do."

He shook his head. "You can't ask me to sit back while the people I," his throat bobbed as he swallowed hard, "love put themselves in danger over and over." He held my focus as that word hung between us. I could convince myself that he was talking only about Lyra. We both knew that would be another lie.

I reached forward and put my hand over his. "And I can't keep letting the people I love get hurt *for* me."

"You can't mix those!"

We both looked around as Leander snapped at Lyra and Wes for the third time in the last forty or so minutes. His normal composure was completely shot, as we were days from Lyra's birthday. He'd given up on trying to convince her to just wait it out, but that meant he was far more irritable than before.

"Go help with dinner," Lyra ordered, pointing to the back room.

"Not if you're going to be—"

"Leander," Wes said calmly. "I understand your concern, but I do know what I'm doing."

Leander's jaw worked at the same time he clenched and unclenched his fists. "Fine," he muttered and stomped off.

"Can we sneak some valerian into his drink?" Lyra asked Wes.

Wes stared at her. "No."

"Damn."

Jax's hands wrapped against mine again, the warmth of his touch drawing my gaze back to his. "I don't have a good feeling about this," he admitted quietly.

I swallowed, my own apprehension sitting at the forefront of my mind. I forced the best smile I could muster. "Once Sadiki and Blythe get back, we'll have a plan," I assured him.

His eyes held mine, and after a moment more, he released my hands and leaned back in the chair with a sigh. "Yeah." He stood and followed his brother to the kitchen.

Crossing my arms on the table, I laid my head down on them and took a deep breath. We'd been hurdling towards this since the Council first demanded I be brought to them. Even without knowing what *this* was, we'd all been positioned to be here, now.

We were so close. Days instead of weeks from success or failure. The end, one way or another.

Chapter 27

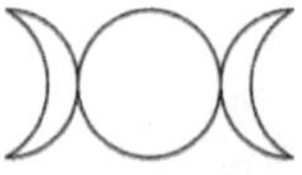

A few low conversations filled the space, hushed enough it was hard to focus on any singular one, but loud enough that I caught my name more than once. Blythe had rounded up others to help us while we'd been fine-tuning Lyra's revised spell.

Sofia, Devya, and Hazel had all shown up, eager to help again. Seeing Hazel made my heart ache. I'd tried to think of something—any-thing—to say to her, but it all felt hollow. It had been the same when mom died. People offered condolences or kind words, but they were empty because *I* had been empty.

Another witch, Astrid, had come with them, but she seemed to be a little separate from the group. She was almost as tall as Lyra, and her dark blond hair was pulled back into double Dutch braids, accentuating her sharp features. Her dark blue eyes never roamed far from Blythe in a way that told me there was a history between them no one was talking about.

Z had come back to town, most likely at Lyra's request. I was genuinely surprised when they walked in. Last time we saw them, it had been clear they were planning on getting out for as long as possible. I wasn't sure what Lyra could have said to get them back, but here they were.

Sadiki had gotten in late last night after his drive up from New York. He looked more tired than I'd ever seen him, and the tension in his shoulders was new, but he'd assured me it was just the hours spent in a car. Something told me that wasn't entirely it, but I hadn't earned the right to pry.

I sat at the bar, facing the group, while Lyra made a few extra notes next to me. It was hard to ignore the scrutinizing gazes that would flick to me before wandering elsewhere in the room an effort to disguise the staring. Whatever Lyra and Blythe had told their friends to get them to come had clearly not been the full truth, and those who had shown up were looking for it from me.

Grace leapt smoothly onto the bar next to me and laid down, her length taking up a considerable amount of space. She crossed her large paws and let them hang over the edge like a panther in a tree, watching the gathered witches.

I absentmindedly stroked her black fur while she purred loudly. Her presence had become a comfort I didn't know I'd needed.

Blythe stepped up next to me, Rhi at her heels. She let out a soft meow that Grace replied to with her own, something that sounded almost like agreed contentment.

Lyra emerged from her notes and books on the bar top to face everyone. "Alright," she started, rubbing her hands together. "First off, thanks for coming."

Leander let out a snort that drew the attention of the crowd.

Jax elbowed him.

"Secondly," Lyra continued, pointed glare focused on the older of her bro—cousins. "The new moon is tomorrow. So, we need to make sure everyone knows the plan by then."

Hurried murmurs filled the room.

"That's not a lot of time," Sofia said.

"Especially if we don't *actually* know what we're doing here," Astrid added, crossing her arms as she leaned back in her chair. "And who we're trying to help." Her glare shifted to me.

Blythe exchanged a look with Sofia. "You're helping me," Blythe answered after a moment.

"If all goes right, it won't take too long," Lyra jumped in before Astrid could say anything else. "The reason we asked for your help," she continued, "is because things around Em rarely go the way they're supposed to."

The back of my neck warmed, and I glanced down at my hands while Grace let out a noise that sounded suspiciously like a chuckle. I knew Lyra was trying to lighten the mood, but she didn't have to say that. It wasn't *my* fault things never went according to the plans I made.

"Still doesn't answer the question," Astrid retorted. I wasn't sure what Lyra had done to earn the harshness, but something told me it was less about Lyra and more about Blythe.

Lyra nodded. "We're trying to undo—no, sorry, *shift* a life binding."

More than one set of eyebrows raised.

"A *life* binding?" Astrid repeated, her gaze catching Blythe's.

I swallowed. "Our ancestors," I said, voice catching slightly as everyone's attention found me, "tried a coven binding that went...badly."

"That's one word for it," Blythe muttered.

"We're trying to correct it before..." I didn't feel the need to finish the thought. *Life binding* was enough for them to figure it out for themselves.

"You two are bound?" Devya said, her words slowing as she pointed between Blythe and me.

"The three of us," I corrected, nodding to Thea, who stood next to Jax. All heads turned to her. To her credit, her stance didn't waver.

"Hold on," Astrid said, putting up a hand as she turned back to us. "I thought *her* family cursed yours?"

"How many people did you tell that to?" I muttered.

Blythe shrugged. "Misunderstanding."

It was Thea's turn to offer a disbelieving snort, and I resisted the urge to rub at the mostly healed bruise on my cheek.

Some of Astrid's defensiveness eased.

Devya's mouth parted in surprise.

"I don't follow," Z said with a frown.

"We thought it was a curse, turns out it was a botched binding," Blythe said simply.

"Three of...but..." Sofia's eyes widened. "Ay, Dios mío."

"What?"

"The prophecy," Sofia hissed. "Three witches binding a coven..." She let the realization hang in the air for a moment, and I braced myself.

"What about Mary Boswell?"

"*Two* Blood Witches?"

"Why didn't the Collective know about this?"

"But the original coven had thirteen witches?"

The questions came so close together, I couldn't tell where one ended and the other started or who was asking what.

Lyra whistled loudly to get the barrage of questions to come to a halt. Everyone looked at her expectantly, as if she was going to answer them.

"All that you need to know right now is that the *actual* original coven fucked up, so now Em, Blythe, and Thea are fucked unless we do this."

I could sense that wasn't a good enough answer for the majority of the people in the room, but no one countered her. I wasn't sure if that was because it came from Lyra or if they figured they could corner one or all of us later to get their answers; either way, I was glad we didn't have to get into the Boswell blame game.

"Now," Lyra continued. "I've gotten the spell as good as I can, but as we all know there's no such thing as a perfect spell on your first try."

Murmurs of agreement rumbled through the club.

"I also wouldn't mind an extra set of eyes on it in case I missed something." She looked at Sofia, who gave her a firm nod. "A pep talk from the cards wouldn't hurt either," Lyra said to Hazel. "If you're feeling up to it."

Hazel took a deep breath and nodded. "I think I can do that."

Lyra nodded her gratitude and turned to Z. "It's probably a moot point since we've been back too long, but Z, if you could lay a false trail for the DRUs to debate over, give us an extra hour or two?"

Z worried their lip piercing. "Not sure what good it'll do, but I can whip something up."

"I'll get you the jet's tail number," Rez offered, pulling out his phone. "I'm sure my pilot wouldn't mind heading out himself if needed."

Z nodded. "Wouldn't hurt."

"What can I do?" Devya asked, sitting up straighter in her chair.

Lyra held up a shoe box of supplies. "Protection charms," she instructed.

Devya smiled. "On it."

"Why do we need charms for you to do one spell?" Astrid asked as Devya took the box from Lyra.

"We've really only got one good shot at this," Lyra explained. "We need to make it count."

"One shot?" Z asked.

Lyra caught my eye. "Charlevoix is going to try and stop this," she said simply.

"Which one?" Sofia grumbled, examining the contents of the box with Devya.

I took a deep breath.

"If it was Sebastian, I wouldn't be worried," Lyra said with half a shrug and a dismissive wave of her hand that earned a few chuckles. "The Councilwoman is another story. She for sure has at least four other

Council members backing her, and who knows how many others she's brainwashed into thinking Em needs to die to save us all."

I flinched.

"What about Castor?" Hazel asked quietly.

Lyra's jaw clenched, her glare landing on Jax and Leander. I didn't need to be an empath to know what passed between them.

I was surprised how quiet they'd both been since Leander's first snort. Maybe they were tired of fighting us on this. Or maybe they'd thought that no one would be willing to help and we'd have to drop the whole idea—and now that they were outnumbered, they didn't see a point.

"If he shows," Lyra said slowly, not taking her eyes off them, "we'll deal with it."

"You'll *deal* with your father?" Astrid said with a slight laugh. "Sure."

"You're more than welcome to do it yourself," Lyra snapped.

"Or leave," I added gently. Their table turned to me. "No one is being forced here. If you want to leave, you can." I took a deep breath. "We could use all the help we can get, but you *do* have a choice." I couldn't emphasize it enough. Because this was the part of the plan I had been against as much as Jax and Leander.

I didn't want to ask *anyone* else to risk their lives or magic for me. But Lyra and Blythe had both insisted we needed more than the four of us to do this, especially if Lenore decided it was the perfect time to take out two Blood Witches from the board.

"That's not what I meant," Astrid muttered, shrinking back slightly in her chair. "I just—Castor has a reputation, is all."

I caught Hazel's eye, but she quickly looked down at her folded hands in her lap. I saw her shoulders shake with a quiet sob.

"We need time," Lyra said. "As much as we can get. Then, it won't matter who shows up."

Thea shifted on her feet.

My heart sped up a little.

Blythe swallowed hard enough I saw her throat bob.

Truth was, we weren't sure that *if* our lives were no longer bound it it would mean anything different. I doubted it would matter at all to Lenore; it would just make getting rid of us harder, not impossible.

Sofia looked between Blythe and Lyra, her mouth parting as if she was going to ask for more. Instead, she shook her head. "You want us there for the spell?" she clarified.

Blythe nodded. "Lyra, Em, Thea, and me will do the transference spell in our own circle," she said.

Lyra held up a piece of paper with a five-pointed star on it. "You five," she said, nodding to Blythe's friends and Z, "will be at the points to form a protective barrier—slash, give anyone that gets too close second thoughts about doing that. Staying at the points ensures any expressed power has an extra little boost."

Lyra clicked a pen and drew a circle around the star. "The witches who have had their expressed power cut off will rotate around the others with the charms and spell bags and give the others a heads up if anyone gets too close."

Five heads turned to the former Emissaries at the back. Lyra could have left out the part about them having their powers bound; it was a tad petty, but she was still pissed, and I wasn't going to be the one to tell her how to deal with that.

"How are we going to do that?" Leander asked. "With our power being *cut off* and all." I'm sure I wasn't the only one who heard the edge in his tone.

"Phones, dumbass," Lyra said with an eye roll.

Z pinched their lips together to keep from laughing, and even Astrid cracked a smile.

Leander let out a long sigh. "Not very reliable."

"If everything goes completely to shit," Lyra continued, as if Leander hadn't spoken, "Astrid'll astral project people clear."

Astrid's smile vanished. "What?" She looked at Blythe. "Are you serious?"

Blythe grimaced. "You're the only one who can."

"It's not an instant thing, you know that," she hissed back.

"That's why it's a last resort," Blythe said.

Astrid shook her head but didn't offer any other argument. She was breathing a little heavier than before, and I could almost see her mind turning as her eyes swept the floor at her feet.

Lyra waited for Blythe to give her an affirmative nod before continuing. "Wes and Chad will run point on primary communication from here," she said. "That way, no one person in the field is responsible for the sitrep."

"We sure she wasn't a good Emissary?" Blythe whispered to me.

I smiled over at her. She was right, Lyra was remarkably good at this for someone who insisted she'd never wanted to do it.

"We'll also be ready in case anyone is hurt," Wes added.

"I can get more supplies from the shop," Sofia offered quickly.

Wes nodded. "That would be great."

"What happens when Charlevoix or one of her puppets figures out where we're meeting and cuts us off from getting back?" Astrid asked.

"Then you're fucked," Lyra said with a shrug.

I aimed a swat at her but missed. Attie's meow-laugh followed.

Rez tapped his ringed finger on the table. "I've made sure there are alternate entry points up and down the block," he said. "They can't watch every one of them."

Astrid looked like she was trying to come up with another argument, but she either couldn't think of one or decided to give up.

"What about after the spell?" Z asked. "How are we going to know if it worked?"

My stomach dropped.

Lyra bit her lip.

Blythe frowned.

"We won't," Lyra admitted.

Everyone in the room shifted in discomfort at that answer. But I wasn't about to start lying to them now.

"For all we know, it could make the problem worse," I acknowledged.

Thea flinched, and Leander took half a step forward.

"We aren't asking for you to ensure it works," I continued. "That's on us. We just need your help to try."

"Our help taking on the Council, you mean?" Astrid said.

"None of you are members of a Collective coven," Lyra said. "So, technically, the Council has no legal recourse."

Z laughed. "Babes, *legal* recourse isn't what we're worried about."

I held their gaze for a moment. "Lenore wants my power," I told them. "Or my life." I took a small step forward and tried to stand as tall as I could, ignoring the anxiety roiling in my gut, as I looked around at the witches who had come to help despite not owing me—us—a thing.

"So, whether our spell works or not, it's me who has to deal with her in the end. And I will."

Grace rubbed her large head against my elbow with a loud purr as surprised looks greeted my words. I could practically feel Lyra and Blythe exchange a look behind me.

But we had to accept it. Facing Lenore was an eventuality that couldn't be avoided any longer.

Chapter 28

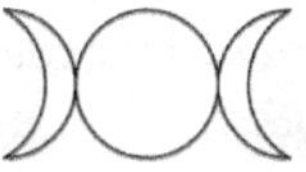

My toes curled in my shoes as I stood on the edge of a metaphorical cliff, not ready to take the leap. Upkept, clean sidewalk against a wild, overgrown lot. A house had stood on these grounds centuries ago. Now, nothing but a layer of dirt and leaves was left to cover the scorched earth where the structure had once stood.

Twelve witches had lost their lives in that fire because of a lie. Twelve witches who just wanted a community. Used—sacrificed—to stop a destiny that had already been realized.

A shiver ran up my arms and I tucked my chin into the high collar of my sweatshirt, breathing hard against the fabric. I stared at the bone-bare trees, nothing about them signaling spring was close to reviving the world.

What did mortals see when they passed by? Lost potential? An unsellable lot? Was their curiosity piqued or did what happened that night taint the ground so much that even they felt the ripple of lingering sorrow?

Taking a deep breath, I took that final half-step onto the soft earth, feet leaden. Tears welled in my eyes, and I wished I could blame the bitter wind of late winter. But the pain that pulsed beneath my feet made it obvious the blame would be misplaced.

Every step further from the concrete weighed heavier and power hummed around me, overwhelming any other sense. It made me sick, knowing the truth behind this piece of family history. I shut my eyes and tried to focus on the whisper of the tree branches in the wind or the distant song of birds that promised the coming of a new season, new life.

But it was removed, like this spot existed out of time, the cycle of life daring not intrude on the tragedy. I wanted to turn and run. I was not welcome here at the site of so much death. Sybil had said it: My magic was Blood. Life.

This place was the opposite. Death had claimed it, and that's why it sat empty and alone—and always would.

I forced myself to open my eyes and look around the barren state of the lot, to stay and feel the gravity of what they'd lost. I couldn't run, not from this. Not anymore. My ancestor—my family—was the villain in this story. We hadn't been running from a prophecy. We'd been running from that truth.

"You seem lost, child."

I didn't turn to face her, not for a long moment. The ground vibrated as if her presence was as equally unwelcome as my own—maybe more.

"I didn't ask you to come," I said, finally turning around.

Amity's smile fell. "I come when I am needed."

I let out a harsh laugh. "The last thing I need is *you*."

She clasped her hands in front of her dark dress. Her face had more lines than the iteration of her I'd seen in the spell. More like the grandmother I'd called on for guidance all those weeks ago. And she'd held onto her lies even then. The idea that I'd once felt a sense of pride in knowing that my power was like hers left a bitter taste.

"I understand your ire," she said.

"*Ire?*" I repeated. "You—" I took a deep breath to keep myself from yelling. "You lied. To everyone." I took a small step towards her. "And sat back, letting generations believe that lie."

She glanced around the trees before looking back at me. "I did not think it a lie," she admitted, voice barely above a whisper on the breeze that sent loose strands of hair spidering across my face.

Sadness creased her features. "I thought my friends were gone," she offered. "I had no conception that what we had done that night changed anything."

"You thought your curse didn't take," I said.

She inclined her head. "What I said in grief, in anger, I never imagined would have any sort of lasting impact."

I shook my head.

"None of us thought the binding took," she continued.

I could still feel the weight of that night, her grief bleeding into raw anger and power. We may not have technically been there, but that didn't mean seeing my own ancestor like that didn't haunt me.

I knew better than most how strong emotions, grief especially, could cloud any sense of logic. So, I knew, deep down, that she was right and probably had no idea how far the backlash of their botched spell reached. But that was her own fault.

"I saw no reason to allow my daughters to inherit my guilt."

I snorted.

"It was not until after I had passed on that I realized what had occurred."

"You're here," I snapped. "You were able to come on Solstice. You told me you watched over us. You could have told us!"

Amity took a silent step towards me. "There is no way to undo it," she insisted. "Putting that burden on you or any of the others would accomplish nothing."

Frustration crawled out of my throat in a growl, and I turned away from her. Long shadows cast from the setting sun brought the city closer to darkness, and I wiped a tear away.

"Why?" I asked quietly, wrapping my arms around myself, desperate for any semblance of comfort among the desolation that surrounded me.

An answer didn't come for so long, I thought she'd left with the stir of wind. I turned back to find her standing with such a deep sadness etched into her features that it made my own chest tighten. The ghost of a tear ran down her cheek.

"I did not know what I was doing," she said, her voice a feather against my skin that made me shiver.

"They were your friends," I said. "Your *coven*."

She blinked as if she was trying to keep more tears from falling. "So was Lydia."

I clenched my fists against my crossed arms. "You all lost her. That shouldn't have been enough to drive them away. To make them hate you. Us."

Her bottom lip trembled. "I never wanted that. My anger got the better of me, and I will not pretend to be proud of what I did." She took a deep breath, despite not needing to. "I was not as strong as you are."

I let out a bitter laugh. "I wouldn't have to be strong if it weren't for you and your lies."

She shook her head. "You would have had to be stronger."

I took a breath against the sob that wanted to escape as more pain from the power in the ground took hold. "Is this going to work?" I asked. "Lyra's spell?"

Wind kicked up the dead leaves that had been trapped by months of snow, sending them swirling around our feet. Another haunting bird call echoed from somewhere in the distance, signaling the end to the day.

Amity took a few steps into the space where even plants refused to grow. She probably could have told me what room we would have been in if the house remained.

She turned to look at me. "I do not know, child."

Anger bubbled in my stomach. "Then why are you here?"

She crouched to flatten a ghostly palm on the ground and closed her eyes, flexing her fingers into the dirt as if grasping for some part of the place she used to reside. The ground did not budge under her touch.

"To remind you that you are not alone," she whispered.

I shivered again as the words chilled my core. "The ruby is gone," I bit out.

She closed her hand against the dirt and held it there for a moment or two before relaxing her fingers and standing. She dusted her hand on her skirt as if something *had* clung to her skin.

"You are not alone," she repeated, facing me again. She held my gaze, but I found no comfort in it—only anger. She turned her face to the sky's waning light. "Never alone," she whispered.

Wind picked up her hair, and it swirled around her like it had that night. Only this time, I didn't feel grief or anger. Resignation washed over the lot, and a sense of clarity like I'd never known nestled inside me.

A smile curved her lips as another tear escaped and fell down the side of her tilted face. In that moment, I didn't see the woman from the portrait in the family book. I didn't see the angry power, or the strongest witch in generations. I saw myself.

And despite her words, I'd never felt more alone.

Chapter 29

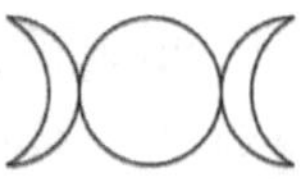

An unnatural stillness settled over Salem Woods, highlighted more so by the fact that the winds from earlier in the day had kept my bones chilled for hours. Now, however, there was no breeze, no rustling trees. Just my heartbeat and my own breath in the moonless night.

A circle of protection charms had been placed while it was still light out, strategically positioned around the space Lyra had designated for the spell. They wouldn't do much against the full force of the Council, but it would slow them enough for us to have a halfway decent warning of their arrival

Five witches at the pentagram points, four former Emissaries on the perimeter, and the four of us to complete the spell. Thirteen. I wasn't sure if that was a comfort or an ill omen.

The brackets of the prophecy ran clear in my mind as we stood in the woods. *With the thirteenth it will begin,* and *it will end with the thirteenth.* We may know now those words had nothing to do with a war among the covens, but that didn't mean they were reassuring in any way. *End* could mean a lot of different things.

Bright white chalk stood out on the forest floor to form Lyra's directional circle. I wasn't sure what she'd done to enchant it to work that well on dirt, but it was one of the few discernible things around us.

Unlike the first time we'd tried this, all four runic points had a witch to correspond with them. Four witches, four sets of offerings to the goddesses—and four ways this could go wrong.

White, unlit candles were the only similarities in our offerings. The offering in front of Lyra included a cup of red wine, a loaf of bread, and a pomegranate. For Hekate.

The one in front of me had a couple of small stag figurines, an effigy of a mother and child, and four apple halves. Diana.

Blythe's had a bowl of water, river stones, and hawthorn branches. For Danu.

Finally, Thea had a cup of mead, edible flowers, and pieces of amber. Freyja.

Hekate, Diana, Danu, Freyja, all the deities our ancestors from well over three centuries ago would have called on for help.

"This looks complicated," Thea muttered, pulling a hat over her ears. Spring was a couple of weeks off, and despite the days warming, night was still cold enough that spoken words sent puffs of white pluming into the air.

Lyra looked up from the ground, pausing in her drawing of chalked runes. "Maybe that's because shifting a three-century-old life binding into a *used* talisman *is* fucking complicated, Thea."

"And you're sure *you* can do it?" Thea snapped back. She glanced around and added under her breath, "I have a bad feeling."

Lyra finished the last rune and stood, dusting her hands on her pants. "As sure as I can be," she said.

I straightened and glanced around the small clearing, unsure what a Death Witch having a bad feeling could mean, and instead focused on the light current of magic I could feel from the protective charms being boosted by our friends.

Every now and then, I could see the bobbing of flashlights, and I counted them every time to make sure none had disappeared. It was a small way to reassure myself that we were still the only ones in the woods.

Lyra tossed the chalk to the side and glanced towards the sky. There was no moon like the first time we'd tried. But that was the point—the new moon to their full, the symmetry of reversal.

"Let's get started," she said. "Before the party crashers show."

I swallowed and took another sweeping glance of the woods, half of me expecting to see Lenore and her supporters charging at us from between dark trees. Z and Rez had worked together to lay down a fake trail that we'd left Salem in his jet, but even if they followed that, it wouldn't take them long to figure out the ruse.

"Scale of one to ten, how likely is this to work?" Blythe asked, shifting on her feet.

Lyra shrugged. "Solid six and half."

My stomach turned over, and I pulled out my phone to send a quick text to Wes telling him where I'd filed the deed to the Sandusky house, adding that I loved him and Chad. I stuffed it back into my pocket without waiting for a reply.

When I looked back up, they were all watching me. "I've been too lucky for too long," I said.

"Appreciate the vote of confidence," Lyra muttered. "Okay. Positions."

It was like watching someone else's dream play out. I barely registered when my arms and legs moved. When it came time to prick my finger, I didn't even feel it. Time slowed and sped abnormally.

I went through the motions without having to think about them. I recited my portion of Lyra's spell and let my blood drip into the cast-iron cauldron. I held the hands of the two witches whose lives were bound to mine, our palms clasped over the offerings.

The first jolt of a new, and different energy shook me out of my stupor. My hands still connected with Blythe and Thea, a warm, dull ache started at my wrists and raced up my arms.

My veins burned bright red. Next to me, the insides of Blythe's wrists turned black beneath her pale skin. Tendrils of purple throbbed under Thea's neck as if synchronized with her heartbeat. Neither looked any more comfortable than I felt.

Lyra passed each of us a piece of the broken ruby, I glanced down at it, it realizing the shard was heavier than it should have been. I met Blythe's eyes and didn't need her to vocalize that she was as scared as I was.

"Don't move from your spot," Lyra said. "Don't step out of the circle, no matter what."

We all nodded in agreement.

Lyra returned the nod and flipped to the page in the notebook where she'd re-worked the spell, adding the new part.

She took a deep breath and used the fire under the cauldron to light a long match.

"Hekate, hear my plea." She lit the first of the white candles, let it flicker for a moment, then returned it to its holder on the ground. "Unbind these daughters three." She lit the second candle, let it flicker, then placed it back at her feet. "Take what was never theirs and allow them to be free."

She handed a fresh match to me, and I lit in the cauldron's flames. "Diana, we call on you." I brought the match to the wick of my first candle and repeated Lyra's motions. "To end the strife of your daughter bound for life." I lit the second candle and set it down.

Thea lit her match and began. "Freyja, we beseech you." Her voice wavered as she lit her first candle. "Release from another's breath," she recited, pausing as she lit her second candle, "your daughter bound by death."

Blythe took a deep breath and lit her match. "Danu, we implore you." Her gaze was focused on the wick as it ignited. "End torment's flood for your daughter bound in blood." After she lit her second candle and set it back down, we all picked up our third and looked to Lyra.

Lyra held her match over her third candle. "Goddesses, we summon your help to shift what cannot be undone."

We each held our matches over our third and final candles and, in one breath, lit them and ended in unison, "So mote it be."

The candles flickered in our hands. The trees stilled, and the hair on my arms rose. Then, nothing.

Lyra frowned down at her notebook.

I made to move, wanting to see what she'd written, but she held up a hand to stop me from leaving spot.

"Hekate," she began, looking at the offerings around her. "An offering you will see, unbind these daughters three." A breeze rustled the flames, and I swore I heard a distant shout.

We all glanced at each other, waiting for something—anything—to happen. But there was just a whole lot of nothing. No surge of power. No pain. The ruby stayed heavy and silent in my hand.

Lyra dropped her notebook in the dirt. "Hekate," she practically growled, as if frustrated with the goddess herself. "Undo this binding." She threw a cinnamon stick into the roiling cauldron. "Because I *fucking* said so!"

Blythe gasped.

Thea gaped at Lyra.

I was having trouble registering that Lyra just cursed at a goddess. I wasn't one for much deity work, but even I knew that probably wasn't the best way to get their help.

One distant shout turned to three. Then more. She was here—Lenore had found us—and we were out of time. The thought of extinguishing the candle in my hand had barely entered my mind when it happened.

A sharp pull deep inside my core, like something was trying to pry my magic from my being, made me flinch so hard I dropped the candle to clutch at my chest. My magic instinctively fought against the intrusion, trying desperately to throw up a defense.

The tug got worse, painful.

It wasn't trying to pull my magic, but something around it. Something that had been embedded so deep, it felt as if it were one with my magic.

A moment passed in a day.

How long had this been inside of me? How long had I mistaken it for my magic? Why didn't I want to lose it?

My magic recoiled, curling around the force like a snake protecting its clutch. Whatever it was, whatever harm it had done, it was a part of me, and I didn't want to lose it anymore than I had lost mom or the talisman.

I inhaled sharply and shut my eyes as my chest tightened painfully. We—no, *I* was wrong. I changed my mind. I didn't need this. Didn't want this. We had to stop.

We'd jumped off this ledge without knowing what waited at the bottom. I was going to lose my magic, my power. Myself.

We're here.

Two words said by a cacophony of voices. Intertwined. Confusing. But, no, I knew them. I knew all of them and none of them at the same time.

Let go.

My magic relinquished some of its hold at the gentle command. It was met with stinging resistance. Whatever had a hold didn't *want* to let go.

I took a deep breath to steady myself and let the spell do its work. This was necessary, I kept reminding myself. We had—I had to do this.

The piece of ruby warmed in my hand, and even through my closed eyes, I could see the bright red glow.

Hot power skittered over my skin, and the tug grew stronger, fighting against the little bit of resistance left. Gasping, I fought the urge to drop the ruby and run.

Rooted to the spot by the smallest prick in the back of my overactive mind was that this was right. This was what was supposed to happen.

We're here.

I wasn't sure if the voices had returned or if it was my own mind replaying them, but I let them soothe the burning in my core that made me want to flee. Gritting my teeth, I held on to the gem tighter, forcing my mind to think of anything but the pain. We'd already been through too much to give up now.

I pushed my thoughts to Thea, and how much it must've hurt to lose her mother, her magic unable to help. Blythe, and how she lived her entire life thinking she was cursed with no way out. Lyra, and having to reconcile that she was lied to about her own family and not given the chance to grieve like the rest of us.

But it wasn't all bad. There was Ian and his determination to make me like my birthday again. Wes teaching me how to use plants and herbs to help and heal. Chad making my favorite meal just to cheer me up when I was down.

Jax's lips on mine.

Anything but the white-hot pain of being ripped apart.

A raw sob escaped as a dark thought intruded: I wasn't going to survive this. I couldn't, not this pain. It was too much. I was burning from the inside.

The pain receded almost as quickly as it started. Somehow, I'd ended up on all fours, heaving against the dirt. I blinked sweat from my eyes as the pang of loss settled. Because something was missing. Something I hadn't even realized was there until it wasn't.

A vise grip that kept the fullness of my power just out of reach. Like I'd been underground my whole life, and I was just now able to take a full breath. The flood of magic in my veins was the pristine air I didn't know my lungs had craved.

I rose on shaky legs, and it only took a second for it to hit me. The wave of magic was everywhere. In my blood, my mind, my chest. A power I didn't know how to wield. It was too much. Thunderous heartbeats and the rush of blood through bodies swarmed my senses.

I clapped my hands over my ears and shut my eyes, trying to drown it out. But I couldn't. It—they—were everywhere. I couldn't distinguish my own heartbeat from anyone else's. I could *feel* the power of the other witches around me.

This was true power. It was what the binding had been holding back. Tears leaked from my eyes as my magic surged, free for the first time ever.

I took deep breaths, searching for the heartbeat that was my own, focusing on the thud against my chest to find it. The others faded to voices, their yelling taking the place of blood rushing in my ears.

The rush dulled as I counted my heartbeats. Now it was just me and the others.

Me.

Blythe.

Thea.

My eyes snapped open as panic seized my throat. Spinning to face the last place I saw her, my knees buckled as Blythe's sob pierced though the haze of magic. I couldn't find—sense her. There was no sign of life.

Lyra was gone.

Chapter 30

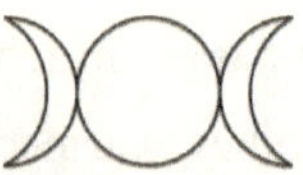

Hot rage surged through my veins. My magic ignited before I fully knew what was happening. It boiled over in a flash of red and a flood of power. A scream, deep and visceral, ripped itself from me, clawing its way out and scorching my throat raw.

Every heartbeat. Every witch in the woods, every witch with magic flowing through them. I sensed them all. And they collapsed as one under my power. Friend or foe, it didn't matter. Not when what mattered was lost.

A red cloud, thick with power, settled around me, coaxing my magic to more. With every thud against my chest, a wave of red magic pulsed forward, reaching further and further.

Searing heat swirled around me, enveloping me, as an unexplainable wind ripped through the clearing, melting candles and figurines. Liquid boiled without need for a flame, and food was turned to ash. My own scream was drowned out by the rush of power.

Lyra was gone.

Dead.

And they were all going to pay.

Needle-like cold wrapped around my arm. My power burned it off in another surge.

Rot assaulted my senses, churning my stomach. Still, my magic pulsed—seeking more to overpower, demanding more to suffer for what they'd cost me.

Shivering against the cold that continued to seep into my space, I lashed out at the invasion, but it crept in further. Tendrils of cold and rot wrapped around me, dragging me down.

It wouldn't budge, no matter how much magic I sent after it.

The red consuming my vision cracked, purple strikes flashing through to clear it. Part of the woods came into view.

A sob that wasn't my own broke through the pounding of heartbeats in my mind.

My vision cleared even more, and I found Blythe. She sat on the ground, cradling Lyra, rocking back and forth as she shook with sobs.

Ice doused my skin, and the dark world came back in a rush. The ground was burned red where our spell circle had been, and purple magic caged me.

Thea stood next to Blythe, eyes burning purple as her magic kept me locked in place. I shook my head, trying to clear it from the swell of magic that had taken over.

The witches I'd taken, laid unconscious from the unbridled wave of my magic, stirred from their states; as I allowed myself to focus, I realized I recognized some. My magic hadn't cared who hurt as long as *someone* hurt.

Thea sent a jolt of magic through me and bile rose at the slickness of death bringing me back from the edge.

When she released me, I collapsed to the ground and dry heaved against the rot still in my system. The ice receded from my arms, the smell fading to a hint like something out of a bad memory.

The purple mist from Thea's magic dissipated as I rocked back on my heels and stared at Blythe, her cries echoing too loudly for the clarity of my returned hearing. The clearing went still, cold.

A grave.

(

Lyra was dead.

Gone.

My raw throat scratched with each attempt to swallow, and my puffy eyes stung. I held my head in my hands, staring at Lyra. There was no fear on her face, no shock, only peace. And that made it worse.

Another sob clutched my chest. My magic stirred as it sensed another witch approaching too close. I hadn't stopped *feeling* them all since the spell unchained it. If this was what my unbound magic was, I didn't want it. Not like this.

The binding wasn't supposed to be undone at *her* expense. It wasn't fair. It wasn't right. She'd been twenty-one for less than an hour before it claimed her. It wasn't fucking *fair*.

Every step ran through in my mind like a bad movie clip replay. Everything we'd done, said. We had tried to be careful. It hadn't been enough.

I winced a second before the shouting got closer. More witches with their magic thrumming against my own. The sickly-sweet tang of too much magic in one place filled the air and coated my tongue. Lenore was here; I could sense her like I could sense everyone else. They were all still alive.

Lyra was dead.

Gone.

It was my fault. All of this was my fault. I should have just given up and gone with them. If I had Lyra would still—

Thea stood motionless, staring blankly ahead as a faint purple mist swirled at her fingers. The hot rush of my own power still burned inside me, like someone had injected my veins with boiling water.

We were unbound. Our power was our own again. But I never wanted it to be like *this*. I would have stayed bound a thousand years more if it meant not losing her.

Cracking branches and hurried steps reached us, and I squeezed my eyes shut against the fresh wave of pain that came as my magic recognized them before they came into view.

"What is the point of phones if no one ans—" Leander's words died, and his heart stuttered

Jax's heart sped up.

Rez's heart dropped.

I felt the moment they all realized what had happened. The vice grip of sorrow tightened around my chest. I waited for it to shatter from the pressure. Waited, unable to get a full breath in. All my fault.

A breath of wind kicked up the honeyed tang of magic again. Witches fighting, casting, holding the line because they didn't know that it was pointless. We'd lost.

I flinched as Leander collapsed to his knees, grief taking what strength he had. His scream ripped at my own heart. Sobs that could have been words heaved from his throat and I forced myself to look at him, to confront what I'd done. Blood stained his face from a wound that left his right eye obscured by gore.

He struggled against the tight hold Rez had on him from behind. He shook, fighting the comfort, fighting his own pain, and with each fresh wave of sorrow it multiplied my own.

"N-n-no," he heaved out. "She can't—she's not—" He shuddered against Rez, those few words taking any fight he had left.

Rez's own face was streaked with silent tears, but his hold on Leander never faltered, never loosened. He pressed himself against Leander as if trying desperately to ground him.

Blythe stared at her cousin, waiting for him to offer her something, anything in the way of a solution. As if he could fix this for either of them. For any of us. My own hot tears spilled over, scorching my skin.

Jax stood still. Staring at Lyra's body, still wrapped in Blythe's arms, as if he hadn't fully grasped what he was seeing. His face was cold stone. He didn't scream, didn't rage at me like he should. I killed his sister. I had ensured their fears were realized and there was only one thing I could do to rectify that.

I pressed the palms of my hands to my eyes, staunching the flow of tears. They left angry welts on my hands, but it didn't matter. Forcing myself to stand I gripped the piece of ruby in my hand so hard my knuckles blanched.

"Get back to the club," I ordered, voice deep unyielding.

They all looked at me.

Rez started to shake his head. "We don't have a clear way out," he said softly, as if afraid Leander would break if he spoke too loudly.

"You will."

Jax started as if I'd yelled, and he tore his eyes away from his sister. "*We* will," he corrected, brows creasing.

"I'm not running," I replied, moving away from Lyra and Blythe and focus the trees on the other side of the clearing. I could feel them getting closer. Their power buzzed in their veins. But it was nothing compared to *mine*.

Jax stepped in front of me. "I'm not leaving you," he said, grabbing my wrists.

I shook him off and placed a hand on his chest. I could feel his magic trapped by the Council's binding. It swirled against the cage, trying to find a way out. His eyes widened when he felt it. My magic, my power radiating through him. It seeped into him, already familiar with his essence. It took no effort. My power took hold as easily as the rise and fall of his chest under my touch.

He shook his head. "Em, please," he implored.

Rez looked between us, eyes going wide.

"Go." I let more of my magic flow into him.

He took a lurching step towards me, "I won't—" he heaved a breath, the effort of trying to both fight my hold and speak becoming too much, "I won't lose you too."

I flexed my fingers against him, my nails digging deeper. "Go." A command he couldn't defy, because I wouldn't let him.

He gritted his teeth, attempting to do just that.

"Em, what are you doing?" Rez asked. He already knew the answer because as Jax took a struggling step away from me, my magic turned on him, along with Leander, forcing them to their feet.

Their magic, like Jax's, was caught behind a wall the Council had forced on them. Leander's golden light beating against it, trying to break it down, and Rez's a mess of white-hot lightning sending strike after strike against the barricade, cracking like a never ending storm. Neither of their magic did anything to it; they were trying to breach a mountain when all they had was a battering ram.

Leander grunted with the effort to stay with his sister. He wasn't going to leave her again. But he didn't understand. He didn't have a choice. I couldn't save her, but I could save them *for* her.

"No," he managed to grind out, even as he retreated from us. He was helpless against me. Even if his magic had been able to come to the surface, it wouldn't have mattered.

Thea let out a soft gasp, realizing what was happening but she made no move to stop me. Because, however she felt about how I made it happen, she knew it had to—knew they couldn't be here for this.

I closed my eyes against the moonless night and felt them retreat. They stopped fighting me and moved quickly through the trees, further and further from us. They met no resistance. The witches Lenore had brought with her lay twitching on the ground, rendered useless by my power.

They found the others. They cleared the woods. The only energies left among the trees belonged to Lenore and those witches foolish enough to stay with her. Good.

Opening my eyes, I turned to Thea, her own eyes a bright purple against the darkness. She was breathing heavily, staring after Jax and Leander. I could see the fear mixed with determination on her face; she was prepared for me to do the same to her. That's where she was wrong.

I opened my palm and looked down at the ruby, jagged edges leaving indents in my flesh. I took it with the opposite hand and turned it over, watching it illuminate in the deep red of my glowing eyes.

Thea's eyes were wide when I looked back up at her.

"Raise her."

Blythe looked up at us. "What?" she breathed before looking back down at Lyra.

Thea shook her head, putting her hands up as if to fend me off. "I—I can't," she said.

"You can try." I took a step towards her.

Thea swallowed and glanced down at Blythe, who was still cradling Lyra against her, lips pressed to the top of her head as if it were her touch that could bring our friend back. "It doesn't work like that," Thea explained slowly. "I can't restore life."

I gripped the piece of broken talisman, wielding it like a knife and pressed it against the opposite palm. "Because death has no power over life," I stated, echoing our ancestors.

Her brows drew together in a deep frown.

"Life has no power over death," I said.

Her frown turned to shock as her gaze flicked between the ruby poised on my flesh and my face.

"That..." She closed her eyes and flexed her fingers at her side. Purple mist swirled up her arms as if her power knew before she did. I watched the choice play out across her features. It was asking a lot, facing the unknown to try and fix what I broke—but I needed her to *try*.

Her eyes met mine again, and with a short nod, she stepped forward until we were level. Holding out her hand, I pressed the ruby harder, working to draw blood. But a firm grip stopped me. Blythe was on her feet, fingers wrapped around my wrist and hard determination in her blood-red eyes.

I hesitated for only a moment before passing her the ruby. She didn't even stop to think, just drew it across her palm, slicing skin and brining a line of her own blood to the surface. Thea and Blythe faced each other. Tendrils of purple mist reached for the blood being offered. Life had no power over death. Death had no power over life. All we needed was time to try.

Because Lyra was dead.

Gone.

But maybe she didn't have to be.

Chapter 31

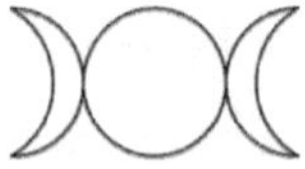

Waiting. Listening. Feeling.

I stood alone in the clearing. Gone were the sounds of Blythe and Thea carrying Lyra's body through the brush. The breeze sent the branches of trees awaiting spring creaking, cooling the sweat that clung to my skin.

The woods were darker, colder than they had been an hour ago. Flowing magic that was not my own caressed my senses. The full force of my unbound power would take some getting used to, but a part of me was already adjusting. Like I'd always known what to do with it, just never given the chance.

Pools of cooled wax collected among the scorched dirt at my feet, and the contents of the toppled cauldron seeped into the ground. The only evidence left from the spell.

I closed my eyes, willing any and all of the deities to bring her back. To give her the chance Lydia never had. To trade my life for hers, if that's what it took. My bloodline started this; *mine* should be the one sacrificed to finish it.

Nothing but the gentle whisper of a breeze answered my call.

I opened my eyes and looked down at my hand, blazing an angry red from where I'd pressed the piece of ruby too hard. The gem that was supposed to keep the spell from taking anyone from us.

Heartbeats.

Magic.

They were here.

I sensed them before they stepped into the clearing. They stood opposite me, moving like they were in control. But I was done running. Done hiding. Done being afraid of my own power. The power that hummed under the surface making me feel more alive than I ever had. My magic was sharper, easier to tap into. It was an extension of me now; it took no effort, no thought. As easy as *being*.

Five of them neared, their magic a different tinge to my system. The acidic burn of Lenore and Sebastian's telekinesis, harsh and unyielding. The warm spice of an Igniter and lingering sourness of a Pyro. And then his, warm, comforting, and savory like Jax's. Castor's magic was similar but held a bitterness Jax didn't have. They were all there, distinct and beautiful in their own way.

Unfortunately, they were here for *her*.

The sharp click of a lighter, a whispered command, and fire erupted in a circle around us, caging me in with them. They thought I was going to run. But as hot and strong as their fire burned, my magic burned harsher and angrier.

"You've lost," Lenore declared, folding her hands in front of her like a disappointed instructor. Her show of power was lessened by the streaks of dirt across her face, torn jacket, and hair out of its slicked bun. She thought she'd face no resistance.

My gaze fell to Castor next to her. His nose so like Jax's, his eyes narrowed like Leander's when he was trying to solve a problem, and the bright blue of them like Lyra's.

I swallowed. "Lyra is dead," I said to him.

His scowl dropped to surprise, and the face of the hardened Emissary broke. "You're lying," he accused, but the quiver in his voice betrayed him. He knew I was telling the truth.

"I'm not the liar here," I said. He retreated the small distance he'd made to level with Lenore again.

"Where is she?" he demanded.

I cocked my head to the side. "With her coven," I said simply.

Lenore's composure flickered as her eyes darted around us. Coven-less, I was an easy target for her, but with the other thirteenth daughters on my side, she knew she'd lose.

"More lies," she said. "Another witch, your friend, is dead because of your insolence," Lenore scolded. "Will his sons pay the price as well?" she asked, waving a hand at Castor.

Castor glanced at Lenore as if that question had been a threat directed at him instead of me. She was pitting him against me. Making me the object of his fears.

"Let them leave," I urged. "This is between us."

Sebastian snorted.

The other two exchanged a confused glance. I didn't know what they'd been told about me and my magic. They all thought I was the trapped one.

No one moved.

I sighed and raised my hands, sweeping them to the sides, my fingers reaching toward the flaming circle.

"*Tenere locum tuum*," I whispered, and my vision burned red, not completely, but enough to know my power was there—always there. The roar of burning fire filled the air as the flames turned blood red, now mine to command, and continued to flicker against the night.

Someone let out a curse.

I locked eyes with Lenore and focused on the two witches behind her. Brainwashed, threatened, or true believers of Lenore's mission, it didn't matter. They weren't needed.

With half a thought and a flick of my index finger, they went down and lay unconscious on the ground. Sebastian let out a gasp and jumped to the side.

Castor glanced behind him; when he turned back to me, his eyes were wide with fear.

Lenore's throat bobbed, but she did her best not to show how much my power scared her.

"You're outnumbered," she stated. "You cannot hold them forever." But she was wrong. A few weeks ago, I would have passed out simply by trying. She had no idea what I was capable of now.

Their magic had tried to fight me, tried to come to their defense, but it had been useless. Butterfly wings in a hurricane.

"Surrender to me, and the rest of your coven will not be punished," Lenore said.

"We don't answer to you," I replied. "And never will."

"Go," Lenore hissed to Sebastian, jerking her head towards the woods behind me.

He hesitated, looking between my—our—grandmother and me before taking a tentative step to the side as if to get around me. As if he could.

He froze a few feet from Lenore and Castor.

"What are you doing?" Lenore snapped.

"He can't move," I replied for him. "Not until I allow him to."

His magic was stilled, beating against a steel door that trapped him. I felt every attempt to throw me out. But it wouldn't work, not this time. The sooner Lenore realized she was no longer in control the better.

Her eyes flew wide. "That's impossible."

"I thought you said without the talisman she was powerless," Castor said, physically distancing himself from Lenore with half a step.

"She was supposed to be," Lenore seethed.

Another essence flickered in the back of my mind. No magic, only life— a mortal.

My magic went to take them. A gunshot rang out. A sting clipped my shoulder, sending me stumbling. My hold on Sebastian faltered and I was sent soaring backwards.

The landing forced the air from my lungs, and I gasped, trying to get it back. Pain exploded in my chest, and the red in my vision flickered. A haze flooded into my mind, causing the world to blur.

I'd felt this before. I knew what it was. Only this was much stronger than at Onyx, worse than what Raven had used. This was far more potent than it should have been.

I rolled to my side and let out a gasp at the twinge when I tried to prop myself up on my injured arm. Lenore strode towards me, Castor and Sebastian behind her.

She crouched in front of me, eyes searching my face as my barrier of flames weakened to a dull glow. The two other witches stirred; I could still feel the faint brush of their magic, but the hold was fading too fast. My magic grappled to keep it from slipping.

I shoved myself onto my knees and swayed as the ground pitched beneath me.

"Give up," Lenore ordered, catching my chin and locking her eyes with mine. I tried to shake my head, but it swam even with that little effort.

She let out a breath of a laugh. "Emaleth, without the connection to your family's magic, you are *nothing.*"

Nostri sanguinis, viribus meis. The words flooded my mind, dousing the white hot pain of the drug that invaded my system.

Nostri sanguinis, viribus meis. They were here. I wasn't alone. Because the power wasn't the talisman or the words, it was *mine.*

My magic coursed through me, coiling around the invading drug and squeezing. It felt like my insides were being pulled, suffocated under the force needed to flush it from my system. I thought I'd buckle before it was clear.

"I've never been *nothing,*" I snarled and grabbed her wrist.

I opened the floodgates and let my magic flow through the connection. My nails punctured skin, and Lenore let out a cry. Her blood seeped into my skin, locking us together. Her magic was mine and she knew it, letting out a trembling gasp as my magic clicked into hers.

Her composure shattered. "Do something!" she screeched.

Castor and Sebastian rushed us. With a wave of my hand, I sent them flying backward, using her own magic against them.

She'd hurt Phoenix, Kane, Vadim. She'd taken Ian from me. And now she was going to hurt like I did. She let out a strangled cry as I forced myself to my feet and stood over her. She wanted power above all else; it was time she learned she'd never have it.

Another shot went off, and another sting in my shoulder sent me stumbling sideways. The flames faltered even more around us, and the two witches were almost completely out of my control. I tried to shake the dizziness from my mind as blood loss and this new drug threatened to send me to the ground.

Lenore threw me aside the second I dropped her arm. Breathing in the dirt I'd landed face-first in, I willed myself to not give in to the power-blocking drug. My whole body shook from fighting it and Lenore. I may have been able to tap into more power than ever before, but my body could only take so much.

"Hunters?" Castor growled as I rolled onto my back, coughing up the debris I'd accidently inhaled. It hurt to breathe. "You never said—"

"Shut up," Lenore snapped, breathing labored. "She has to *die*." Her voice was so laced with venom I flinched.

The dark sky looked down at me, firelight flickering in and out as my vision began to tunnel. Once I passed out, that was it—I'd be dead. But at least now Blythe and Thea wouldn't share my fate.

With a grunt and shaking arms, I pushed myself off the ground to face them. The clearing swirled around me as unconsciousness got closer. Another shot echoed through the trees. No pain came. Another shot. The ground swirled higher, reaching my knees. A long hiss sent the hair on my arm rising. A second hiss joined the first. Then a third. More shots. The flames around me turned purple, then black, then back to red before burning all three colors at once.

Grace—now the size of a large dog—appeared in front of me. She looked back at me, red eyes blazing as her hiss turned to an unearthly growl that caused the ground to shudder. Rhi joined her, then Attie a second later. The ground violently enough under their unified growls, I expected it to open under us.

"Sebastian!" Lenore shouted.

The flames around us grew higher with new colors.

"Sebastian!" she called again, panic flooding her tone. Lenore's continued confused shouts mingled with Castor's and the clamor of hunters as they fled from our familiars and the mist that was now almost to my chest.

They were here.

Grace stomped a paw on the ground as a hunter tried to rush her. I stumbled but Blythe ducked under my arm and kept me upright as she dragged me away from the chaos unfolding in the clearing.

"The fire," I muttered pathetically.

"Doesn't work on other coven members, apparently," she said with a slight smirk. We stumbled through the ring of flames, and Blythe slowly lowered me to the ground. I leaned against a tree and let out a long breath.

Thea jumped through the flames, a second later and hurried over to us. "You look like shit," she said, crouching down to examine my arm.

I opened my mouth to gargle some kind of response but shut it quickly as black edged into my vision.

Blythe snapped her fingers in front of my face. "You can't pass out on us," she said. "We can't carry both of you out of here."

I glanced to the side to see Lyra still lying on the ground. My chest tightened, knowing what that meant. My mind wanted to see more color in her cheeks and the soft rise and fall of her chest, but that's all it was—wishful thinking.

I shook my head. "Lenore needs to be stopped, here, now."

"And how do you propose we do that?" Thea asked.

I looked at Blythe. "Bind her," I said.

Blythe blinked at me. "What?"

"If I get some of her blood, you can bind her."

She shook her head. "Even if I could—"

"You can," I insisted. We'd been unknowingly bound for so long that second-guessing our capabilities was our first reaction. But I knew they had to feel it too, the untethered power we all had.

"*Even if*," she said a little louder. "Doing a binding in the perfect conditions is tricky. Like this, there's too much room for mistakes."

I swallowed and closed my eyes against the nausea that surged in my stomach. "It's the best chance we're going to get," I said, opening my eyes to look at her.

She bit her lip and glanced at Thea. "Em," she said slowly. "It could...she's..." Blythe took a deep breath. "*You're* part of her bloodline."

My stomach dropped when the reality of her words sank in. If she wasn't careful and it wasn't perfect, my magic could be bound—again.

My magic flared angrily at the thought. It had been locked away my entire life and wasn't going to be again, not without a fight.

I put my hand on her shoulder. "I trust you," I said, and her own eyes burned red. "Can you handle Sebastian and Castor?" I asked, turning to Thea.

The color drained from her face. "I—they don't know..."

"I think it's time we all stop hiding," I said as gently as I could.

She glanced at the ring of fire, still holding the others in place, and looked back at me before nodding. "Okay."

They helped me to my feet. I closed my eyes and took a deep breath to clear my head. With half a thought and a whip of power, the two witches that had been freed from my control went down again. They weren't a part of this.

Head clear, I was able to find the mortals, four of them searching for me. My magic latched onto their blood, and they, too, crumpled within two seconds of the command. Extensive blood loss wasn't doing me any favors, though, and that command was enough to pitch the ground underneath my feet.

Our cats, back to their realatively normal size, appeared next to us. Attie curled up next to Lyra while the other two stood guard. Grace gave me a small, encouraging meow.

I swallowed and faced the flames again. "I'll get you as much as I can," I told Blythe.

She nodded and squared her shoulders, stepping up next to me.

Thea came to stand on my other side and tightened the tie around her hair, jaw set.

We stepped through the flames together. They parted for us, the fire nothing but a feather-light touch against my magic. Comforting.

The scene before us a vastly different one than when I'd been pulled out of the clearing a minute ago: Lenore, bravado gone, clutched her arm where my nails had drawn blood while Castor bent over it working to repair the damage. Sebastian had a significant gash above his eye and was ready to bolt the moment he saw us.

Castor froze, golden magic fading as he watched us move closer. Lenore had the good sense to look afraid for once.

Alone, we were formidable. Together we were unstoppable.

Chapter 32

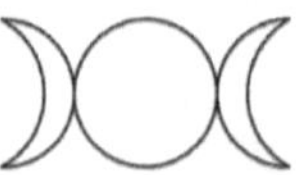

Lenore didn't hesitate and raised her hand at us. Blythe ducked to the side, reaching for what little supplies were left from the unbinding to use for her own spell. Thea called every dead branch to her in a swipe of her hands and a swirl of purple mist before sending them hurtling towards the three witches. Burning leaves and the rot of death filled the air and made my eyes water.

My magic caught Lenore's before she could get a hold on any of us. Sebastian let out a scream and dove out of the way of Thea's magic as Castor stepped in front of Lenore, throwing his own hands up, and his golden magic collided with Thea's. The impact echoed like thunder in the small clearing and sent Castor stumbling away.

His eyes widened as he stared at her. "You—" But she didn't let him finish, as roots shot forward under her power. He leapt out of the way and Thea rushed at him, magic swirling around her arms in purple bands.

Lenore sent a crystal dagger soaring towards me; I ducked in time to keep it from lodging in my neck, but not quickly enough to stop it from it grazing my skin. I rounded back to her and saw her eyes darting around in panic. She'd counted on the hunters taking me out before she had to face me.

I charged. She threw up her hands. I braced for the sensation of being thrown back again—only, it never came. A root shot up, catching my foot. I tumbled over and caught myself with my outstretched forearm. The snap came at the same time as the shooting pain.

Letting out a cry, I rolled over, cradling my wrist against my chest, sure it was broken. My eyes blurred from pained tears. Sucking in a breath, I twisted to my feet and faced her again, keeping my injured wrist tight against myself.

Thea had drawn Castor's attention, and Sebastian crawled away from the fight as the fullness of what Thea's power was became evident. I didn't blame him for wanting to get as far away as he could.

Castor held his own, sending bolts of golden power at her to keep the touch of her death magic from getting too close, but I could see the effort took a toll.

Lenore crooked her finger towards herself, and the knife whirled past my ear as it soared back into her open hand. She wrapped her slender fingers around the hilt and pointed it at me.

"This would be easier for everyone if you'd just give up," she said through a sneer. She couldn't take my power with that knife unwillingly. That's what she still fought for. Compliance. Obedience.

The dagger hovered above her outstretched palm, vibrating as if waiting anxiously to do what it was made for. My magic latched into hers, keeping her from sending it anywhere. She was stronger than any witch I'd held before, even now. Her magic was pushing back, and I wasn't sure I'd be able to get close enough to do what I needed to.

Her arm trembled, ready to use that knife against me as soon as her magic won out.

Cold sweat broke out on my back as I took a shuddering step closer to her. Closer. Like wading through wet sand, my feet dragged slowly closer. My magic held onto hers, but the sheer force of it set my teeth on edge.

Then, I was in front of her, and the dagger was in my hand.

My hold collapsed.

I struck.

She sucked in a breath against the pain, and I knew what was coming. I tackled her to the ground and pressed the sleeve of my sweater against the cut I'd made in her arm, holding it there as long as I could before she sent me flying off of her.

I landed in a crunch on the burnt ground. Blythe scooted over, eyes roaming over me. "Are you okay?"

I grunted, the only response I could muster after being thrown around again. Sitting up, I hooked the edge of the knife under my sleeve and ripped. The fabric fell away, and I nodded towards it.

Blythe picked it up by the torn edge, careful not to get any of Lenore's blood onto her own skin, and hurried back to the small circle she'd made for her binding.

Now I just had to give her time. Taking a deep breath to steel myself, I rose and squared my shoulders, the movement angering the gunshot wounds in my arm. I closed my eyes, breathing in through my nose, against the pain, against the sorrow, against any thoughts of hopelessness that desperately wanted to bleed in.

I wasn't able to help Phoenix. I'd lost Vadim. I'd failed Kane. I couldn't bring Lyra back.

But I could save *them*. The friends who came without hesitation. Hazel, Sofia, Devya. Z, and Astrid. The Emissaries abandonad by the Council they swore to protect. Rez, Sadiki, Leander, Jax. My family. Wes, Chad, Ian. My *coven*. She would never hurt any of them ever again.

Blythe's hushed spell reached me, and I opened my eyes to take a step forward, then another, and another. I was facing Lenore once again. Her hair a mess, her face enraged. This was not the order she wanted—demanded—of us.

Sebastian had fled. I no longer felt his magic nearby. Castor was in a losing fight with Thea's powerful death magic, and she was holding back.

Lenore stepped out to meet me. She'd always wanted my power for herself; we both knew that truth. But, if she wanted to stop me now, she was going to have to kill me.

Her eyelids fluttered, and her hand went to her chest at the same time I felt a tug at my magic. It made me flinch so hard that my knees almost buckled. A grip tightened around my core and I gasped, trying to stay upright.

Blythe's binding.

I swallowed, hard. It had been a risk. But a risk worth taking. Lenore stared at me, eyes flashing with rage and hatred. She clawed at her chest as if she could rip away the spell.

Her breaths heaved as her mind and magic fought against what was happening. My own magic clawed at the binding that wanted to re-cage my power. It dug in, refusing to be buried again. It was like losing mom all over again. Tears leaked from my eyes, and I let out a breath; this was what had to be done. This was a punishment we would share. Penance for the harm we'd both caused.

Only, atonement never came for me. My magic didn't curl into a ball to be locked away. The uncomfortable tug was gone and my magic flared hot through my veins, free and full. Lenore continued to scrape at her herself, but she had fallen to the ground, screaming.

Castor ran to her, sliding to her side as he called his magic to heal her. But there was nothing he could do. This wasn't something he could fix.

Thea came to stand next to me, power radiating from her and her eyes glowing a bright purple even against the light from the boundary fire.

"Do something," Lenore hissed to Castor.

His hands were caged in golden light as he searched for something to heal.

"There's nothing he can do," I said. "You've been bound by a Blood Witch. Only she can reverse it."

Lenore glared up at me, hand shooting out weakly as if to use her magic, but nothing happened.

Castor looked up at us and made to move, but Thea's hand twitched and the purple mist solidified into a scythe in her grip.

He settled back on the dirt, sitting protectively with Lenore, whose hard expression lost its strength as her eyes welled with tears. I tried to muster sympathy for her, for what she lost. But nothing came.

Blythe stepped up on the other side of me, her own power thrumming through her and eyes as red as the flames around us.

"It's over," I said simply, exhaustion threatening to take over as the abuse my body had taken started to surface. My wrist ached. My vision blurred, and I could feel at least one bullet still in my arm.

Lenore's lip quivered, and Castor looked to her as if waiting for instructions. She heaved a deep breath and hung her head. She had no choice to accept it. She'd lost.

The Triple Moon Coven had returned.

Chapter 33

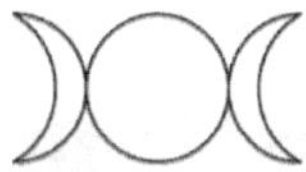

Flickering candlelight sent shadows dancing across the polished surface of the round oak table. Everyone could see everyone, and there was no head. In the center stood a slightly raised platform for petitioners or appellants to make their case.

The large table had belonged to the Mother Witch—my ancestor—Mary Boswell. It had survived the sham trials the hunters used to try to wipe out the bloodlines and seen many disputes settled among witches since. Now, it was only used on major conflicts that involved both the Collective and the Outliers.

This was the first time in over three hundred years that thirteen witches sat at the table. The first time since Amity that her coven was represented. Each seat had a carving in front of it to symbolize the coven present. A triple moon symbol in front of me, a flame in a five-pointed star for Ignis, hands circling a spiral for Prudentia, and so on.

The high-back chair was old and probably important, but incredibly uncomfortable. Blythe was on my left, given a small stool to sit on, and Thea on my right with a wooden folding chair that let out a creak with each shift in movement. I doubted they were any more comfortable than

I was, probably less so since they were on the receiving end of more than one glare from the others.

Only one representative from each coven was welcome at the table. That had been the topic of argument for some time after I'd made it clear I wouldn't attend alone. Lenore may have been powerless against me now, the full Council was another story—and I wasn't about to give them my trust any time soon.

"It's simply not what is done," Xavier—head of Viatores—said for what felt like the thousandth time. His clasped hands tightened on each other as if he were resisting the urge to use whatever magic he had to punctuate his point.

"It's hardly the most unconventional part of this meeting," Melantha—head of Ventus—said.

Xavier let out a huff. "It disrupts the rulings of the Congregation," he continued. He unfolded his hands to point at me. "She has already caused enough trouble. If we allow her to—"

"I am more than willing to leave," I said.

Some of his fight dissipated at that. "That's not what I meant," he said.

"If I stay, they stay," I declared, crossing my arms and doing my best to believe my own act of belonging. Despite the symbol in front of me and the power vibrating under my skin, I felt small and young in the too-large room.

"That's not how things are done," he repeated like he was scolding a toddler. That didn't help my nerves, but it also made me angry enough that my magic stirred, itching to show him how *I* did things.

But, unlike before we'd been unbound, I was able to keep it in check. It may want to force him to shut up, but that's because so did I. It didn't feel separate anymore; I had an easy control, a strange sensation I was still getting used to.

"Considering more than half of you were fine with Lenore killing me..." I began. More than a few heads dipped down to avoid eye contact, "I won't stay if they're not here."

"A rift like this needs to be repaired, quickly," Cyrus—head of Videntis—said. Or maybe he was Viatores and Xavier was Videntis. I couldn't keep them straight.

All I knew was that Xavier had been an open supporter of Lenore until recently. Cyrus was an unknown as far who he had sided with when my grandmother plotted to kill me, but the way he spoke and held himself was far too much like a smarmy politician for my taste.

"It's not my job to fix what you broke," I stated, straightening as much as I could against the chair. "I'm only here to make sure Lenore doesn't get off the hook, *again*."

Nicholas, Lenore's replacement at the meeting, shifted in his seat.

"This meeting is for coven leaders only," Xavier insisted.

"Then you get all three of us," I said firmly. "We don't have a leader."

He wasn't the only one unable to hide their surprise. I even felt Blythe's piercing eyes on me, as if she was trying to send a silent question through the side of my skull.

"That is unwise," Cyrus said calmly.

"So is pissing me off," I snapped before I could stop myself. I'd planned on staying calm, reasonable. But we'd been going back and forth on this for almost an hour, and I was ridiculously over it.

"Is that a threa—"

"Xavier," Martin interjected. "Let us not forget that Emaleth is here as a courtesy."

"A courtesy! She is required—"

"To do nothing," Martin finished. "She is neither a member of a Collective coven nor an Outlier. You cannot require anything of her any more than I can."

I bit back the reminder that he had *required* something of me when he thought I would help him keep Blythe from trying to unbind our lines. If we hadn't succeeded in that, there'd be no way he'd be backing me right now.

Of course, if we hadn't succeeded in unbinding the lines, we'd all be dead.

"I am more than content to allow her cooperation to be on her terms. If Emaleth will not sit without her coven members, you will hear no argument from me."

"Nor me," Ambrose agreed.

"Tenebris takes no issue with their attendance," Agnes offered. The other covens of the Outliers chimed in with their agreement and the gap in the vote grew closer.

"You know my feelings on the matter," Selene said. The edge to her voice invited no argument—and even if she'd sounded more herself, I doubted anyone would dare. She'd lost a granddaughter to Lenore's attempted power grab; there was nothing she'd hear to change her mind.

I swallowed and looked down at my hands to avoid her bright blue gaze.

Melantha and another Collective coven leader—Yvette—came next, and with that Lenore's supporters were outnumbered. I wasn't sure how far what had happened in the Salem Woods had spread by this point. Far enough, at least, that everyone at this table knew what I'd done, what my power had done. Blythe's identity as another Blood Witch was public knowledge, and Thea had been outed as a Death Witch to the Council.

But, just how powerful we all were now that we were unbound? Even *I* wasn't sure of that yet.

Xavier let out a huff. "Very well," he conceded and refolded his hands. He glared at me but kept his mouth shut.

Martin stood. "Seeing as there is no way to find a true arbitrator in this, I move to cast judgment by vote."

"I will second that motion." Cyrus inclined his head to Martin. "But with the caveat that the Triple Moon Coven only receives one vote," he said. "That all its members agree to."

An unease settled in my gut at the implication laced in his words. Would we agree on our vote? Thea and I hadn't seen eye to eye on a lot since we first met. I caught Blythe's eye as she gave me a small nod. I looked at Thea, who sat with her arms crossed over a suit jacket like she'd expected a job interview and gotten an interrogation instead. I swallowed.

"Seeing as no other coven is allowed other members, it seems the only fair recourse," Cyrus continued.

"No one is disagreeing with you on that point, Cyrus," Martin said coolly.

I glanced around, trying to gauge reactions. As I'd never been in a meeting like this before, I wasn't sure if this was a normal thing. It didn't feel normal; the way both Martin and Cyrus were having some kind of stare-off, I knew I'd stepped into the middle of something between them. Even if they allowed us three votes, that would still make one of us the tiebreaker. I couldn't imagine they'd want to be deadlocked forever.

Nods and affirmative murmurs swirled around the room after Martin spoke. Every eye turned to us, and Blythe nodded to the two leaders first. I took a deep breath and agreed. Thea's fists clenched against her crossed arms, but after a painfully long second, she inclined her head in concession.

Martin gave me what I could only assume was a proud smile and sat down. I swallowed, and my heart sped up as I waited. I didn't know what to expect now that it had finally been decided that Blythe, Thea, and I were staying.

This all was very official. It felt a little like after mom died, when we had to go court to finalize Wes and Chad taking me in. Except that had been one mortal judge, not twelve critical witches.

"First order of business," Cyrus started, pulling out a tablet and tapping the screen a few times, "is the petition to release the three Emissaries from their oath's punishment."

Martin cleared his throat.

Cyrus's yellow eyes darted to him. "Assembly member Foster?"

"I believe there should be four names in the petition," Martin corrected.

Cyrus cleared his throat and glanced back down at the tablet. "Three Emissaries and one dissenter," he said with a pointed look back at Martin.

Martin's jaw ticked, but he didn't say anything.

"The names, for the record, are," Cyrus continued, "Sadiki Ochola, Leander Tsipras, Ajax Tsipras, and Reznor Dorsey." He paused as if waiting for an invisible scribe to record them. He looked around the table. "Do we have any arguments for keeping bound the four named forementioned?"

My heart stopped for a moment, waiting for Cyrus or Xavier to say something, and I mentally prepared my own reasons to undo their magical binding. I wasn't sure what I'd do if they chose not to side with me in the end.

"The dissenter," Yvette asked. "Did he give a reason for his abandonment of his duties?"

Cyrus looked to Martin.

"He felt as if his personal morals were at odds with the assignment given to him," Martin explained. "He chose to leave service at that time."

"Could he have not pursued a petition to this Council to be given leave?" Xavier asked.

"He was young," Martin replied. "Had he sought my advice, I would have directed him to do just that."

"It sounds as if he let his emotions overrule his sense," Cyrus offered.

Martin opened his mouth.

"He chose to leave," I interjected. "And *he* didn't resort to attempted murder to try to regain his power."

Cyrus looked over at me like he was evaluating a new car for flaws. A bitter tang filled the air for a moment—one I vaguely recognized.

"We do not weigh one witch's actions against another's here, Ms. Boswell," he said slowly.

I folded my hands on the table in front of me, black brace on my wrist making it hard to feel like the gesture was a strong one. "Rez has spent how many years bound?" I asked.

Cyrus checked his notes. "Seven," he answered, looking back up at me.

"Seven years, and have you ever had an issue with him?"

Cyrus raised an eyebrow.

"*Other* than helping me," I added.

"No," Selene answered before Cyrus could. "Reznor has caused this Council no issue since his departure," she said. "And his business has brought jobs and additional revenue to Salem."

"A club he neglected to let our unit into when it sought a fugitive," Xavier offered.

"They didn't have the proper paperwork," Martin countered with a shrug. "My own lawyer looked it over after you improperly closed the establishment, as you will remember, Councilman Delacourt."

Xavier's grip on his own hand tightened, his knuckles blanching. "I remember," he through gritted teeth.

Martin inclined his head but said nothing else.

Cyrus watched the exchange curiously. When no one else spoke for a moment, he continued. "Are there any other arguments against?"

No one offered anything.

"Very well," Cyrus said, tapping on the tablet. "A vote. In favor?"

All but two raised their hands.

"Opposed?"

Xavier and Cyrus raised their hands.

"Petition is granted," Cyrus stated. "Their marks will be cleared and their magic untethered within twenty-four hours of these proceedings' end."

He tapped a few more times on the tablet. "Next order," he began. "Regarding the knowledge of one Chadwick Bell in matters concerning witches and witchcraft."

"Excuse me?" I blurted.

Cyrus looked up at me. "It is a concern of this Congregation how much a mortal knows about our—"

"This *Congregation* doesn't need to be concerned with my uncle," I shot, a faint red mist forming around my clasped fists.

"It is our job to protect witches, Ms. Boswell," Cyrus said. "Exposure to mortals threatens our safety."

The mist grew heavier, turning into a crackling red electric current.

Cyrus's eyes went to my hands.

"This concern was not brought to my attention," Selene said.

"Nor mine," Martin added.

"It was my own finding," Cyrus said flatly. "One I want discussed."

I felt Blythe's hand on my arm, a subtle reminder that attacking someone here and now was a terrible idea. But that didn't stop me from wanting to shut Cyrus up. If he thought I'd let *them* vote on whether or not Chad got to keep his memories of me—of Wes—they had a fight worse than words on their hands.

"Note the record of your discomfort," Selene said. "We are not here to determine how Em and her family chose to operate."

Cyrus opened his mouth to argue.

"Any vote you bring forth on this matter, I will abstain from," Selene snapped. "Next item."

Cyrus glared at her for a long moment before giving up and tapping the screen a few more times. "Very well." He picked up an obsidian gavel.

"Present the accused." His voice amplified and echoed around the room as he banged the gavel.

My skin pricked, and the magic around my hands flared. I rolled my fingers into my fists as I hid my hands underneath the table.

Three bells chimed, and the platform in the center of the table sank into the floor, only to return, a few moments later, Lenore standing on it. Her expression was hard, eyes filled with anger, and her posture upright and stiff. Almost as though, despite the situation, she held onto the belief that she was still in control.

Her glare fell on me.

"Lenore Jeanne Charlevoix," Cyrus said. "You stand accused of treason, attempted pilferage, and wrongful death."

Thea shifted next to me, and I had to resist the urge to turn to her. She'd been exposed as a Death Witch—but as far as we were aware, no one knew that she was a Necromancer or what we'd attempted in the woods that night. And we needed to keep it that way if the three of us wanted to stay off that platform ourselves.

"How do you answer?" Cyrus asked.

Lenore stuck her chin in the air. "Self-defense," she stated.

I couldn't stop the snort, and Martin shot me a warning glare.

"Noted," Cyrus said. "You may proceed."

Not reacting was the hardest part. We all sat there while Lenore defended herself—what she'd done to try and get my power. Some of the gaps were filled in for me. She'd decided I was a danger to witch kind after I'd used my power on Kane and Leander the day we'd encountered Armin the first time. Their report to the Council after leaving Portland was the catalyst for her campaign. Lyra had clocked that.

From there, Lenore worked to get others on her side using Isobel Jacob's words and the proof Kane had brought them. As she spoke, it dawned on me that she *actually* believed what she'd done was for the greater good of the covens. She'd thought the prophecy applied to me, that I would start the war to end all the covens.

And she still did. Even with Blythe and Thea sitting on either side of me—two other thirteenth daughters—she honestly thought *I* was the ultimate ruination.

In her case, maybe I was. She had started out a powerful coven leader and a Council member. Now her power was bound, and she was being forced to defend herself to the very witches she used to lead. I had been *her* undoing, prophecy or not.

She had a harder time justifying working with the hunters. Even Xavier's questions regarding her feeding information to Armin and Sasha were accusatory. No matter what her reasoning, she wasn't able to convince a single one of them *that* had been necessary.

Hearing her rehash her version of the last few months made it clear we were never going to be anything other than enemies to each other. She certainly never wanted to be family.

Once she finished telling her story and answering the few questions the others had, the platform descended again, and we were left to discuss.

I didn't listen too closely, didn't offer anything, and no one asked me to elaborate on any one point. It didn't matter what Lenore said; I'd decided already. Perhaps it wasn't fair to ignore the arguments of her supporters, but she hadn't earned fairness from me.

Because too many people had died because of her. Phoenix, Vadim, even Kane.

Lyra. Nothing would justify that.

After what felt like hours, the Congregation called for a vote. No one bought the self-defense plea, but her punishment was another story. The decision wasn't what I would have chosen had it just been me, but it would have to do.

Lenore returned to the center of the table, her chin high and confident. A smirk touched her lips—she thought she'd won. She thought her supporters had done right by her.

Martin cleared his throat and stood at the same time Cyrus did. "You have been found guilty on two of three counts," Martin announced.

Treason had been the hold out. It was a hard one to prove, considering I hadn't declared for either Collective or Outliers. Apparently, you couldn't commit treason on a freelancer.

Martin continued. "As your power has already been bound, that punishment will remain for a minimum of twenty years."

Lenore's smirk vanished.

Cyrus clasped his hands in front of him. "You will serve ten years at Stromford," he stated. "After which time, you will be evaluated for release. If this Congregation determines you are eligible, you will be remanded to the custody of Senann Coven to focus on healing that which you have wronged for the remainder of your sentence."

Selene stood. "Once your sentence has been completed, you will present yourself again to determine if your power will be restored."

Lenore's glare focused on Selene. "And who decides if I've *earned* my power back?"

"This Congregation," Martin replied. "Whomever may sit on it at the time."

Her eyes flashed to Blythe. "What if the Osborne girl disagrees with their decision?"

That was the issue in the very end. Blythe had been the one to bind Lenore; she'd used her blood to ensure that no other witch could undo it, no matter how powerful. If she decided to keep it in place against the Congregation's orders, there wasn't much anyone could do about it.

This whole meeting, they'd all acted as if they had the power, but we all knew how wrong they were.

"She will be made to," Cyrus said.

Blythe let out a soft breath of a laugh.

"I assure you," Martin began, "Blythe has no intention of defying the Congregation."

I turned slightly to catch Blythe's eye, and she gave me a slight eyebrow raise. I turned back to face the table, biting my lip to keep my smile from spreading. We'd been defying the Congregation for weeks.

Chapter 34

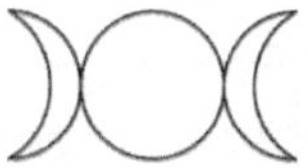

Selene sat in the center of the stage with Lyra's parents on either side of her. Jax sat next to his mother, Leander on the other side of his father. They were on display; the family of the fallen witch for all the mourners to stare at.

They all wore black with hints of yellow. Lyra's favorite color. Castor's tie, Selene's silk scarf, Jax's pocket square. We all followed the same wishes of the family. Blythe swapped her black nail polish for yellow, Thea had worn a chunky yellow necklace, and I had a set of citrine bracelets on the wrist not covered with a brace. Dots of yellow in a sea of black—Lyra would have thought it ridiculous

She would have, however, loved the turnout. I knew she was popular, but this was impressive. I recognized a few witches from the Solstice party and even a few sprites scattered among the seated guests. Lyra had been one easily drawn to.

Bright spring sunlight bore down on the tops of our heads and perfectly illuminated the golden trumpet tree planted in Lyra's memory. Its growth sped up, so the flowers were in full bloom by the time the service started.

The Council sat directly in front of the stage with a few Outlier leaders behind them. Most were here for show only, a way to pretend like they hadn't seen what Lenore was doing and could have stopped it. Lenore and her supporters may have been outed, but that hardly absolved the others.

They'd asked me to sit with them for the memorial after the Congregation finished its meeting. I'd given them hard pass—on both the offer of a seat on the Council and a seat with them at the memorial. If they honestly believed I'd want anything to do with them after everything, they were more delusional than I thought.

"She was such a beautiful person," the red-headed woman sitting on the other side of Blythe sobbed, dabbing a yellow kerchief to the corner of her eye. I tried not to roll my eyes too hard.

Blythe put her hand over her mouth and bent her head to hide her laugh. This had been a bad idea; we should have skipped altogether.

"Did you know her well?" the woman asked, leaning over to us.

"Shhh," I admonished as Selene stood to address the crowd.

Her eulogy was nice, proper, dignified, as was fitting for someone in her position. I knew she was staying poised for the benefit of the rest of the family. If she broke, they would. And this was not the place they were allowed to grieve. That was to be kept private.

Lyra's mother sobbed quietly, clutching Jax's hand as he stared straight ahead. Castor's jaw was clenched so hard I imagined teeth cracking, like the lake outside the house back in Ohio as the weather warmed. Anything to keep up appearances. Hopefully, the guilt of facing what he'd tried to avoid Lyra's whole life because Lenore forced our hand was enough to eat away at him.

I wondered if he was replaying every choice he'd made. Lying to her about who her mother was—about the rest of her family's fates—and forcing her to train as an Emissary while knowing she hadn't wanted it.

Neither of us would ever know if one of those choices led to why we were ultimately sitting here.

I wondered, because that's exactly what I was doing. Running through everything we'd done since meeting at Onyx. Wondering if I'd taken the right path when given a fork in the road. If I hadn't let her come with me that night would there be a golden trumpet tree magically growing in her memory? *What-ifs* were all I seemed to have left these days.

Castor stood to speak after his mother and delivered a mechanical description of Lyra, one that failed to truly capture her. Had his speech been written for him? He'd been with Lenore in the woods and, as of now, his punishment had yet to be decided.

It would be a Council decision now that Lenore had been found guilty. His guilt wouldn't be influenced by any *external* forces. I didn't care if I got a say about what happened to Castor in the end. His mother could protect him if she chose to.

Sebastian was missing from the memorial. He had been, essentially, given a slap on the wrist: sixty days bound and ninety no contact with Lenore or his coven while he did their version of community service. I may not have liked it, but in the end, he had only done what his family told him to; I couldn't really fault him too much for that.

A gentle brush on my ankles made me reach down instinctively and scratch Grace's head. She'd appeared under my chair once we'd sat down, lounging quietly while we listened to the speeches and the ripple of sniffs and soft sobs. After the woods, I'd expected them to vanish, their job done. But she stayed.

Rhi was under Blythe's chair and Attie squeezed between them, eyes unblinking and forward, but every now and then those eyes would narrow on the red-headed woman with displeasure.

As long as she stayed under the chair, we'd be fine, but I didn't need her wandering around and drawing more attention to us.

Soft applause rustled through the air after Castor's speech, and then Cyrus climbed the steps to the stage to give words of encouragement to the gathered witches. As most were Collective members, I was sure it was part memorializing Lyra and part campaigning. With Lenore out and her temporary replacement hardly the shark she was, there was a power vacuum to fill. And Cyrus knew it.

American goldfinches chirped the end to the service as they danced from branch to branch of the golden trumpet tree. As her immediate family descended from the stage, the rest of us stood and the quiet murmur of dozens of conversations started to fill the lawn.

I smoothed out the skirt of my black dress and scrunched my toes in my shoes. I'd borrowed black heels from Sofia, as the last time I wore black heels was at mom's funeral, and Devya had lent me the dress. I'd avoided buying or wearing black dresses since mom, so I was thankful Blythe's friends were willing to loan me clothes.

Blythe and Rhi went to get lemonade that was set out further from the center of the seating; meanwhile, with the wave of a few hands and murmured spells, the chairs were replaced with round standing tables.

I moved to the edge of the mingling, Grace and Attie next to me. The tables, refreshments, and black attire reminded me a lot of the Esbat at Martin's, only sunnier.

Jax, Leander, and their parents stood near the stage to shake hands and thank people for coming. Everyone's hand would feel the same—numb. That's how it had been. Condolences and apologies for their loss would be said so often the words would lose all meaning before the day was over.

Thea stood near Jax while he gave short smiles to people. Rez stood next to Leander, acting as some sort of bouncer, daring people to say more than they were allowed.

My wrist had been healed enough by Wes and Sofia that I didn't need a full cast, but the scar that ran from Leander's forehead to his chin would be there forever. It dimmed the bright blue of his right eye into a cloudy mess. No one knew what spell had caught him to cause it, but he hadn't been as sharp as he was before.

My eyes caught Sadiki on the opposite edge of the crowd, watching the family as well. I hadn't seen him shed a tear, but I knew he was grieving in his own way. The playfulness I'd come to love was gone, his face hardened to stone. He'd been given a nasty burn on his upper arm that night. A scar, he said he would wear with pride for doing what was right, but that didn't mean my heart couldn't ache for him.

His eyes turned to me. He gave me a small smile and a nod that I reciprocated before he turned and walked away. I had no idea if I'd ever see him again. I hoped I would. But unlike Jax, he had chosen not to return to service after his power had been restored. A decision the Council had no choice but to respect.

Attie slunk away and closed the distance between Blythe and me faster than any normal cat could. I watched her go as the red-headed woman cornered Blythe in a patch of grass near the table of refreshments. No matter how much Attie swiped at the woman's ankles, she wouldn't take the hint and leave.

Grace sat next to me and let out a disapproving meow. A chilled breeze that opposed the sunlight swept through the courtyard, sending a shiver running up my bare arms.

"I find that unusual," Cyrus said, stepping up next to me.

I crossed my arms to keep the chill from spreading. "You're going to need to be more specific," I advised, not looking at him.

"That her familiar has stayed," he noted. "They usually return to the Otherworld when their witch passes."

Grace let out a soft hiss.

"I hardly think either of us knows enough about the Otherworld to decide what's *normal*," I countered, keeping my eye on Attie as she sat and practically pouted at the redhead.

His silence could be seen as a concession to my observation, but I knew better. He wasn't here for small talk. Blythe glanced around as the redhead said something that she didn't like.

Grace leaned her long body against my leg as if in support, and I tried not to draw attention to the scene unfolding. As much as I hated it, Cyrus's attention needed to stay focused on me.

"I've been sent to ask you to reconsider," he said.

I sighed and turned to face him, but not before noticing the way Jax was watching the exchange between Blythe and the woman. We didn't need him paying too close attention either.

"They thought you were the best choice for that?" I asked. Selene would have been the obvious choice. Yvette, even. One I liked, and the other I didn't know well enough to have an opinion, yet.

He inclined his head to my point. "We thought it best to keep up appearances that we are of one mind in this endeavor."

I let out a soft snort.

"I do not believe you are sorted for it," he continued. "But that does not mean I don't believe your decision unwise." Thea caught my eye through the crowd, and I nodded towards Blythe as subtly as I could. She frowned but followed my hint, letting out a huff and excusing herself from the greeting line once she saw the two of them.

"I really don't care what you think," I said, looking back to Cyrus. "The Assembly has their representative, and you have yours. I don't know why you feel the need to continue talking about it."

Blythe closed her eyes and let out a long breath at something the woman said as Thea appeared at her side and began speaking to them.

Cyrus put his hands in his pockets. "Traditionally, the seat is taken by the coven leader."

"We've already told you," I said. "We don't have a leader."

"That is—"

"Unwise," I finished for him. "So, you've said." I took a breath as the woman continued to talk to Blythe and Thea in a way that had them both looking around, panicked.

"You've given up the ability to have significant influence—"

"I don't need influence on *your* Council," I snapped.

He shook his head, his yellow eyes searching my face. "If either of them chooses to decide against you," he said, "you'll have no power to protect your family." He straightened his black tie and ran a hand along it, smoothing non-existent wrinkles. "You must understand, Ms. Boswell," he continued. "Your coven has dominion over life, death, and power itself. That makes you *all* targets." He put his hands in his pockets and stood to his full height as if trying to emphasize the difference in our statures. "There isn't a witch living that does not fear you."

I held his stare for long enough he shifted on his feet, clearly uncomfortable with the prolonged silence. "Good." Without giving him the chance to answer, I turned back to Blythe, Thea, and the redheaded woman. The three of them were now openly having a hushed argument while Rhi and Attie rolled around in the grass with each other.

Allowing a small thread of my magic to reach towards him, it connected with his easily, like taking a breath without thinking. Hex magic greeted my own power, but mine latched on stronger. His magic came to his defense quickly, yet it was barely a knuckle brush against a brick wall.

His breath caught, and he took a half-step away from me, hand going to his chest.

"My power doesn't come from a seat at a table," I told him. The muscles in his neck strained as he struggled to throw off my magic. I sent it deeper, strangling his ability to use his against me, and held him in place even as I felt his need to run.

I turned my red gaze to meet his bewildered yellow eyes, burning with his magic's attempt to mount a defense. "And today is *not* the day to threaten me." I released him.

He gulped down a breath, the cracks in his confidence obvious.

"I wasn't—"

"Come near me, my family, or my coven, and the Congregation won't be the one deciding your fate," I said, voice low and deep with power.

His eyes widened with alarm, but I didn't give him the chance to have the last word and hand out more veiled threats. I wasn't in the mood, and by the looks of things, Blythe and Thea weren't having any luck with the redhead who refused to be ignored and—in my opinion—was being far too obvious to stick around any longer.

We'd all told her it was a bad idea, but Lyra had insisted on attending her own memorial.

Chapter 35

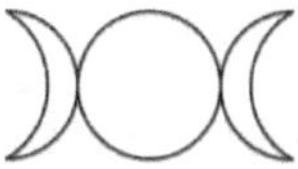

The Boston Emissarial Post was a lot like a college campus. Administrative buildings, conference rooms for briefings, training facilities that were basically specialized gyms, and blocks of dorms for the trainees and visiting units. In the center of the manicured lawns and walkways stood a bronze cast statue of the Mother Witch, hair flowing wildly behind her as she wielded her power to drive the hunters out of Salem.

They'd given me a room to stay in while the Congregation met, and Lyra's memorial was held. Blythe had gone back to her apartment, and Thea already had an assigned room at the post. Calling it a "room" didn't do it justice, though. Mine was set up more like a studio than anything else: small kitchen with an eating space, full bathroom, and a wall separating a living area from the sleeping arrangement. The windows overlooked the statue of Mary Boswell, but I was high enough to see the outline of the harbor just beyond campus.

Early morning sunlight had woken me before my alarm, and that gave me too many free hours before Blythe came to pick me up. I didn't have much to pack after only five days and a couple changes of clothes, so that task didn't keep me nearly busy enough.

Instead of staying cooped up, I decided to head out for fresh air. Being in this room felt a little too much like when they'd tried to keep me locked in my own house.

A group of young witches jogged by in all-black athletic wear embroidered with the post's trainee emblem, teasing each other on their pace. Their laughter echoed off the walls of the buildings around us as I stared at the statue.

Mary had been sculpted with her chin held high, proud. Her hand outstretched towards the long-gone threat of the Salem hunters. An image of strength and protection.

Did the other schools or posts named for her daughters have similar monuments to her? Were there any memorials for the witches she sacrificed to keep her youngest daughter's life? An empty, unsellable lot on the outskirts of Salem was the only thing that came to mind.

I squinted up against the early sun at her face. Stoic, cold and hard. It wasn't difficult to imagine how accurate this depiction was. I only had Amity's records to go off of, but Mary never struck me as the warm and affectionate type.

"Kane's great-great-grandfather was the sculptor."

I didn't need to turn around to know it was Jax. My magic sensed his, warm and golden and no longer locked away.

"He pretended like it was no big deal," Jax continued, coming to stand right next to me. "But he was proud of it."

I hadn't seen him since the memorial. And even that had been the first time since the Salem Woods. Units had converged on the clearing after Lenore's power had been bound. Jax, Leander, and Sadiki had all been detained under Council orders. Between that, my own meetings with various coven leaders, and the memorial, this was the first real chance we had to speak.

He stood with his hands in his pockets. The cuts and bruises he'd gotten while in the woods all healed, with only a light scar on his chin left to show for it. His eyes had returned to their bright blue with cracks of gold now that his magic had been released.

His black button-up was open at the collar, the sleeves rolled up to expose his forearms, and the pocket had his Emissarial ensign on it. A bright white hawk with its wings spread, clutching a holly branch in its talons, over a witch knot stitched with golden thread.

I'd seen the symbol a few times since being here—the same for every Emissary, except for the color of the thread used to stitch the knot. A symbol of strength and protection. What the Emissaries were supposed to be.

I looked up at Mary's face one more time before turning my back to her and looking out over the quad. "Makes sense."

He shifted on his feet. "I went by your room," he said.

I shrugged. "Woke up early."

He sighed. "Want to grab some tea?" he asked with a small smile. "I have a little time before my next briefing."

"Sure," I said, slinging my bag over my shoulder. We fell into step with each other as he led me from the center of campus down the walking path. More witches jogged by, giving us room by cutting onto the grass.

A few Emissaries dressed like Jax passed us, nodding to him as they did, with more than one giving me a wary glance—something I was going to have to get used to. I'd kept myself hidden for so long that even if I had encountered other witches, they likely wouldn't have known anything about me.

Now, however, everyone here knew who I was. The witch that took Lenore Charlevoix down. The witch who ended the Scholz family of hunters. The last Boswell. Blood Witch. Stares were to be expected.

But it wasn't just stares. I'd inherited more than the family name and power; I'd inherited centuries of fear about Blood Witches, and my display of power in the woods only fed into that fear. But what made it hard to sleep some nights wasn't that I was feared, but that a too large part of me enjoyed it.

One of the dining halls had a walk-up window for drinks at the opposite end of the quad from the dorms I'd stayed in. Jax got his coffee, and I got lavender tea with extra honey. As we walked back down the path in silence I watched as the quad filled with more trainees starting their day and had to wander if this is what my life would have looked like if I had been raised like them. I didn't think it would be better, just different.

"Rumor is you turned down a seat," Jax said, breaking into my thoughts.

I took a stalling sip. "I did."

He nodded slowly. "Most wouldn't."

"Cyrus beat you to it."

He frowned.

"You're going to tell me it was a mistake," I said simply. "I've been told, multiple times, by people I like a lot less than you."

He stepped in front and turned to face me, stopping our progress along the path. "I just think you would be good on the Council, that's all."

I picked at the edge of the plastic lid. "They wanted someone from the coven, they got Thea."

He frowned. "I know, I just—"

"Want me in the club," I finished for him. "But I'm not, Jax. And trying to force me to play by their rules after everything just isn't going to happen."

He swallowed and glanced at his feet.

"You wanted to be an Emissary again, despite what they put you through," I continued. "That's your choice, just like turning down their pathetic attempts at placation is mine."

His jaw tensed. He was the only one who had chosen to take his position back after the Council's ruling. Leander surprised me in that; I thought for sure he would have jumped at the chance to be an Emissary again. But since his injury and Lyra's death, he wasn't the same. Rez was doing his best to be there for him, as having his own magic unbound helped to heal whatever had split them up in the first place. But I doubted, even with that, Leander would ever be the same.

"They want me on their Council so they can keep an eye on me, not so I can change things," I added.

"I don't think that's entirely fair," he countered. "With Lenore gone, there's a better chance of making things better."

"And Thea will be right there if that chance presents itself," I said. "I'm not part of the Collective or the Outliers, and I won't start answering to them now."

He opened his mouth as if to add another argument but closed it again with a shake of his head. "You really are stubborn," he muttered.

I shrugged. "One of my more charming faults."

He fell back next to me, and we continued walking towards the main gates where Blythe was due to pick me up soon. I took a long, stalling drink of tea to brace myself for my next words.

"I'm sorry," I said quietly. "For forcing you to leave."

His lips pursed and he kept his eyes forward.

"It wasn't right." I took a deep breath. "But I couldn't have done what I needed to with you there."

His throat bobbed. "I know."

He only knew half of it. Facing Lenore with the possibility of him getting hurt after what had happened to Lyra would have been nearly impossible for me. But I'd also needed them gone so Thea could try raising Lyra. We had no way of knowing if it would have worked in the first place—the fewer people who knew we'd tried, the better. *Especially* if it hadn't worked.

I'd wanted to tell him and Leander as soon as Lyra had come back. As soon as it sank in that magic had succeeded in returning her to us. But

Lyra refused to let them in our secret and Thea begged us not to reveal her as a Necromancer.

I thought they deserved to know, but in the end, it wasn't my decision. But that did mean there was, once again, a secret lingering between Jax and me, another deception being kept to protect him from having to lie to his Council.

"Where does this leave us, then?" he asked.

I shrugged. "You could try being mad at me," I offered.

He hung his head with a sigh. "That would make this easier," he admitted.

My stomach tightened. "I never..." I paused to swallow the slight crack in my voice. "I never meant to hurt you."

He shook his head and put a hand on my arm to stop me. "You didn't," he said firmly.

I stared at him, taking in the image of him as the Emissary he'd been raised to be. He was still the man I'd met on my birthday, but we'd both been through too much in the last few months to remain the same. And that was the problem.

"It's just all a little too..."

"Raw?" he offered.

I nodded.

"I just can't right now," I explained. I wanted him to understand that this had nothing to do with anything he'd done or said. But what we—Lyra, Blythe, and I—needed to do could not get back to the Council, especially Cyrus.

He smiled. "Not never," he said with a slight incline of his head.

I let out a small huff of a laugh. "Not never," I agreed. My phone buzzed in my pocket and after glancing at it, I turned back towards the front entrance to the post. Blythe was here and parked in loading zone.

Jax threaded his fingers through mine and walked me to the gates, where Blythe leaned against her new black 4Runner, arms crossed. Her eyebrows shot up, sending her sunglasses riding up her nose when she saw us.

I frowned when I noticed the woman hanging out of the passenger seat window with a giant grin on her face. Today she had cropped violet hair tucked behind one ear, green eyes, and a half-sleeve tattoo featuring a large rose and a snake.

She winked at me as Jax and I got closer. "Well, don't y'all look cozy," she teased in a soft southern lilt.

Jax frowned. "Who—"

"Astrid's cousin," I lied quickly, giving Lyra a pointed glare. While her glamour had come out perfected after she'd been raised, she seemed to have forgotten to disguise the personality.

Pulling my hand free from Jax's, I handed Blythe my bag. "I thought she was staying in Portland," I hissed.

"Apparently, she's having too much fun with her improved glamour," Blythe whispered back.

She smiled around me at Jax and gave him a half-wave, but he was too busy staring at the disguised Lyra in the front seat, his brows drawn together.

"I guess this is it," I said, stepping back up to Jax, blocking his view of Lyra as best I could.

He nodded and tore his gaze away from the car to look at me. "I guess so," he said with a small smile. "Try not to get into too much trouble."

I shrugged. "You know me, trouble-free."

He let out a soft chuckle that made my heart tighten. I wrapped my arms around his neck and hugged him. His arms pulled me closer and gave me a tight squeeze as I inhaled him. Fresh cedar with a soft snap of mint, and then the faintest hint of honeyed spice that was the magic at his core. I wanted to solidify this in my memory. Just this.

The moment was over too soon. The air rushed between us once he let go. He took a step away, towards the open gates of the post, and put his hands back in his pockets.

I slid into the back seat and groaned as Lyra gave him a mock salute from the front. His eyes widened ever so slightly, but Blythe hastily pulled away from the curb.

"What happened to being careful?" I muttered to Lyra as she propped her bare feet up on the dash, legs significantly shorter in this glamour.

"I got bored," she offered simply. I bit back the urge to remind her that if the Congregation ever found out what our coven had done in those woods, we'd be in Stromford with Lenore for the next twenty years, but she'd just blow it off like she had the other half-dozen times I'd reminded her.

I sat back against the seat and let out a long breath, forcing myself not to turn around and look back at him. We were in too different of places right now, it would never work. And until Lyra and Thea were on board with telling the Tsipras brothers the truth, that secret would linger between us. No, this was what we needed, and we couldn't be anything more, not now.

But, maybe not *never*.

Chapter 36

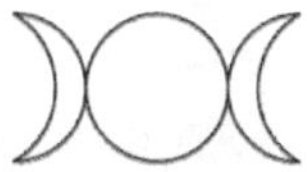

Spring had barely arrived, but it was the first day the city had seen the temps reach sixty in months, and everyone was taking advantage. Dogs were out with their owners for more than the minimum walk time, runners wore short sleeves and left their warm hats at home, and my neighbors were happily back from their impulsive stay in Florida.

It had been almost two weeks since the Congregation passed Lenore's sentence, since I'd turned down the seat on the Council, and since Jax and I ended whatever we'd tried to start. I'd been left alone as promised, not that I expected them to break their word this soon.

And not that they didn't have other things to worry about. Lenore's betrayal was having lasting effects on being able to keep witches safe from hunters. Whatever they'd added to the drug in their latest batch was making the rounds throughout the country. And the formula for the antitoxin the Council had stolen from Ian wasn't doing much against the newest concoction the hunters had.

Thea kept us updated on everything the Council discussed and any operations the Emissaries were sent on, just in case they were coming near enough that someone might recognize Lyra—something very much against their rules, but thankfully for us, they were learning that Thea was a more obstinate force than they'd bargained for.

And she wasn't the only one coming into her power over the last couple weeks. Blythe strengthened the blood wards on the Portland house without any issue. She even over-did it and had to reel it back when the magic tried to keep the mail carrier from stepping onto the stoop.

I'd managed to find the control I needed, too. At first, being able to sense the magic and energy of every living thing around me had sent me into a spin. Once the focus of stopping Lenore and not dying was gone, it all came back to me in a rush that had me worried I'd loose my mind. But now, I could block it out completely.

At night I'd lie in bed and listen to essence of those in the house, finding ways to differentiate among them as they slept. Chad was the easiest to pick out as the only mortal. But after a few days, I was able to discern between Wes, Lyra, and Blythe within seconds. I knew the more I practiced, the faster I would get.

I parked Wes's Subaru in front of the house and grabbed the bags of groceries out of the back. Walking through the door—left open in an attempt to entice the fresh spring air inside—I felt Blythe's wards on my magic, filling me with that same relief you'd get when you finally got home after a long trip.

And it *was* a relief to be back home after weeks of running. It had taken a lot to get it back to feeling normal after the Emissaries had left it a wreck. Although some of the state it had been left in was my fault, a casualty from when we'd broke in to get Amity's book back.

I'd smoke cleansed twice, and Lyra had cleaned the walls of scorch marks using one of Lydia's spells which worked better than any cleaning solution I could've found. I bought new sheets, trashed the old ones, and steam cleaned the couch. Chad and Wes had tried to tell me they'd already washed everything before we'd gotten back, but there was still a lingering vibe to the house I couldn't shake when we'd gotten in from Boston.

Restocking the fridge had been one of the last things on my to-do list. Wes insisted he could take care of it, but I wasn't going to take off again until I knew they were settled. It was as much to calm my own anxiety about leaving them so soon as it was for their comfort.

Blythe rounded the corner out of the kitchen to help, taking one of the grocery bags out of my hands as she met me in the doorway. I cut through the living room and stopped as Lyra flicked on the giant TV she'd had installed.

"That thing is obnoxiously huge," I commented, skirting around her to set the bags down on the island.

"If Chad's going to watch cooking vids from in there," she said, jerking the remote over her shoulder at us, "then he needs to be able to see it."

"We have a tablet for that," Wes grumbled from inside the butler's pantry. He was making a list of everything we'd have to get from the co-op to restock what had been used up. He'd also been vocally anti-huge TV when Lyra had gone looking. Our old one had been large enough, but after the exploding herb bags I'd let go off in the house, it had been damaged beyond repair.

"You people are no fun," Lyra muttered, flipping the ends of her shoulder-length chestnut brown hair at us. For weeks, she'd been trying out various hair colors and styles to see which one she liked the best as her "go-to" disguise.

Attie popped out of thin air to stretch out along the back of the couch and watch Lyra program the new TV. She'd been the familiar that hung around the most these days. The others were still here, though. We could all sense when they were around, watching over us. Why Attie was the one to show herself the most often wasn't a complete mystery. She was checking in on Lyra to make sure she was still alive—or still *her*.

Something we were all looking out for. So far, Lyra seemed very much the same Lyra she had been before being raised. With one notable exception, she'd woken up with different eyes. One was now a deep purple and the other a bright red, something we couldn't find a reason for in any of the books. I could only assume it was a biproduct of mixing blood and death magic.

After we'd gone through Sybil's book looking for an answer to her eye color change, we learned we, also, needed to be on the lookout for any drastic personality changes, which could mean Lyra wasn't the one we raised after all. Yet, another consequence I hadn't considered

"Any signs of a Council raid?" Blythe asked, pulling herself onto the counter next to the fridge as I put the produce away.

I shook my head. "Between the hunters and Castor, Thea said they're too busy to care about us."

"Kinda wish I could see Selene and Cyrus fight it out," Blythe muttered.

I nodded. The Council still hadn't decided on a punishment for Castor. He'd been following orders from a Council member, which was his job, but he also hadn't reported Lenore's qestionable methods to the rest of the Council as was his duty.

Selene was torn between protecting her son and acknowledging the need to not show favoritism, while Cyrus wanted Castor stripped of all rank and his powers bound for a time. Apparently, losing his daughter—niece—wasn't punishment enough.

"I just want it to keep them busy long enough we can get this done," I said, handing her the dark-chocolate-covered pretzels.

She ripped open the bag and took a few out.

"I thought those were for the flight?" I teased.

She shrugged and nodded at Lyra. "Think they know where we're headed?"

I glanced over my shoulder at Lyra. "Thea hasn't mentioned any-thing." I folded up the empty reusable bag. "And she's not going to let them get a jump on us."

"Weird to hear you all trusty about Thea," she said around a mouthful of pretzel.

"She has as much to lose as we do," I pointed out. "More, if you think about it. Besides, she's really good at this Council stuff."

Blythe huffed. "Yeah, don't know how she deals with it," she said. "Martin is constantly trying to get me to go to boring Assembly meet-ings."

I pulled out the jars of sauces from the other bag. "You agreed to be on it," I reminded her with a laugh.

"Yeah, 'cause I thought it came with a paycheck," she admitted.

"Whoa, that's massive," Chad said, walking into the living room.

"You like?" Lyra asked with a proud smile.

He nodded. "I do, thank you."

She passed him the remote. "Quick tutorial..." She walked him through the apps he'd use, settings he might like, and helped him log into his accounts while I finished putting the groceries away.

Wes emerged from the butler's pantry, list in hand and looking like he'd just cataloged a library. But the damage wasn't too bad, according to him. He turned down my offer to go to the co-op for him, offering the excuse that he wanted some normalcy back into his own life. Not exactly something I could argue with.

"Did you tell Martin where we're headed?" I asked Blythe, putting the bags away and wiping off the counter as Wes grabbed his keys from the sideboard.

She shook her head. "Told Rez we were going to '*Europe,*'" she said, adding air quotes to the destination, "because he was being annoying about it."

"He worries," Wes said, turning to face us. "And he's not the only one."

"I think we've made it pretty clear we can handle ourselves," Blythe teased.

Wes shot her a look that I thought he only reserved for teenage me, and I pursed my lips against the laugh that wanted to force itself out.

"I mean it," he warned. "Be careful."

"We will," we said together.

He'd warned us already that European covens played by completely different rules than we knew. They're laws were older and, as the roots of our own ancestors were there, there was no telling what kind of magic we could tap into, intentionally or not.

I knew it was risky going oversees to find what we needed—almost as risky as trying to get Ian's memory back without Kane. It was entirely possible that, even if our trip went entirely to plan, trying to get back what the Council took would do more harm than good. But I owed Ian enough to try.

In lieu of involving Martin again, we'd gone with another plan and tried to find a different witch who could help. Our search had turned up the name of a Hex Witch who dealt exclusively in memory modification—Callum Weir. He had a, questionable, reputation depending on who we asked we got both negative and positive reviews.

After persistent pressing and a solid guilt trip from Blythe, Leander confessed to knowing who Callum was: a powerful Hex Witch, *and* Lyra's biological father. Seeing as coincidences were rarer than Blood Witches these days, we could hardly ignore the sign.

Problem was, Callum Weir had disappeared without a trace fifteen years ago while working for a client near Trim, Ireland.

According to Meg's contacts in the area, the most widely accepted explanation for this was that he took a misstep at the Hill of Tara and been stuck in the Otherworld since. Kidnapped by faeries or running around Ireland with amnesia from a head injury seemed equally as likely a fate. Either way, we needed to find him.

"Did you see that thing?" Chad asked, setting his bag from SKORDO on the counter. He'd made his own run to get the spices he needed for our farewell dinner.

"Unfortunately," Wes said, giving Chad a peck on the cheek before headed out for the co-op.

Lyra climbed onto one of the stools and picked a piece off one of the doughnuts left from this morning and tossed it in her mouth. "Think of how big our faces will be for the video chats."

"Don't go promising we're going to check in every hour," I said. "We don't need to be broadcasting our every move over the internet."

Lyra waved the suggestion away. "I'm dead, remember?"

I rolled my eyes. "And you need to stay dead so we don't get in massive trouble."

"Again, no fun," she teased and tossed a chunk of doughnut at me.

Chad kicked us out of the kitchen before we made too big a mess for him to cook around and got to work on dinner, a recipe of Grandma Geri's he'd found while in Ohio that he wanted to try out.

We went upstairs to finish packing. Everything had to fit in a carry-on backpack, as we weren't sure how much we'd have to move between places in order to find Callum.

Lyra had worked to consolidate the spells from as many books as she could into one so we wouldn't have to pack all of them. It wasn't as organized as I would have liked, but it was her book so I kept my opinions to myself.

That, the new TV, and my rearranged room were all evidence of her restless energy. She claimed to be fine and acted annoyed every time we asked if she was. But her need to be doing *something* told me she wasn't as fine as she pretended to be.

Dinner was a success, and after Blythe and I finished the dishes, Wes triple-checked that we had everything we needed from our newly fake passports—courtesy of Z—boarding passes, and all the contact information for the witches Meg arranged for us to stay with.

He even tried to repack my bag and add more sweaters than I needed. He was worried I'd get too cold and I had to remind him that they did, in fact, have washing machines in Ireland. Chad, thankfully, distracted him with a Bruins game on the new TV, allowing me to fix what he'd messed up.

Blythe did one final check on the wards and got reassurance from Rez that he and Leander would check in on the uncles while we were gone before she and Lyra turned in for the night.

Silver light from the full moon bled through the crack in my curtains as I lay in bed, waiting for sleep to come. Once again, I let energies of everyone in the house fill my mind.

Chad's steady heartbeat, like a soft drum against my core.

Wes's magic, the first sip of honeyed chamomile after a stressful day.

Lyra, the warmth of a perfect sunny afternoon and soft grass under bare feet.

Blythe's magic, similar to mine, was the rush of salty ocean waves cleansing sticky heat from skin.

Together, the rhythm of their essence pulled me towards sleep like a lullaby I never wanted to end. Alive and safe.

☾

We stopped at Becky's for breakfast after saying goodbye to Wes and Chad. It was busy, but it didn't take too long for us to get a table. Darlene gave me a nod of acknowledgement as she passed by with steaming plates, and we slid into a booth by the window.

It was crowded and noisy, thanks to it being late enough in the day that most people were up and hungry. Our flight didn't leave until evening, so I'd convinced Blythe and Lyra we had time to stop before heading to Boston.

Ian and I would always get Becky's after spring break. Especially if one of us went somewhere with our family. As soon as classes resumed, it was back to Becky's—a tradition I didn't want to bring up today. This was our place, and if this trip ended up being futile, I wanted one last time eating here with hope.

Lyra downed the last of her mimosa and stood up with a stretch. "I see the appeal," she said. "This place is good."

I swirled my tea around in my mug, the temperature now well below hot. "I'm aware," I teased.

"We'll get the car," Blythe said, scooting out of the booth. The busyness of the morning had forced us to park a few blocks down. She and Lyra—looking a lot like Meg these days—left while I fished out a twenty to leave on the table.

I grabbed the ticket and made my way to the register to pay the rest of the bill. After I paid and signed the receipt, I turned to scan the posters and adverts for all the upcoming events around Portland, giving them time to get to the car.

Once the weather turned closer to summer, the Old Port would be flooded with tourists for weeks. That's when a lot more events would take place—outdoor concerts, festivals, and dining specials that would entice people to stay and spend their money just a little longer. It could become unbearable, the traffic and chaos interrupting day-to-day life, but there was a charm in it that made it *home*.

Once Lyra's text came through, I went to leave, knowing if I waited outside they wouldn't have to technically park. I wasn't paying enough attention, though, and smacked right into a man walking through the door when I turned.

"Oh my God, I'm so sorr—" The apology died in my throat as Ian gave me a large smile.

"No worries," he said. His smile turned into a small frown, brows creasing. "Do we—sorry, you look familiar. Do I know you?"

My heart jumped and my breath caught. "Um, I..." I swallowed, my throat suddenly dry. "I don't know."

He nodded slowly and then snapped his fingers. "Intro to Anthro," he said as if he'd solved the hardest puzzle. "We had class a couple years ago."

I nodded. "Yeah, that's probably it," I agreed.

"Right, yeah." The rest of the group he was with edged in around us. "Well, see ya around." He ducked by me, following the rest of his friends as they added their party to the waitlist, and I couldn't stop myself from staring after him.

We'd taken Intro to Anthropology together for our core humanities course during our first semester. It was a memory of *us*. Maybe not solid enough for him to remember he hadn't taken a single note himself because mine were always better. Maybe not firm enough for him to remember us arguing over sitting in the front or the back, so we'd gone with the middle. It wasn't perfect, but it was something.

I slid into the back seat of the car, and Blythe made a most definitely illegal U-turn that earned a honk or two. As she sped down Commercial Street, Lyra argued with her over who would get the window seat on our flight.

I didn't process who won in the end—because it didn't matter. I had my family back, and they were safe. My friends.

My coven.

EPILOGUE

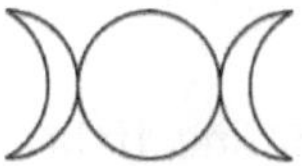

Three Years Later

Wolfe's Bend hadn't changed since we'd last been there. The first week of October, however, made it look entirely different than before. Trees with bright leaves welcomed visitors as they crossed the bridge onto the stone-paved street that ran through the center of town. The surrounding woods had more red, orange, and yellow trees that seemed to outnumber the evergreens.

Small tents lined each side of the closed Main Street for artisans, local shops, and food vendors. Already, and in spite of the relatively early hour, throngs of people moved from stand to stand. Lyra had made reservations so far in advance, I was surprised they let her. By some fluke or intervention of the universe, we ended up in the same room at the Wolfe's Bend Inn we had three years ago.

The ice machine on our floor was working this time.

We were running a little behind to meet Wes and Chad—an annoyance Lyra voiced often, despite her being the one who had snoozed the multiple alarms she'd set.

The crisp fall air was layered with hints of cinnamon, fresh coffee, that didn't quite overtake the prickly coolness if the surrounding cedars. The rush of the river behind the inn could be heard over the conversations and hum of food truck generators.

I took a deep breath and zipped my fleece up over my long, red, velvet dress. Sticking my hands in my pockets, I glanced around just as I saw a sleek black form dart among the trees. One of the cats, Attie by the looks of the gait. It had taken years, but I was getting better at telling them apart from a distance now.

"Where to?" I asked, squinting, trying to confirm I was right about which cat it was. They didn't latch onto us anymore, instead popping in and out when they wanted—a welcome, ever-present comfort.

Lyra stepped up next to me, the train of her golden dress hanging over her arm and the sparkling bodice partially hidden by a black leather jacket. Her blonde hair, streaked with black, had been curled and twisted into a loose knot at the back of her head.

She peered down at the festival map the front desk had given us. Vendors, events, local shops hosting specials were all marked on there. She looked back up and squinted towards the large cast bronze statue of a wolf howling in the center of the square ahead of us.

She pointed. "I think just behind that thing."

"You *think*?" Blythe asked through a yawn. The hem of her black spider-web lace dress was just short enough to show off the tops of her black heeled boots underneath and her long, solid black hair, was swept in front of her, pinned away from her face on one side with the help of a spider lily clip.

I swept a strand of hair that had fallen out of my attempt to style my long bob away from my face and checked the message on my phone. "Wes and Chad just parked."

"The Salem crew?" Lyra asked.

"I told Sofia we'd meet them at the diner," Blythe said.

Lyra nodded and folded the map. "Why didn't we have everyone meet there?"

"Because you didn't let me plan," I muttered with a half-smirk.

"Well, next time we do a hand-fasting ceremony, I'll let you do all the planning you want," Lyra said with an eye roll.

I stepped off the curb. "You meet up with Ian, I'll get the others," I directed. "I need a tea anyway."

"Get me a coffee!" Blythe called.

"Me too!" Lyra added.

I gave them a wave of acknowledgment over my shoulder, and I weaved through the early morning festival-goers crossing the street, my heels clicking on the stone as I went.

Earthshine didn't have an extensive tea selection, but it was better than the two options in the hotel room. Inside, it was warm and cozy; hints of pine and fresh cinnamon rolls filled the air, giving the place that homey feel other places might not have had. Every bit of this town was a little unbelievable sometimes, but I supposed that was part of the appeal.

It was also partly why Lyra and Blythe had chosen it for their hand-fasting. Secluded, themed, and highly unlikely anyone they didn't want there would show up. Even with time, Lyra hadn't fully forgiven her cousins or uncle for lying to her. They all still thought she was dead. Selene had too many friends and she had learned about our journey to Ireland, and some of our less than desirable encounters while there. She'd kept the secret, though, and was setting up the altar while we gathered the guests.

It wasn't the party we would have come to expect from Lyra. But, as she kept joking, dying had given her "perspective." So, she'd only invited a few people. Ian—now that his memories had been restored—Wes and Chad, Callum, and Z. Blythe invited Sofia, Devya, and Hazel, and went back and forth about Rez.

He and Leander had held their own hand-fasting about a year ago, which had been a bigger affair thanks to Martin and Selvina's interference. Something Blythe desperately wanted to avoid. As she was still our coven's representative at the Assembly, her union would be a bigger deal than Rez's if they found out about it.

In the end, she decided against telling him—both for not wanting Martin to find out, and not for not being willing to tell Rez he could only come if he didn't bring his husband.

We'd all wanted Sadiki there, but no one had heard from him since the memorial. Normally, that would have worried me, but something told me he had found his own way. He'd left on his terms and stayed gone on his terms. But I still wished he'd answer *one* of my emails.

The line moved a little slowly, but no one had shown up to meet us by the time I got to the ordering counter. I got a London Fog for myself, Blythe a black coffee, and Lyra a triple-shot maple latte for the festivity of it.

By the time the drinks were done, Sofia, Devya, and Hazel had arrived and were able to take the two drinks with their own to meet up with the others at the statue while I waited for my uncles.

I squeezed my way back outside to the sidewalk, giving the people inside more space to eat and wait for their drinks. Metal tables for outdoor dining sat off to the side, and I took a small one far enough from the building where I could still see the entrance to the street.

Cupping my hands around the paper cup, I shivered against the hair rising on my neck. Something—or someone—powerful was nearby. I let my magic fan out, searching for the source. There was a lot of power in the town itself, but my mind was drawn to two girls close by, probably only a few years younger than me.

One had silver hair with light roots peeking out in the autumn sunlight and a large scar on her neck. The other had short brown hair with a streak of white around her face. The one with short hair caught my eye, sending a pulse of power running through me, but my magic couldn't find hers. She had to be a witch, but her magic was unlike anything I'd encountered. Soft moonlight on freshly fallen leaves with a wildness I couldn't quite place.

My phone buzzed on the metal table, and I broke our brief eye contact to pick it up and read the message quickly: a congratulations from Thea and another apology for not being able to come. As it turned out, she was a natural at handling the politics of the Council. Cyrus had under-estimated her, and she'd used that to her advantage, gaining more power and influence than he thought possible.

It kept her busy, but I think she finally found the kind of respect she'd wanted when she tried to be an Emissary. Only this time, everyone knew what kind of power she had. She'd kept us updated on the Council and their movements for years, ensuring Lyra was glamoured if there was a chance we'd run into someone who knew her.

She'd been invited to the handfasting, but thanks to the Council taking a steep turn downward over the last few years, she didn't feel comfortable leaving Boston. Lenore's replacement and Cyrus were of similar minds on most issues, our coven's lack of governance being the major one. Selene had resigned a year after Lyra's death and the witch who had taken her seat was afraid of confrontation, apparently.

Thea held her own against the group, but even she wasn't able to fight a full Council on the regular. Whispers of a disunion in the Collective were swirling faster than they could be stamped out. But, despite the Council trying to keep all those rumors under control, the ripple of friction was impossible to ignore. Maybe the return of our coven was a catalyst for a division amongst them after all.

I took a sip of tea; when I didn't see Wes or Chad for a few minutes, I picked up my phone to see how long they thought they'd be and if they needed coffee.

Halfway through typing out the message, metal scrapped against con-crete as the chair across from me was pulled out. Honeyed spice magic that was warm and golden flooded through my system. I looked up to meet bright blue eyes cracked with gold and a wide smile.

"You're a hard witch to find," Jax said.

Acknowledgements

I can't believe this is the end to Em's story. I started this project years ago and to see it finished is both exciting and bittersweet. From the elation of completing that first draft, to late night revision sessions, to getting that final product, it has been quite the ride. A ride that would never have come this far on my own.

I have a terrible habit of sending completely out of context messages to friends and family, but I am so thankful you all just took them in stride. An extra special thanks to my sister, Colleen, for giving me all sorts of theories (some more outlandish than others) about where she thought this story was going to go that helped with the revision process.

As always, my first readers were invaluable in getting feedback on the entire project. Not only have they been helpful in the process, but some of my biggest cheerleaders when things got rough.

Thank you once again to the team at Blue Pen Books for the cover design. They are great to work with and make the process easy to navigate for someone who is still learning all the ins-and-outs of the industry.

I can never stop singing the praises of my marvelous editor Kate Murray Theibauth, who has made sure this novel is as polished as it can be. Not only is her input indispensable, but her enthusiasm for Em's story makes her an absolute joy to work with.

Once again, I can't thank my wonderful parents enough for always supporting me throughout everything. There aren't words to express how much you both mean to me.

Finally, a special shout out to the staff at Scarborough Grounds Cafe for their amazing service, great food and drinks, and for letting me take over my usual corner table for (many) hours every weekend.

ABOUT THE AUTHOR

E. O'Meagher has long been drawn to worlds with their own rules and characters that challenge societal "norms."

After spending most of her childhood escaping into the fantasy realms and adventures of her favorite books, she now works to develop what she loved from those stories in her own works.

Raised in Western Montana, she currently calls Southern Maine home where she revels in a good rainy day on the beach. Aside from writing, she enjoys traveling, exploring lighthouses (both haunted and not), wandering through a forest, and a good cup of tea on a chilly autumn morning.

She holds a Bachelor of Arts in Creative writing with a minor in Irish Studies from the University of Montana.

The Forgotten Daughter **is the third and final installment in her debut series: The Lost Coven Trilogy.**
Find her on Instagram and TikTok (@omeagherstories) and visit her online at www.omeagherstories.com